Communities of Cultural Value

Communities of Cultural Value

Reception Study, Political Differences, and Literary History

Philip Goldstein

LEXINGTON BOOKS

A member of the Rowman & Littlefield Publishing Group
Lanham • Boulder • New York • Oxford

LEXINGTON BOOKS

Published in the United States of America
by Lexington Books
4720 Boston Way, Lanham, Maryland 20706

12 Hid's Copse Road
Cumnor Hill, Oxford OX2 9JJ, England

Copyright © 2001 by Lexington Books

All rights reserved. No part of this publication may be reproduced,
stored in a retrieval system, or transmitted in any form or by any
means, electronic, mechanical, photocopying, recording, or otherwise,
without the prior permission of the publisher.

British Library Cataloguing in Publication Information Available

Library of Congress Cataloging-in-Publication Data
Goldstein, Philip.
 Communities of cultural value : reception study, political differences, and literary history / Philip Goldstein.
  p. cm.
 Includes bibliographical references (p.) and index.
 ISBN: 0-7391-0261-3 (cloth : alk. paper) – ISBN 0-7391-0262-1 (pbk. : alk. paper)
  1. English literature—History and criticism—Theory, etc. 2. American literature—History and criticism—Theory, etc. 3. Politics and literature—Great Britain—History. 4. Politics and literature—United States—History. 5. Orwell, George, 1903–1950. Nineteen eighty-four. 6. Hurston, Zora Neale. Their eyes were watching God. 7. Austen, Jane, 1775–1817. Pride and prejudice. 8. Shakespeare, William, 1564–1616. Hamlet. 9. Multiculturalism—English-speaking countries. 10. Social values in literature. 11. Culture in literature.

PR21 .G67 2001
820.9'358—dc21

2001029434

Printed in the United States of America

⊖™ The paper used in this publication meets the minimum requirements of American National Standard for Information Sciences—Permanence of Paper for Printed Library Materials, ANSI/NISO Z39.48–1992.

I wish to thank Leslie, my loving wife, for her encouragement, my good friends Mark Amsler Tom Leitch, and Jim Machor for their support of my work, and my many readers and commentators, especially Anthony Cascardi, for their invaluable assistance. Also "Orwell as a Neoconservative: The Reception of *1984*" was published in *The Journal of the Midwest Modern Language Association* (Winter 2000), and "Critical Realism or Black Modernism?: The Reception of *Their Eyes Were Watching God*" appeared in *The Reader* (Spring 1999). I thank those journals for giving me permission to reprint these articles.

I wish to thank Leslie, my loving wife, for her encouragement, my good friends Mark Amsler Tom Leitch, and Jim Machor for their support of my work, and my many readers and commentators, especially Anthony Cascardi, for their invaluable assistance. Also "Orwell as a Neoconservative: The Reception of *1984*" was published in *The Journal of the Midwest Modern Language Association* (Winter 2000), and "Critical Realism or Black Modernism?: The Reception of *Their Eyes Were Watching God*" appeared in *The Reader* (Spring 1999). I thank those journals for giving me permission to reprint these articles.

Contents

Introduction: Reception Study in a Multicultural Era	1
1 Cultural Value and Poststructuralist Theory: The Case for a Left-Wing Reception Study	31
2 Marxism and/as Humanism: The Reception of *Hamlet*	53
3 Feminism and Poststructuralist Criticism: The Reception of *Pride and Prejudice*	83
4 Conformity and Resistance in High Art: From Thomas Hardy to Toni Morrison	113
5 Gender, Spies, and Art: Ian Fleming, John Le Carré, Mickey Spillane, and Sara Paretsky	141
6 Orwell as a Neoconservative: The Reception of *1984*	165
7 Critical Realism or Black Modernism? The Reception of *Their Eyes Were Watching God*	181
Conclusion: The Limits of Reception Study	199
Bibliography	209
Index	235
About the Author	241

Contents

Introduction: Reception Study in a Multicultural Era	1
1 Cultural Value and Poststructuralist Theory: The Case for a Left-Wing Reception Study	31
2 Marxism and/as Humanism: The Reception of *Hamlet*	53
3 Feminism and Poststructuralist Criticism: The Reception of *Pride and Prejudice*	83
4 Conformity and Resistance in High Art: From Thomas Hardy to Toni Morrison	113
5 Gender, Spies, and Art: Ian Fleming, John Le Carré, Mickey Spillane, and Sara Paretsky	141
6 Orwell as a Neoconservative: The Reception of *1984*	165
7 Critical Realism or Black Modernism? The Reception of *Their Eyes Were Watching God*	181
Conclusion: The Limits of Reception Study	199
Bibliography	209
Index	235
About the Author	241

Introduction: Reception Study in a Multicultural Era

In the 1990s what were commonly termed the "theory/culture wars" sharply fragmented the humanities, undermining the autonomy of theoretical norms and aesthetic practices and discrediting professional literary study. The very success of literary theory, cultural and multicultural studies, and feminist, gay, African American, and Marxist criticism produced entrenched divisions which have constituted normal literary study, not a temporary disintegration certain to vanish once the leaders of the profession reassert the norms of "rationality." Assimilating these new programs to a field, concentration, or minor, departments have muffled but have not eliminated these conflicts; as John Carlos Rowe says, "The 'culture wars' of the late 1980s and early 1990s are by no means over; they have simply warped into new and less publicly visible struggles for control of educational funding, curricula, 'standards' (or 'competency levels'), and pedagogical authority."[1] Indeed, the bitter polemics defending traditional literary study or the new programs and studies have led to hostile new professional organizations, which, like the National Association of Scholars, discredit the humanities, increasing public distrust and financial reductions. Of course, the broad reductions of federal support, the rapidly increasing costs of prisons and other state programs, and the consolidation and downsizing of departments and programs explain why, as the rest of the American economy has boomed, the humanities have remained a depressed area, with growing percentages of part-time faculty teaching first-year courses and over half of all new Ph.D.s unable to find tenure-track jobs. Still, the professional divisions and theoretical polemics also explain these difficulties. Michael Bérubé points out that what "truly endangers the future of higher education . . . are the PC wars in tandem with the growing mad-as-hell taxpayer outrage at the professional autonomy of faculty." He adds that with "extraordinary ease . . . anyone can ridicule or demonize professors, largely because no one outside academe has any clear idea of what professors do."[3]

This book examines the theory and types of reception study as well as the historical reception of major and minor types. The argument is that the divisions and conflicts of the 1990s justify a reevaluation of reception study because it explains and defends the contemporary humanities.

Consider the evolution and the influence of these divisions. They emerged in the 1980s, when the humanities' new programs in women's, African American, gay, cultural, multicultural, and theoretical studies were first established. Irate conservatives made the well-known argument that, supported by affirmative action and militant student demonstrators, the defenders of cultural studies and literary theory demand political "correctness" and obfuscating jargon, not the genuine standards of literary value, positive knowledge, or rational thought ensured by the study of the traditional Anglo-American canon.[4] Although communism has collapsed, a left-wing outlook prevails in university life because the radical feminist, African American, gay, and poststructuralist critics of the 1960s lost the revolution in the streets and in the legislatures but mean to win it in the English classroom.[5] On the other hand, the proponents of the new cultural programs debunk the traditional claim that, largely white, male, and European, canonical Anglo-American literature represents universal values, rather than the establishment's middle-class interests.[6] The proponents, who assume that the increasing ethnic and sexual diversity and the democratic accessibility of Anglo-American higher education justify the new programs, maintain that African American, women's, or multicultural literatures address the experiences and the traditions of the university's changing student body. The proponents add that, by manipulating the general reader's ignorance of and hostility to obscure terminology, repressive political ideals, and privileged elites, the conservatives support the right-wing movements undermining affirmative action, social welfare, women's rights, and other liberal policies begun under Presidents Lyndon Johnson and Franklin Roosevelt.[7] To discredit these policies, the conservatives made communism their scapegoat. When communism ended and the Cold War collapsed, they treated the humanities' cultural programs and poststructuralist theory as a new scapegoat.[8]

Most accounts of the humanities' conflicts and divisions assume that this opposition of conservatives and radicals explains why the "culture wars" began, persisted, and, to an extent, still persist; however, many liberal, feminist, Marxist, and radical proponents of the new cultural and multicultural studies voiced the methodological concerns of the conservatives. Surprisingly enough, these progressive critics also object to "extraneous" polititical criteria or obfuscating theoretical jargon, what Edward Said calls the disciplines' "totalizing concepts," "reified objects," "guilds, special interests, imperialized fiefdoms," "orthodox habits of mind," and "organized dogma."[9] As Murray Kreiger points out, since poststructuralist theory successfully influenced educational practice and formed interdisciplinary programs, the "repressive" influence of this theory has provoked the opposition not only of traditionalists but also of liberals and radicals.[10] Conservatives and radicals have formed a loose coalition which, despite their very different literary and political agendas, preserves traditional notions of objective truth, formal authorial or textual criticism, and public responsibility, and opposes poststructuralist discourse, subjectivity, or literary politics.[11] As I will show, the coalition shares the nostalgic belief that the humanities are in a state of decline.

That conservatives and radicals have formed what I am calling a loose coalition suggests, however, that persistent methodological differences explain these conflicts more fully than the political differences of right- and left-wingers. The disputes of conservatives and radicals preoccupied daily newspapers and middlebrow magazines in the 1980s and 1990s; this book will show, however, that these methodological conflicts pervaded "normal" literary activities, including the interpretation of canonical and noncanonical texts, the recovery of forgotten works, the distinction between popular and high art, and the practice of African American, women's, and cultural studies. As Josephine Guy and Ian Small said, "[I]t is precisely because political controversy has so dominated discussion of the teaching of English that other aspects of disciplinary knowledge—its philosophical condition and social nature—have been neglected."[12]

These "other aspects" include pervasive methodological conflicts, which imply that theories of art's objective truth or aesthetic autonomy can no longer transcend the profession's divisions or reconcile its antagonistic parties. The recent divisions and conflicts have produced a crisis of theory. On the one hand, since critics in all fields defend different epistemological methods and aesthetic practices, theory acquires a new explanatory force. On the other hand, aesthetics cannot preserve its traditional autonomy if critics employ contrary methods.

Robert Holub rightly says that American criticism has repeatedly failed to appreciate the historical profundity of reception study;[13] however, this crisis of theory gives reception study a new validity. Initiated by Hans Robert Jauss, reception study challenges the aesthetic norms of formal and historical criticism and explains the historical import of the reader's interpretive practices. Jauss makes these practices the ground of revitalized historical method but preserves the transformative force of aesthetic norms. Poststructuralist reception study also maintains that the interpretive practices of the reader ground a rejuvenated historical method; however, instead of defending art's aesthetic autonomy, the poststructuralist approach examines the interpretive communities governing the reader's practices.[14] A left-wing or Marxist version of poststructuralist reception study, what I call post-Marxist reception study to indicate its debts to Ernesto Laclau and Chantal Mouffe's poststructuralist Marxism, also examines these communities or reading formations but goes on to show that the changing sociohistorical conditions of modern literary study explain the evolution of its contrary schools, movements, or "communities" and clarify their progressive and conservative aspects. These versions of reception study defend the humanities' new programs better than the coalition of conservatives and radicals does because reception study repudiates the theoretical polemics by virtue of which the coalition means to ensure the humanities' conformity with the classical tradition, the national culture, middle-class morality, the working class, the women's movement, or ethnic or racial minorities. As I will shortly show, post-Marxist reception study also appeals to broad social movements, whose progressive import it defines as a radical extension of the Enlightenment's democratic practices; however, instead of engaging in polemics (or, at least, only in a polemic against polemics), this reception study examines the historical development of criticism's interpretive communities.

Modern Reception Study

Scholars initially believed that reception study was an aspect of an author's development, not an independent form of literary history. They assumed that, since an author's work often responds to commentary provided by friends, reviewers, or formal critics, the study of these responses may help explain how and why the style, ideas, aims, or forms of a writer evolved.[15] Jauss showed, however, that reception study does much more than explain the author's development; beyond that, reception study examines the reader's changing horizons and sociohistorical contexts and reveals literature's historical influence, what Jauss terms the "coherence of literature as an event."[16] Although the modern reception study of Hans Robert Jauss preserves the transformative force of the great text, his reception study establishes the interpretive practices of the reader as the effective ground of literary history.

In the influential essay "Literary History as a Challenge to Literary Theory," he maintains that the reader's constructive activity, not the author's intention nor the text's language, explains the significance of a text because the reader's activity brings together the author's historical context and the reader's "horizon of expectations." Derived from Martin Heidegger's notion of world and Hans-Georg Gadamer's notion of an event, the "horizon of expectations" stipulates that, to experience or interpret a text or a society in a meaningful way, readers must bring to bear the subjective models, paradigms, beliefs, and values of their necessarily limited background, what his colleague Wolfgang Iser calls a "repertoire" of strategies.

That is, Jauss accepts the Heideggerian belief that, because understanding is circular, hermeneutic experience requires openness or letting be. A text constructs a world but not a totality which cancels and preserves partial methods or distinct historical periods, as Hegelian and Marxist critics claim. The Heideggerians maintain, however, that, bringing "what is into the clearing," a text undermines traditional Western notions of truth or value and discloses the unique import of being, whereas Jauss adopts Gadamer's belief that, just as a festival exists only in its celebration, so a text exists only as an event which reveals the reader's self, not being's unique import.

In literary terms, the author's historical context explains the original meaning of the text, but the reader's activity accounts for its subsequent interpretations or continuing reception. Jauss shows, for example, that Rousseau's *Nouvelle Héloïse* put in place a new horizon which enabled readers to rediscover what Jauss terms the lost "naturalness" and exemplary virtue of the autonomous self, while Goethe's *The Sorrows of Young Werther* accepted and transformed that horizon, providing readers another "option for healing a denatured society."[17]

David Perkins claims that reception study of Jauss has no advantages over the traditional historical method because they both construct elaborate categories of texts or readers and they both fail to reconcile their general descriptions of an epoch and their specific accounts of its divisions or a text's readers.[18] Such methodological objections to reception study's categories and general descriptions do not address the practical difficulties which Jauss takes reception study to solve.

As Jauss indicates, these difficulties stem from the rise of the formal method, which claimed that the close textual analyses of a text's figural devices, not the scientific study of an author's life or social context, explained a work's unity. Of course, René Wellek and Austin Warren, who accepted the formal belief that the symbols, ironies, paradoxes, and other devices of a text effectively unify it, granted that the reader's responses or "concretizations" explained the history of the text's structure.[19] Similarly, as Jauss, Tony Bennett, and John Frow point out, Russian formalism maintained that a text defamiliarizes generic conventions and reveals thereby the evolution of literary forms and devices as well as the reader's changing repertoire of interpretive practices. It is still true, however, that most American New Critics and British Leavisites considered the text's "intrinsic" structure autonomous and unchanging and repudiated "extrinsic" social, historical, or biographical accounts.

The traditional historical method maintained, by contrast, that the author's intention gave a text its meaning and that what explained this meaning is the author's life and historical context. For example, E. D. Hirsch Jr., argues that, since "meaning" is a "constant, unchanging pole" of the "relationship" binding the text and the reader, the critic must establish a text's "objective" meaning before he or she assesses its subjective psychological, biographical, feminist, or Marxist "significance."[20] Similarly, traditional Marxists believe that objective, public "understanding" precedes and transcends "interpretation"; however, while the liberal Hirsch considers the author's intention an autonomous, universally binding norm, the Marxists, who expect the critic's understanding to overcome the historical and institutional changes alienating the reader from the author, maintain that an objective account of the author's social conditions reveals the historical import of the author's meaning. Georg Lukács showed, for example, that in Homer's *Iliad* the shield of Achilles represents Greek society as a whole, whereas modern fiction, alienated from society, loses this capacity, which the literary historian must reinvent.

It is not surprising that the historian's accounts of an era's conventions and ideals insightfully explained the emergence of realism, naturalism, modernism, and other literary movements; at the same, most historians neglected the impact of the artist's and the reader's productive activities.[21] As a result, the historians' accounts of the social conditions explaining a work's virtues and limitations were reductive by modern formal standards. Raymond Williams points out that during the 1940s and 1950s American New Critics and British Leavisites considered Marxist explanations of an author's socioeconomic context the worst sort of reductive or "totalitarian" determinism, but they severely condemned all historical study because, instead of analyzing the work itself, the historians provided causal analyses of a work's sources and influences or an author's development.[22]

In response, many Marxist and non-Marxist literary historians simply dismissed the formal critiques, which they attributed to what Lukács derisively labeled "shop talk" and Hirsch called "cognitive atheism." Other historians have preserved the traditional method but sought more complex textual accounts of a writer's style; as Jerome McGann says, to overcome the "disciplinary crisis" resulting from the historians' defeat, critics "integrate the entire range of sociohistorical and philological methods with an aesthetic and ideological criticism of individual works."[23]

For example, like Lukács, Lionel Trilling expected great art to produce complex insight into sociopolitical life, but he formulated this insight as a matter of the subject's individual authenticity and not of realism's historical development. While Lukács argued that modernism shows only the disintegration of the subject, Trilling extended art's adversarial character to modernism too. In a New Critical fashion he found in it a congenial opponent of liberal intellectuals and democratic writers whose Stalinist proclivities led to simplistic abstractions and stylistic ineptitude.[24]

Raymond Williams supported progressive ideals, but, like Trilling, he defended the historical method and rejected the reductive Marxism of Lukács. Williams believed, as Lukács does, that the author's experience of new social conditions explains his or her creation of new literary forms, yet Williams dismissed the dualism implicit in Lukácsian mediation. Just as the superstructure does not reflect the base, so too literary practices do not mediate between predetermined literary or social wholes. Literary practices produce their own meanings and values because cultural signification is a productive activity.[25]

Jauss' reception study also overcomes the opposition of formal and historical approaches, but Jauss faults both the historians' objectivity and the formal critics' subjectivity. He claims that, while traditional historians rightly emphasize art's social insight, they ignore their biases or subjective involvement; as he says, they set themselves "outside of history and beyond the errors of . . . the historical reception."²⁶ Although he appreciates the formal critic's subjective emphasis on values and method and the Russian formalist's historical accounts of generic conventions, he complains that most formal critics ignore the author's original audience. These critics evaluate texts and canons, overturn old traditions, introduce new ones, but dismiss the genre's history and the writer's life and era.²⁷ René Wellek and Austin Warren also consider the text's structure a historical product of the reader's interpretations, yet Wellek and Warren emphasize the structure's normative, autonomous status because, as Wellek says, "Men can correct their biases, criticize their presuppositions, rise above their temporal and local limitations, aim at objectivity, arrive at some knowledge and truth";²⁸ by contrast, Jauss, who rejects what Hans-Georg Gadamer aptly terms the Enlightenment's prejudice against prejudice, claims that the reader's prejudices do not distort or misconstrue the text's meaning or the author's intention; rather, readers who open themselves to the historical or cultural other revealed by a text engage in an open-ended dialogue. As Robert Holub points out, Jauss's hermeneutic method "calls upon the experience, not the neutrality, of the interpreter, defining the writing of literary history in a Gadamerian fashion as the 'fusion of horizons.'"²⁹

Jauss's reception study indicates that the interpretations of the reader show his or her predispositions and still open a dialogue with the historical other. Interpretations reveal the commitments, beliefs, and aesthetic ideals of the reader and his or her era because the figures of the text or the intention of the author are not autonomous norms but changing sociohistorical constructs. Commentary and criticism no longer reduce to secondary bibliographical matter aiding the reader's close textual analysis; they provide the primary evidence of the reader's interpretive practices, aesthetic ideals, and ideological commitments. Jauss claims, nonetheless, that reading is not an entirely subjective process because a text can resist its reception and transform readers and society. Largely negative, the great text fuses the historical meaning of the original author and the radically incommensurate interpretation of the contemporary reader.³⁰ Critics object that Jauss inconsistently preserves the historical objectivity which his hermeneutic method opposes;³¹ the problem is, however, that Jauss endows canonical texts with the power to escape their original reception and to establish a new paradigm as well as new beliefs and values. In his terms, a new work can "result in a 'change of horizons' through negation of familiar experiences or through raising newly articulated experiences to the level of consciousness."[32]

In *Sensational Designs* (1985), Jane Tompkins examines the reception of Hawthorne's work but denies that it acquired high canonical status because it emancipates readers from their established beliefs. She points out that in the 1840s and 1850s critics praised both the forgotten Susan Ashton-Warner and the well-known Nathaniel Hawthorne for depicting idealized childhood, sentimental domesticity, and Christian virtues.[33] What distinguished Hawthorne from Ashton-Warner was not the critics' terms of praise but Hawthorne's position in society. Thanks to his family, his education, his publishers, and his politics, he possessed close ties to American cultural elites, whereas Ashton-Warner had no such ties. As a consequence, he acquired what Ashton-Warner lost—a position in the American literary canon.[34]

Although Tompkins explains the reception of Hawthorne's work, she shows that, contrary to Jauss, Hawthorne's social position, not his work's emancipatory force, explains its canonical status. Such differences divide reception study into types. The work of Jauss establishes modern reception study, which maintains that the changing horizons of a text's many readers explain the history of the work but still claims that a text can transcend its original reception and establish new paradigms or values. Tompkins's work illustrates, by contrast, the poststructuralist approach whereby reception study undertakes the historical study of a text's diverse readings but repudiates the transformative force of aesthetic norms and theoretical critique. As I explain in the next chapter, poststructuralist reception study, which includes the liberal or empiricist approaches of Stanley Fish, Steven Mailloux, and Barbara Herrnstein Smith and the post-Marxist approaches of Tony Bennett and John Frow, maintains that the activity of diverse readers addresses equally diverse interpretive communities or reading formations whose norms and values determine the validity of the reader's interpretation. In the post-Marxist version this reception study goes on to explain these formations' historical development.

Robert Holub complains that the poststructuralist criticism of Paul De Man or Stanley Fish expresses a corrosive negativity which "undercuts" reception theory "without offering much in the way of an alternative."[35] It is true that, like De Man, who claims that the diverse readings allowed by a text may open up undecidable aporias subverting the centering force of interpretive norms and theoretical ideals,[36] the poststructuralist approach critiques the "foundational" aesthetic norms accepted by Jauss; still, poststructuralist reception study repudiates this transformative force and goes on to depict the changing socioeconomic contexts of literary study and to defend its specialized disciplines and new cultural programs. In the next chapter I explain more fully these differences of liberal, empiricist, and post-Marxist proponents of this reception study; here I mean to outline the philosophical assumptions in keeping with which post-Marxist reception study explains the historical development of literary study's reading formations yet, unlike the conservative/radical coalition, which engages in harsh theoretical polemics denigrating contemporary literary studies, clarifies their conservative and progressive aspects.

Post-Marxist Theory: Ernesto Laclau, Chantal Mouffe, and Michel Foucault

In literary terms, post-Marxist reception study repudiates the autonomous norms and values of traditional aesthetics and, instead of engaging in harsh polemics, explains the reader's sociohistorical contexts, what Tony Bennett calls "reading formations." In philosophical terms, post-Marxist reception theory repudiates the teleological history of Marxist aesthetics and the scientific neutrality of Althusserian theory and reveals the changing sociohistorical contexts and the conservative or progressive import of the reader's interpretive practices. In other words, post-Marxist theory examines the institutional reproduction of the literary subject and defends the democratic politics of a radical Enlightenment tradition

As I indicate in the next chapter, some post-Marxists accept the institutional reproduction of the subject but reject the democratic politics of the Enlightenment tradition, while others reject the subject's institutional reproduction but accept the Enlightenment's democratic politics; however, a full post-Marxist reception theory adopts both theoretical notions: the institutional determination of the subject and the radical extension of the Enlightenment tradition. The notion of institutional determination comes from Michel Foucault, who argues that the authoritative strategies, methods, and tactics of a discourse explain its historical development. The notion of a radically democratic politics comes from Ernesto Laclau and Chantal Mouffe, who suggest that, by deepening the Enlightenment tradition, post-Marxist theory can bring together women's, African American, postcolonial, gay, working-class, and other "new social movements."

To an extent, Laclau and Mouffe accept Louis Althusser's critique of traditional Hegelian Marxism, according to which society evolves in distinct historical stages realizing a predetermined telos—the communist society. Althusser rejects the Hegelian notion that the working class will achieve full humanity once it overthrows the capitalist system. More negative, Laclau argues that traditional Marxism treats the working class as a privileged agent achieving "full presence" in a "transparent" communist society because the "rationalist naturalism" of traditional Hegelian Marxism preserves the apocalyptic ideals of the Christian theology which this Marxism opposes.[37]

In *For Marx*, Althusser admits that Marx initially adopted Hegelian humanism but maintains that Marx eventually rejected this humanist view and established a scientific Marxism; as Althusser says, the "rupture with . . . all philosophical humanism is not a secondary detail; it is one with the scientific discovery of Marx."[38] That Marx breaks with "all philosophical humanism" means that the scientific Marxism which Marx discovers distinguishes science and ideology and, as a result, opposes both Hegelian and Marxist humanism. Laclau and Mouffe also critique the Hegelian belief that predetermined historical stages and contexts explain social development. They too say that the ideological apparatuses of the state interpellate or construct a subject and thereby reproduce themselves, as Althusser claims; however, they defend Gramsci's notion of ideological hegemony because they deny that a Marxist science resists its ideological practices and grasps the objective truth. They adopt, in addition, the poststructuralist belief that, since objects do not simply or literally mirror their sociohistorical contexts, the distinction between object and context, discursive and nondiscursive practices, or "thought and reality" breaks down; in Laclau and Mouffe's terms, "Synonymy, metonomy, metaphor . . . are part of the primary terrain itself in which the social is constituted."[39]

Most Derridean or poststructuralist Marxists also claim that concepts or logic do not exclude convention, rhetoric, or ideology, yet these poststructuralists maintain that the figural devices of a text subvert the encrusted conventions of institutional life.[40] Laclau and Mouffe also take hegemonic ideological discourses to construct stable but partial identities or dislocated subjects, but Laclau and Mouffe maintain that the antagonisms produced by the new social movements ensure that these discourses fail to achieve closure. In traditional terms, the discursive conflict in which contending political parties seek to impose their hegemony explains values and identities more fully than ruling-class interests or social structures do because, incomplete or dislocated, such structures produce only partial identities. The social antagonisms or dislocations produced by the oppositional social movements do not imply a positive new context or

Hegelian *aufhebung*, as traditional Marxists say; rather, these antagonisms keep hegemonic ideological practices or social relations from constructing the literal import, full identity, and contradictory forces reflecting history's predetermined stages.[41]

Critics complain that, by granting discourse "an absolute autonomy" or "central role in social and political life," Laclau and Mouffe "find no alternative short of total contingency, indeterminacy and randomness."[42] Laclau does consider "the social" an indeterminate or irreducible discourse, not economic structures reproduced by institutional practices; however, he rightly maintains that, to win the support of the new movements, a successful politics requires strategic argument whose success working-class or other socioeconomic contexts cannot ensure in advance. Since the antagonisms of the working class, women, minorities, and others expose the fissures within the literal meanings and conservative identities imposed by hegemonic ideological practices, the contingent, fragmented state of the modern subject reflects contemporary social movements.

Laclau and Mouffe's account of hegemonic discourse radically extends the Enlightenment tradition to previously excluded women's, African American, postcolonial, gay, and working-class movements; just the same, because Laclau and Mouffe fear that institutional practice imposes a functionalist conformity, they defend theoretical critique and dismiss not only Stalinist communism or bureaucratic working-class organizations but all established progressive groups, including trade unions, left-wing political parties, and the humanities' newly instituted women's, African American, ethnic, or gay studies and programs. Jürgen Habermas complains that the postmodernist attack on Enlightenment reason destroys the liberal consensus legitimating art, ethics, science, and other public spheres.[43] Laclau and Mouffe do not accept these disciplinary divisions but do not reject Enlightenment reason either; rather, Laclau and Mouffe assume that poststructuralist theory, rather than the divisions of these spheres or of a discourse's historical development, exposes the antagonisms, dislocations, fissures, or equivalences undermining the modern subject. Richard Rorty rightly objects that it is Laclau's poststructuralist metalanguage, more than the new social movements, which reveals the modern subject's fragmented and decentered character.[44]

Michel Foucault does not extend the Enlightenment tradition, but he accepts the institutional determination of discourse, rather than the independent ideals of theoretical critique. He discusses the breakdown of the phenomenological tradition, not Marxism's humanist or Stalinist limitations. Indeed, he says that the study of the Gulag exposes the limits of Marxism.[45] In *The Archaeology of Knowledge* (1969), he rejects Althusser's antihumanist account of science and ideology because he considers science "one practice among many," not a privileged discourse.[46] He rejects as well the Hegelian theory of historical development. He says that contradiction has many levels and functions within and between discursive formations and does not represent a difference to be resolved or a fundamental principle of explanation.[47] In *The Order of Things*, he argues, just the same, that the impersonal or "subjectless" science of the modern disciplines overturns the empirical science of the eighteenth century and the rationalist humanism of the nineteenth. In the twentieth century, however, the modern episteme, which breaks into the mathematical sciences, the social sciences, and philosophical disciplines, subverted the human figure grounding the nineteenth-century disciplines and allowed them to establish their formal autonomy. Invented in the nineteenth century, humanity remains an indifferent effect of impersonal discourse, not the genuine foundation presupposed by phenomenology.

Like Laclau and Mouffe, Foucault dismisses humanist notions of theoretical self-consciousness and Althusserian ideas of an autonomous science, but he does not reduce established configurations of power and knowledge to a functionalist conformity; rather, he maintains that ideology or discourse imposes conformity but resists ruling-class purposes. Just as Althusser claims that ideology is rooted in institutional rituals which reproduce it, so Foucault maintains that institutional or disciplinary power establishes and maintains its corresponding knowledge. Unlike Foucault, Althusser says that the rituals and practices whereby an institution constructs or "interpellates" the subject work within the subject's unconscious, but he still claims that "an ideology always exists in an apparatus, and its practice, or practices."[48]

Similarly, in his early *Madness and Civilization*, which preserves a Hegelian sort of underlying episteme, Foucault argues that institutional changes, not scientific enlightenment, explain the modern treatment of the insane. Medical historians discover in ancient treatises examples of pathologies, neuroses, paranoias, hallucinations, and so on, as though these forms of madness were eternal and unchanging, whereas actually the altered institutional arrangements of the eighteenth and nineteenth centuries allowed these scientific forms of madness to emerge.

In *Discipline and Punish* Foucault preserves this institutional determination of knowledge but, repudiating the totalizing episteme of

The Order of Things, he claims that the discourse of judges, psychiatrists, anthropologists, and criminologists forms a "scientific-juridical complex" which resists the interests of the dominant class but ensures the class's domination all the same. While Althusser also shows that the ideological apparatus of the state resists ruling-class ends but ensures ruling-class domination, Althusser inconsistently retains the economy as an absent cause unifying disciplines and institutions; by contrast, Foucault indicates that, impersonal and anonymous, a discipline is not an institution or an apparatus but an anatomy of power used by different institutions, including the family. Moreover, it is the historical evolution of the "scientific-juridical complex" which disrupts ruling-class aims but still constitutes a docile, obedient subject faithful to rules and to authority.

A left-wing or post-Marxist theory adopts this Foucauldian concept of a discourse's history and institutional determination, not Laclau and Mouffe's fear of functionalist conformity, because that fear dismisses the humanities' newly established programs, whereas the Foucauldian concept explains a discourse's methodological conflicts and historical changes. Post-Marxist theory also adopts Laclau and Mouffe's notion of ideological hegemony, which undermines the Hegelian humanism of traditional and Stalinist Marxists and justifies a broad democratic alliance of trade unionists, feminists, minorities, and other "new social movements" emerging since the 1960s.

The reception study based on this post-Marxist theory explains the schools, movements, or "reading formations" which constitute readers as subjects and explain the history of a text's reception. Both Stanley Fish and Tony Bennett say that the norms, ideals, and methods of diverse readers' interpretive communities or reading formations explain a text's diverse interpretations. Bennett goes on to claim, however, that "[t]o think critically about criticism requires that account be taken of the actual mechanisms of the literary-pedagogical apparatus . . . inducting the reader into the socially constructed interior of the text as a space in which to exhibit not correct readings but a way of reading."[49] Most Derridean or post-structuralist Marxists also claim that a text provides "a space in which to exhibit . . . a way of reading" but maintain that reading does not reveal "the actual mechanisms of the literary-pedagogical apparatus"; reading subverts the ideological assumptions of the text.

Since post-Marxist reception study accepts the Foucauldian notion that the institutional contexts of a discourse determine its practices, reception study argues, by contrast, that literary study's authoritative mechanisms or "reading formations" govern the reader's interpretive activity and limit the play of figural language. Unlike the Derridean's figural language, a reading formation explains the reader's interpretive practices but imposes the Foucauldian discipline of established schools and methods. In schematic methodological terms (more fully described in the upcoming chapters), these schools and movements include the objective authorial approach, which seeks a unifying intention derived from the text and from the author's life and sociohistorical context; the textual or formal approach, which claims that the symbols, metaphors, ironies, and other rhetorical devices of a text explain its unity and autonomy; the generic neoclassical approach, which takes a text's conformity with and opposition to the conventions of the text's genre or type to show its import; the subjective reader-oriented approach, which attributes the meaning of a text to the conventions and beliefs of the competent reader; the systematic structuralist approach, which shows that a text illuminates the forms and conventions of narrative and other discourses; and the poststructuralist figural, discursive, or rhetorical approaches, which indicate that the figures and devices of a text both assert and undermine its themes and values as well as its era's historical, sexual, or political discourses. As the traditional literary histories point out, what initiates and elaborates these approaches are broad cultural movements, including humanism, whose faith in a universal human nature and in art's conceptual truth opposes fragmentary commodity production as well as specialized, modern disciplinary study and justifies neoclassical generic conventions; romanticism, whose commitment to the artist's autonomous imagination opposes neoclassical generic conventions and justifies the intentional, authorial approach and the formal, textual approach; liberal empiricism, whose philosophical realism—the belief in factual truths independent of human discourse and preconceptions—preserves the imagination's autonomy but endows it with historical truth and ethical and social justifications; modernism, whose defense of art's aesthetic autonomy repudiates the humanist faith in art's conceptual truth and the liberal belief in art's ethical and social justifications and warrants the specialized formal, textual approach; and postmodernism, whose assimilation of popular culture and commodity production as well as the poststructuralist notions of discourse and rhetorical figures opposes neoclassical generic conventions, the artist's autonomous imagination, art's ethical and social justifications, and the text's aesthetic autonomy and warrants the Derridean or New Historical approaches. In the upcoming chapters, which discuss these movements more fully, I show that, established in universities and other institutions, these schools and movements do not evolve in a continuous or linear fashion; rather, as a Foucauldian sort of history suggests, they rupture with and oppose each other,[50] yet they still assimilate each other's techniques and methods and acquire feminist, Marxist, psychoanalytic, African American, gay, or multicultural variants as well.

From René Wellek's four-volume *A History of Modern Criticism* to Vincent Leitch's *American Literary Criticism*, traditional literary histories detail the leading figures and central concepts of these schools and movements but rigidly divide the concepts and ideals of their theoretical discourse from the textual truth or empirical objectivity of practical interpretation. Reception study repudiates this conventional opposition of theory and practice because, far from adopting the norms of literary theory, practical critics accept and elaborate the methods and theories of the established schools and movements. Literary theory remains relevant and even therapeutic insofar as these established methods explain the persistent differences and conflicts revealed by the practical critics' accounts of a text.

The New Historical approach also critiques the foundational norms governing traditional historical study and describes the anonymous, dispersed discourses organizing society as well as the body. In a poststructuralist fashion, Hayden White has argued, for example, that historical study does not escape the ambiguities of rhetorical tropes, because, as an art as well as a science, historical study requires interpretations, not just facts, and rhetorical modes or genres, not formal logic alone. As he says, "[H]istorians interpret their materials in two ways: by the choice of a plot structure . . . and by the choice of a paradigm of explanation."[51] Similarly, Stephen Greenblatt says that the literary historian does not examine formal poetics alone; in addition, he or she examines the "practical strategies of negotiation and exchange" whereby a text generates "the pattern of boundary making and breaking, the oscillation between demarcated objects and monological totality."[52] As Claire Colebrook says, New Historicists consider "the cultural/aesthetic domain . . . an area of contestation where various forces (aesthetic, political, historical, economic, etc.) circulate";[53] however, instead of explaining the historical contexts and modern import of readers' interpretive activities, this approach preserves the autonomy of the text, which may assert both subversive and dominant discourses, and/or the critic, who may freely "affiliate" with established or oppositional institutions.[54] White complains, for example, that "absurdist" Derridean or Foucauldian criticism reduces the text to language and language, in turn, to silence or babble. More importantly, he fears that this criticism fetishizes the reader: "Mystification of the text results in . . . the narcissism of the reader. The privileged reader looks everywhere and finds only texts and within the texts only himself."[55] Similarly, Greenblatt accepts the traditional belief that Shakespeare's text constructs alien, subversive outlooks which anticipate and resist modern views, doctrines, and beliefs. As he says, "It was true that I could only hear my own voice, but my own voice was the voice of the dead."[56] He too complains, in addition, that reception study reduces literary history to the professorate's bureaucratic will.[57]

Roger Chartier rightly suggests that such fears of the reader's "narcissism" divorce "the historical imagination" from the "historical forms of rhetoric, understood as the art of discourse and persuasion."[58] In other words, such fears justify a formal neutrality, rather than a strategic engagement, but since the 1990s, when the theory/culture wars first divided the profession, such neutrality has been open to question because it fails to address the issues posed by these wars. For that reason, post-Marxist reception study, which describes the changing sociohistorical contexts of literary study's schools, movements, or reading formations repudiates this neutral objectivity, which is incompatible with the Foucauldian belief that the historical knowledge of the critic does not escape the effects of disciplinary power. Although the New Historical approach also analyzes the cultural discourses organizing society and the body, this approach preserves the autonomy and neutrality of the literary text and the critic; by contrast, the post-Marxist approach situates criticism within its evolving schools and movements, and still defends the progressive aspects of the humanities' specialized disciplines and new cultural programs.

Defenses of Realism: From Allan Bloom to Edward Said

While this reception study defends the humanities' specialized disciplines and new cultural programs, the conservative/radical coalition laments them. In *The Rise and Fall of English*, for example, Robert Scholes nostalgically recalls how in the 1950s and 1960s his many close relationships with distinguished literary scholars profoundly motivated his research. Turning to the 1990s, he says that now "we" literary scholars "feel bad because we do not believe in the significance of the research that is required of us . . . and because we are confused about what we should be teaching, and how, and why."[59] This painful sense of confusion and loss echoes the conservative and radical complaint that the humanities have suffered a painful fall from grace. That is, since at least World War I, the immense growth of radio, television, cinema, popular fiction, and other commercial products has undermined the unifying cultural force of traditional literature. So have its new technical undergraduate majors and specialized literary fields, which divorce literature from rhetoric or composition, teacher training, and other public duties. In the 1980s and 1990s, Marxist, poststructuralist, feminist, African American, and other new programs and studies have added to this fragmentation, dividing not only established English departments but also university administrations and their public and private supporters. Unlike reception study, whose sociohistorical accounts of the humanities' specialized disciplines and new cultural programs defend their integrity, scholars as diverse as Allan Bloom, E. D. Hirsch Jr., Gerald Graff, Fredric Jameson, Terry Eagleton, Sandra Gilbert and Susan Gubar, and Edward Said lament the humanities' decline and fragmentation and blame subjective, Marxist, or "politically correct" poststructuralist theory, "complacent" reception study, as well as the university's expanding disciplines, new programs, indiscriminate admissions policies, or multicultural clientele.[60] From very different perspectives, Hirsch, Bloom, Graff, Eagleton, Gilbert and Gubar, Jameson, and Said attribute this growing fragmentation to modern criticism's obscure jargon, narrow specialties, and careerist aims; the university's expanding disciplines and co-opted programs; and popular culture's conformity and vacuity.

Scholars have shown, however, that the disciplinary divisions and cultural programs of the humanities have progressive import because the vast expansion of working-class, female, racial, and ethnic student populations of the late twentieth-century university greatly enhance the humanities' influence. As Stanley Aronowitz indicates in *Science and Power*, the disciplinary academic study fostered by modern industrial capitalism gives the specialized professional intellectual a political importance unknown to the gentlemanly, traditional intellectual cultivating humanistic knowledge for its own sake.[61] To an extent, the sheer growth of higher education explains this new importance. Since the mid-nineteenth century, when the development of new technology and the fierce competition of Western countries broke up the apprentice system of eighteenth-century crafts and guilds, the working- and middle-class population have pursued more and more advanced education. Because of the high school programs established in the 1870s and 1880s, the disciplinary university curriculum begun in the 1880s and 1890s and greatly expanded after World War II, and the community colleges instituted in the 1960s, American higher education has greatly increased its populations of middle- and working-class and, more recently, minority and female students. In the United States, more than 55 percent of people between eighteen and twenty-two years of age attend some form of higher education. In England, since the 1990s "one in three young people go to university, a proportion which is continuing to rise."[62] Of course, most colleges and universities have adopted a "supermarket" of courses and programs whereby a student who majors in, say, computer programming may never have to take a literature or cultural studies course; still, the huge student body created by higher education's explosive expansion has made the humanities' new programs more widely available and has increased their influence. The specialized majors adopted by modern colleges and universities have enabled working-class and middle-class students to rise in socioeconomic status;[63] at the same time, women's studies, cultural studies, and even literary studies have grown in importance. Tied to education, journalism, advertising, communications, and other professions, literary studies too has fostered this social mobility, what Evan Watkins terms the "distribution and certification of human capital."[64]

The democratic expansion of the university justifies the specialized character of literary study, enabling it to include the nontraditional female, minority, and working-class students and programs excluded hitherto. Thanks to this expansion, feminist and Black scholars were able to secure the student enrollment necessary to justify courses in women's or African American literature and to establish women's, Black, or cultural studies programs. In other words, student interest, not administrative fiat, warranted such courses and programs. Watkins adds that

> Women's studies programs, to take a very visible example, not only work to challenge a literary canon, reorder the curricular priorities of course offerings, contest the dominance of patriarchal ideologies. They also recruit women into English, as ethnic studies programs recruit socially designated "minority" populations.[65]

The new curriculum, programs, and pedagogy of feminist, Marxist, African American, or postcolonial critics may not reinstate the unified public culture of the pre-Enlightenment era, but, as Watkins indicates, these programs still challenge established practices and accommodate excluded groups. Indeed, these programs have made the modern university what Lawrence Levine calls "one of the more successfully integrated and heterogeneous institutions in the United States."[66]

To be sure, the coalition of conservative and radical scholars does not simply condemn literary study's academic contexts or defend the norms of traditional or speculative theory; rather, the coalition means to ensure that a unified public culture overcomes the fragmented, withdrawn, or "reified" character of literary study's disciplinary divisions and even the decline of the nation-state and the international character of the capitalist economy.[67] Derrida rightly objects, however, that the "guardians of the humanities" ignore "the history and the system of norms specific to their own institution, the deontology of their profession."[68] That is, the coalition assumes that the grounds of a unified, coherent criticism must lie not in its institutional or academic contexts but outside them, in our human nature, the public sphere, the underlying totality, or the oppositional women's or postcolonial movements.

The work of Foucault suggests, however, that the internal coherence of literary studies lies in its fractured or ruptured historical development, not in a linear fall from or a gradual acquisition of cultural plenitude. It is the origins and the evolution of literary study's many established schools and movements, not their broad, public contexts, which explain the coherence of conflicted modern literary studies. Since these schools and movements may originate in public contexts and can exercise hegemonic institutional power, their struggle to dominate a text reveals the changing history of literary study.

In this book, the reception of *Hamlet, Pride and Prejudice, 1984, Their Eyes Were Watching God*, detective and spy fiction, and modernist and postmodernist art shows the schools' and movements' evolution and development. Chapter 2 indicates that, even though the Marxist and the non-Marxist approaches to *Hamlet* sharply oppose each other, they both dismiss poststructuralist or New Historicist accounts and justify the ideals of modern humanism, which defends the unified human self against the fragmentation imposed by sociohistorical change, commodity production, disciplinary divisions, and so on. The reception of *Hamlet* shows, moreover, that in a progressive manner the poststructuralist approaches promote contemporary interests in race, class, and gender and oppose but do not escape the humanist formal, authorial, and historical approaches from which the poststructuralist accounts evolve.

In chapter 3, which examines the development of feminist criticism, not neoclassical humanism, the reception of *Pride and Prejudice* shows that, contrary to Austen's traditional critics, who consider the sheer diversity of contemporary interpretations an embarrassment, the many approaches to this novel have progressive import. The Victorian liberals and the modern authorial critics, who establish Austen's high canonical status, high moral authority, and good "Aunt Jane" stereotype, considered her novels a humble chronicle of her era's customs but still endowed the study of them and, more generally, of English literature with broad political ends: to promote the New Rhetoric, liberal agenda, moral values, or separate spheres of middle-class British society. The neoclassical humanists assumed that an educated gentleman would study great art for its own sake; by contrast, the liberals, who considered the study of "rhetoric and belles lettres" a useful enterprise which would improve the reader's mind and the nation's civility and prosperity, justified the educational reforms which made the fiction of Austen and other English writers a legitimate object of a university education. In addition, even though the authorial, formal, and historical approaches evolved out of the liberal Victorian view, they acquired progressive feminist import once women students and faculty broke down the liberals' "separate spheres" and gained equal status and independent programs. The poststructuralist feminists, who emerge within the established English department and women's studies programs, acknowledge the novel's diverse and incompatible interpretive frameworks and its forceful social criticism, yet these feminists preserve the formal autonomy of literary study and accommodate the fragmented character of modern culture.

Chapters 4 and 5 show that the reception of the high modernist and postmodernist fiction of Thomas Hardy, Vladimir Nabokov, Milan Kundera, Philip Roth, and Toni Morrison opposes the optimistic liberalism and humanist ideals of the Enlightenment era, as the New Critics, the New York intellectuals, the Frankfurt School, and others maintain; however, this fiction does not exclude popular stereotypes and established doctrines and conventions. Reception theorists maintain, however, that, far from precluding subversive aesthetic practices, popular spy and detective fiction also undermines itself, resisting its generic forms and chauvinist and anticommunist stereotypes. In addition, the vast expansion of the modern university has positive import: it greatly increases the accessibility and influence of literary studies, and it enables literary studies to intervene in both high art and popular culture.

In chapter 6, I show that the public cultural criticism of the New York intellectuals dominates the reception of *1984*.[69] This cultural criticism highly esteems the novel's sociohistorical critique of totalitarian communism and of Western culture's decline and fragmentation and, like the traditional critics of *Hamlet, Pride and Prejudice*, and high modern art, bitterly opposes the subjective, "irrational" views of postmodern theory. Among the originators of totalitarian theory's nightmarish communist other, this public criticism has neoconservative import: it fiercely opposes not only communist parties in and out of power but also "naive" liberals, "power hungry" intellectuals, "misguided" feminists, the "complicit" media, or "irrational" postmodernists. Formal, feminist, Frankfurt School, and postmodern accounts of the novel resist but do not consistently overcome this neoconservative import.

While chapter 6 critiques such neoconservative views, chapter 7 justifies the feminist and African American revaluation of Zora Neale Hurston's *Their Eyes Were Watching God*. The conventional explanation of why the novel was forgotten blames Richard Wright and other Marxist or social realists because they denied that it protested racial prejudice or social injustice; however, literary historians, the New Critics, the New York intellectuals, and other critics and scholars also neglected *Their Eyes*. It was not until the 1960s and 1970s that African American literary study, established in major Anglo-American universities, went on to revalue Hurston's novel. Traditional scholars condemned this new nationalist or separatist movement, yet it made possible the revaluation of *Their Eyes*.

Conclusion

These studies of major and minor works illustrate and justify reception study's belief that what explains the coherence of modern literary study is not human nature, the public sphere, or the women's, Black, or postcolonial movement, as the conservative/radical coalition says, but criticism's history, especially the origins and development of modern literary schools or "reading formations." These studies also show that, more sharply than the political differences, the methodological divisions of the modern schools and movements divide literary study, pervading its everyday practices.

In this book's conclusion I will discuss various objections to reception study; for now, I would like to consider John Guillory's fear that such a post-Marxist account of criticism's divided schools and movements suffers from a vitiating relativism. Even though he recognizes how destructively conservative and radical scholars have disputed the established canon, specialized study, literary language, aesthetic judgment, and foundational theory and advocated or opposed alternative feminist, African American, or postcolonial literatures, he considers the disputes to a tempest in a teapot because he shares the widespread fear that to critique the foundations of aesthetics and to acknowledge criticism's diverse schools and movements, as reception study does, is to lapse into a corrosive "relativism" whereby the schools, based on consensus and not on binding aesthetic norms, readily degenerate into anarchy.[70]

Post-Marxist reception study certainly denies that aesthetics limits interpretive practice or changes anything; still, the reading formations governing interpretive practices do not foster anarchy because, as a pedagogical apparatus, they exercise authority and do not require consensus. More importantly, while reception study examines the rich history of modern criticism's many interpretive communities or literary schools, Guillory, who defends universal aesthetic norms, reduces literary criticism to one function: to provide the credentials of the successful few and to exclude the unsuccessful many. Guillory dismisses the reception study as well the conservative/radical coalition, but his defense of a universal aesthetics accepts the coalition's belief that the modern technocratic university promotes its own bureaucratic interests and excludes working people, African Americans, women, and ethnic groups, who are given little access to and less comfort from the old traditional or the new feminist, African American, or postcolonial literatures.[71]

Certainly some Anglo-American colleges and universities show the elitist tendencies whereby only the privileged few learn to appreciate the new theories and literatures; still, many colleges and universities also show progressive tendencies, which include, as I noted, greatly expanded populations of minority, female, and working-class students as well as increased accessibility of women's, cultural, and, more generally, literary studies. As Bérubé says, "'literature' may indeed have declined in cultural authority but 'English' remains a potentially valuable career asset."[72] In addition, if the modern university has progressive tendencies, then reception study can have democratic import as well. To illustrate and clarify that import, this book argues that, despite conservative tendencies, Marxist, New Historicist, feminist, poststructuralist, and African American interpretations of Shakespeare's *Hamlet*, Austen's *Pride and Prejudice*, and other canonical and noncanonical works have progressive import because their interest in race, class, gender, and discourse opens these works to the modern university's multicultural clientele.

Initially a way of explaining an author's development, reception study has become an important mode of historical inquiry because reception study limits or rejects theory's transformative force, examines the readers' "reading formations" or "interpretive communities," and, in the post-Marxist version, fosters a coalition of the "new social movements" established in the multicultural university. As I explain in the next chapter, poststructuralist theorists of reception, who include Tony Bennett, Stanley Fish, John Frow, Steven Mailloux, and Barbara Herrnstein Smith, maintain that the activity of diverse readers addresses equally diverse interpretive communities or reading formations whose norms and values determine the validity of the interpretation. These theorists deny that literary theory can improve readers, resolve interpretive disputes, or transform institutional practices but do not go on to defend the progressive aspects of modern literary study; still, unlike the loose coalition of conservative, liberal, feminist, radical, and Marxist critics, these theorists justify the specialized study and new programs of the humanities.

Notes

1. John Carlos Rowe, *Culture*, 4.
2. See *MLA*, 6-9.
3. Michael Bérubé, *Public Access*, 20-22.
4. See Bernard Bergonzi, *Exploding English*, 178-80; Avrom Fleishman, *The Condition of English*; Harold Fromm, *Academic Capitalism*, 17-18, 21-24; and E. D. Hirsch Jr., *Cultural Literacy*, 18-24.
5. See, for example, John Ellis, *Literature Lost*; Avrom Fleishman, *The Condition of English*; or Roger Kimball, *Tenured Radicals*.
6. See Terry Eagleton, *Literary Theory*, 1-16.
7. See, for example, Michael Apple, *Official Knowledge*; Paul Lauter, "Political Correctness;" and John Wilson, *The myth of political correctness*.
8. See Michael Bérubé, *Public Access*, 20-27.
9. Edward Said, *The World*, 29; Patrick Brantlinger, *Crusoe's Footprints*, 1-26; Paul Lauter, "History," 157; and Cary Nelson, "Against English," 47-51, and "Always Already Cultural Studies," 25.
10. Murray Kreiger, *The Institution of Theory*, 22.
11. See Stanley Fish, "Being Interdisciplinary," 15; Jerry Herron, *Universities and the Myth of Cultural Decline*, 39; and Bruce Sarchett, "Russell Jacoby," 134-37.

12. Josephine Guy and Ian Small, *Politics and Value*, 3.

13. Robert Holub, *Crossing Borders*, 5-13.

14. Initially the term "poststructuralist" indicated a theoretical critique or deconstruction of structuralism, especially its systematic accounts of the conventions and codes governing the implications of texts, as well as totalizing accounts of history and referential accounts of truth. Such critiques have subsequently extended to phenomenology, analytic philosophy, pragmatism, Marxism, or psychoanalysis, especially their attempt to establish theoretical foundations for their practices. I use the term in this more general sense to indicate the rejection of interpretation's broad theoretical foundations in favor of local practices, conversations, or discourses (see Michael Ryan, *Literary Theory* 67-76). In this general sense, the term overlaps postmodern philosophy, which rejects the foundational norms of traditional philosophy, literary theory, or historical study but goes on to challenge the grand Christian and Marxist historical narratives as well; as Horace Fairlamb says, "In . . . these cases one finds a rejection of the traditional epistemological quest for a foundation of knowledge, truth, or meaning . . . [and] a movement toward a more conventionalist or relativist model of cognitive or hermeneutic authority" (*Critical Conditions*, 57). The term "postmodern" also characterizes the modern literature which continues the modernist subversion of established ethical, historical, or political values but not of popular culture (see, for example, Andreas Huyssen) as well as accounts of the contemporary historical epoch which challenge the traditional distinctions between surface and depth or parody and pastiche (see, for example, Jameson, "Regarding Postmodernism"). To minimize confusion, I use the term "poststructuralist" to indicate the philosophical critique of foundations and save the term "postmodernist" for the modern literary movement and the contemporary sociohistorical epoch.

15. For example, in *The Beauty of Inflections* (1985), Jerome McGann says that a work's "critical history . . . dates from the first responses and reviews it receives. These reactions . . . modify the author's purposes and intentions, sometimes drastically, and they remain part of the processive life" of the work "as it passes on to future readers" (24).

16. Hans Robert Jauss, *Toward an Aesthetic of Reception*, 22.

17. Hans Robert Jauss, *Question and Answer*, 160-66.

18. David Perkins, *Literary History*, 25-27.

19. René Wellek and Austin Warren, *Theory of Literary Production*, 155-56.

20. E. D. Hirsch Jr., *Validity in Interpretation*, 8.

21. See Pierre Macherey, *Theory of Literary Production*, 18-19.

22. *Writing in Society*, 197. Similarly, Jerome McGann says, "[A] text-only approach has been so vigorously promoted during the last thirty-five years that most historical critics have been driven from the field" (*Beauty of Inflections*, 17). See also David Shumway, *Creating American Civilization*, 189-90.

23. *Beauty of Inflections*, 3; see also *Marxism and Literary Criticism* (1976), in which Terry Eagleton insists that, to explain a poem like *The Wasteland* "as a poem which springs from a crisis of bourgeois ideology," one does not reduce "the poem to the state of contemporary capitalism"; rather, "Marxist criticism looks for the unique conjuncture" of such elements as "the author's class-position, ideological forms and their relation to literary forms, 'spirituality' and philosophy, techniques of literary production, aesthetic theory" (15-16); see also Lionel Trilling, *The Liberal Imagination*, which puts together an Arnoldian grace and balance and historical objectivity, and Fredric Jameson, *Political Unconscious*, 10.

24. Lionel Trilling, *The Liberal Imagination*, 285-86.

25. Raymond Williams, *Problems in Materialism and Culture*, 31-50.

26. Jauss, *Toward*, 9.

27. Jauss, *Toward*, 16-18.

28. René Wellek, *Concepts of Criticism*, 14.

29. Robert C. Holub, *Reception Theory*, 65.

30. In the later *Question and Answer*, he accords literature both traditional affirmative and modern negative functions, for the autonomous aesthetic practices of the modern era evolved from the platonic realism that dominated them in ancient times (1-10); see also Holub, *Reception Theory*.

31. See David Perkins, *Literary History*, 26.

32. Jauss, *Toward*, 25.

33. Jane Tompkins, *Sensational Designs*, 17.

34. Tompkins, *Sensational Designs*, 32-33.

35. Robert Holub, *Crossing Borders*, 34; see also Brook Thomas, *The New Historicism and Other Old-Fashioned Topics*, which says that reception study's critique of theory discredits the "very possibility of a new historicism"(79).

36. In *The Resistance to Theory*, Paul De Man says, "Literature involves the voiding, rather than the affirmation, of aesthetic categories" (10). De Man also claims that Jauss's "synthesis" of "poetic figures and hermeneutic meaning" breaks down ("Introduction,"xix) because De Man denies that one can reduce the play of literary language to an event or happening which implicates the reader and, as a result, provides historical insight.

37. Ernesto Laclau, *New Reflections*, 76-78.

38. Louis Althusser, *For Marx*, 234.

39. Ernesto Laclau and Chantal Mouffe, *Hegemony*, 110.

40. See Gayatri Spivak, "Revolutions That As Yet Have No Model," 40; and Michael Sprinker, *Imaginary Relations*.

41. *Hegemony*, 122-34. See, for example, Laclau and Mouffe's explanation of Soviet communism. On the one hand, Laclau and Mouffe grant the totalitarian theorist's belief that the Leninist account of the vanguard party explains the Stalinist features of Soviet communism (See, for example, Zbigniew Brzezinski

and Carl J. Friedrich, *Totalitarian Dictatorship and Autocracy*). The Soviet party grew more and more dictatorial because Leninist theory gave the party the exclusive possession of the scientific truth and the exclusive right to define and represent the working class and its interests (*Hegemony*, 56-57). On the other hand, Laclau and Mouffe accept the liberal historians' belief that, more than Marxist theory, the authoritarian character and the socioeconomic difficulties of late nineteenth-century Russia explain the growth of the Stalinist system (see Stephen Cohen, *Rethinking the Soviet Experience*, and Moshe Lewin, *The Gorbachev Phenomenon*). That is, emerging simultaneously, not in chronological succession, Russia's diverse groups created an anomalous situation in which the frail bourgeoisie could not undertake the modernizing tasks assigned it by established historical schema. These tasks, which included educating and industrializing Soviet society and creating large urban centers and even an independent and democratic civil society, fell instead upon the Russian working class (*Hegemony*, 50-54). In other words, since the Soviet communists articulated diverse democratic demands and simultaneous socioeconomic structures, the communists' ideological hegemony, not the fixed class identity and distinct historical stages of traditional Marxism, explain the Soviet experience.

42. See Jorge Larrain, *Ideology*, 104.
43. Jürgen Habermas, *Philosophical Discourse*, 26-28.
44. Richard Rorty, "Response."
45. Michel Foucault, *Power/Knowledge*, 134-37.
46. Michel Foucault, *The Archaeology of Knowledge*, 186.
47. Foucault, *Archaeology*, 149-56.
48. Louis Althusser, *Lenin and Philosophy*, 166.
49. Tony Bennett, *Outside Literature*, 189.
50. Michel Foucault, *Power/Knowledge*, 8-10.
51. Hayden White, *Tropics of Discourse*, 67.
52. Stephen Greenblatt, "Towards," 8.
53. Claire Colebrook, *New Literary Histories*, 24.
54. See Howard Horwitz, "Skepticism," 799-800.
55. *Tropics*, 265. Other poststructuralist historians argue that the Foucauldian approach lacks theoretical self-consciousness or accepts a black conformist functionalism. For instance, in *Foucault, Marxism and History*, Poster claims, as post-Marxists do, that Marxists address only the past era of factory production, not the modern era of electronic communication. By contrast, Poster esteems the work of Foucault, who, contrary to traditional scholars, preserves resistance either as local opposition within evolving discourses or as rupture between a discourse's ancient and modern versions. All the same, Poster laments Foucault's lack of historical and methodological self-consciousness even though such self-consciousness dismisses the specialized contexts of Foucault's work and reaffirms the systematic, totalizing thought of the traditional intellectual. In *Soundings in Critical Theory*, Dominick LaCapra voices many of the post-

Marxist criticisms of Althusser: his subtle "positivist" scientism locates ideology in the subject, makes ideology necessary or inevitable, treats the theorist's transcendence as unproblematic, ignores or denies the ideological character of objective, subjectless science, erases the institutional roots of historical inquiry, and occludes the totality of modern society (13, 166). By contrast, LaCapra praises Foucault and Derrida because he believes that they have worked out the "discursive and social practices" making possible new accounts of text and context. He grants that Foucault's concept of power-knowledge forcefully reveals "the complicity of forces that are often neatly separated, especially in defense of a value-neutral, unworldly contemplative idea of research" (21). In a paradoxical manner, he admits that disciplinary knowledge entails sociopolitical power, yet he still assumes that disciplinary knowledge takes a fetishized form undermining resistance and occluding the social totality. As a result, he criticizes what he calls the "black functionalism" of Foucault, who has, LaCapra says, revived an "indiscriminate, late 1960's idea of 'the system' or the 'dominant ideology' that necessarily" co-opts "everything it touches, including all forms of resistance" (21).

56. Stephen Greenblatt, *Shakespearean Negotiations*, 1. See also Claire Colebrook, *New Literary Histories*, which says that New Historicists preserve the traditional notion that historical texts are referential or that, as "self-fashioning," representation is fundamental to human experience (226-27).

57. Stephen Greenblatt, "What Is," 470.

58. Roger Chartier, *On the Edge of the Cliff*, 32-33.

59. Robert Scholes, *The Rise and Fall of English*, 44.

60. For instance, in *The Closing of the American Mind*, Bloom says that, while the classical tradition of Plato and Aristotle preserved the ideal of absolute knowledge and fostered the quest for the universal good, the modern university encourages a tepid openness, minority factions, and pluralist tolerance; accepts relativist, feminist and Marxist views; and, as a result, blindly promotes the collapse of the West (25-43). In *Cultural Literacy* (1987), Hirsch discusses the national culture of American public schools, not the classical tradition of elite universities. He too says, however, that schools which model their texts and dictionaries on this national culture facilitate easy communication, national unity, and socioeconomic progress (91), whereas the "modern" school, whose texts and policies, by contrast, encourage linguistic and cultural diversity, only "increases cultural fragmentation, civil antagonism, illiteracy, and economic-technological ineffectualness" (92). In *The Function of Criticism*, the Marxist Terry Eagleton also condemns the specialized disciplines, but he laments modern criticism's withdrawn state, not the dissolution of the classical or the national curriculum. In the late nineteenth century, after criticism entered the university, professional specialization destroyed the Victorian man of letters, and, isolated from the public sphere, criticism grew too technical to exercise any significant political force; as he says, "Criticism achieved security by committing political suicide; its mo-

ment of academic institutionalization is also the moment of its effective demise as a socially active force" (65). In *Professing Literature*, the liberal Gerald Graff examines the history of American literary studies, not British criticism nor the classical curriculum, yet he too regrets that the specialized fields of the modern department; however, more optimistic than Bloom or Eagleton, he maintains that, by dramatizing the theoretical conflicts, literary studies can escape its dreary history, overcome its specialized character, and regain its lost public. In *The Madwoman in the Attic*, Sandra Gilbert and Susan Gubar fault the chauvinist biases, rather than the specialized character, of established criticism, but these feminist critics expect women's literature to overcome these biases and to reestablish a lost public culture. By recuperating the "verbal fertility" stolen from the mother artist, women writers can overcome their professional and institutional oppression and reinstate writing's broad, mythic import: "[T]he path to the Sibyl's cave has been forgotten, the coherent truth of her leaves has been shattered . . . [and] the whole meaning of the sibylline leaves can only be remembered through . . . translation, transcription, and stitchery, re-vision and re-creation" (97). Fredric Jameson also considers modern literary study oppressive, but he credits what he calls the "fragmentation and compartmentalization of social reality in modern times" (*Fables of Aggression*, 6). Jameson complains, moreover, that the university's commitment to specialized, "scientific" disciplines turns theoretical discourse into reified commodities presenting themselves as sui generis, autonomous, and sacred and concealing thereby the mode of production from which they stem (*Marxism and Form*, 392-416). Edward Said also condemns specialized knowledge and disciplinary divisions, but he complains that systematizing Marxist theory and obfuscating postmodern jargon alienate the oppositional scholars from the postcolonial artists and critics who can and do resist Western colonial and imperialist domination. Even though Said considers feminism, Marxism, and postcolonial studies genuinely subversive, he fears that the modern university renders them toothless: "The irony is that it has been the university's practice to admit [them] in order to some degree to neutralize them by fixing them in the status of academic subspecialties" (*The World, the Text and the Critic*, 321).

    61. Stanley Aronowitz, *Science as Power*, 208.

    62. Anthony Smith and Frank Webster, *The Postmodern University?*, 2.

    63. Christopher J. Lucas, *American Higher Education*, i-xviii.

    64. Evan Watkins, *Work Time*, 249. See also Tony Bennett, *Outside Literature*, 239-42.

    65. Watkins, *Work Time*, 9.

    66. Lawrence Levine, *The Opening of the American Mind*, 32.

    67. See John Guillory, *Cultural Capital*, 44-46; See also Bill Readings, "The University without Culture?," 465-83.

    68. Jacques Derrida, "The Principle of Reason," 15.

    69. Vincent Leitch says that the most important New York intellectuals in-

cluded Richard Chase, Irving Howe, Alfred Kazin, Philip Rahv, and Lionel Trilling (*American Literary Criticism*, 81).

70. See *Cultural Capital*, 270-75. Similarly, although Jacques Derrida complains that conservative "guardians of the humanities" ignore "the history and the system of norms specific to their own institution, the deontology of their profession" ("The Principle of Reason," 15), he too condemns the professional orientation of the modern university. He argues, however, that it destroys the Kantian division between the practical ends of the university administration (the "technicians" of the "higher faculty") and the autonomous reason of the lower faculty (philosophy). Military research, data banks, information centers, and calculating machines all implement the false mastery of what he terms technical competence and the Frankfurt School terms instrumental reason, not the formal autonomy of rational thought ("The Principle of Reason," 14). See also *Secular Vocations*, wherein, unlike Derrida, Bruce Robbins considers professional activities a positive, "secular vocation" that enables progressive reforms. He rejects the polemics of conservative and radical scholars on the grounds that they deny the public responsibility or "secular vocation" of the modern academic. That is, he recognizes that the traditional belief in the "apolitical" disciplines ignores the positive import which reception study attributes to them but only because classical rhetoric implies that all disciplinary wisdom requires some justifying public values or political ideals. More importantly, he argues that the literary study of Williams, Said, and other Marxist and radical theorists defends radical political commitment and progressive left-wing values more successfully than disciplinary study can. In other words, he considers professional criticism positive but still takes the conservative and radical polemics dividing the discipline to show that it lacks the political commitment and self-consciousness achieved by the great Marxist scholars.

71. Guillory, *Cultural Capital*, 6-10, 38-47.
72. Michael Bérubé, *The Employment of English*, 22.

Chapter One
Cultural Value and Poststructuralist Theory: The Case for a Left-Wing Reception Study

As I indicated in the introduction, Hans Robert Jauss's modern reception study as well as poststructuralist and post-Marxist reception study maintain that the interpretive activities of readers explain the meaning of a text and, more generally, the history of literary studies; however, unlike Jauss, poststructuralist and post-Marxist reception study repudiate the transcendent status of the great text and justify the humanities' new programs. The leading poststructuralists, who include Stanley Fish, Steven Mailloux, and Barbara Herrnstein Smith, and the leading post-Marxists, who include Tony Bennett and John Frow, maintain that the activity of diverse readers addresses the equally diverse personal economies or interpretive or rhetorical communities whose norms and values determine the validity of the interpretation. Bennett and Frow go on to show, however, that the contrary norms and ideals of modern criticism's schools, movements, or "reading formations" establish what Bennett terms an educational "technology" forming the literary subject. While Smith opposes modern literary study because of its aesthetic "axiology," Bennett, Fish, Frow, and Mailloux justify its specialized disciplines and/or its new cultural programs; still, Fish and Mailloux question or deny altogether the value of a literary politics and preserve a positivist view of language or a utopian notion of social progress. Bennett and Frow describe the reading or value formations governing interpretive practices but inconsistently adopt the positivist or liberal view, instead of clarifying literary study's conservative and progressive aspects or fostering the radical extension of the Enlightenment tradition, as Ernesto Laclau and Chantal Mouffe do. Still, while conservatives and radicals engage in polemics designed to ensure the conformity of literary study with ideals, movements, groups, or values outside professional literary study, reception study, which repudiates the transformative force of such polemics, produces histories of a text's reception preserving the integrity of professional literary study.

The Neopragmatism of Stanley Fish

Fish shows that the "interpretive community" of the reader limits the subversive force of figural language and theoretical critique and establishes the legitimacy of the reader's interpretation and, more generally, the profession's fields and programs. Fish goes on, however, to dismiss a literary politics, including post-Marxism's radical democracy, and to defend a neutral, positivist view of literary study.

Fish's positivist view evolves from his earlier reader-response criticism. In early works, he argues that the irreducible effects of language move readers to produce interpretations, and, like Jauss, he construes the author as a normative force teaching or fashioning the reader. For example, in "Affective Stylistics," he says that reading is a temporal process in which the reader constructs interpretations and, when they mislead him or her, repudiates them in favor of new ones. Such construction and reconstruction reveal to the reader the kind of text he or she is experiencing, rather than the unifying figures of the text or the intention of the author.

In later work Fish abandons the assumption that competent readers discover one "deep structure" or generic type because that assumption did not enable him to explain why some readers interpret a text one way and others interpret it another. Adopting the pragmatist's belief that the community of inquirers establishes the truth of a theory, Fish claims instead that the norms, ideals, and methods of the reader's "interpretive community" determine an interpretation's validity. In "Interpreting the Variorum," for example, he says that Milton's sonnets pose conundrums to which readers have consistently offered the same sorts of solutions. What explains these persistent solutions is the formal requirements of the readers' different "interpretive communities."[1]

Fish denies that to reject the absolute ground of an author's intention or a text's structure is to consider any interpretation as good as any other or to lapse into a vacuous relativism, as critics say, because we cannot get outside of our beliefs in order, to treat them as relativist and because the reader's community determines the validity of facts and interpretations.

Post-Marxist reception study also maintains that, precluding a vacuous relativism, the reading formation establishes the validity of his or her interpretations. In Bennett's terms, interpretations require warranted assertability, rather than perfect certainty; however, while the post-Marxist defends the Foucauldian notion that authoritative discourse constructs or interpellates a subject, Fish maintains that the contextual indeterminacies of language open a text to multiple interpretive practices. Scholars complain that Fish rejects the ideals of the literary and philosophical community,[2] but he derives this account of textual language from analytic philosophy, especially John Austin's speech-act theory.

In the *Meditations*, René Descartes's famous claim "I think, so I am" aptly summarized his belief that his ability to doubt false as well as uncertain beliefs ultimately justified his existence and his conceptual framework, what he called the ideas which he found within himself. Because analytic philosophers consider such self-consciousness nonsensical, they seek to reduce abstract ideas to empirically observable behavior. For example, according to the "logical atomism" established by Bertrand Russell, the early Wittgenstein, and others, linguistic analysis divides the meaning of a proposition from the particular entity to which the proposition ostensibly refers. If the analysts can acquaint themselves with this entity or if a description can enable them to know it or to deduce its features, they treat the assertion as a sensible statement. If they cannot know this entity either by acquaintance or by description, they dismiss the assertion as rhetorical or metaphysical.[3] Hence, the statement "The king of France is bald" makes no sense because there is no king of France.

Gilbert Ryle also argued that to construe concepts like "love" or "spirit" as independent or substantial entities was to make a "category mistake." Just as there is no team spirit apart from the team's enthusiasm, so there is no love apart from a lover's passion.[4] Ryle went on to maintain, however, that this mistake derives from Descartes's belief that the mechanical laws of the body must be very different from the reflexive, self-determining character of the mind. Ryle derisively labeled this Cartesian belief in such self-conscious thought "the ghost in the machine" because he feared that, freezing the self in its mirroring mind, this mechanical ghost imposed an infinite regress in which, if I recognize that I am aware that I see an object, then I must also be aware that I am aware of seeing an object, and so on. John Austin, Ryle's colleague at Oxford, also reduces abstract concepts to empirical behavior, but he makes some provision for rhetorical conventions. Like the later

Wittgenstein, who insisted that, in addition to naming or denoting, language involves many sorts of "games," he says that "constative" assertions describe facts whereas performative assertions must meet conventional requirements if they are to indicate action authoritatively.[5]

Fish also repudiates the Cartesian self-consciousness, but he argues that the linguistic analysis of abstract concepts cannot exclude the auditor's conventions. Like Derrida, who maintains that Austin's distinction between constative and performative assertions cannot effectively exclude misfires, failures, or literary figures,[6] he claims that the distinction breaks down. He says that no assertion can have a purely factual, descriptive, or constative status because, as Austin admits, all assertions presuppose a conventional social context in which they represent actions.[7]

John Searle objects that a few misfires or a little metaphorical slippage does not destroy a conceptual distinction or undermine a writer's intentional act.[8] This objection denies that linguistic acts generate concepts; rather, in Russell's analytic fashion the objections assume that concepts mirror facts or lapse into metaphysical nonsense. Barbara Johnson grants, by contrast, that the misfires or metaphorical slippages destroy the referential capacity of language, but she argues that they allow mutually incompatible meanings undermining the seriousness of the assertion.[9] In keeping with Paul De Man's paradoxical belief that "[t]echnically correct rhetorical readings . . . are theory and not theory at the same time, the universal theory of the impossibility of theory,"[10] Johnson assumes that her formal reading of Mallarmé's *La Déclaration foraine* justifies a textual indeterminacy subverting the reader's practices.

Like Johnson, Fish says that the breakdown of the distinction destroys the referential capacity of language, but he maintains that the breakdown effectively establishes the reader's conventions as the authoritative basis of speech's meaning, rather than speech's inability to make any assertions. Fish shows, however, that, if all assertions, even ostensibly factual ones, affect hearers or readers, their conventions, not the language's conceptual rigor or denotative clarity, explain the felicity of the assertion.[11] As he says, "[S]entences emerge only in situations, and within those situations, the normative meaning of an utterance will always be obvious or at least accessible, although within another situation that same utterance, no longer the same, will have another normative meaning that will be no less obvious and accessible."[12] This contextual indeterminacy allows the sentences of a speech or a text a normative meaning but not one normative meaning.

Moreover, Fish opposes the theoretical self-consciousness whereby, in De Man's terms, "[t]echnically correct rhetorical readings" can be "theory and not theory at the same time." In "Consequences," he grants that literary theory has acquired its own practices and fields; just the same, he argues, as Ryle does, that theory does not ensure a reader's self-consciousness, govern interpretive practice, or change anything at all. He admits that theorists may examine the rhetorical figures of a text, the unifying intention of its author, its play of gender differences, or its critiques of ideology; however, he considers these diverse interpretive practices a matter of local, Derridean, authorial, feminist, or Marxist beliefs, not of valid theory, whose general rules or universal norms cannot determine correct interpretations. Fish does not reduce values to emotive feelings, as some positivists do; still, just as the positivists divide personal values and public fact, so Fish claims that the project of literary theory inevitably fails because practical interpretation is a matter of local beliefs, not general or universal truth.[13]

Post-Marxism also maintains that facts, concepts, and logic do not exclude convention, rhetoric, or ideology and that theoretical norms do not govern institutional practices; post-Marxism claims, however, that the authoritative reading formations established in literary institutions construct the literary subject and allow a radical democratic coalition of new social movements. Fish assumes, by contrast, that the contextual indeterminacy of a text's language, not the hegemonic influence of authoritative schools or movements, explains the interpretive communities governing a text's readers. For example, Fish limits Milton's interpretive community to specialized Miltonist or Renaissance scholars, who know the generic conventions of pastoral poetry, because he believes that these contrary generic conventions, not the changing sociohistorical contexts of literary study, explain the contextual indeterminacies of Milton's work.[14]

Moreover, Fish dismisses multicultural criticism in both its feeble "boutique" and its strong serious version because he attributes its critiques of American ethnocentrism to theoretical polemics, not institutional politics.[15] Theory alone may not change ethnocentrism, as he claims, yet the politics of multicultural criticism involves institutional conflict and change, not just theoretical critique. In general, he claims that "in our society interpretations of literary works . . . do not connect up strongly with the issues being debated in the larger political arena . . . there is just too much distance between" literary criticism and "legislative, journalistic, juridical" public forums."[16] Fish may be right to deny that the generic conventions of Milton's pastoral poetry have much to do with such "public forums"; however, the establishment of the humanities' new theories and programs involved and still involves intense political conflict, which informs contemporary discussion of department curriculum, course requirements, faculty hiring, remedial programs, and university admissions policies. Fish may mean that, if, like Milton scholarship, the humanities' new cultural or multicultural programs meet professional standards, their politics should not matter. In that case too, Fish would be right, yet their politics still do matter, especially in light of the culture wars, corporate downsizing, graduate student unions, nationally publicized curriculum disputes, hiring policies, rising tuition costs, and so on.

Unlike post-Marxism, which extends the Enlightenment tradition to the women's, African American, and other social movements, Fish excludes politics from literary study because he accepts not only analytic philosophy's critique of referential statements and of Cartesian self-consciousness but also its positivist distinction between personal values and public or factual truth. Critics object that the reception study of Fish allows incompatible interpretive communities because it rejects the transcendental entities or universal ideals needed to account for other minds, avoid solipsism, or learn from experience.[17] To an extent, the critics are right: since positivist analytic philosophy reduces values to private feelings or dogmatic beliefs, Fish allows the contextual indeterminacies of a text's language, not authoritative reading formations, to explain the text's contrary readings. Fish's opponents claim, however, that this limitation of his view invalidates reception study and justifies figural or theoretical critique. Daniel O'Hara even warns us that "a Stanley Fish can all too readily be taken, even by [oppositional] critics who should know better, as a plausible representative of the academic left."[18] This claim goes too far. In the divided 1990s, when the successes of African American, women's, cultural, multicultural, theoretical, and gay studies have so sharply fragmented the humanities, a post-Marxist reception study also argues against theoretical critique or political jeremiads because no aesthetic theory or literary method transcends these divisions and reconciles its antagonistic parties or interpretive communities. This reception study goes on, nonetheless, to explain the changing historical contexts of the antagonistic parties and to clarify the conservative and progressive aspects of the humanities' new programs.

The Hermeneutics of Steven Mailloux

Like Fish's reception study, Steven Mailloux's "rhetorical hermeneutics" debunks the subversive pretensions of literary theory and explains literary study's diverse "rhetorical" communities. At the same time, his hermeneutics explains the historical origins and rhetorical practices of literary study's diverse professional communities and promotes the democratic reform of literary study more fully than Fish's analytic theory does. Mailloux argues, however, that the critique of theory need not imply incommensurable or "relativist" interpretive practices or preclude a rational consensus. Instead of acknowledging that established literary schools and movements divide modern literary study or defending their progressive import, as post-Marxists do, he advocates a utopian liberalism which sets his postmodern hermeneutics above the humanities' "culture wars."

He maintains, as Fish and Jauss do, that authors communicate meanings to readers and in this way teach readers how to read. The conventions adopted by readers, not the foundational aesthetic norms of a text nor the unifying intention of an author, explain established interpretive practices.[19] Mailloux objects that the empiricist Fish consigns too much to the reader's beliefs and too little to theory, which, Mailloux says, has at least unexpected consequences: it directs research, precludes unacceptable views, and exposes concealed interests,[20] yet he too argues that the rhetorical practices of a community or discipline, rather than the norms of "foundational" theory, justify or limit the reader's interpretive practice. Derived from Jonathan Culler's *Structuralist Poetics*, not Austin's speech-act theory,[21] this broad notion of rhetoric repudiates the Platonic belief that, trapped in the dark cave, rhetoric takes shadows for truth, while, coming into bright daylight, theory grasps objective reality. Mailloux too claims, however, that different readers produce different interpretations and even different texts because their diverse conventions govern their interpretive practices. As he says, "rhetorical hermeneutics" uses the "widespread acceptability" of established literary methods "to explain the rhetorical dynamics of academic interpretations in late twentieth-century America."[22]

For example, he considers the conclusion of *Huckleberry Finn* progressive because it requires the reader to provide a liberal solution to the racial issues raised by Huck's travels with Jim. These travels have taught Huck to appreciate Jim's deep humanity, yet, when Tom turns Jim's escape into a ridiculous and dangerous adventure, Huck does not object. Critics claim that this turn of events vitiates Twain's critique of slavery;[23] Mailloux says, however, that the turn of events poses important conundrums for the reader, who must decide for himself or herself whether Twain has abandoned his liberal critique of slavery and reconstruction. Mailloux maintains, moreover, that nineteenth-century readers ignored these racial issues because these readers meant to stop a spreading juvenile delinquency, what they termed the "bad boy syndrome," whereas twentieth-century readers debated these racial issues because those readers disputed the politics of the newly established formal criticism.[24]

This account of the reader's conundrums shows how insightfully Mailloux's hermeneutics explains a text's reception; still, by assimilating the criticism of the novel to these determinate historical contexts, this account implicitly denies that contrary schools and movements seek to dominate the text. Gunn insightfully suggests that, "while acknowledging the historicity of all interpretive acts, including its own," Mailloux's hermeneutics "in effect denies the possibility of critically comparing and evaluating them."[25] In addition, both Fish and Bennett discount the objection that, by rejecting the absolute ground of an author's intention or a text's structure, they inevitably treat any interpretation as good as any other. By contrast, Mailloux argues that, while the reception study of Fish and Jauss betrays an incoherent "relativist" incommensurability or precludes rational communication or professional improvement, as critics say, his rhetorical hermeneutics escapes these limitations and fosters an enlightened liberal community.

One of his reasons is that he accepts Rorty's troublesome belief that the neopragmatist critique of philosophy's epistemological foundations cannot be relativist because it moves beyond traditional philosophy—Carl Freedman considers Mailloux a liberal of a similar but more genial kind than Richard Rorty.[26] Joseph Margolis rightly objects, however, that Rorty's repudiation of foundational epistemology does not obviate such criticism of his relativism because the repudiation does not exclude epistemological questions about what makes our knowledge possible.[27] Rorty may still discuss knowledge claims, as Mailloux says,[28] but his discussion of them does not avoid relativist import because the discussion cannot exclude epistemological questions.

Mailloux also argues that the sophistic rhetoric of Protagoras, who in Plato's famous dialogue claims that man is the measure of all things, justifies his claim that, unlike Fish's or Bennett's reception study, his hermeneutics overcomes relativism and transcends criticism's divided communities. Mailloux says that, taken as social and not as individual, Protagoras's claim implies that "all we have to deal with as situated observers are the webs of belief and desire that constitute our rhetorical contexts."[29] In this social sense, that claim does not reduce to a vacuous relativism, as critics charge, because no privileged standpoint enables us to maintain that our culture is superior to other cultures or to stigmatize our cultural others. He still argues, however, that "it is better to keep the issue of foundationalism versus antifoundationalism logically separate from the issue of reactionary versus progressive politics."[30] This politically neutral "antifoundationalism" divorces the critique of philosophical and aesthetic foundations from the divided historical context established by the culture/theory wars. To ignore or dismiss such contexts is, however, to lapse into the self-refuting Protagorean relativism whereby the claim that the truth of a statement is always relative to its context amounts to a universal truth, not a strategic assertion.

Mailloux grants that theory does not transcend these divisions but, to overcome the relativist incommensurability of Fish's or Bennett's reception study, establishes a utopian "no man's land" where, transcending relativist incommensurability, the humanities form an enlightened liberal community. As a consequence, he recognizes that "realists," who, like Bloom, Hirsch, and Eagleton, expect criticism to conform to the demands of the text, the author, or the public world, oppose "idealists," who, like Fish, Frow, or Bennett, expect the conventions and discourses of literary study to explain interpretive practice. He claims, however, that the "way to answer the realist/idealist question 'Is meaning created by the text or by the reader or by both?' is simply not to ask it, to stop doing Theory."[31] He does not dismiss universal theory in favor of local beliefs or ideologies, as Fish does, or the Hegelian totality in favor of a partial horizon, as Jauss does. He simply urges critics to put aside theory and engage in "therapeutic" rhetorical analyses.

Since theoretical critique warrants the jeremiads dividing the profession, Mailloux is right; at the same time, even though he denies that there is an "ahistorical, nonrhetorical 'neutral ground' from which historical arguments can be made,"[32] this ecumenical call for an end to the theory wars presupposes just such a neutral space—what else would explain why critics who "stop doing Theory" turn to "therapeutic" rhetorical analyses, rather than epistemological critique or political argument? He says that to reject theory is to focus "on the rhetorical dynamics among interpreters within specific cultural settings ... theory soon turns into rhetorical history,"[33] yet "theory soon turns into rhetorical history" only if history constitutes a neutral space outside literary study's "incommensurable" divisions.

Like the post-Marxists, Mailloux favors a more democratic criticism—he grants that his "sophistic rhetorical pragmatism can promote and be promoted by democratic forms of political organization."[34] He even allows that, because of our enlightened, liberal traditions, interpreters who learn the beliefs of other cultures enable our society to overcome its entrenched ethnocentrism. More fully than Fish's empirical reception study, Mailloux's rhetorical hermeneutics opens the interpretive methods of modern literary criticism to historical study and to democratic reform, yet on the utopian grounds that a liberal society overcomes its "relativist" or incommensurable communities, abolishes its others, and preserves its wholeness, Mailloux sets reception study outside the theory/culture wars dividing modern literary study.

The Post-Marxist Reception Study of Tony Bennett and John Frow

Like Fish and Mailloux, Tony Bennett and John Frow examine the interpretive practices of readers and their governing reading formations but go on to explain the institutional reproduction of the literary subject. Although Bennett and Frow initially elaborate Althusserian theory and Russian formalism, not analytic philosophy or liberal neopragmatism, they subsequently repudiate the scientific neutrality of the Althusserians and in a post-Marxist fashion reveal the authoritative contexts of the reader's interpretive practices. More fully than Frow, Bennett critiques the theoretical norms of aesthetic theory, yet Bennett and Frow both accept the neutral positivism or liberal optimism of Fish and Mailloux, instead of the radical democratic politics extending Enlightenment traditions to excluded groups.

Initially, Bennett and Frow maintain that Althusserian theory and Russian formalism explain the reader's interpretive practices as well as what Frow terms their governing "regimes of reading" and Bennett their "reading formations." In *Marxism and Literary History* (1986), Frow adopts the Althusserian belief that literature does not imitate an independent reality; literature produces the effects of realism. He maintains that, since a text reworks the conventions and practices of its discourses, it produces a "knowledge-effect," not cognitive truth.

The Althusserian view elaborated the structuralist belief that, by providing the "object-language" for which structuralism represents a "meta-language," writing becomes science, just as science becomes writing. In *Mythologies* (1958), for example, Roland Barthes suggested that, like science, literature demystifies popular culture. Writers like Flaubert are not formalists erasing the presence of the author but scientists analyzing the object-languages of popular culture. Elaborating this structuralist view, Pierre Macherey argued that the ordinary reader falls victim to ideology, which presents itself as historical truth, whereas the rigorous, scientific critic recognizes the formal gaps and aesthetic incoherence revealing the work's ideological import.[35] Similarly, in *Criticism and Ideology* (1976), Eagleton claims that literary texts rework the signs of ideology, exposing their gaps, speaking their silences. The critic who possesses a science of ideologies escapes their influence, transcends his or her own arbitrariness, and perceives the reader's and the text's "true" relationship.[36] Frow complains that this Althusserian science of ideology preserves the transcendent force of sociohistorical reality,[37] but he grants that, unlike the Lukácsians, who efface literary discourse in order to grant historical reality an unmediated presence, the Althusserians rightly construe realism as an effect of literary discourse.[38] Similarly, Bennett claims that great literature does not conform with an external sociohistorical context or origin; it produces the effects of realism, as the Althusserians say. In *Outside Literature*, he also complains that the scientific stance adopted by Althusserian antihumanists does not enable the subject to overcome the arbitrary or subjective character of aesthetic judgments and to perceive a text's "objective" ideological incoherence, distortion, and gaps. Bennett denies that an ideological subject can adopt the subjectless standpoint of science especially if, as Althusser says, science does not constitute a subject.[39] He rejects as well the traditional Marxist "dualism" whereby an objective history grounds an indeterminate text or culture. He argues that traditional Marxists explained canonical works in profound, sociohistorical terms but mistakenly believed that, when history ends and communism begins, the universality of a text's values will be self-evident.[40] Since the "inevitable" march of progressive social forces does not ensure the triumph of socialist ideals, the objective historical contexts of a work do not explain its value or limit its meaning. He accepts, instead, Laclau and Mouffe's claim that the hegemonic force of established discourse undermines the fixed stages and predetermined contexts in terms of which Hegelian Marxists have so narrowly explained historical change. As he says, "It becomes difficult to see how the idea of society can be regarded as supplying a conceptually 'fixed' or stabilized object."[41]

As I noted in the introduction, Jauss, who also critiques the traditional historical method, goes on to adopt Russian formalism, whose notion of defamiliarization explains the historical relationship of a text and its readers' activity. Similarly, Bennett and Frow defend Russian formalism, especially its notions of estrangement and innovation. In *Formalism and Marxism* (1979), Bennett argues that, since traditional Marxism neglected matters of literary form, it can learn from Russian formalism, whose accounts of defamiliarization, estrangement, or intertextuality situate texts in a literary context but still subvert established ideological discourses.[42] "Bourgeois" critics assume that literature possesses a timeless essence which includes only a few established genres and reveals the universals truths of our human nature, whereas Bennett denies that the notion of literature has such formal, authorial, or essential properties; rather, literature is a historical construct whose canonical genres and texts and whose opposition to non-literary discourses has changed markedly especially in the twentieth century, when the media have been so influential.[43] In a similar fashion, Frow argues that Russian formalism places a text in a "literary series" in which it ruptures with official generic norms and literary codes and affirms its own vision. A modernist practice fostered by commodity production, the estrangement or, in structuralist terms, "intertextuality" of the Russian formalists subverts the conventional opposition between intrinsic literary practices and extrinsic scientific, legal, political, religious, or economic discourse. Literature is not an autonomous entity composed of a few unchanging genres; literary texts acquire an ideological or sociohistorical import and changing genres and types.[44]

Frow also claims that intertextuality opens a place for reading, which constitutes the text's references to codes, genres, other texts, and nonliterary discourses. Like Fish, who argues that a reader's misleading interpretations reveal the text's enabling conventions, not mistaken views, Frow says that criticism does not refute wrong interpretations; rather, it illuminates the intertextual literary system or "regime of reading" governing a reader's interpretations. Bennett too maintains that the intertextuality of Russian formalism or contemporary semiotics opens a place for reading, but he claims that authoritative institutions of criticism, not the transcendent force of the great text, regulate the reader's activity. In *Bond and Beyond*, for example, he and Janet Woollacott show that established "reading formations" situate and construct the reader's norms and ideals.[45] To interpret a text is to contest its terrain, to vindicate one's methods and ideologies, and, by implication if not by explicit assertion, to debunk opposed methods and ideologies.[46] In addition, he maintains that during the nineteenth century, when the schools turned literature into a "moral technology," the ideal teacher and subsequently the many-layered text made the reader's interpretive activity the basis of his or her unending ethical improvement.[47] The Marxist critic expects this endless interpretive activity to ensure the reader's ideological improvement, but the Marxist critic too ignores the power of this institutional technology to constitute a self-improving subject.

In *Culture: A Reformer's Science* (1998), Bennett goes on to dismiss the Gramscian notion that, creating political assent or imposing "hegemony," culture emanates from a centering social formation and integrates and mediates diverse levels of social organization;[48] rather, in a Foucauldian fashion, various technologies produce various cultural resources and impose equally various forms and kinds of discipline or governmental organization.[49] As Toby Miller suggests, such technologies produce cultural resources imposing equally various forms of normality. Libraries, television, movies, or academic disciplines, especially economics, political science, and literary criticism, constitute subjects loyal to what he terms the "cultural-capitalist state." Since this state is not absolutist, these disciplines and cultural forms do not form a unified subject functioning as a coherent agent of social change; they form subjects with diverse economic, political, or literary kinds of loyalty or normality. Miller also argues that cultural critics ignore the power of this technology to constitute a self-improving subject; however, while Bennett construes a text as a meaningful terrain in which the reader defends one method and refutes others, Miller, who accepts the conservative and radical belief that the humanities have suffered a decline in the modern era, argues that the ethical norms imposed by a text's incompleteness or indeterminacy simply ensure that, to complete themselves, readers accept the ideals of the state.[50]

Eagleton also repudiates Althusserian antihumanism and adopts a poststructuralist account of discourse, but, unlike Bennett and Frow, he defends traditional notions of realism.[51] When the poststructuralist era begins, Eagleton confesses that the scientific formalism of *Criticism and Ideology* is "elitist," and, even though he considers deconstructive discourse anarchistic and insubstantial, he accepts a poststructuralist textuality preserving the subversive force of literary language. In the Althusserian work, the lapses produced by ideology's inability to reduce literary language to programmatic ends reveal the text's ideological commitments; in the poststructuralist work, the gaps induced by figural language's ability to escape the text's "centering voice" reveal those ends.[52]

Eagleton grants that this poststructuralist theory subverts the capacity of literature to depict its sociohistorical contexts objectively but defends the traditional realism of Theodor Adorno, who argues that the public, sociohistorical contexts of a text overcome its disciplinary limitations and determine its objective meaning;[53] Eagleton's defense of Adorno's realist approach does not square with his poststructuralist view of literary language, which does not by any means imply that discourse conforms with the social totality or with traditional generic or social conventions. Moreover, as Habermas argues, the Enlightenment tradition embodied by the modern university overcomes the reification of disciplinary discourse by making expert knowledge accessible to the public, not by speculatively reconstructing the immanent social totality.[54]

While Bennett, Eagleton, and Frow all repudiate Althusserian science and adopt poststructuralist theories, Eagleton inconsistently preserves the public ideals of traditional realism, whereas, like Fish and Mailloux, Bennett and Frow take the "reading formations" or "regimes of reading" established in literary or pedagogic institutions to govern the interpretive activities of readers because Bennett and Frow accept the post-Marxist belief that institutions construct their own social relations and do not simply mirror or accept a predetermined cultural center or social context. Bennett and Frow go on, nonetheless, to reject the radical democratic politics of post-Marxist theory and to accommodate the positivist autonomy or utopian liberalism of Fish and Mailloux.

For instance, like Mailloux, Frow sets reception study beyond the conflicts and divisions of modern literary study because he fears that, because the "regimes of reading" which govern the reception of diverse literatures or cultures are incommensurable, these regimes generate a vitiating relativism; however, Frow argues that only theoretical self-consciousness can overcome this relativism. As he says:

> [T]he disjunctions between the organizing aesthetics of European and non-European cultures, between 'men's' and 'women's' genres (in so far as this opposition can be sustained), between religious and 'aesthetic' functionalizations of a text, between literate and oral cultures, between the cultural norms of different age-classes or different sexual subcultures or different national regions, and so on, can be taken as indications of a vastly more complex network of differentiations which is not, or is no longer, reducible to a single scale.[55]

Frow adds that to insist upon a "single scale" or a "uniform criterion" is not to transform the reader but to repress "the differences and specificity of other practices."[56] He fears just the same that these incommensurable regimes generate a vitiating relativism which renders all judgments of value equivalent, ignores differences within communities, and permits no "critique of everyday processes."[57] Although Mailloux also fears this relativism, he repudiates the transformative power of theory; by contrast, Frow defends the aesthetic self-consciousness enabling "cultural intellectuals" to grasp their determining sociohistorical interests as a class and readers to resist the established codes, genres, and norms of their regimes of reading. As he says, "The productive role of the reader ... represents a break with a dominant regime of reading and with the institutional context which directly or indirectly sustains this regime."[58] The claim that the aesthetic self-consciousness of intellectuals and readers enables them to "break with ... the institutional context" of literary study contradicts his belief that, as a "regime of reading," that context validates their interpretive practice. If readers can break with their institutional contexts, they function in a realm above criticism's divisions and conflicts, as Mailloux shows.

While Frow resists the relativism of the regimes of reading and preserves the theoretical self-consciousness of the reader, Bennett denies the transformative force of theory but still considers literary institutions apolitical. Indeed, he and Barbara Herrnstein Smith critique "foundational" aesthetics in a similar manner. Smith emphasizes the individuality of the reader, whose personal "economy" of values justifies his or her judgments and interpretations, and faults modern literary study, whose oppressive aesthetic "axiology" precludes such individual judgments of value,[59] while Bennett says that established reading formations enable schools and universities to discipline readers, ensuring that they constitute proper subjects; still, Bennett and Smith both claim that the traditional aesthetics of David Hume, Immanuel Kant, and other modern theorists requires but fails to establish absolute norms of universal value.[60]

Peggy Kamuf complains that Bennett's and Smith's critique of traditional aesthetics treats the concept of aesthetic judgment as real, not hypothetical: "They tend . . . to read Kant as invoking a substantive understanding, our own."[61] This objection mixes up theoretical ideals and institutional practices. It is not Bennett or Smith but the received aesthetic "axiology" which affirms the universal truths of common sense or our human nature or considers them our "substantive understanding." Kamuf assumes, moreover, that in a Kantian manner Bennett means to free literature from its institutional technology.[62] It is true that in the relatively early "Texts in History" (1985) Bennett takes Marxist reception study to disrupt the institutional reproduction of established ideologies and to situate texts in "different reading formations," which he identifies with working-class, feminist, and African American struggles; nonetheless, in later work, he considers the institutional technology of literary study positive or enabling, not oppressive or "functionalist."

While Stuart Hall argues that cultural studies must resist its disciplinary contexts if it is to avoid cooptation, Bennett esteems its established institutional status, which includes not only academic programs with specific course requirements but also a growing industry of classroom textbooks and scholarly journals and studies.[63] Fredric Jameson expects cultural studies to form a historic block of progressive academic and public radicals, whereas Bennett argues that in most colleges and universities, which are under strict state regulation, cultural studies can, at best, contribute to a student's general education requirements and employment prospects.[64] As he says, work in educational institutions "is in no way to be downgraded or regarded as less vital politically than the attempt to produce new collective forms of cultural association."⁶⁵

Unlike Frow, who preserves traditional notions of theoretical self-consciousness, Bennett forcefully demonstrates that, in defense of such self-consciousness, radical theorists reduce educational institutions to a political instrument or to a threatening cooptation and ignore their positive features; nonetheless, like Fish, who divides literature from politics in a positivist manner, Bennett maintains that the "institutional placement" of modern intellectuals in "tertiary educational institutions" allows only formal policies, rather than a progressive politics.⁶⁶ This claim, which involves what Miller terms "redemption through a neo-Wittgensteinian concept of rule rather than neoromantic elevations of resistance,"⁶⁷ goes too far. As I argued in the introduction, the humanities' new cultural and multicultural studies raise sexual, literary, ethnic, racial, and theoretical issues which preclude the traditional neutrality of criticism. Like Fish's defense of a positivist literary autonomy, Bennett's notion of "institutional placement" implies that criticism remains neutral and independent even though the "theory/culture" wars have so sharply divided the humanities.

Bennett, Fish, Frow, and Mailloux all critique the foundational norms established by aesthetic theory and examine the "interpretive communities," "rhetorical practices," or "reading formations" governing contemporary literary studies; however, while post-Marxism defends the progressive aspects of the humanities, Fish's poststructuralist speech-act theory divides literary study and political activity, Mailloux's rhetorical hermeneutics sets reception study above criticism's "relativist" conflicts and divisions, Frow's theoretical self-consciousness counters the regimes of reading's vitiating relativism, and Bennett's notion of intellectuals' "institutional placement" precludes a literary politics.

Conclusion

The next chapter, which examines the reception of *Hamlet*, shows that the opposition of Marxist and poststructuralist or postmodern criticism has its roots in modern humanism, which defends the unified human self against the fragmentation imposed by commodity production, historical change, or specialized disciplines. That is, while traditional Marxist and non-Marxist accounts of *Hamlet* oppose each other, these traditional accounts defend the humanist ideal and reject poststructuralist accounts, whereas the poststructuralist accounts raise progressive issues of gender and textuality. Chapters 4 and 5 examine theorists who, like Eagleton, adopt a poststructuralist account of art but, to remain responsible to the public sphere, preserve a version of traditional realism, instead of fostering the progressive reform of the humanities. Those chapters also show that, to reform the humanities, the post-Marxist emphasizes the subversive import of popular culture, while the poststructuralist defense of realism inconsistently retains the privileges of high art and traditional theory.

In this chapter, I have argued that Bennett, Fish, Frow, and Mailloux develop a reception theory which maintains, for the most part, that interpretive communities or reading formations govern the interpretive practices of readers and that literary theory cannot improve readers, resolve interpretive disputes, or transform institutional practices. Fish and Mailloux adopt a positivist view of language or a utopian notion of social progress, whereas Bennett and Frow accept a Foucauldian or post-Marxist notion of authoritative literary formations but not the radical democracy of post-Marxism. Eagleton also adopts a poststructuralist account of discourse, but he complains that post-Marxist theory disables radical opponents of the capitalist system just when that system has gotten more powerful than ever;[68] however, he admits that his poststructuralist realism grants only high modernist art oppositional force. By contrast, Bennett, Fish, Frow, and Mailloux defend the humanities' disciplines and/or new programs. Although Fish's positivist approach restricts the legitimation of disciplinary practices to professional expertise, he still demonstrates that the liberal and conservative opposition to established literary or cultural studies itself reflects the disciplinary contexts of modern professional life.[69] Mailloux grants that the context of this opposition is the profession, as Fish says; still, his rhetorical hermeneutics promotes democratic reforms like the reformed curriculum which Syracuse University instituted under his leadership.[70] Bennett's critique of a radical self-consciousness justifies academic disciplines and established cultural studies programs, including their textbooks, graduation requirements, and occupational utility.

Notes

1. Stanley Fish, *Is There a Text in This Class?*, 147-73.
2. See Suresh Raval, *Grounds of Literary Criticism*, 98-100.
3. See, for example, "On the Nature of Acquaintance" (1914), wherein Bertrand Russell identifies two legitimate kinds of knowledge: knowledge by acquaintance and knowledge by description. Knowledge by acquaintance assumes that the knower observes, describes, and even names the objects or experiences

conceptualized by the knowledge. Such knowledge enables one to get to know the particulars to which a proposition refers. One attains the immediate certainty provided by proper names and by pronouns like "this." By contrast, knowledge by description allows the knower to assent to objects and to experiences even though he or she has not encountered or observed them. Since one knows only the language used by a proposition, inference and deduction from what one knows by acquaintance justifies one's assent.

    4. Gilbert Ryle, *The Concept of Mind*, 16-18.

    5. John Austin, *How to Do Things with Words*, 3-9.

    6. Jacques Derrida, "Signature, Event, Context," 385-87.

    7. Fish, *Is There*, 67, 91.

    8. Searle makes this claim in "Reiterating the Differences: A Reply to Derrida." In the 1987 Romanelli Phi Beta Kappa Lectures in Philosophy, which were published as "Literary Theory and Its Discontents," Searle elaborates his argument. He says that, little more than a "tissue of confusions," the Derridean critique of Austin mixes up such plain distinctions as type/token, use/mention, literal/figurative, and convention/intention. For example, Searle says that the Derridean notion of "iterability" confuses intention and convention. He grants that, say, Derrida's example, "green is either," can make no sense in one context but perfect sense in another context. However, he denies Derrida's conclusion that language is iterable or that distinct codes or conventions and not a writer's intention govern meaning; the fact that language makes no sense in one context and perfectly good sense in another only shows that in different contexts writers have different intentions. The Derridean critique of Austin takes for granted, however, the phenomenological notion that pure, autonomous concepts do not mirror the features of linguistic facts; these concepts explain the possibility of such facts. To insist that "we can already recognize the phenomenon before we begin the investigation" is simply to ignore the ability of language to constitute the "facts" which analytic philosophers consider independent.

    9. Barbara Johnson, *The Critical Difference*, 59-66.

    10. Paul De Man, *The Resistance to Theory*, 19.

    11. Stanley Fish, *Is There*, 198; see also Sandy Petry, *Speech Acts and Literary Theory*, 22-41, 138, and 149.

    12. Fish, *Is There*, 307-8.

    13. Stanley Fish, "Consequences," 433-38; See also Steven Knapp and Walter Benn Michaels, "Against Theory," 738-40.

    14. Stanley Fish, *Professional Correctness*, 1-17.

    15. Stanley Fish, "Boutique Multiculturalism," 384.

    16. Fish, *Professional*, 51.

    17. See, for example, Richard Rorty, *Consequences of Pragmatism*, 14-17 and Reed Way Dasenbrock, "Do We Write the Text?," 18-30.

    18. Daniel O'Hara, *Radical Parody*, 7 and 133-43; see also Paul Bové, *In the Wake*, 5, 33; Reed Way Dasenbrock, "We've Done It," 182; Christopher Norris,

What's Wrong with Postmodernism, 107-9; and Michael Sprinker, "The War Against Theory," 155.

19. See, for example, Steven Mailloux, *Reception Histories*, 47.
20. Steven Mailloux, *Rhetorical Power*, 151-66.
21. Steven Mailloux, *Interpretive Conventions*, 56-7.
22. Mailloux, *Rhetorical Power*, 17.
23. Jonathan Arac argues, for example, that Twain attacks slavery, which was a safe target, but not racism, which was not, and fails to acknowledge the abolitionist or antislavery movements which he must have known about. See *Huckleberry Finn as Idol and Target*.
24. Mailloux, *Rhetorical Power*, 86-99 and 104-29.
25. Giles Gunn, "Approaching the Historical," 62.
26. Carl Freedman, "Rhetorical Hermeneutics," 124.
27. Joseph Margolis, *Pragmatism Without Foundations*, 165.
28. Mailloux, *Reception Histories*, 64.
29. Steven Mailloux, "Articulation and Understanding," 12.
30. Mailloux, *Reception Histories*, 40.
31. Mailloux, *Rhetorical Power*, 14.
32. Mailloux, *Rhetorical Power*, 68.
33. Mailloux, *Rhetorical Power*, 144-45.
34. Mailloux, *Reception Histories*, 41.
35. Pierre Macherey, *A Theory of Literary Production*, 1-14.
36. Terry Eagleton, *Criticism and Ideology*, 96.
37. John Frow, *Marxism and Literary History*, 28, 38, and 47.
38. Frow, *Marxism*, 13-15 and 22.
39. Tony Bennett, *Outside Literature*, 63-4.
40. Bennett, *Outside*, 31-33; see also "Marxism and Popular Fiction," 140-41, and "Texts in History," 13.
41. Bennett, *Outside*, 21.
42. Tony Bennett, *Formalism and Marxism*, 42-43.
43. Bennett, *Formalism*, 15.
44. Frow, *Marxism*, 101-2.
45. Tony Bennett and Janet Woollacott, *Bond and Beyond*, 59-60.
46. See also *Formalism*, where he says that the "literary text has no single or uniquely privileged meaning . . . that can be abstracted from the ways in which criticism itself works upon and mediates the reception of the text" (137).
47. Bennett, *Outside*, 177-80.
48. Tony Bennett, *Culture: A Reformer's Science*, 76-77.
49. Bennett, *Culture*, 69-70.
50. Toby Miller, *The Well-Tempered Self*, 68-83.
51. Similarly, in *The Object of Literature* [*A quoi pense la littérature* (1990)], Macherey maintains that a great period of history elaborates what Foucault terms an underlying episteme or structuring mythology. Like Foucault, he considers this

mythology a functional necessity, not the improved understanding nor the distorted representation required by the Althusserian opposition of science/ideology; however, Macherey's belief that a Foucauldian episteme structures an era preserves the traditional belief that determinate historical eras resolve interpretive conflicts, rather than the Foucauldian notion that, because discourse is divided, its history shows gaps and ruptures. In addition, the Foucauldian episteme denies the agency and autonomy of the subject, whose "self" is constituted by the discursive practices disciplining it. Macherey argues, just the same, that a Foucauldian conception of knowledge explains a work's influence on contemporary life, not a work's reception by diverse readers (95). Macherey claims not only that an era's functional mythology exercises historical influence but also that a text can overcome what he calls the "essentialist" division of literature and philosophy (9-10). While Post-Marxism denies the aesthetic autonomy of the text, Macherey argues that it subverts the "foundational" assumptions whereby philosophy appropriates the right to speak the truth about literature and literature presents itself as the repressed other or concealed truth of philosophy. Weaving the two together, the great text produces a unique insight but transcends disciplinary boundaries and preserves aesthetic autonomy.

52. Terry Eagleton, *Walter Benjamin*, 66-78.

53. In *The Ideology of the Aesthetic*, he argues that the immanent critique of Theodor Adorno undermines oppressive notions of history and totality as fully as the poststructuralists do, yet, still responsible to the public, this critique distinguishes between the good and the bad whole (354-55). Eagleton also claims that Adorno's critique appreciates nonidentity, multiplicity, and difference as fully as the poststructuralists do but still recognizes that the traditional principles of identity effectively regulate thought (334-35).

54. Jürgen Habermas, *The Philosophical Discourse of Modernity*, 112-14.

55. John Frow, *Cultural Studies and Cultural Value*, 132.

56. Frow, *Cultural Studies*, 132.

57. Frow, *Cultural Studies*, 132.

58. Frow, *Marxism*, 229; see also his *Cultural Studies*, 165-69.

59. Barbara Herrnstein Smith, *Contingencies of Value*, 30-42.

60. For instance, Smith and Bennett expose the inconsistency of David Hume, who claims that different persons, cultures, and eras show a remarkable diversity of taste, but who insists that humankind also shows an equally remarkable uniformity of judgment. Hume argues that the sensitivity, training, and impartiality of an authoritative critic ensure the universal validity of his or her judgments, yet he admits that even these critics may not agree. Smith and Bennett find a comparable inconsistency in Kant, who claims that individual judgments of value must employ the universal terms "good" and "bad" even though these judgments are subjective and hypothetical. Critics talk as though everyone must share their taste, yet only the hypothetical assumption of a common human nature or a common sense gives these subjective judgments their universality. Both Smith and Bennett also fault the

critical theory of the Frankfurt School, whose accounts of ideological distortions or false consciousness preserve bourgeois notions of universal truth, as well as traditional Marxists, who expect judgments of value to possess universal validity but whose historical "grand narrative" also fails to overcome the opposition between universal values and a critic's subjective taste. See Smith, *Contingencies*, 54-84, and Bennett, *Outside*, 143-66.

61. Peggy Kamuf, *The Division of Literature*, 33. See also John Guillory, *Cultural Capital*, 273.

62. Kamuf, *Division*, 31.

63. Bennett, *Culture*, 20.

64. Bennett, *Culture*, 32.

65. Bennett, *Outside*, 239.

66. Bennett, *Culture*, 32.

67. Toby Miller, *Technologies of Truth*, 72.

68. Eagleton, *Ideology of the Aesthetic*, 381.

69. See Stanley Fish, "Anti-Professionalism."

70. Mailloux, *Histories*, 164.

Chapter Two
Marxism and/as Humanism:
The Reception of *Hamlet*

Poststructuralist and post-Marxist reception study maintains that the activity of diverse readers addresses the equally diverse interpretive communities or reading formations whose norms and values determine the validity of the interpretation, but post-Marxism goes on to clarify the conservative and progressive aspects of these formations. The reception of *Hamlet* illustrates and elaborates this post-Marxist approach as well as its Marxist opposition. To address this opposition, I adopt the traditional Marxist interpretation, which says that the play engages in forceful criticism of the Renaissance court and society but faults the idealism whereby Hamlet leaves to time and conscience the reforms which require organized action. Moreover, in defense of Hamlet's manhood or humanism, traditional Marxists fault non-Marxist authorial, formal, and historical accounts, which, in turn, condemn the Marxist's economic determinism. During the Cold War, Arnold Kettle acquired the dubious status of the Marxist whom Anglo-American critics most loved to hate; just the same, both the traditional Marxist and non-Marxist accounts share the humanist ideal of a unified or autonomous human self which resists historical differences, commodity production, or disciplinary divisions. Moreover, these accounts oppose Derridean, Foucauldian, New Historicist, or cultural materialist views even though these "antihumanist" views defend progressive notions of gender, class, or nationality.

Of course, the many studies of *Hamlet*'s reception have clearly shown that, opposed to each other, the authorial, formal or textual, and historical schools of criticism have interpreted the play in contrary ways; however, these studies demand that the critic transcend his or her school and accept the plain text, the common view, or the public truth.[1] By contrast, in keeping with the radical democracy of the Enlightenment tradition, post-Marxist reception study takes sides. That is, on the one hand, traditional Marxist and non-Marxist accounts defend conservative humanist ideals and condemn the radical subjectivity or "political correctness" of the "antihumanist" Derridean, Foucauldian, New Historicist, or cultural materialist accounts. Indeed, the Marxists insist that there is nothing Marxist about these accounts, while the non-Marxists maintain that the poststructuralist language cannot conceal the antihumanists' essential Marxism.[2] On the other hand, the "antihumanist" accounts do not consistently resist the authorial, formal, and historical accounts but still have progressive import because they examine the play's treatment of gender, class, or nationality.

The Traditional Marxist Reading

I will briefly outline the traditional Marxist account, which in a neoclassical generic manner emphasizes the tragic consequences of Hamlet's flaw—the idealism whereby he leaves to time and conscience the reforms which require organized action. This account claims that, because of Gertrude's "o'erhasty" marriage and the ghost's horrible revelations, Hamlet discovers a shocking corruption and brutal inhumanity pervading Danish society. As Victor Kiernan says, "Sins of individuals open his eyes to deep faults in the society he has hitherto taken for granted."[3] A melancholy, speculative, or negative Hamlet does not prove incapable of decisive action, nor does the figural language of the play resist its generic conventions or sociohistorical contexts, as non-Marxists say; rather, faced with this pervasive inhumanity, Hamlet hesitates but still takes decisive action. In Arnold Kettle's terms, he ceases "to behave as a prince ought to behave and begins behaving as a man, a sixteenth-century man."[4] As he says after he sees the ghost, "The time is out of joint. O cursèd spite / That ever I was born to set it right!"[5]

The Marxist argues that, "to set it right," he tries but fails to reform the Danes. For example, when Polonius asks Hamlet if Hamlet recognizes him, Hamlet calls Polonius a fishmonger. This epithet belittles Polonius, who considers Hamlet "far gone," yet Hamlet also urges him to acquire honesty: "I would you were so honest a man" (2.2.175). He mimics the ostentatious gestures of Osric but still asks him to put his "bonnet to his right use"

(5.2.91). When he instructs the players, he tells them not to overstep the "modesty of nature" (3.2.20) and during the play scene complains when they do so. Once Rosencrantz and Guildenstern admit that they were sent for, he warns them that "when the wind is southerly," he "knows a hawk from a handsaw" (2.2.349-50), but they ignore his warning. More importantly, after he sets up a spiritual "glass" to show Gertrude her "inmost part," he urges her not to go to his "uncle's bed . . . Refrain tonight /And that shall lend a kind of easiness / To the next abstinence; the next more easy" (3.4.19-20). He berates Ophelia in an even harsher way but still urges her to go to a nunnery to escape "calumny" (3.1.134). He arranges the play within the play to "catch the conscience of the king" because he has "heard / That guilty creatures sitting at a play / Have . . . / Been struck so to the soul that presently They have proclaimed their malefactions" (2.2.545-49). After the king calls for light and flees the room, a jubilant Hamlet takes the "strucken deer" to weep, if not reform, and, as a result, refuses to kill the king as he tries to pray for forgiveness; "Why, this is hire and salary, not revenge" (3.3.79).

Hamlet's reforms fail. Instead of improving, the other characters consider him mad: as Ophelia says, now I "see that noble and most sovereign reason / Like sweet bells jangled, out of time and harsh" (3.1.151-54). Unable to pray for forgiveness, Claudius fears that the "lunacy" of Hamlet makes him dangerous: "For like the hectic in my blood he rages" (4.3.62). Instead of proclaiming his own "malefactions," Claudius orders that Hamlet's head "should be struck off." In Act V, after Hamlet returns from England, he admits that his "deep plots" did "pall": as he says, "There's a divinity shapes our ends, rough-hew them how we will" (5.2.9-10). He still dies, but not before he declares his love of the drowned Ophelia, reconciles the hotheaded Laertes, avenges his poisoned father, and, urging Horatio to live on, preserves his princely name and the royal succession: "I do prophesy th' election lights on Fortinbras" (5.2.354-55).

In keeping with the generic model, which requires that the hero recognize his fault and, to complete his fall, suffer a reversal, the Marxists claim that, once Hamlet grasps that his idealist reforms have failed, he accepts traditional values and acts fully and decisively; the Marxists go on to argue, however, that Hamlet's criticisms of the court and the era voice what Kettle calls the "new humanism" of sixteenth-century England. A Marxist critic of traditional Marxism, Terry Eagleton speaks of Hamlet's "bourgeois individualism," not his manhood or humanism, yet Eagleton too claims that "we glimpse in him a negative critique of the forms of subjectivity typical of . . . the traditional social order to which he is marginal, and a future epoch of achieved bourgeois individualism which will surpass it."[6]

The trouble with this claim is that Hamlet voices elitist, misogynistic views. For example, he faults his mother's lack of devotion and good judgment—"a beast that wants discourse of reason / Would have mourned longer" (1.2.151-52), yet Fortinbras's attack on Denmark justifies Gertrude's "o'erhasty" marriage to Claudius, who, by informing Old Norway of Fortinbras's true aims, avoids an unnecessary war. Even though Gertrude is a loving wife and solicitous mother, Hamlet and the ghost condemn her "unseemly" lust: "Frailty—thy name is woman" (1.2.146). In the closet scene Hamlet's misogynistic condemnations grow so strident that the ghost has to remind him to destroy Claudius, not Gertrude. When he warns Ophelia that her beauty corrupts her honesty, he grows equally strident: "[W]ise men know well what monsters you make of them" (3.1.135-36).

I also grant that Hamlet's praise of his father's manhood—"A' was a man, take him for all in all, I shall not look upon his like again" (1.2.187-88)—establishes a forceful ideal of manhood which Machiavellian courtiers and rulers like Claudius and Polonius do not match; still, the ideal justifies the internecine warfare and military rivalry of the older feudal era, not the diplomacy of the Renaissance state. The ideal also justifies Hamlet's remarkable contempt of enterprising middle-class individualism and social mobility, what he calls the "weary, stale, flat, and unprofitable . . . uses of this world!" (1.2.133-34).

Hence, to explain why he has "of late" "lost all of" his "mirth," he delineates man's virtues—"how noble in reason, how infinite in faculties" (2.2.288-89)—only to dismiss man and woman: "to me, what is this quintessence of dust?" (2.2.292). Sidney Finkelstein says that this speech illustrates Shakespeare's humanist despair,[7] but it shows Hamlet's disgust with the upwardly mobile. He also condemns the opportunistic Rosencrantz and Guildenstern, who, to please the king, mean to play upon Hamlet, and the conniving Polonius, who would "by indirections find directions out (2.1.35). By contrast, he praises the loyal Horatio, "Whose blood and judgment are so well commeddled / That they are not a pipe for Fortune's finger / To sound what stop she please" (3.2i.60-62); still, seeking no advancement at all, the stoic Horatio accepts "Fortune's buffets and rewards . . . with equal thanks" (3.2.58-59). The famous "To be or not to be" soliloquy laments the heavy burdens and pervasive injustice of everyday life, but the melancholy "dread of something after death" does not just keep ordinary people grunting and sweating "under a weary life"; it destroys the "native hue of resolution" as well as "enterprises of great pitch and moment" (3.1.79-86).

Hamlet's and the ghost's abuse of women shows that they find female sexuality disgusting.[8] Leonard Tennenhouse says that the abuse anticipates Jacobean tragedy, where Hamlet "would favor extravagant scenes of mutilation."[9] In addition, his jeux de mots, his ridicule of courtly ambition or opportunism, and his defense of his "mystery" voice the rhetoric of courtesy employed by the Elizabethan aristocracy to distinguish the true from the many sham would-be courtiers hoping to benefit from the court's vast wealth and patronage.[10]

The Marxists ignore the play's hostility to middle-class individualism and female sexuality and its rhetoric of courtesy and defend the play's advanced humanism because the Marxist accounts assume that the humanist ideals originated in the Renaissance and evolved into modern humanism, what Eagleton calls "a future epoch of achieved bourgeois individualism"; however, Hamlet could not anticipate or critique modern humanism because it originates in the eighteenth century, not in the Renaissance era.[11]

It began in the eighteenth-century Enlightenment, when Kant argued that the subjective categories of human reason and the categorical imperatives of the human will dominate nature,[12] whereas Renaissance humanism was little more than a loose collection of peregrinating scholars whose friendships concealed their many differences. The Renaissance humanists esteemed classical eloquence as well as the ancient Greeks and Romans but never formed a coherent movement or overcame chauvinist sentiments and adopted truly universal human ideals.[13] Early Renaissance humanists, including Rudolph Agricola and Desiderius Erasmus, claimed that the study of classical rhetoric would ensure that the good speaker is a good man. These humanists argued that, unlike the dry scholastic logic of the medieval era, classical rhetoric fostered the religious, moral, and civic virtue of the good orator. This Latinate humanist theory justified the aristocracy, the clergy, and the Tudor court, whose vast patronage made it a central route to wealth and power, not the grounds of social criticism.[14] More importantly, this Latinate humanist theory was ensconced in the endowed private schools and great universities, where, as Walter Ong points out, until the twentieth century Latin instruction amounted to "a form of ritual male combat centered on disputation."[15]

Later humanists also believed that good rhetoric promotes virtue, decorum, or civility; however, inspired by Ramus, these humanists treated rhetorical techniques as useful skills applicable to law, government, and other areas.[16] More importantly, the later humanists justified the use of the "vulgar" vernacular languages, rather than the learned Latin. Successful in the marketplace, the church, dissenting adult schools, commercial academies, and female seminaries, but not in the university, the later humanist defense of a vernacular rhetoric promoted the English language and literature of the nationalist middle class. In Alvin Kernan's terms, eighteenth-century humanist criticism "swept away" the Tudor's "older system of polite or courtly letters—primarily oral, aristocratic, amateur, authoritarian, court-centered."[17]

Codifying the practices of Renaissance humanism, this neoclassical humanist criticism flourished in the eighteenth century, when it was able to unite the aristocracy and the middle classes and to define the educated public or, as Jürgen Habermas says, the public sphere;[18] however, in the nineteenth century, when the middle classes acquired more power, partisan journals formed diverse publics, and the modern disciplines acquired formal autonomy, the neoclassical ideal lost its ability to unite the aristocracy and the bourgeoisie.[19]

The Marxists claim that the play critiques the Renaissance court and ruling elites because they deny that modern humanism differs substantially from Renaissance humanism or that it breaks down in the twentieth century, when, as Foucault says, the disciplines acquire autonomy. As a result, most scholars consider the Marxists reductive socioeconomic or "totalitarian" determinists. It is true that Kettle, Kiernan, and other British critics and scholars, including the historians Christopher Hill and E. P. Thompson, supported the British communist party in the 1940s and 1950s and in the 1960s and 1970s adopted independent leftist stances, but they represented a humanist opposition to scientific Stalinism and, in the 1970s and 1980s, to scientific or structuralist and poststructuralist Marxism, which Thompson derisively labeled the "poverty of theory."[20] In other words, the reason the Marxists ignore Hamlet's hostility to women and to the enterprising middle class but esteem the play's critique of Renaissance society and of Hamlet's idealism is that the Marxists oppose not only literature's formal autonomy but also scientific Stalinism as well as structuralist and poststructuralist Marxism; as Kettle says, Hamlet's dilemmas are "essentially the dilemmas of the modern intellectual." Since authorial, formal, and historical accounts of the play ignore or deny the play's humanist critique of social life or preserve the autonomy of literary study, the traditional Marxist faults those accounts too, but they too defend modern humanist ideals and oppose poststructuralist views, which, as I will argue, evolve out of the traditional views and voice progressive interests in race, class, gender, and nationality.

The Authorial Reading

Certainly the approach which I call authorial because it appreciates Hamlet's analytical mind, Shakespeare's autonomous imagination, or tragedy's generic features defends humanist ideals taken in the broad Enlightenment sense. This approach, which evolves Romantic, Victorian, modern, and psychoanalytic versions as well as feminist poststructuralist versions, claims that Hamlet believes the ghost, wants to take revenge, but, because of the world's evils, his speculative mind, his melancholy nature, or his mother's unseemly sexual appetite, grows too depressed to do anything. As Samuel T. Coleridge said in *The Lectures on Shakespeare (1811-1812)*, Hamlet demonstrates a dangerous "aversion to action" which "prevails among those who have a world of their own."[21] The Marxists complain that this approach neglects the historical conflicts of the Renaissance era; however, the authorial account shares the neoclassical generic conventions of the Marxists. Moreover, initiated by Coleridge and other Romantic critics, this account made the play accessible to the new reading public which emerged in the nineteenth century and integral to the neoclassical academic humanism established in late nineteenth-century universities.

Initially, the authorial account discredited the eighteenth-century neoclassical account, which defended ethical propriety, generic conventions, and biographical or historical truth, not Shakespeare's profound insights.[22] For instance, the neoclassical account faults Hamlet's madness, cruelty, and delay. Samuel Johnson, who accepts the neoclassical ideals of decorum, propriety, and generic form,[23] condemns the prayer scene, where Hamlet utters what Johnson considers sentiments "too horrible to be read or to be uttered," and the ghost scenes and the conclusion, which lack the "poetical justice" and "poetical probability" of great tragedy because the ghost's revenge miscarries and Ophelia and Hamlet die.[24] Johnson admits that the play's mixture of comedy and tragedy violates the generic norms of tragedy, but, unlike Tillyard, who, as I will show, belittles the play for that reason, Johnson allows it "the praise of variety."[25] As he says, Shakespeare, like Johnson himself, "was not to be depressed by the weight of poverty, nor limited by the narrow conversation to which men in want are inevitably condemned" but "has been able to obtain an exact knowledge of many modes of life."[26]

In the judicial manner neoclassical critics like Johnson fault the improprieties of Hamlet but appreciate the generic form of the play and the sociohistorical context of Shakespeare's life; by contrast, the Romantics defend the play's characterization of Hamlet and dismiss its generic forms and historical context. William Hazlitt claims, for example, that Shakespeare created an "original text" of nature, not an illustration of historical or ethical truths.[27] As Hazlitt says:

> Whoever has become thoughtful and melancholy through his own mishaps or those of others; whoever has borne about with him the clouded brow of reflection . . . whoever has seen the golden lamp of day dimmed by envious mists rising in his own breast . . . he who has felt his mind sink within him, and sadness cling to his heart like a malady . . . this is the true Hamlet.[28]

Similarly, Coleridge explains Shakespeare's "brilliant" characterization of Hamlet as a matter of one who, possessed of a world of his own, "has become thoughtful and melancholy through his own mishaps or those of others" or "has borne about with him the clouded brow of reflection." Moreover, he rejects Johnson's belief that Shakespeare's account of Hamlet's voyage to England simply followed the extant sources of the play; rather, the penetrating Shakespeare, who, Coleridge claims, never "followed a novel because he found such and such an incident in it," "saw at once how consistent" the voyage was "with the character of Hamlet."[29]

Coleridge also denies that the play should illustrate ethical or moral truth. For instance, he says that, when Hamlet refuses to kill Claudius because Claudius is praying and might go to heaven, Hamlet does not show an "atrocious and horrible" sentiment, as Johnson claimed; rather, the withdrawn Hamlet simply "seizes hold of a pretext for not acting."[30] Hamlet's misogynistic abuse of Ophelia does not show "useless and wanton cruelty," as Johnson also says; rather, like J. Dover Wilson, Coleridge argues that Hamlet addresses the speech to "the listeners and spies," not to Ophelia, "who was not acting a part of her own."[31]

In *Shakespearean Tragedy* (1904), A. C. Bradley also accepts the Romantic belief that Shakespeare's insightful characterization of Hamlet raises the play above conventional ethical values, but, far from opposing the generic conventions of the neoclassical humanists, as the Romantics do, he adopts them. He grants that Hamlet's "intellectual genius," "forever unmaking his world and rebuilding it in thought," gives the play its tragic interest.[32] Bradley claims, however, that, initially frank, courteous, kindly, cheerful, and trusting, Hamlet discovers what Bradley terms the "astounding shallowness" and "coarse sensuality" of his mother, his "whole mind is poisoned," and he grows too disgusted with life to take revenge. That is, Hamlet shows an extraordinary disgust with life, rather than a purely speculative nature, because he can take decided action in healthy moments and at other times be averse to action and even give way to painful bursts of "savage irritability," "self-absorption," "callousness," "hysterical emotion," and "dull, brooding gloom."[33] As Gottschalk points out, this claim anticipates the Freudian reading in which Hamlet's disgust with his mother's sensuality betrays unconscious desires undermining his opposition to the overly despised Claudius.[34] What's more, since Bradley maintains that Hamlet's disgust and ensuing procrastination establish his "tragic flaw" and that pity, fear, sadness, waste, and mystery create the play's "tragic impression,"[35] Bradley preserves the neoclassical generic approach rejected by Coleridge and Hazlitt.

The psychoanalysts also appreciate Shakespeare's insightful characterization of Hamlet but explain it in terms of unconscious conflicts of identity, not the faulty strategies of an idealist intellectual nor his possession of a world all his own; however, authorial psychoanalytic accounts accept, while the feminist poststructuralist versions reject, the neoclassical generic conventions of Bradley and the Marxists. For example, Janet Adelman says that, because Gertrude's sexuality disturbs Hamlet, his repressed Oedipal desires keep him from defining himself or taking forceful action. The ghost's revelations arouse in Hamlet repressed male fantasies making his mother's body repugnant and his own identity unclear. Adelman argues, however, that Gertrude's independent body violates his patriarchal rights and, as his maternal origin, corrupts his male integrity. Turning misogynistic, he rages at his mother's inconstancy and lust, instead of avenging his father's murder. In keeping with the generic norms, Adelman grants that in Act V he affirms his kingly identity and takes positive actions, as the generic account requires, but only because in the closet scene, when Hamlet censures his mother's behavior so severely, he overcomes his misogyny and reconstructs the ideal mother enabling him to act.[36]

The poststructuralists Jacqueline Rose and Marjorie Garber also claim that Hamlet's unconscious disillusionment and misogynistic rage keep him from avenging his father's murder; however, while Adelman gives the generic authorial account a feminist import, they consider the generic account chauvinist. Rose and Garber argue that the text's figural language undermines the neoclassical generic form whereby traditional critics establish that in Act V Hamlet overcomes his melancholy disillusionment and affirms his kingly self or, as the Marxists say, abandons his idealist schemes and takes concrete action. Rose, who assumes that the rhetorical devices of the play reveals a feminine subjectivity subverting its formal design, complains that the authorial generic account fails to depict Gertrude objectively because this account assumes that artistic form limits human desire, especially women's sexuality.[37]

In defense of the authorial generic account, William Kerrigan grants that Hamlet's disillusionment and misogynistic rage keep him from acting but maintains that the rage stems from man's divided nature, which degrades women to mere whores or elevates them to ideal virgins, rather than Hamlet's repressed Oedipal desires. Although the poststructuralist feminists expose the chauvinist import of the neoclassical generic approach, not the play, Kerrigan treats their critique as vain moralizing because like Bradley he esteems the play's insights into man's nature, not generic conventions. Just as Coleridge and Hazlitt fault the judicial criticism of Johnson and praise Shakespeare's autonomous imagination, so Kerrigan, who titled his book *Hamlet's Perfection*, dismisses the feminist critiques and praises Shakespeare's purely artistic brilliance.[38]

The traditional Marxist also dismisses the poststructuralist feminist critiques but argues that the authorial/psychoanalytic accounts embrace abstract notions of human nature and divorce the play from its historical context whose corruptions justify Hamlet's rage and delay as well as his actions. That is, the play's humanist critique of Hamlet's idealism and of the Renaissance court and aristocracy, not the play's insights into female sexuality, misogynistic anger, or unconscious desire, explains *Hamlet's* profound import. In general, the Marxist believes that in our fallen capitalist society only concrete historical analyses can reveal a work's universal truth;[39] nonetheless, the Marxist and the authorial views converge not only because they both oppose the feminist critique of Hamlet's misogyny and disgust with life but also because the Marxist implicitly accepts the neoclassical generic ideal whereby the characters and insights of great tragedy transcend their era and demonstrate universal truths.

This convergence, in turn, suggests that the influence of the authorial view stems not only from Hamlet's character or the play's insights but also from the nineteenth century's greatly expanded reading public and new "disinterested" humanism. In the late eighteenth and early nineteenth centuries, circulating libraries, steam printing, and new technologies made cheap newspapers, magazines, tracts, serials, and editions more widely available. The growth of commerce and trade gave the middle classes more leisure for reading. Despite conservative opposition, Sunday schools, charity schools, adult mechanics institutes, and other institutions succeeded in teaching the traditional rural peasants and the new urban, industrial workers how to read.[40] To foster and consolidate these new readers, both the Romantic and the neoclassical critics repudiated what Kernan terms the Tudors' "older system of polite or courtly letters—primarily oral, aristocratic, amateur, authoritarian, court-centered";[41] however, the neoclassical critics expected readers to attend the lavish productions mounted by the British theaters and to consult the detailed and expensive commentary produced by Johnson and other eighteenth-century scholars.[42] By contrast, the accounts of Hazlitt, who doubted that a theater could adequately perform the play, and of Coleridge, who believed that Shakespeare's plays would give the divided nation a united "national personality," made the play accessible and instructive to these new middle- and working- class readers.[43] To appreciate it, they had only to read it themselves.

As I show in the next chapter, in the middle and late nineteenth century, parliamentary reforms gradually forced the exclusively male and narrowly classical Cambridge and Oxford to teach the English language and literature (and prospective female teachers of English) excluded in previous centuries.[44] One of the first English professors to specialize in Shakespeare, Bradley preserves the Romantic belief in Shakespeare's autonomous imagination but, eliding the Romantic opposition to generic approaches, identifies the play with the neoclassical humanism established by the Tudor court and the aristocracy. The resulting authorial humanist account influences not only the psychoanalytic view but also, as I will shortly show, the formal and the historical accounts. Although the Marxist account opposes the authorial and the psychoanalytic view and defends concrete historical truth, the Marxist account accepts the generic form and the universal values of the authorial approach and implicitly accommodates the neoclassical humanism established by the Tudor court. Moreover, while both the Marxists and the authorial critics consider the poststructuralist psychoanalytic accounts retrograde, these accounts expose the repressive, chauvinist import of the humanist's neoclassical form.

Formal Readings

The formal account, which denies that Hamlet takes meaningful action, occupies a world of his own, or experiences a disabling disgust with life, also elaborates modern humanist ideals, but this account defends the Romantic faith in Shakespeare's autonomous imagination and rejects the universal truths and generic forms of Marxist and authorial humanism. As F. R. Leavis bragged, in the 1930s and the 1940s the new formal criticism of Shakespeare showed "the academic world . . . how inadequate and wrong the Bradley approach was."[45] This formal criticism includes a textual version, which says that *Hamlet's* images of poison, disease, corruption, and death endow the play with a unifying tone; a generic version, which grants that Hamlet delays but considers the delay a convention of Renaissance revenge tragedy; and a Derridean or poststructuralist version, which claims that the play's figural language undermines the language's literal import, the text's unity, tragedy's generic conventions, and the traditional critic's ideological commitments. The Marxist argues that these textual, generic, and Derridean accounts divorce the language of the play from its Renaissance contexts, especially the conventions and ideologies of the court and the theater; however, as I indicate more fully in the next section, the formal accounts develop historical import. Moreover, even though the formal accounts repudiate the generic form and universal truth of the authorial humanist and foster the disciplinary specialization and professional autonomy of Shakespeare criticism, these accounts still preserve the Romantic ideal of Shakespeare's autonomous imaginations.

For example, in the influential *The Wheel of Fire* (1930), G. Wilson Knight praises the court's "healthy and robust life, good-nature, humour, Romantic strength, and welfare" and faults Hamlet, whom he considers "the ambassador of death walking amid life."[46] Knight claims that Gertrude's sensuality and the ghost's revelations blacken Hamlet, whose reactions are excessive; Knight argues, however, that Hamlet's "consciousness of death insidiously undermines the health of the state . . . until at the end the stage is filled with corpses."[47] Moreover, Knight dismisses the "intellectual" "intentions, causes, sources, characters" and "ethical ideals" of Bradley and other authorial critics, but he esteems the formal unity of the play, what he calls "a visionary whole, close-knit in personification, atmospheric suggestion, and direct poetic-symbolism."[48] Wolfgang Clemens and other textual critics describe Hamlet's intellect more positively than Knight does, but they too dismiss the intentions and causes sought by the authorial critics and examine the motifs of corruption, disease, and death revealed by the play's unifying images and metaphors.[49]

By contrast, in "Hamlet and His Problems" (1919), T. S. Eliot, who wrote a laudatory introduction to *The Wheel of Fire*, adopts Bradley's belief that Hamlet's "disgust is occasioned by his mother,"[50] but argues that Hamlet overreacts to his mother, whose insignificant personality does not justify Hamlet's melancholy disgust or represent, in Eliot's famous terms, an adequate "objective correlative." Eliot complains, moreover, that Bradley and Coleridge substitute "their Hamlet for Shakespeare's,"[51] yet, unlike Knight or Hubler, he analyzes the play in generic terms. He restricts his analysis to Renaissance revenge tragedy, rather than tragedy as a whole. As a result, while Coleridge and Bradley praise Shakespeare's insightful characterization of Hamlet, Eliot calls the play a failure because "Shakespeare was unable to impose" his story of Gertrude's guilt and Hamlet's disgust "upon the 'intractable' material" of Thomas Kyd's lost revenge tragedy.[52] As Eliot says, "[U]nder compulsion of what experience, he attempted to express the inexpressibly horrible, we cannot ever know."[53]

In "Updating Revenge Tragedy" (1951), William Empson accepts the formal belief that "Hamlet himself is a problem" (Cited in *Hamlet* 284), rather than Bradley's belief that Hamlet's mother causes his delay and disgust, but he too situates the play in the historical context of Renaissance revenge tragedy; as he says, the "real 'Hamlet problem' . . . is a problem about his first audiences."[54] That is, like Knight, Empson considers Hamlet's mind of death, rather than the Renaissance court and society, the play's problem, but Empson claims that the rhetorical conventions of Renaissance revenge tragedy justify Hamlet's delay. Empson argues that, familiar with campy revenge tragedies, the audience prepared to laugh when the hero clamored for revenge but did nothing. Both Empson and Eliot esteem formal unity over character development or sociohistorical insight; however, while Eliot complains that Shakespeare failed to impose his story on Kyd's intractable material, Empson says that he designed Hamlet's delay so that the play represses its theatrical qualities and forestalls the audience's knowing laughter.[55]

Kettle says that Hamlet sees "what, from the point of view of an advanced sixteenth-century humanist, the Renaissance court is actually like,"[56] whereas the textual critics insist that the repressed generic conventions of revenge tragedy or the unifying figures of death, decay, corruption, and poison make the play great. In other words, even though the formal critics reject the universal authorial and the Marxists' historical account, the formal critics preserve the humanist ideal of Shakespeare's sui generis imagination. Richard Halpern denies that Knight, Clemens, and other formal or textual critics "choose decontextualizing over contextualizing approaches";[57] however, the formal critics deny that Hamlet takes meaningful action or that his character develops significantly because, as such a "totalizing context," the text and/or its Renaissance conventions preserve the humanist ideal of Shakespeare's sui generis imagination, not the objective historical truth defended by the Marxists.

Derridean poststructuralists also esteem the play's textual language and, by implication, Shakespeare's sui generis imagination; however, instead of establishing a unified whole, they say that the many, delightful puns, tropes, and ambiguities of the play undermine the generic conventions of tragedy as well as the traditional methods and ideologies of the critics. On this figural ground the Derridean approaches, like the formal, textual approach, oppose but do not escape authorial humanism because the figural indeterminacy which undermines the generic account of the play also preserves its aesthetic autonomy.

For instance, Margaret Ferguson shows that "Lamord," the name of the skillful French horseman so taken with Laertes' fencing, puns on death (la mort), whose import Hamlet forgets, and on love (l'amour), whose comic meaning undermines the tragic form of the play.[58] Unlike the traditional textual formalist, who values aesthetic unity over character development, Ferguson grants that at the end, when Hamlet takes positive action, he forcefully affirms his princely identity, as the Marxist claims. The difference is that she considers this affirmation decidedly unheroic and even deathly because it suppresses the individualizing indeterminacy of the figural devices and reinforces the generic conventions of revenge tragedy. The indeterminacy preserves, in other words, the sui generis character of Shakespeare's imagination because, as James Calderwood shows, Hamlet's figural play enables him to negate his paternal identity and individualize himself, and the "semi-autonomous episodes, tableaux-like scenes, insets, stylistic pauses" of the play individualize it.[59]

Similarly, Terence Hawks maintains that the play allows both the traditional generic reading, in which it has a clear beginning, middle, and end; a logical progression; and distinct character development, and an inverse reading (Telmah), in which the beginning and the ending display a symmetrical form, the interpretation and reinterpretation of the play continue endlessly, and the performance of the play never begins and never truly ends.[60] Indeed, more radical than Ferguson and Calderwood, Hawks shows that, since the play supports both the inverse reading and the established, sequential reading, the play contradicts itself and exposes and violates, thereby, the Eurocentric order and presence of the traditional critic;[61] at the same time, Hawks's account does not escape authorial humanism because the paradoxical formal features preserve the aesthetic autonomy and imaginative uniqueness which the Romantics attribute to the play.

Traditional Marxists grant that the language of the play resists its generic conventions and public contexts but still argue that the play accepts its public contexts. For instance, Robert Weimann says that the figural, reflexive language of the play undermines its authoritative representations of historical life; he maintains, just the same, that such language also confirms authoritative Elizabethan discourses and the theater's dramatic practices. He insists, moreover, that not only deconstruction but all formal concepts of literary language fail to explain both the mimetic truth and antimimetic illusions of the play or of Shakespeare's theater.[62] Similarly, Alvin Kernan says that, by criticizing Hamlet's idealist strategies, the play exposes the inadequacy of the Elizabethan belief that art reforms social life.[63] More negative than Weimann, Kernan, who claims that neoclassical criticism, with its scrupulous devotion to the author's intention, the common reader, universal values, rational thought, and market-oriented enterprise, has "remained fundamental to letters in western society,"[64] objects that Romantic, modernist, and postmodernist approaches have fostered subjective, anarchic practices; as he says, one does not "stand helplessly by thinking that the end of the world has come, or opportunistically conceive that anything goes."[65]

Moreover, to defend the unified self fragmented by commodity production or sociohistorical differences, Marxist and non-Marxist authorial humanists have derisively labeled the textual and the Derridean accounts careerist professionalism.[66] Ironically, this label indicates that what justifies the formal readings is not only its claims about language, the text, the theater, or the traditional critic but also its relationship to literary study's new disciplinary divisions and professional associations. As I noted, in the late Victorian era, when the study of English literature entered Anglo-American universities, the criticism of Bradley and others repudiated the Romantics' middle-class nationalism and adopted established neoclassical humanism. In the twentieth century, when literary study gained independent departments, graduate programs, distinct fields, and professional associations,[67] formal readings opposed the broad Romantic and Victorian humanism and produced highly specialized readings promoting this new disciplinary context. Gerald Graff summarizes these conflicts as follows: "classicists versus modern-language scholars; research investigators versus generalists; historical scholars versus critics; New Humanists versus New Critics; academic critics versus literary journalists and culture critics; critics and scholars versus theorists."[68] Graff assumes, however, that these conflicts largely reiterate the initial conflict of the neoclassical humanists and the modern department's scholarly specialists; actually, as formal criticism came to dominate the rapidly expanding Anglo-American universities of the mid-twentieth century, the formal readings adopt historical analyses. That is, the early figural readings of Knight and others divorce the language of the play from its theatrical or historical contexts, as the Marxists say, but the formal accounts of the play's Renaissance conventions and the Derridean readings of Renaissance tropes and figures undermine this opposition of formal and historical accounts—I explain this breakdown more fully in the next section. Moreover, while the figural readings preserve the humanist ideal of aesthetic

Historical Readings

Like the authorial and formal accounts, the historical approach preserves the neoclassical humanism of Coleridge and Bradley, but the historical account says that the public or sociohistorical contexts of the play—not the textual imagery, unifying symbols, figural devices, generic conventions, or autonomous structures of the formal approach, nor the transcendent characters, universal themes, or profound insights of the authorial approach—explain its import. Most historical critics adopt the scientific or "positivist" belief that a critic must set aside his or her modern sensibility and adopt Shakespeare's or the Elizabethans' social context and original terms. These historical critics still accept Bradley's account of the play and ignore Hamlet's misogynistic and anti-middle-class attitudes, but these critics claim that the Elizabethan audience would consider the ghost a devil who "abuses" Hamlet so as to "damn" him; revenge a damnable violation of the religious law leaving justice in God's hands, and Hamlet himself a mad, satanic Vice speeding to his doom.[69] Influenced by Johnson and the neoclassical critics, other historians adopt the rhetorical belief that historical study reveals the historian's subjective values, rather than the positivist belief that objective fact supports some views but not others; as Helen Gardner says, the play does not permit an easy distinction between objective history and contemporary values.[70] Some of these historical critics go on, however, to reconcile the formal, authorial, and positivist historical approaches despite their differences. Others, especially the New Historical and cultural materialist critics, oppose the "humanist essentialism" of those approaches because, like the psychoanalytic feminists and the Derrideans, they believe that the play expresses a poststructuralist subjectivity expressing differences of gender and class.

Traditional historical critics adopt the positivist assumption that objective historical fact supports some views and not others and reject the "postmodern" claim that the critic's rhetoric reveals his or her subjective values or the play's misogynistic and anti-middle-class values; however, these historians still accept the modern authorial belief that Hamlet occupies a world beyond ethical values and fails to act or to change. For example, in *Shakespeare's Problem Plays* (1947), E. M. W. Tillyard restates Bradley's belief that Hamlet never overcomes his shock at his uncle's duplicity or his mother's infidelity, yet he says that the play affirms the Elizabethans' "powerfully traditional and Christian" "world picture," whereby the great "chain of being" reflects the hierarchic structure of Elizabethan society.[71] Like the Marxist, Tillyard grants that in Act V Hamlet grasps his failure—he has not caught "the conscience of the king" or restrained the desires of his mother—but takes this recognition to affirm the Elizabethan's religious belief in divine providence, not the limits of the idealist intellectual. As a consequence, even though Tillyard accepts Bradley's interpretation, he rejects Bradley's high estimation of the play: "[W]ith no great revelation or reversal of direction or regeneration, the play cannot answer to one of our expectations from the highest tragedy."[72] Samuel Johnson also objects that the play does not meet the formal demands of tragedy, but he claims that the play's great variety of experience makes it valuable. Tillyard says that he describes the play's objective Elizabethan context, not the modern sensibility; however, Tillyard, whose *The Muse Unchained* praises the founders of Cambridge's first English department, defends tragedy's generic forms in Bradley's modern fashion—Hugh Grady derisively terms Tillyard's criticism a "modernizing and positivist ideology" "housed in the new research universities."[73]

In *What Happens in* Hamlet (1935), J. Dover Wilson also means to recover the history of the play, not impose modern values or acknowledge its misogynistic and anti-middle-class attitudes. As he says, "Apparent obscurities may be explained and elucidated through the recovery" of "lost and forgotten" elements.[74] Like Tillyard, Wilson accepts Bradley's humanist belief that the depression and shocks produced by Gertrude's hasty and incestuous marriage and the ghost's frightful revelations keep Hamlet from acting; however, Wilson argues that Shakespeare's audience believed in the ghost's reality, took Claudius for a usurper, judged Gertrude guilty of adultery, and in general, considered Gertrude, Ophelia, and others treacherous and Hamlet responsible and sympathetic.[75]

In a positivist fashion Wilson denies that historians interpret historical fact, yet these historical claims support the authorial approach. So do his accounts of the play's texts. For instance, to explain the first quarto, he claims, as many scholars do, that an actor-reporter reconstructed the play from memory; in his vituperative terms, this "wild ass" produced a "ridiculous text."[76] Scholars have recently suggested, however, that, since the speeches of all the characters, not just those attributed to the mythical actor-reporter, show irregular variations, the first quarto may be a legitimate version of the play.[77] Scholars have also suggested that, since the second quarto may have provided the working text for the first folio, Shakespeare and his company revised the second quarto during the play's many performances;[78] by contrast, Wilson deems the second quarto a "typographical facsimile" of Shakespeare's lost, original "autograph manuscript."[79] Like Wilson's Bradleyan interpretation of the play, this claim supports the modern Romantic/authorial faith in Shakespeare's original genius.

On similar grounds Wilson complains that the obscurities, ambiguities, and unassimilated materials which textual critics like Eliot find in the play discredit the genius of Shakespeare and that the Freudian's unconscious Oedipal complex cannot explain Hamlet's blurred rationality because Shakespeare "did not think in these terms."[80] Other historians, who acknowledge the influence of their interpretive rhetoric, assimilate the contrary authorial and formal views, instead of refuting them and dismissing modern values, as Wilson and Tillyard do. These eclectic historians synthesize these contrary views, yet, except for Gardner, who attributes to Hamlet the liberal, modern dilemma that one cannot take action to secure justice "without outraging the very conscience which demands" action,[81] these critics too ignore the play's modern import, including its misogynistic and antimiddle-class attitudes.

For example, in *The Question of Hamlet* (1959), Harry Levin ignores the modern import and reconciles the positivist historical and the formal views. On the one hand, in the historical fashion, he maintains that Hamlet has good reason to doubt the ghost and the court and to postpone his revenge. Gertrude's infidelity does not render him incapable of action, as Bradley claimed;[82] his cynical views do not show the evils of rational thought, as Knight said; rather, historical matters, including the theological concerns of the Elizabethan era, the bloody justice of revenge tragedy, and the philosophical skepticism of Montaigne, Shakespeare's contemporary, justify Hamlet's hesitations.[83] On the other hand, in the formal fashion, he considers the play a "verbal structure" defined by the rhetorical tropes of interrogation, doubt, and irony, not by the suffering and purgation of the classical hero, as the Marxists and the authorial critics say. Because of the interrogative rhetorical tropes and the positive historical doctrines, he, unlike Tillyard, allows the play the status of a great tragedy which, as Eliot said, explores the mysteries of "painful experience," not Hamlet's hatred of women and contempt of the middle classes.[84]

Known as a systematizing structuralist, Northrop Frye also dismisses the subjective modern evaluations, which, he fears, make criticism too much like the stock market, and reconciles not only the historical and the formal but the authorial views too.[85] Like Tillyard and Wilson, Frye accepts Bradley's belief that the remarriage of Gertrude, not the murder of Hamlet's father, renders Hamlet too melancholy to take action. Like G. Wilson Knight, his former teacher and colleague, Frye refuses to identify the "sick" views of the melancholy Hamlet with those of Shakespeare; rather, echoing T. S. Eliot, Frye says that Hamlet "sees what's there, but there's an emotional excess that's reflected back to him."[86] In the historical manner, Frye claims that the ghost acts more like a threatening devil than a purgatorial spirit even though this belief implies that the dangerous ghost, not Gertrude's remarriage nor Hamlet's "sick" views, makes Hamlet hesitate. In an equally contrary way, Frye's account attributes to the play's conclusion a heroic element, which restates the historical critic's belief that Hamlet manifests "a torrent of abilities and qualities" and "would have been a great king and warrior too," and an ironic element, which restates the formal, Romantic belief that the play depicts "consciousness as a withdrawal from action."[87] In contradictory ways, as a generic tragedy and a mixed type, a potentially great action and withdrawal from action, Frye's structuralist reading dismisses modern evaluations and accommodates the authorial, formal, and historical accounts.

In very different ways, cultural materialists and New Historicists also accept the neoclassical rhetoric or "discourse" reconciling subjective values and historical truth, rather than the "foundational" historical fact objectively confirming or refuting interpretive frameworks; however, instead of reconciling the authorial, formal, and positivist historical approaches, cultural materialists and New Historicists acknowledge their modern subjectivity and attack "humanist essentialism," especially the coherent characters, substantial plots, unified culture, and historical continuity of the authorial, formal, and historical approaches. Some scholars object that this critique of humanist "essentialism" mistakenly dismisses the authorial/formal/historical approach.[88] Others complain that the cultural materialists and New Historicists lack the objectivity of traditional historical approaches.[89] It is true that these "antihumanist" critics eschew the traditional objectivity and recognize their modern subjectivity, but, like Johnson and the neoclassical critics, they adopt a rhetorical version of historical criticism.[90]

For example, in *Faultlines* (1992), Sinfield shows that Hamlet tries but fails to achieve the stoic ideal of rational self-control. He believes that God "gave us not That capability and godlike reason/To fust in us unus'd" (4.4.38-39), but fails to control himself because he holds incompatible stoic and Puritan views. Emulating Horatio, he means to control his emotions in a stoic fashion. As a result, he treats his revenge of his father's murder as a matter of duty, not grief. That he also considers man just a "quintessence of dust" means, Sinfield tells us, that the godlike independence provided by stoic self-control violates the Puritan belief in human wretchedness.[91] More importantly, after he returns from England, he adopts the Puritan's fatalistic doctrine of divine providence because he takes the complicated events, from the ghost's appearance to his rescue by the pirates and escape from death, to show that "[t]here is a special providence in the fall of a sparrow"(5.2.194-95). Like the Derrideans, who take the play's figural devices to undermine its literal meanings, ideological commitments, and generic conventions, Sinfield argues that these incompatible views give Hamlet only a "continuous subjectivity," not the unified self which humanist essentialism attributes to "dramatis personae."[92] The Marxists, who accept his unified self, fault his idealist illusions, not his incompatible views, yet argue that, to reform the court, Hamlet seeks (but fails to achieve) rational control of his own and others' feelings and actions and that in Act V he recognizes his errors and changes his views.

In general, the Marxists and Sinfield both claim that the play reflects the discourses and beliefs of the Elizabethan era, but Sinfield denies that these incompatible discourses and beliefs implicitly assert the universal truths of humanism. Rather, like the era's Protestant theology, which urges acceptance of divine predestination but fosters subjectivity and restlessness, or like Puritan doctrine, which values the truths of the Bible and still appreciates and teaches the "heathen" classics, the play reveals conflicts, tensions, and ruptures which deny the legitimating universality sought by traditional humanist critics; still, just as the Marxists assume that Hamlet's changes subvert his idealist faith in time and conscience, so Sinfield says that his newfound fatalism discredits Protestant Christianity: "Members of an audience watching *Hamlet* may come to feel that, insofar as the protestant deity is distinguished by an intricate determination of human affairs, it is intrusive and coercive; and that such a tyrannical deity need inspire no more than a passive acquiescence."[93] This critique of the "protestant deity" also suggests that Hamlet is wrong to leave social reforms to God, time, and conscience, rather than organized human action. Moreover, the critique gives Sinfield's account the contemporary import sought by traditional Marxists as well.

The New Historicist Leonard Tennenhouse also examines the play's conflicting discourses and repudiates but does not escape the humanist "essentialism" of the Marxists or the authorial critics. For example, he admits that, obsessed with Gertrude's sexual desire, Hamlet turns misogynistic, as authorial/psychoanalytic critics say; however, Tennenhouse argues that Gertrude's rejecting patrilineal succession, not Hamlet's sensitive nature or unresolved Oedipal conflicts, explains his obsession; as Tennenhouse says,

"Merely by inciting sexual desire, the queen's sexuality becomes a form of corruption . . . an assault on the whole concept of patriarchy."[94] Tennenhouse situates the queen and Hamlet in their sociohistorical contexts but in the rhetorical fashion interprets the queen's sexuality in modern feminist terms.

Like the psychoanalytic feminist and the Derridean formal critics, Tennenhouse takes the play to undermine neoclassical generic conventions, but he argues that the play dramatizes the Elizabethans' concern with Queen Elizabeth's impending death and the royal succession and its justification, not the corruptions of the Danish court, a melancholy disgust with life, nor the subversive force of puns and other figural devices. He says that the "aristocratic body" of Gertrude stands for two different political ideals. In the first, the "natural" female body and the body politic ("metaphysical body") are identical; in the second, the two bodies are distinct. More importantly, the first preserves patrilineal succession based on blood; the second, which makes the aristocratic female body an object of sexual desire, allows succession on other grounds. The play enacts the tragic conflict of Claudius, whose marriage into the aristocratic body represents succession based on desire, and Hamlet, whose blood justifies his claim to power.[95] In rhetorical terms, the stoic Hamlet exerts the symbolic "magic of blood" but lacks the authority to exercise power, while the pragmatic Claudius can exercise force but cannot legitimate his authority.

Unlike the Marxist, who argues that Hamlet acts but until the last act leaves to time and conscience the changes which require concerted action, Tennenhouse accepts the authorial, formal, and historical belief that Hamlet fails to take meaningful action; more negative, Tennenhouse says that the equivalent claims of Claudius and Hamlet ensure that neither one could "become the legitimate sovereign of Denmark."[96] Far from justifying Hamlet, the play equates Claudius's crime and Hamlet's revenge, and, as a result, undermines the neoclassical generic form. The feminist psychoanalytic and formal Derridean critics also claim that the play undermines the generic neoclassical conventions, but Tennenhouse gives this subversion a political, rather than a sexual or a figural import: in his terms, "[B]oth acts of violence assault the sovereign's body rather than establish the absolute power of the aristocratic body over that of its subject."[97]

In the traditional Marxist fashion, Francis Barker complains that, influenced by the Elizabethan patriarchal monarchy, Tennenhouse, Sinfield, and other New Historians or cultural materialists reduce cultural power to benign theatrical displays repressing objective history. As he says, "in some deep complicity with" the Shakespearean text, which occluded and domesticated the "coercive apparatus" of Elizabethan power, these critics efface the historicity of the present and erase the signs of domination, including the brutal and barbarous violence with which power actually rules.[98] Richard Levin also believes that such critics lack objectivity, but he complains that their antihumanist rhetoric conceals their Marxist beliefs. Killing off Shakespeare the author, these "antihumanists" empower texts to perform the functions which the defunct Shakespeare used to perform. The critics' rhetoric does not obscure the violent coercive apparatus of the Elizabethan ruling classes, as Barker says, but, on the contrary, the rhetoric reveals the ideological truths of Marxism "without making Shakespeare a premature Marxist."[99] Both Barker and Levin assume, nonetheless, that traditional "formalist-humanist" critics achieve an impersonal objectivity and theoretical rigor foreign to poststructuralist theory. I have argued, by contrast, that such positivist historical criticism conceals its commitment to Bradley's modern humanist view. Moreover, by subverting "essentialist" distinctions between text and context, discourse and historical fact, or literature and history, the antihumanist historians, who explain the play's treatment of class, gender, nationality, and other modern values, elaborate the rhetorical kind of historical criticism established in Johnson's era and developed by Frye and other eclectic modern critics.

In other words, like the feminist psychoanalysts and the Derridean formalists, the New Historical and cultural materialist views oppose but still evolve out of the traditional "formalist-humanist" criticism. The reason is that, even though the formal and historical readings opposed each other, the nineteenth century's new reading publics and "disinterested" academic humanism and the twentieth century's specialized departments and professional associations eventually legitimated both of them. Grady rightly suggests that in England and the United States, where Tillyard's views were exceptionally influential, professional English departments encouraged both the historical stance of Tillyard and the formal approach which he opposed.[100] This intense opposition persisted until the 1950s and the 1960s, when rapidly expanding Anglo-American universities encouraged various sorts of approaches. At the same time, eclectic critics like Empson, Frye, and Levin brought the formal and historical readings of *Hamlet* together, establishing what scholars term "objective" or purely "literary" methods and concepts and opening literary study to poststructuralist or New Historical readings.[101] Halpern, who believes that the modernist New Criticism of Knight, not the authorial humanism of Bradley, dominates twentieth-century Shakespeare studies, rightly claims that "certain continuities tie even the most recent forms of Shakespeare criticism to the fundamental problematic" of these twentieth-century studies.[102]

Conclusion

In sum, the Marxists claim that the play critiques the (Christian) idealism but not the hostility to women nor the contempt of middle-class enterprise shown by Hamlet, who perceives the corruptions of the Danish court but leaves to time and conscience the reforms which require organized action. To justify this account, the Marxist defends the play's Renaissance humanism and on that historical ground opposes the non-Marxist authorial, formal, and historical views. The traditional non-Marxist views also defend humanist ideals, which evolve in the nineteenth century, not the sixteenth, and, like the Marxist, reject the subjective "political (in)correctness" of poststructuralist approaches. It is true that the poststructuralist psychoanalytic, figural, cultural materialist, and New Historical readings oppose the universal truth, textual unity, generic conventions, and positivist facticity of the authorial, formal, and historical approaches. These readings reveal, nonetheless, the feminist, class, or nationalist values of the play and foster, thereby, the multicultural practices of the modern university and state. Lastly, the "impersonal" authorial, formal, and positivist historical readings from which the poststructuralist accounts evolved fostered the professional unity of the modern English department and of independent English associations and the national unity of Britain and the United States and their empires. The authorial, formal, and historical readings themselves evolved from the neo-classical humanism and Romantic formalism by virtue of which Coleridge, Hazlitt, Johnson, and other early modern critics resisted the aristocratic classical ideals of the Renaissance humanists and the Tudor court and promoted the language and the literature of the British middle classes.

Notes

1. For example, C. S. Lewis grants that the play has had many, contrary readings, but they embarrass him because he fears that absurdities and weaknesses in the play must explain them. See "Hamlet The Prince or the Poem?" 170-87. In *Shakespeare and the critics* A. L. French also blames the many readings on the play's lapses, incoherence, and failures. What's more, he complains that, to vindicate Shakespeare, critics produce coherent accounts obscuring the play's many faults. See also Cedric Watts, Hamlet (London, 19-88). In Hamlet *and the Philosophy of Criticism*, Morris Weitz also admits that critics have interpreted the

play in diverse and even contrary ways, but, instead of blaming the play, he maintains that "there is no true, best, correct, or right explanation, reading, interpretation, or understanding of *Hamlet*, nor can there be" (258). Weitz still expects critics to overcome their differences and arrive at a consensus but only if they accept Wittgenstein's rigorous distinctions between description and evaluation, explanation and understanding, and fact and interpretation. Similarly, in *The Meanings of* Hamlet, Paul Gottshalk also says that "no interpretation can explain *Hamlet* utterly," but he still argues that many interpretations "may be coordinate... the possibilities of cooperation [among critical schools] are great and the impediments less than many seem to feel" (131). Similarly, in Hamlet*'s Perfection*, William Kerrigan grants that a "finite number" of conceptual frameworks explain the play's many readings (2) but denies that these many frameworks justify our abandoning the pursuit of a "coherent understanding" (3). He even calls *Hamlet*'s poststructuralist critics "decadent" because their "new methods and concerns" give these critics "no way to solve its mysteries and unravel its cruxes" (3). Terence Hawkes rejects the possibility of such a definitive solution to the play's mysteries and acknowledges the incompatibility of the play's many readings. He recommends that we perceive a text as an "intersection or confluence" of "different and opposed readings," rather than a convergence of objective readings; all the same, he expects close textual analysis, which undermines not only the "definitive significance" of diverse readings but also their pursuit of "ideological power," to limit interpretive differences (*Meaning by Shakespeare*, 8).

2. Louis Montrose, "Professing the Renaissance," 19.

3. Victor Kiernan, *Eight Tragedies*, 68 and 198; see also Arnold Kettle, "From Hamlet to Lear," 238; Alvin Kernan, *The Playwright as Magician*, 93; David Margolies, *Monsters of the Deep*, 66-67; and Paul N. Siegel, *Shakespeare In His Time and Ours*.

4. Kettle, "Hamlet to Lear," 238; see also Margolies, *Monsters of the Deep*, 59-61; and Kernan, *Eight Tragedies*, 85-77.

5. William Shakespeare, *Hamlet*. Edited by Cyrus Hoy, 2nd edition, 1.5.187-88.

6. Terry Eagleton, *William Shakespeare*, 74.

7. Sidney Finkelstein, *Who Needs Shakespeare?*, 17.

8. See Rebecca Smith, "A Heart Cleft in Twain" and Marilyn French, *Shakespeare's Division of Experience*, 141-45.

9. Leonard Tennenhouse, *Power on Display*, 120.

10. See Frank Whigham, *Ambition and Privilege*, 1-47.

11. See, for example, *The Order of Things,* in which Foucault says that the figure of man "is a quite recent creature, which the demiurge of knowledge fabricated with its own hands less than two hundred years ago." Similarly, in *Humanism*, Tony Davies maintains that the nineteenth century invented "the myth of essential and universal Man" (24) and projected it "back onto the writings of the fifteenth- and sixteenth-century umanisti"(19). Applied to the working-class movement, this myth explains Marx's belief that wage-labor alienates the worker

from what Feuerbach termed his or her species-essence. Applied to literary study, the myth formed what Matthew Arnold called "disinterested" humanism, which, by appealing to the reader's "best" self, would reconcile the social classes and unify the state.

12. Davies, *Humanism*, 117-24.

13. Davies, *Humanism*, 72-104.

14. See Richard D. Altick, *The English Common Reader*, 173-87; and Frank Whigham, *Ambition and Privilege*.

15. Walter J. Ong, *Rhetoric, Romance, and Technology*, 17; See also Thomas M. Conley, *Rhetoric in the European Tradition*, 134, and Richard Waswo, *Language and Meaning in the Renaissance*, 134-35.

16. See Ong, *Rhetoric, Romance, and Technology*, 6; Conley, *Rhetoric in the European Tradition*, 109-10; and Anthony Grafton and Lisa Jardine, *From Humanism to the Humanities*, 161-200.

17. Alvin Kernan, *Samuel Johnson and the Impact of Print*, 4.

18. See Erich Auerbach, *Literary Language and Its Public*, 333; Gerald Newman, *The Rise of English Nationalism*, 67-87; Patrick Parrinder, *Authors and Authority*, 8; and René Wellek, *A History of Modern Criticism*, I, 5-11.

19. See Auerbach, *Literary Language and Its Public*, 333, and Roger Chartier, *The Cultural Uses of Print*, 71-108. Other scholars have suggested that, instituted in the public schools, where Matthew Arnold was chief inspector for twenty years, this humanism stifled the rebellion and the opposition of women and the working-class, imposed bourgeois forms of national unity, and, by the 1880s and 1890s, adopted racist and anti-Semitic tones (See Chris Baldick, *The Social Mission of English Criticism*, 82; Martin Bernal, *Black Athena* I, 347-66; Doyle *English and Englishness*, 12; and Gerald Graff, *Professing Literature*, 13). See also *The Order of Things*, where Foucault shows that the breakdown of humanism enables the disciplines to acquire a formal autonomy contrary to humanist ideals. He says that in the nineteenth century the study of the familiar philology, biology, and political economy replaces the eighteenth century's strange study of language, riches, and history. Knowledge has not grasped its objects more precisely or uncovered new objects; it has acquired new figures—production, life, language. Foucault shows that, at the same time, nineteenth-century disciplines develop an opposition between positive knowledge and transcendental critique. On the one side, the forms of rationality detach and reattach themselves to the positive disciplines; on the other, transcendental philosophy subjects the disciplines to critique, exposing the subjectivity, finitude, and being of the knower. In this way the nineteenth-century episteme invents the figure of man, whom the eighteenth century does not discuss. In the twentieth century, however, the modern episteme, which breaks into the mathematical sciences, the social sciences, and philosophical disciplines, subverts the human figure grounding the nineteenth-century disciplines and allows them to establish their formal autonomy.

20. See Dennis Dworkin, *Cultural Marxism*, 10-44. For a contrary view, see Ivo Kamps, *Materialist Shakespeare*, which maintains that "poststructuralist theory"

made it possible for the "so-called 'vulgar' Marxism to rethink the relationship between principles of determination, human agency, and the creation and reception of works of art"(1).

21. See Edward Hubler, ed., *The Tragedy of Hamlet*, 165, 167; similarly, in *The Characters of Shakespeare's Plays* (1818), William Hazlitt says that Hamlet, whose "ruling passion . . . is to think, not to act," acknowledges only "the tribunal of his own thoughts" (Cited in Hubler, ed., *Hamlet*, 167).

22. See David Farley-Hills, *Critical Responses to Hamlet, 1790-1830*, 2, xxii.

23. See Charles Hinnant, "Steel for the Mind," 184-85, and Thomas Woodman, *A Preface to Samuel Johnson*, 111.

24. Johnson, cited in Brian Vickers, *Shakespeare: The Critical Heritage*, V, 159.

25. Johnson, *Hamlet*, 148; Similarly, in *Some Remarks on the Tragedy of Hamlet* (1736), the first extended study of the play, Sir Thomas Hanmer—some say the author of this anonymous work is George Stubbs—censures the mad Ophelia, the comic gravediggers, Polonius's "low jokes and punns," and Hamlet's harsh satire of women and undignified comments on the ghost's movements, Claudius's praying, and Polonius's dead body. In addition, Hanmer praises the convincing ghost, the guards' speeches, Ophelia's modesty, decency, and simplicity, and Hamlet's speech to the ghost and reflections on his mother's hasty marriage. In general, Hanmer admits that the play's "Gold is strangely mixed with Dross," but, like Johnson, denies that "our Poet" should be "so much blamed for giving a Loose to his Fancy" because, unlike the French, whose aristocratic government has turned "their Rules of Criticism" into "an unnecessary Slavery," the English esteem such liberty (66-68).

26. Samuel Johnson, "Preface," 439; For an alternative view, see Edward Tomarken, who argues in *Samuel Johnson on Shakespeare* that Johnson praises the play's variety because Johnson accepts the "interruptive nature of death" (148-49).

27. Hazlitt, cited in *Hamlet*, 165.

28. Hazlitt, cited in *Hamlet*, 164-65.

29. Coleridge, cited in Edward Hubler, ed., *The Tragedy of Hamlet*, 194.

30. Coleridge, cited in Hubler, ed., *The Tragedy of Hamlet*, 194.

31. Coleridge, cited in *Hamlet*, 160.

32. Bradley, cited in Hubler, ed., *The Tragedy of Hamlet*, 205.

33. Bradley, cited in *Hamlet*, 172-75.

34. Paul Gottschalk, *The Meanings of Hamlet*, 79.

35. A. C. Bradley, *Shakespearean Tragedy*, 21-23.

36. Janet Adelman, *Suffocating Mothers*, 33.

37. Jacqueline Rose, "Sexuality in the Reading of Shakespeare." Similarly, in *Shakespeare's Ghost Writers,* Marjorie Garber says that, animated by the language with which the characters address him, the ghost orders Hamlet to remember him, but that command traps Hamlet, who, to take revenge, must forget his Oedipal desires, not endlessly remember and restate his mother's and uncle's crimes (162). Garber too rejects the play's neoclassical form but in a Derridean fashion claims

that Hamlet's successful revenge, Fortinbras' and Laertes' suppressed revenges, and the play's many other revengers, fathers, brothers, and Hamlets show that the play compulsively repeats the notion of revenge, not that Hamlet effectively overcomes his misogynistic rage nor that justice is finally done (129). This compulsive repetition enabled Freud to discover the modern notion of an Oedipal complex but renders Hamlet passive and even possessed, not active or responsible, as the Marxists claim.

38. William Kerrigan, *Hamlet's Perfection*, 63-93.

39. See Arnold Kettle, "From Hamlet to Lear," 10, 15, and Robert Weimann, "Mimesis in Hamlet," 275-91.

40. See Raymond Williams, *The Long Revolution*, 156-72, and Robert Altick, *The English Common Reader*, 30-77.

41. Alvin Kernan, *Samuel Johnson*, 4.

42. Gary Taylor, *Reinventing Shakespeare*, 115-33.

43. See David Simpson, *Romanticism*, 62, and Howard Felperin, *The Uses of the Canon*, 12.

44. See Brian Doyle, *English and Englishness*, 3.

45. Leavis, cited in Katharine Cooke, *A.C. Bradley*, 218.

46. Knight, cited in *Hamlet*, 185.

47. Knight, cited in *Hamlet*, 186.

48. G. Wilson Knight, *The Wheel of Fire*, 12.

49. Clemens, cited in Hubler, ed., *The Tragedy of Hamlet*, 221-23; see also Nigel Alexander, *Poison, Play and Duel*.

50. Eliot, cited in *Hamlet*, 183.

51. Eliot, cited in *Hamlet*, 180.

52. Eliot, cited in *Hamlet*, 181, 184.

53. Eliot, cited in *Hamlet*, 184. Carolyn Heilbrun complains that Eliot demeans the forceful and the vigorous character of Gertrude and dismisses the conventions of the Elizabethan stage and the beliefs of the Elizabethan audience (cited in Hubler, ed., *The Tragedy of Hamlet*, 265). In *T.S. Eliot on Shakespeare* Charles Warren defends Eliot's attack on the grounds that it allows Eliot to shift critical attention to Shakespeare's less famous plays or to less familiar Elizabethan playwrights and thereby to elaborate the motifs of his poetry (5-22).

54. Empson, cited in *Hamlet*, 284.

55. In *The Business of Criticism* (1959), Helen Gardner also says that authorial critics like Coleridge or Bradley ignore the conventions of Elizabethan revenge tragedy, which assumes that the villain creates the tragic situation, takes the initiative, and thereby gives the waiting hero his opportunity for revenge (40-41).

56. Kettle, "Hamlet to Lear," 241.

57. Richard Halpern. *Shakespeare Among the Moderns*, 40.

58. Ferguson, cited in *Hamlet*, 246-62.

59. James Calderwood, *To Be and Not to Be*, 144-52.

60. Terence Hawkes, "Telmah," 312, 327.

61. Hawks, "Telmah," 300.

62. Robert Weimann, "Mimesis in Hamlet," 276.

63. Alvin Kernan, *The Playwright as Magician*, 85-94, 105-6; see also David Margolies, *Monsters of the Deep*, 62-65.

64. Alvin Kernan, *Samuel Johnson*, 287.

65. Kernan, *Johnson*, 286.

66. For example, in *Appropriating Shakespeare*, Brian Vickers complains that "[o]nce upon a time the student of Shakespeare could read a wide range of books and articles devoted primarily to interpreting the plays in a modern critical-analytical way" (ix). By contrast, in the "contemporary critical scene," Vickers finds only "a great amount of pushing and shoving for attention, commercial promotion, indeed self-promotion, by forming or supporting a group, praising other members of it, denigrating rival groups" (x). Similarly, Richard Levin complains that professors of literature publish just to get "raises, promotions, tenure, fellowships, invitations to speak, recognition by professional associations, and the like" (See *New Readings vs. Old Plays*, 197-98). In *The Modernist Shakespeare* the radical Hugh Grady voices a similar concern; in the nineteenth century, when the study of Shakespeare "passed out of the sphere of public discourse properly speaking, becoming instead a knowledge/power of new bureaucratic institutions," more and less "virulent" forms of "professionalism" emerged, most of which were "housed in the new research universities" (28-30). Similar fears come from Gary Taylor, who complains in *Re-inventing Shakespeare* that "[t]he courtier/critic's 'candied tongue,' in Hamlet's withering description, will all too readily 'licke absurde pompe / and crooke the pregnant hindges of the knee'" (411). See also Vincent Leitch, *American Literary Criticism*, 25-26.

67. Gerald Graff, *Professing Literature*, 6-7.

68. Graff, *Professing*, 14.

69. See Maynard Mack, "The World of Hamlet," in Hubler, ed., *The Tragedy of Hamlet*, 234-56; Arthur McGee, *The Elizabethan Hamlet*; E. E. Stoll, *Hamlet: An Historical and Comparative Study*, in Joseph Price, ed., *Hamlet: Critical Essays*, 9-38; and Eleaner Prosser, *Hamlet and Revenge*.

70. Helen Gardner, *The Business of Criticism*, 50.

71. E. M. W. Tillyard, *Shakespeare's Problem Plays*, 23.

72. Tillyard, *Shakespeare's Problem Plays*, 28.

73. Hugh Grady, *The Modernist Shakespeare*, 169, 28-30.

74. J. Dover Wilson, *What Happens in Hamlet*, 140.

75. Wilson, *What Happens*, 33-34, 44-46, and 58.

76. Wilson, *What Happens*, xiii, 20.

77. Steven Urkowitz, "Well-sayd olde Mole," 259-66, and Paul Werstine, "Narratives About Shakespearean Texts," 81.

78. John Jones, *Shakespeare at Work*, 76.

79. Wilson, *What Happens*, xiii.

80. Wilson, *What Happens*, 218.

81. Gardner, *Business*, 50.

82. Harry Levin, *The Question of Hamlet*, 73.

83. Levin, *The Question*, 84.
84. Levin, *The Question*, 42.
85. Vincent Leitch, *American Literary Criticism*, 136.
86. Northrop Frye, *Northrop Frye on Shakespeare*, 83.
87. Frye, *Frye on Shakespeare*, 99.
88. See Michael Bristol, *Big-time Shakespeare*, 21.
89. See Francis Barker, *The Culture of Violence*, and Richard Levin, "The Poetics and Politics of Bardicide."
90. For an account of the cultural materialists' and New Historicists' origins, see Evan Watkins, *English Departments*, 201, and Bernard Bergonzi, *Exploding English*. For a full explanation, see Claire Colebrook's *New Literary Histories*, which says that, influenced by Foucault and other poststructuralists, these critics consider "the cultural/aesthetic domain . . . an area of contestation where various forces (aesthetic, political, historical, economic, etc.) circulate" (24), yet these "antihumanist" critics defend the traditional notion that historical texts are referential or that, as "self-fashioning," representation is fundamental to human experience (226-27); see Louis Montrose, "Professing the Renaissance," 17-22, and Jonathan Dollimore, *Political Shakespeare*, 2-3, for a more positive account of New Historicism's and cultural materialism's poststructuralist character.
91. Alan Sinfield, *Faultlines*, 224.
92. Sinfield, *Faultlines*, 226.
93. Sinfield, *Faultlines*, 230.
94. Leonard Tennenhouse, *Power on Display*, 114-15.
95. Tennenhouse, *Power*, 89.
96. Tennenhouse, *Power*, 93.
97. Tennenhouse, *Power*, 92.
98. Francis Barker, *The Culture of Violence*, 38-51, 200-201, 203, 209-10, and 230-33; see also Annabel Patterson, "The Very Age and Body of the Time His Form and Pressure," 56-57.
99. Richard Levin, "The Poetics and Politics of Bardicide," 501; See also Graham Bradshaw, *Misrepresentations*, 1-33; Brian Vickers, *Appropriating Shakespeare*, x; and Edward Pechter, "The New Historicism and Its Discontents," which also consider the New Historicists and cultural materialists Marxist, as well as Carolyn Porter, "Are We Being Historical Yet?"; and Louis Montrose, "Professing the Renaissance," which argue that Pechter and others conflate Marxism and New Historicism.
100. Grady, *Modernist*, 184.
101. Graff, *Professing*, 14-15, and 204-8.
102. Halpern, *Shakespeare*, 16-17.

Chapter Three
Feminism and Poststructuralist Criticism: The Reception of *Pride and Prejudice*

As I noted in the last chapter, which examined the strengths and limitations of traditional Marxist criticism, the Marxist and non-Marxist critics of *Hamlet* defend the play's humanist ideals and dismiss poststructuralist accounts even though they promote contemporary interests in class and gender. Similarly, this chapter argues that *Pride and Prejudice*'s traditional critics defend the moral truth of the novel and oppose poststructuralist accounts of its feminist social criticism and that the poststructuralist accounts reveal but do not fully describe this social criticism. Indeed, *Pride and Prejudice* criticizes social life more forcefully than most of its traditional and poststructuralist critics recognize; as Edward Neill says, "Jane Austen's fictional discourse is much more politically destabilized and destabilizing than the critical convoy for Austen's work has been at all eager to acknowledge."[1] For example, not only does the novel satirize the middle-class vulgarity of Mrs. Bennet, the childish frivolity of Lydia and Kitty, the aristocratic snobbery and arrogance of Darcy, Miss Bingley, and Lady Catherine, and the servile pomposity of clergymen like Mr. Collins, the novel also exposes the self-indulgent sarcasm, permissiveness, or dependence of middle-class gentlemen like Mr. Bennet and Mr. Bingley and the cynical conformity or complacent indifference of middle-class women like Jane Bennet and Charlotte Lucas.

Neither traditional nor poststructuralist accounts of the novel fully acknowledge this forceful social criticism. More precisely, traditional accounts of the novel deflate the social criticism and praise the novel's positive moral truth, while poststructuralist critics acknowledge the social criticism and question but do not consistently reject the positive moral truth. Moreover, the traditional critics consider the sheer diversity of contemporary interpretations an embarrassment because it denies the transcendent objectivity of critical practice. As Roger Gard says, "I dread that moment . . . when a natural delighted esteem [of Austen] might give way to the limitation of her appeal by arguments that are only historical, Marxist, Freudian, generic, feminist, etc."[2] Traditional feminist critics also maintain that, escaping literary study's schools, fashions, and currents, their interdisciplinary "gynocentric" criticism or engaged public stance resists cultural fragmentation and preserves what Elaine Showalter terms "the prospect of theoretical consensus."[3] Susan Guber complains, for example, that poststructuralist feminist, African American or postcolonial criticism, which indicts "the feminist universal and the grounded subject" for neglecting race and class, denies the transcendent objectivity of feminist theory, but Gubar adds that this criticism threatens "the relationship feminists within the academy have sought to maintain with one another and with women outside it."[4]

Instead of engaging in theoretical polemics against such diversity, post-Marxist reception study clarifies the conservative and progressive aspects of a work's main interpretations. In the last chapter I argued that the "antihumanist" accounts of *Hamlet* foster contemporary interests in race, class, or gender; in this chapter, I will show that, far from a divisive embarrassment or an irresponsible abdication, the diverse authorial, formal, and historical accounts of the novel have progressive import—their traditional and poststructuralist feminist versions justify programs in women's studies or enhance the disciplinary status of feminist criticism. The poststructuralist feminist accounts of the novel do not consistently oppose the traditional belief in the novel's unifying moral authority or support the humanities' new African American, gay, or multicultural literatures and programs, yet these accounts do reveal the novel's diverse interpretive frameworks and their implicit feminist social criticism.

Social Criticism in *Pride and Prejudice*

It is well known that *Pride and Prejudice* is a romantic comedy whose depiction of the characters' confusions and difficulties forcefully satirizes middle-class ideals of romance and marriage; at the same time, the novel develops less familiar but more subversive notions of reading and interpretation. For example, Mr. Collins will not read a novel to the Bennet family because he considers novels too frivolous to improve their readers. He reads, instead, Fordyce's *Sermons* in a loud voice, but, when he fails to retain the interest of Lydia and Kitty, he says, "I have often observed how little young ladies are interested by books of a serious stamp, though written solely for their benefit. It amazes me, I confess . . . But I will no longer importune my young cousin."[5] To his amazement, such serious public reading proves pretentious and boring. In an equally pretentious way, Lady Catherine is shocked to learn that no governess taught the Bennet sisters to read, whereas Elizabeth is pleased that they were left to read if they so wished. More intelligent, Mr. Bennet considers his library his private domain and spends much of his time there reading his books and avoiding his family and his neighbors. He calls all of his daughters silly and, except for Elizabeth's occasional agreement, needs no company to share his appreciation of Mr. Collins's absurdities and his wife's, his daughters', or his own. As he says, "For what do we live, but to make sport for our neighbors, and to laugh at them in our turn?" (233). Although the scholarly Mary also reads privately, she usually draws pedantic or obtuse moral generalizations, whereas Mr. Bennet's private reading and enjoyment demonstrate his intelligence. His daughters Lydia and Kitty prove silly, as he says, because, like Mrs. Bennet, they would rather entertain soldiers than peruse books. Miss Bingley, who claims that the accomplished woman is conversant with the modern languages, praises Darcy's library but does little reading herself. When Elizabeth would rather read a book than play whist, Miss Bingley charges that Elizabeth loves only reading. Elizabeth denies it, and, like Lady Catherine, Miss Bingley proves pretentious and even cynical.

    The novel assumes, in other words, that serious public reading ends up boring and pretentious, while skeptical private reading can demonstrate genuine intelligence. This assumption reveals what Roger Chartier calls the late eighteenth century's new manner of reading. This new manner fostered the individual, private consumption of multiple texts and displaced the older public reading, which was based mainly on the family and on a few religious texts. Moreover, while the older, public reading demanded serious moral reflection and personal improvement, the new kind of reading implied an intimate, private mode of interpretation.[6]

    This new reading involves not only skeptical, individual views but also subjective interpretations of the world, what Foucault terms the book of nature. In keeping with this broad sense that reading requires not only private views but also individual interpretation, the novel sets apart the discerning Elizabeth, who criticizes her society, from her sister Jane, who consistently finds only good in her society, and from the other characters, most of whom lack Elizabeth's discernment. For example, when Mrs. Bennet insists that Elizabeth marry Mr. Collins and secure the family estate, both Mrs. Bennet and Mr. Collins believe that Mr. Bennet will compel Elizabeth to accept his hand. Elizabeth recognizes, however, that her father will never agree to the marriage. His amusing announcement—"An unhappy alternative is before you, Elizabeth . . . Your mother will never see you again if you do not marry Mr. Collins, and I will never see you again if you do" (75)—proves her correct. Similarly, when Elizabeth warns Mr. Bennet not to let Lydia go to Brighton Beach, Mr. Bennet imagines that Elizabeth fears the loss of suitors but ends up acknowledging that she was right.

Elizabeth reads the book of nature very well; still, even though her friend Charlotte Lucas indicated that she was not romantic ("Happiness in marriage is entirely a matter of chance"[16]), Elizabeth is amazed to discover that Charlotte accepted Mr. Collins's offer of marriage. To Elizabeth's surprise, not only does Charlotte, who faces spinsterhood and economic dependence, marry to gain economic security, she adroitly adjusts to Collins's absurdities and even to Lady Catherine's officious attentions. Similarly, Elizabeth confidently ridicules and rejects the pompous Mr. Collins and the snobbish Darcy, but Darcy's letter refuting her criticisms of him depresses her terribly. In disbelief Elizabeth reads and rereads the shocking letter in which Darcy depicts Wickham's unprincipled character, Jane's serene manner, and her family's obnoxious behavior. To her amazement, she discovers that his treatment of Wickham and of her sister "was capable of a turn which made him entirely blameless throughout the whole" (133), and, retiring to her room, she experiences a depression "beyond anything she had ever known before" (136).

It is well known that this depressing discovery, central to the novel, changes her. For example, before the discovery, the skeptical Elizabeth freely disputes the opinions of one and all and inadvertently wins, thereby, the ardent admiration of Darcy. After she marries him, she teaches his sister to laugh at him too; still, once she can no longer hate Darcy, she loses her enthusiasm for witty disputation ("It is such a spur to one's genius, such an opening for wit to have a dislike of that kind" [145]). Before the discovery, she considered herself witty and shrewd; Jane, sensible and good; Bingley and Wickham, handsome, amiable, but abused; and her father, a gentleman of ability. She recognized, nonetheless, the middle-class vulgarity of her mother, who publically discusses Jane's impending wedding even though Bingley had not proposed to Jane; the adolescent frivolity of Lydia and

Kitty, who do little besides pursuing and entertaining soldiers; the servile pomposity of Mr. Collins, who compulsively flatters the powerful; and the aristocratic arrogance of Darcy, who will not trouble to please his society, and of Lady Catherine, who rudely intrudes in Charlotte's domestic affairs and in Elizabeth's marital arrangements. After the discovery, she faults the judgment of the dependent Bingley, who lets Darcy separate him from and reconnect him with Jane; the irresponsible behavior of Wickham, who cynically pursues wealthy women and persistently fails to live within his means; the complacent serenity of Jane, who conceals her feelings too adroitly; and the self-indulgent sarcasm and permissiveness of her too-liberal father, whose "continual breach of conjugal obligation and decorum . . . was so highly reprehensible" because it exposed "his wife to the contempt of her own children" (152).

Because of her depressing discovery and ensuing changes, she grows so critical of her society that, when Mrs. Gardiner invites her to travel to the Lakes region, she exclaims, "Adieu to disappointment and to spleen. What are men to rocks and mountains?" (102). She visits Pemberley, where a reformed Darcy, not rocks and mountains, delights her, but her growing delight with Darcy does not obviate her criticism of her family or her community. When her father reads her the letter in which Mr. Collins warns against her marriage to Mr. Darcy, she woodenly acknowledges the absurdity of Collins's warning but is privately mortified by her father's amusement. Similarly, when Lydia elopes with Wickham, the novel criticizes her fun-loving nature, Wickham's financial irresponsibility, and Mr. Bennet's permissiveness. Thanks to Darcy, Lydia marries Wickham and briefly returns home, but her ensuing joy does not obviate the novel's criticisms of her: "Lydia was Lydia still; untamed, unabased, wild, noisy, and fearless" (201). Jane and Bingley and Elizabeth and Darcy also end up happily married, yet Elizabeth still expects Pemberley to provide her and Darcy a welcome relief from her society: "She looked forward with delight to the time when they should be removed from society so little pleasing to either" (247).

Liberal Victorian Reading

Despite the happy ending, the novel's views of private reading and of individual interpretation imply forceful social criticism; nonetheless, while the liberal Victorian account establishes the canonical status of Austen's fiction, institutes progressive reforms of academic life, this account adopts a literal realism whereby a humble Austen simply but accurately chronicles rural eighteenth-century society. Although the interpretive practices of Elizabeth and others reveal the faults of the arrogant aristocratic and gentlemanly middle-class characters, the Victorian liberals, who include Richard Whately, Sir Walter Scott, Thomas Babington MacCauley, George Henry Lewes, Julia Kavanaugh, and Goldwin Smith, esteem the salutary realism whereby the novel provides what Sir Walter Scott terms a "correct and striking representation of that which is daily taking place."[7] Indeed, the liberal Victorian account accepts the good, humble, withdrawn Aunt Jane stereotype so assiduously promoted by Austen's family; in Henry Austen's words, "Faultless herself, as nearly as human nature can be, she always sought, in the faults of others, something to excuse, to forgive or forget.... She was tranquil without reserve or stiffness; and communicative without intrusion or self-sufficiency."[8]

Because the liberal account ignores the novel's artistic devices and emphasizes the novel's realism and the Aunt Jane stereotype, scholars dismiss it. Some say that the Victorian liberals praised the salutary effects of Austen's realism because they meant to counter conservative fears that novel readers, especially young, leisurely females, simply indulged escapist sexual fantasies.[9] Other scholars complain that the realism of Whately, Lewes, and other liberals amounts to little more than informal impressionism and chauvinistic stereotyping and lives on only in the movie adaptations and English tourism promoted by the Austen industry.[10]

To an extent, these criticisms are right: the liberals considered Austen a humble chronicler of her society's customs and neglected her artistic development as well as her social criticism. For example, in "Modern Novels" (1821) Richard Whately says that "certainly no author has ever conformed more closely to real life, as well in the incidents, as in the characters and descriptions."[11] More negative than Whately, who says, "Her fables appear to us to be in their own way, nearly faultless,"[12] Thomas Babington MacCauley, George Henry Lewes, Julia Kavanaugh, and Goldwin Smith complain that Austen fails to evoke grand passions, to explore the concrete details of life, or to plumb its profound depths; however, these Victorian critics also praise her discriminating realism. For instance, Lewes says, "Her dramatic ventriloquism is such that, amid our tears of laughter and sympathetic exasperation at folly, we feel it is almost impossible that she did not hear those very people utter those very words."[13] Goldwin Smith, who wrote the first formal study of Austen's life and work, considers Darcy's derogatory comments on Elizabeth's looks a flaw of his otherwise good characterization. He too says, however, that in a brilliant, untutored way Austen's work simply chronicles the lives of the rural eighteenth-century

British middle class and gentry; in his terms, "[T]here is no hidden meaning in her."[14]

The liberals' belief that the novel chronicles the lives of the rural eighteenth-century British middle class and gentry neglects the novel's aesthetic devices and feminist social criticism, as scholars say, but the liberals' belief in the novel's realism still has progressive import. To begin with, the belief moved them to establish the canonical status of Austen's work. Until the 1870s, when Austen's nephew Austen-Leigh wrote a popular biography of her, her fiction was financially unsuccessful. A publisher who purchased an early version of *Northanger Abbey* refused to bring it out; others required her to pay the costs of printing her novels. While she was alive, she was able to publish only four novels, and those four earned much less money and won much less acclaim than the financially successful novels of Fanny Burney or Maria Edgeworth, her more or less forgotten contemporaries.[15] The Victorian biographer and writer Mrs. Oliphant points out that it was the liberals, not the market, that made the work of Austen a classic with which "it is now the duty of every student of recent English literature to be more or less acquainted . . . 'The best judges' have here done the office of an Academy."[16]

More importantly, the realism praised by the liberals resists the elevated Ciceronian rhetoric of the Renaissance and neoclassical humanism maintaining *Hamlet*'s high status and in an empiricist manner emphasizes the speech of everyday life and the truths of individual experience. Like the Renaissance humanists, eighteenth- and nineteenth-century "new rhetoricians," who include Whately as well as Adam Smith, Hugh Blair, and George Campbell, maintained that the English language and English literature were capable of the same systematic grammar and stylistic subtlety as the established Greek and Latin classics. For example, in *Elements of Rhetoric Compromising an Analysis of the Laws of Moral Evidence and of Persuasion, with Rules for Argumentative Composition and Elocution,* which reached its sixth edition in 1828, Whately argued that good rhetoric followed objective experience, imitated proper English elocution, and promoted the reader's individual responses. Nancy Streuver, who interprets Austen's realistic conversations, descriptions, and analyses as a version of this "new" rhetoric, rightly says that it explains why Victorian liberals praised her fiction so highly.[17]

Moreover, since the new rhetoricians accepted David Hume's and John Locke's empiricist belief that significant language conforms with experience, they made the speech of educated and cultured upper-class persons the ideal speech and dismissed the "rude" speech of poor, uneducated persons as substandard dialects.[18] Certainly, in keeping with this linguistic ideal, Austen treats the propriety of English diction and the norms of English grammar as legitimate signs of a character's character and status.[19] As Tony Tanner says, "[T]he language of Jane Austen's novels excludes not only the unassimilable roughness and dissonance of working class speech but also any of the potential discordance of colloquial or vernacular discourse."[20] No wonder Mark Twain wanted to "dig her up and hit her over the skull with her own shinbone."[21]

The neoclassical humanists, who appreciated the serious social, political, or moral questions raised by *Hamlet*, assumed that an educated gentleman would study great art for its own sake; by contrast, the Victorian liberals esteemed Austen's literal realism, rather than any probing social criticism, yet they considered the study of "rhetoric and belles lettres" a useful enterprise in which the cultivation of good taste, rather than the action of the court or the state, would improve the reader's mind and the nation's civility and prosperity.[22] The conventional wisdom tells us that it was not until Charles Dickens and others made huge fortunes by writing fiction that the novel rose in canonical status; however, the Victorians' study of "rhetoric and belles lettres" justified the educational reforms whereby the liberals made the fiction of Austen and other English writers a legitimate object of a university education. Eighteenth-century educators working in dissenting academies or secondary schools taught their students that, as Trevor Ross says, "the true pleasures of reading could only come in relation to texts of an intellectually demanding nature."[23] These educators feared, however, that novels, which one could consume "too easily and rapidly," had "injurious effects." The Victorian liberals also expected reading to improve the reader, but, to improve intellectual standards, they went on to foster the academic study of Austen and other modern English fiction writers. Harold Orel points out that Lewes, who rejected Matthew Arnold's belief that the Greek and Roman classics formed a genuine critical standard and that modern literature was hopelessly enervated, praised the realist fiction not only of Jane Austen but also of George Sand, George Eliot, and others.[24] Lewes did not participate in mid-century university reforms, but *The Westminster Review*, to which Lewes was a frequent contributor, sharply opposed the classical education demanded by the church and imposed by the state. Smith, who campaigned for a competitive, secular Oxford, was appointed secretary of the government commission which prepared the university reform acts of 1854 and 1856.[25] Thomas Miller points out that, because of these acts, "English studies became a formal part of the curriculum, and professorships in English literature were widely instituted."[26] Similarly, in "The London

University," Thomas Babington Macaulay, who called Austen the Shakespeare of English prose, defended the grammatical norms and "chaste" diction of the national language, the reforming, elevating powers of modern British literature, and the benefits of a secular, liberal education. Elected to Parliament several times, Macaulay, whom Jonathan Arac considers "one of the most publicly powerful literary individuals that one can readily imagine,"[27] produced the 1853 East India Act. It is not surprising that the competitive civil service examination established by the East India Act enabled tutors at Oxford and Cambridge to teach English for the first time or that the *Civil Service Handbook of English Literature* required candidates to master Austen's fiction.[28]

Scholars rightly complain that the late Victorian Oxford and Cambridge where the study of English literature was finally established represented what Martin Wiener calls the "ethos of later-Victorian Oxbridge, a fusion of aristocratic and professional values," which "stood self-consciously in opposition to the spirit of Victorian business and industry" and which, in Mary Poovey's terms, "helped legitimize both England's sense of moral superiority and the imperial ambitions this superiority underwrote."[29] In the early and the mid-nineteenth century, when newly established Anglo-American colleges began to teach English literature, the study of English fiction promoted, just the same, the progressive views of disenfranchised middle and working classes and even the "radical" or feminist assertion of the "separate spheres."[30] In this era women's colleges and the newly founded Ladies Educational Associations also fostered the study of English fiction; however, thanks to the liberal reforms, Britain's elite, exclusively male universities accepted the "separate spheres" in which "tough, disciplined" men preparing to be lawyers, theologians, or administrators studied the difficult and rigorous Latin and mathematics while in the university extensions "soft, motherly" women preparing to be elementary and eventually secondary school teachers studied and taught the "unchallenging" English.[31] In keeping with the new rhetoric, the liberals attributed to the novel a literal realism excluding social critique, yet the liberals effectively instituted the study of Austen's fiction and that of other British writers. In addition, even though the authorial, formal, and historical approaches which evolved out of the liberal Victorian view do not consistently oppose the improving virtues of the liberals' realism, these approaches acquired progressive feminist import once women students and faculty broke down the Victorians' "separate spheres" and gained equal status and independent programs.

Modern Authorial Critics

For the most part, modern critics whom I call authorial because they assume that the intention of the author explains a text's meaning also accept Austen's realism but, setting literature above social, linguistic, or methodological differences, defend Austen's moral truth, not her social criticism and dismiss the reader's subjective responses. Bradley and the authorial humanist critics of *Hamlet* esteem Shakespeare's profound insights into human nature but, to justify the play's high status, accommodate the neoclassical tragic form rejected by their romantic predecessors; similarly, early modern authorial critics argue that Austen's limited range only heightens her depiction of what Lord David Cecil terms the "fundamental problems of human conduct" and her "complete understanding" and "criticism of life."[32] These critics ignore or dismiss the social criticism implicit in the characters' diverse interpretive frameworks and in Cecil's grand Arnoldian manner emphasize the great moral authority whereby *Pride and Prejudice* can unify society; as Cecil says, "[W]ere Stendhal to rebuke me, it would only convince me I had done right . . . [but] I should worry for weeks and weeks, if I incurred the disapproval of Jane Austen."[33]

Later authorial accounts also emphasize Austen's moral authority. These critics claim, however, that, while the novel initially permits highly divergent responses to Darcy or to Wickham, responses that implicitly criticize social life, Austen has ironically depicted the characters' misconstructions of each others' motives or personalities in order to teach Elizabeth and the reader the universal truth, which is, in Alistair Duckworth's terms, that the "best solution, clearly, is neither society alone, nor self alone, but self-in-society, the vitalized reconstitution of a social totality, the dynamic compromise between past and present, the simultaneous reception of what is valuable in an inheritance and the liberation of the originality, energy and spontaneity in the living moment."[34]

Feminist authorial critics reject the good Aunt Jane stereotype and the novel's "vitalized reconstitution of a social totality" but still appreciate the novel's ironic depiction of Elizabeth and Darcy's misunderstandings and the novel's assertion of a unifying moral truth, not its implicit social criticism. Still other critics, whom I call poststructuralist authorial feminists because they deny the good Aunt Jane stereotype and the novel's moral realism, acknowledge the characters' and the reader's diverse frameworks because these critics take the rationalist truth of the narrator and the subjective, feminine responses of Elizabeth and other characters to diverge sharply.

Consider Marvin Mudrick's authorial account. In the widely reviewed *Jane Austen: Irony as Defense and Discovery* (1952), he appreciates the self-conscious irony whereby Austen insightfully depicts the socioeconomic biases and pressures of an acquisitive society and in the process teaches Elizabeth the unifying moral truth; however, he faults the wooden male stereotypes whereby "Aunt Jane" the withdrawn spinster excludes sexuality from her world. Mudrick says, for instance, that Elizabeth represents Austen's comic irony, not her moral insight. Like Austen, Elizabeth understands that for the simple characters, who, like Mrs. Bennet or Lady Catherine, never have to worry about growing up, love is straightforward.[35] For the complex characters, who, despite the pressures of economic needs or social hierarchy, preserve free choice, love requires learning and discrimination. Betrayed by her "youth and inexperience and emotional partiality," Elizabeth ignores the moral context of her "acquisitive society," including the socioeconomic pressures on a Charlotte or a Wickham.[36] Elizabeth eventually learns, however, that, despite the pressures, the complex characters retain their free choice, while the simple characters, bound to the social hierarchy, do not.

As this lesson suggests, Mudrick faults Elizabeth's acquisitive society, which puts such pressures on the characters; still, he ultimately dismisses this social criticism and emphasizes the characters' free choice and the author's moral truth. Moreover, like the New Critic Reuben Brower, who complains that, after Elizabeth and Darcy recognize the truth, the novel turns literal and hastens to a happy but conventional ending, Mudrick finds the ending disappointing. He argues, however, that the reason the last third of the novel lacks subtlety, "density," or "originality" is that, when Austen tries to depict "sexual experience outside marriage," her irony fails. Austen does not critique Darcy's snobbery or Wickham's opportunism; rather, unable to manage the "personally involving" aspects of sex, Austen "too obviously" takes the "wooden and lifeless" Wickham and Darcy "from books."[37] Preserving the Aunt Jane stereotype, Mudrick reduces Austen's social criticism to a stereotypical spinster's rigid defense against a condemning world, but Mudrick's belief that Austen's irony teaches Elizabeth to esteem the complex, rather than the simple, conformist characters forcefully emphasizes the author's moral truth.

The feminist Mary Poovey also appreciates Austen's ironic moral truths, but she maintains that Austen humbles Elizabeth because Austen's conservative notion of romance opposes Elizabeth's liberal individuality, not because, a defensive spinster, she cannot handle the disturbing aspects of sexuality. Poovey says, for example, that Elizabeth's subversive wit defends her against the emotional vulnerability which she shares with all unmarried women. At the first ball, when Darcy insults her, touching her fear of spinsterhood, she responds with hostile wit, whereas when Wickham flatters her, dishonestly encouraging her hostility to Darcy, she responds with romantic fantasies. In other words, Poovey grants that Elizabeth mistakes both Darcy and Wickham, as the modern authorial reading says; Poovey argues, however, that Darcy marries because of his sexual desire, not because he learns to appreciate the Bennet family. Similarly, Elizabeth, who mistakenly assumed that her superior mind preserved her individual autonomy, marries not because she discovers the true Wickham, Darcy, and Lydia but because her mistakes mortify her individualist pride.

The rationalist Mary Wollstonecraft argues that, weakening women, romance fosters their desire for sensual pleasure and their pursuit of beauty, whereas reason makes them the equal of men; similarly, Poovey claims that the novel faults the liberal individuality and romantic fantasies of Elizabeth but preserves the liberal ideal in which the marriage of Elizabeth and Darcy represents the perfect resolution of individual pleasure and social responsibility, or moral relativity and common social values.[38] Anne Ruderman, who shares Whately's belief that Austen's status as a novelist "does not mean that she cannot be a great moralist," claims that Austen attributes to moral virtue a "permanent, objective content" incompatible with modernity's liberal individualism, human "plasticity," and feminist "extremes."[39] Poovey also maintains that the absolute moral values of the novel's liberal ideal overcome the relativism and individualism of the characters, but, instead of repudiating "feminist 'extremes,'" Poovey takes the novel to undermine the good Aunt Jane stereotype in Wollstonecraft's rationalist fashion.

Poststructuralist authorial feminists also claim that at first the novel attributes to the characters diverse interpretive frameworks; as Martha Satz says, Jane is steadily optimistic; Mr. Collins, always laudatory; Mr. Bennet, inevitably detached and satirical; and Elizabeth, satirical but endowed with empiricist skepticism. These feminists emphasize the characters' subjective outlooks but deny that by the end the author defeats the characters' "relativist" perspectives and imposes the moral truth. Although Austen intervenes to defend the truth of established social conventions, Elizabeth and other characters do not accept this arrogant authorial intervention or abandon their private, critical outlook. Satz grants, for instance, that the last third of the novel exposes the errors and the limitations of Elizabeth and other, subjective characters, as Mudrick, Poovey, and other authorial critics say. Satz denies, however, that the novel's last third presents cardboard villains or restates disappointingly conventional themes; rather, in the last third

Elizabeth learns how painful and difficult it is to overcome the comic detachment which she acquires from her father and to grasp the power and the virtue which Darcy and Pemberley represent. Satz also grants that the concluding affirmation aesthetically displaces the limited relativism of the characters, but Satz argues that the reader still resents the presumptuous arrogance of Austen's platonic outlook.[40] More radical, Susan Morgan, who also appreciates the characters' interpretive perspectives and personal relationships, says that the conclusion does not fault Elizabeth's individualist pride in the rationalist manner, as Poovey and Ruderman claim; the conclusion affirms only Elizabeth's subjective processes of engaged learning, not the public, liberal ideal of a balanced energy and hierarchy.[41]

Such defenses of the character's "processes of engaged learning" do not dismiss the subjective, feminine responses and social criticism of Elizabeth and other characters or reduce them to biases or misunderstandings. Feminist and nonfeminist authorial critics complain, however, that the feminist poststructuralists promote the very anarchic subjectivity which the moral truth of the novel overcomes.[42] In defense of their views, the poststructuralist feminists do not advocate bisexual relationships; still, just as Irigaray says that, if the "object" speaks and sees, the subject splits into (male) self and (female) other, so the poststructuralist feminists maintain that the "greatest evil" is the unselfconscious realism of the liberal Victorian and the modern authorial critics, who expect the characters and readers to mirror experience, instead of interpreting and criticizing it.[43]

In other words, while the traditional and feminist authorial critics oppose each other, they defend the novel's moral truth, not its social criticism, because they resist the anarchic or fragmented subjectivity of much contemporary literary study, whereas, preserving the novel's social criticism, the poststructuralist critics reject the novel's moral realism and emphasize the characters' and the reader's subjective frameworks. The incompatibility of these traditional and poststructuralist views indicates that modern literary study has grown too diverse for traditional moral realism to dominate it. As I noted, to establish Austen's canonical status, the Victorian liberals promoted the stereotype of a withdrawn, limited Austen whose untutored genius humbly but accurately chronicled eighteenth-century rural England. The liberals also fostered the reform of the elite British universities, imposing the "separate spheres" of male and female students.

After World War I, when the rapid growth of secondary education enhanced the importance of literature, authorial critics, who like Cecil instituted the modern English department, promoted literary study's high moral ideals in order to ensure that literature overcame class and linguistic differences and unified society. Claudia Johnson maintains that, little more than enthusiastic Janeites, Cecil and other early modern critics violate the protocols of professional criticism;[44] in an Arnoldian fashion they maintained, however, that literary study demands a subjective aesthetic response going beyond factual knowledge and imposes a broad moral authority overcoming narrow class interests and linguistic "degeneration."[45] After World War II, authorial critics like Mudrick also assumed that canonical Anglo-American literature exercises a broad moral authority but in the Cold War style went on to repudiate economic determinism and to defend liberal ideals.[46] Authorial feminists also defend literature's broad moral authority; however, these feminists expect literary study to promote the equal rights of women, rather than ideals of cold war liberalism because in a remarkable way feminist literary study evolved from the liberals' "separate spheres" to independent women's studies programs and departmental literature courses and concentrations.[47]

As Robert Young suggests, since the Victorian era academic literary study has paradoxically adopted such "useful" reform and disinterested or autonomous aesthetic ideals and moral truth. In Irigaray's fashion the poststructuralist authorial feminists have gone on, however, to emphasize the subjective processes of interpretation and deny the equality or universality of both women's and men's truth. As a result, these feminists subvert the paradoxical structure of aesthetic autonomy and practical reform and acknowledge the humanities' diverse programs and the twenty-first century's fragmented culture. Since formal accounts of the novel also undermine this paradoxical structure and accept modern culture's fragmentation, I turn now to the novel's formal readings.

Traditional and Feminist Formal Readings

Critics whom I term formal because they believe that, by unifying the text, its figural devices render it autonomous deny that Elizabeth's discovery teaches (or fails to teach) her and the reader universal moral truths; rather, the formal critics maintain that we value *Pride and Prejudice* for its good plot, effective irony, indirect discourse, or satiric comedy, not for its moral truth, liberal values, realistic depictions, feminist beliefs, or social criticism. Many formal critics, who include D. W. Harding, Q. D. Leavis, and Sandra Gilbert and Susan Gubar, describe a savage but aloof Austen, who outwardly accepts yet privately or unconsciously disdains modern life's conventional practices or chauvinistic customs. For the most part, these critics accept the modernist belief that what Fredric Jameson calls the narrow, commodified character of bourgeois modernity empties it of any genuine significance;[48] however, some of these critics dismiss the diversity of the characters' or the readers' views and reconcile this savage Austen and the authorial critic's unifying moral truth, while others defend her literary techniques and feminist import but emphasize literature's formal autonomy, not its engaged social criticism.

In the modernist fashion, D. W. Harding and Q. D. Leavis deny that the novels state explicit morals or themes, as the authorial critics argue. In "A Critical Theory of Jane Austen," a series of essays written from 1941 to 1944, Leavis does not say what problems the novels dramatize; rather, she says that their meaning lies in Austen's "exploring her own problems by dramatizing them."[49] In "Regulated Hatred: An Aspect of the Work of Jane Austen" (1940), Harding makes a similar but more specific claim: the novels dramatize the unconscious, fairy tale motifs in which the "delicate," "inborn" "sensitivities" of the motherless Cinderella or the adopted princess enable her to win the hand of the prince.[50]

In addition to this unconscious mythology, Harding brings to light textual ambiguities and harsh caricatures which reveal the novel's social criticism but only as the grounds of Austen's aesthetic autonomy. He ingenuously accepts the liberal/authorial belief that family-oriented Jane Austen was a contented, secure, and instinctively artistic spinster. At the same time, he uncovers an altogether different, much more alienated Austen, one who needed, he says, "to keep on reasonably good terms with the associates of her everyday life" but who could not tolerate their "crudenesses and complacencies."[51] Once Austen discovered that "good natured" exposés of people's faults would make people laugh, she produced serious caricatures who, like Mr. Collins or Lady Catherine de Bourgh, readily turn their victims' lives into "fantastic nightmare."[52]

Leavis shares Harding's belief that contextual detail subverts the authorial belief in Austen's unifying moral truth and reveals the ambiguities preserving the text's autonomy; however, she construes Austen as a devoted, professional writer, rather than a savage social critic or a positive moral force. Leavis argues that, far from showing the intuitive genius with which the Victorian liberals and authorial critics so enthusiastically endow her, Austen spent many years slowly and laboriously revising and perfecting her novels and maturing as an artist.[53] Leavis describes how *Pride and Prejudice*, for example, gradually evolved from Austen's youthful parodies, her many letters, and her extensive family experiences. Her greatness lies not in her self-effacement or self-restraint but in what Leavis calls "this power of seizing on every trifle at her command . . . [and] using it in the one place and context where it will tell and do exactly what is required of it."[54]

In *The Madwoman in the Attic*, Sandra Gilbert and Susan Gubar also praise Austen's revisions not only of her own work but of eighteenth-century fiction as well. What's more, Gilbert and Gubar also argue that, instead of teaching a moral, the novel dramatizes Austen's unconscious conflicts, but Gilbert and Gubar say that these conflicts reveal an angry Austen's repressed feminist sentiments. Sympathetic to women's independence, she warmly depicts witty, creative, self-authoring young women like Elizabeth and still severely humiliates them, forcing them to accept the conventional, repressed female role.[55] Austen indulges the unconventional autonomy of these women only to subjugate them, when they marry, to the patriarchal structures which romance idealizes.

Despite this forceful critical insight, Gilbert and Gubar accept the authorial belief that in a rationalist, egalitarian manner Austen exposes the seductive illusions whereby romantic fiction leads women to devote themselves to romantic love and to marital bliss; Gilbert and Gubar maintain that a divided Austen inconsistently accepts the underlying truth of these illusions, ironically parodying the illusions and the conventions which her works extend and perpetuate. Such divided practices do not indicate that the novel accepts or rejects the liberal ideal of an egalitarian union or a balanced society, as Poovey and the authorial critics say; these practices illustrate the struggle of the nineteenth-century female artist to escape what Gilbert and Gubar term "male houses and male texts" and establish a purely female artistic identity and literary tradition.[56]

Susan Fraiman also maintains that, instead of asserting positive moral truth, the novel dramatizes Austen's unconscious sentiments, but, more radical than Harding, Leavis, and Gilbert and Gubar, she claims that these sentiments protest patriarchal "violence against women."[57] More importantly, instead of preserving the text's and the tradition's autonomy, Fraiman adopts the poststructuralist feminist belief that characters interpret experience in diverse ways; in her terms, like authors, they write their own texts. For instance, she considers Mr. Bennet a Lockean liberal whose comic detachment and suspenseful actions make him an authorial figure able "to frame a moral discourse and judge characters accordingly."[58] An "honorary boy" or "castrated" girl, Elizabeth, who identifies with Mr. Bennet, acquires his comic detachment and even his authorial powers; however, because "heterosexuality" remains "compulsory," he betrays her, reducing her to a possession available for exchange on the marriage market. Although witty Elizabeth resists this "grammar of exchange" and competes with Darcy, another authorial figure, for control of the text, Darcy's painful letter and unseen influence defeat her, vitiating her authorial powers. Elizabeth condemns the reckless Lydia and the pragmatic Charlotte, but she too cannot resist the allure of Darcy's wealth and power. In other words, like Gilbert and Gubar, Fraiman grants that, celebrating the marriage of Darcy and Elizabeth, the novel subordinates Elizabeth to patriarchal norms but still claims that, allowing diverse frameworks or interpretive perspectives, the novel protests the "complex mechanism" trapping women.

Other formal critics, who include Mary Lascelles and Ian Fergus, also appreciate Austen's artistic achievements but, instead of acknowledging the novel's diverse frameworks or perspectives and their implicit feminist social criticism, preserve Austen's moral truth. In *Jane Austen and Her Art* (1939), which, according to Southam, put Austen studies on a whole "new footing,"[59] Lascelles claims that the brilliance of Austen's early work has blinded critics to her "gradual and steady development," as Leavis suggested;[60] however, Lascelles argues that Austen's forceful parodies and ingenious stylistic devices do not reveal the novel's diverse interpretive frameworks and implicit social criticism; the parodies and devices betray her considerable indebtedness to contemporary novelists, essayists, and poets, especially Samuel Johnson, to whom, more than to other writers, Austen owes what Lascelles calls her "pregnant abstractions," "parallel phrasing," and "mimicing idioms."[61] Like the liberal Victorians, she claims that Austen effaces herself in order to speak through her characters and to make the idiomatic speech of the characters differentiate them.[62] In Lascelles's Jamesian terms, Austen restricts her story to Elizabeth's point of view and engages in free indirect discourse.[63] Lastly, Lascelles maintains that, far from undermining each other, the story's satiric moral truth and the plot's romantic ideals legitimate each other. For instance, Collins reveals a monstrous character but has positive functions: he "has to draw and hold together Longbourn and Hunsford . . . to confirm Elizabeth's ill opinion of everything connected with Darcy . . . to draw Elizabeth to Hunsford when the time is ripe, and eventually to send Lady Catherine to Longbourn on her catastrophic visit."[64]

In "The Comedy of Manners" (1987), Jan Fergus also appreciates Austen's formal achievements and still accepts the novel's moral truth, not its feminist social criticism. In the formal manner, she praises Austen's grasp of the dialogue, compliments, linear and structural irony, comic and emotional incongruity, and other conventions defining the comedy of manners.[65] In Leavis's fashion, she maintains that Austen, a master of this genre's conventions, discriminates her characters more finely and describes conduct more precisely and more comically than Fanny Burney, Samuel Richardson, and other eighteenth-century novelists do.[66] Like Lascelles, she claims that these conventions reveal Austen's moral truth, not the characters' diverse perspectives. For instance, she says that the comic scene in which the Bennet sisters respond very differently to Mr. Collins's letter of introduction do not show that the novel allows incompatible interpretive frameworks, as poststructuralist critics claim; rather, these scenes contrast the characters' foibles, manners, and affectations in a conventional eighteenth-century manner. In addition, since Fergus esteems the novel's ironies of structure, including the emotional incongruities and sexual antagonisms of Darcy and Elizabeth, she denies that in several key dialogues Elizabeth rightly faults Darcy's "pride, conceit, and ill temper." Feminists claim that, because of this criticism, Darcy recognizes his mistakes and improves his manners, whereas Fergus maintains that, "[w]hile a prejudiced mind, like Elizabeth's, can see these qualities in Darcy's remarks," a reader with "an open mind" will recognize Darcy's amiable qualities.[67] Karen Newman says that as "critics and feminists, we must refuse the effects of" the marriage ending the novels;[68] Fergus celebrates the marriage because it "confirms that in life and literature" established conventions "need not be limitations."[69]

Like Harding and Leavis, Lascelles and Fergus appreciate the novel's aesthetic devices, but their accounts of the novel's literary conventions dismiss the novel's diverse interpretive frameworks and preserve the unifying authority of Austen's moral truth. The formal feminists also appreciate the novel's aesthetic devices, but their account of the novel's feminist insights defends an autonomous female literary tradition. These differences imply that the formal approach has evolved a conservative and a radical branch. During the 1930s and the 1940s, *Scrutiny*, to which Harding and Leavis were important contributors, stridently opposed the authorial humanists' abstract evaluations, class biases, and academic privileges.[70] Just as G. Wilson Knight and other formal critics repudiated the authorial humanist account of Hamlet's character and Shakespeare's profound insight, so Leavis engaged in what Francis Mulhern considers "a comprehensive and unrestrained assault on the intellectual and social character of traditional English studies."[71] As I noted, such assaults justified the highly specialized studies which were fostered by the modern English department's increasingly independent fields, areas, and programs but which undermined literature's moral authority and fragmented the modern curriculum.[72] In the 1950s and 1960s, when the formal method had successfully established itself, rapidly expanding Anglo-American English departments reconciled what scholars call "objective" formal and authorial views.[73] In this era, critics of *Hamlet* synthesize the authorial and the formal reading and thereby defend Shakespeare's autonomous imagination. Similarly, eclectic critics like Fergus and Lascelles emphasize Austen's artistic development but accommodate the formal and authorial views, thereby preserving Austen's (and the traditional department's) cultural authority.

Once women's studies programs are instituted, feminist critics like Fraiman and Gilbert and Gubar, who emphasize Austen's artistic practices and reveal the novel's feminist insights, revive Harding and Leavis's radicalism. More precisely, like Morgan and Satz, Fraiman accepts the novel's poststructuralist diversity of interpretive frameworks and their implicit social criticism and cultural fragmentation, whereas Gilbert and Gubar assume that the literary language produced by Austen and other women writers recuperates their literature's lost mythic import. More than Fraiman, Gilbert and Gubar resist the diversity of the modern curriculum and defend the public authority of women's literature and women's studies, rather than, say, feminist, Black, gay, or multicultural literatures. The historical account also does not foster such diversity; however, since this account rejects both the moral truths of the authorial critics and the autonomous aesthetics (or purely women's tradition) of the formal critics, I turn now to this account.

Historical Readings

The traditional historical account claims that objective criticism of Austen interprets the novel in eighteenth-century, rather than in modern terms, yet the traditional account implicitly accepts the unifying moral realism of the Victorian liberals and the modern authorial critics and rejects the autonomous text or literary tradition of the formal critics and the interpretive diversity of the poststructuralist critics. For instance, Julia Prewitt Brown says that Elizabeth suffers humiliation because the eighteenth century held conservative views of sex, men, and marriage, not because Austen cannot accept Elizabeth's rebellion nor because she and Darcy recognize the ironic truth.[74] Historical feminists like Nina Auerbach and Judith Newton also say that Elizabeth suffers humiliation because the novel accepts conservative eighteenth-century views but still claim that the novel reveals the oppressed status of eighteenth-century women. Poststructuralist or New Historical feminists like Claudia Johnson grant that Elizabeth suffers humiliation, yet they say that Elizabeth also defends her equality in an egalitarian fashion.

Neither the traditional historical nor the poststructuralist historical feminists consistently acknowledge the novel's diverse interpretive frameworks and implicit social criticism or oppose the authorial critic's belief in Austen's unifying truth; still, the poststructuralist feminists show that the novel faults conservative eighteenth-century views of men and marriage.

Traditional historians expect critics to accept the historical context of Austen but preserve the modern authorial critic's liberal assumptions and unifying moral truth, what Kenneth Moler terms an eighteenth-century neo-classical "concordia discourse" describing not only the motivating forces of the French or the American Revolution but also the universal conflicts of "order and energy, calm and warmth . . . reverence for the status quo and impatience with it."[75] Historical feminists also insist that the reader accept the historical context of Austen, but in Poovey's egalitarian style these feminists depict a rationalist Austen opposed to a "concordia discourse" which reconciles established patriarchal traditions and energetic liberal individualism.

In the authorial manner, Moler says that, identified with "nature," Elizabeth shows strong emotions, deals with people individually, and distrusts social rank and material wealth, whereas, identified with "art," Darcy preserves distinctions of rank and deals with people and society rationally. Marilyn Butler, Nina Auerbach, and Judith Newton object that historical critics like Moler exaggerate the radical import of Elizabeth's emotional spontaneity, which did not resist the social hierarchy. For example, in *Communities of Women* (1978), Nina Auerbach maintains that the novel's women lead devalued and diminished lives because, far from granting them an energetic individuality, Austen's era forced them to wait for men to bring substance and vitality into their empty world.[76] More radical, Newton argues that the French Revolution did not move Austen to esteem the secular, democratic outlook of the enterprising individual, as liberal historical critics say; rather, the Industrial Revolution, which greatly increased the power, status, and wealth of eighteenth- and nineteenth-century middle-class men, made Austen, Charlotte Brontë, and other women writers conscious of the inequities suffered by women.[77]

Despite this forceful feminist insight, the historical feminists accept conservative eighteenth-century values. For example, Auerbach acknowledges that, when Lady Catherine insults and rebukes Elizabeth, she effectively defends her rights and her equality, but Auerbach points out that this defense of her rights defeats Lady Catherine's "matriarchal principles."[78] Moreover, Auerbach denies that a self-determining Elizabeth reforms Darcy or even recognizes his virtues and her illusions. The absurd authority of a

Lady Catherine or a Mrs. Bennet implies that what Elizabeth chooses or what she learns does not matter because Austen shows that only the male authority of a Darcy or a Mr. Bennet can effectively legitimate a woman's claims. Similarly, Newton says that in Austen's era women found sexual men threatening because they compromised the active autonomy which the women sought;[79] she grants, however, that, concealing her discontent with social life, Austen makes Elizabeth defensive and Darcy wooden and inconsistent, as Mudrick says. Newton also argues that, although eighteenth-century women writers take women to exercise positive force, including the power to define and to control themselves and to achieve success,[80] Austen accepts the courtly gentility, female dependency, self-sacrifice, and private influence of a conservative outlook.

These historical feminists defend the novel's feminist insight, yet they accept the conservative views and experiences of the eighteenth century and, like traditional historical critics, go on to reject fragmentary poststructuralist views.[81] Poststructuralist or New Historical feminists acknowledge, by contrast, the novel's diverse interpretive frameworks and, as a result, radically undermine conservative eighteenth-century views; at the same time, the poststructuralist feminists accept the objective historical truth and oppose the cultural fragmentation of the eighteenth century's "complex web."

For example, Maaja Stewart says that the comic wit of Elizabeth, a heroine in the Restoration tradition, voices the satiric detachment which she shares with her father. Showing women's dominance of the drawing room, Elizabeth's wit expresses what Stewart terms the aggressive female sexuality of Restoration comedy. A patrician hero, Darcy shows discomfort and confusion in the drawing room, but his power ensures that, despite his mistakes, his judgment still governs social life. In other words, Stewart claims that, since men retain the power to fulfill women's desires, the novel does not balance feeling and reason, as Moler and the authorial critics say. The claims of reason dominate, yet Elizabeth's wit still deconstructs the categories of male judgment.[82] Like Paul De Man, who takes John Locke's account of wit and judgment to imply that "among the serious affairs of men" wit or rhetoric is "a disruptive scandal," Stewart says that "wit opens up the closed enlightenment system that equates knowledge and power with new energy."[83]

Stewart claims that, at the same time, the novel tames Elizabeth's wit, which finally aims only to enliven or soften Darcy. Feeling reverence and gratitude, Elizabeth eventually abandons the subversive force of wit and learns to respect and even to dread the gaze of Darcy and the power of his silence, his secrets, and his idealized estate. Stewart suggests, however, that

Elizabeth changes so drastically not because the novel ironically reveals her confusions, balances spontaneity and tradition, or condemns Elizabeth's pride and individuality in a rationalist manner; rather, the degraded economic position of women and the growing division of the feminine domestic sphere and the masculine economic sphere required the virtuous sentimentality adopted by Elizabeth. In a "difference" feminist's subversive manner Stewart shows that Elizabeth's wit deconstructs the chauvinistic rationality of Darcy and others, yet, to oppose modern fragmentation, Stewart grants that, like Fanny Burney and Maria Edgeworth, Austen accepted the virtuous sentimentality of the middle classes, not the frank sexuality of Restoration heroines. In Stewart's historical terms, paralleling the economic autonomy of the landed estate, women's sentimental virtues provided a utopian refuge from the brutal capitalist market.

In an equally contradictory manner, Claudia Johnson argues that, because the conservative reaction to the French Revolution repressed Austen's feminist sentiments, the novel's irony, double plotting, central female consciousness, and other figural devices reveal her positive feminist beliefs. Johnson also argues, however, that the novel reworks eighteenth-century discourse, including philosophical systems, feminist radicalism, conservative moral handbooks, political treatises, and economic policies. That is, the novel assimilates both conservative male conduct books, which urged women to show passive kinds of physical movement, trust in male judgment, and devotion to male pleasure, as well as radical feminist treatises and novels, which repudiated the sensual, pleasure-loving female promoted by the conduct books and in Wollstonecraft's fashion defended the rational character and good judgment of well-educated women.[84]

The claim that the novel's figural devices reveal Austen's feminist sentiments defends Gilbert and Gubar's modern formal belief that literary devices, not positive moral truth, expresses Austen's repressed feminist beliefs, but, like Auerbach and Newton, attributes the repression to conservative eighteenth-century views, not to a repressed feminist anger. Since Johnson adopts the skeptical Nietzschean belief that the text undermines the historical discourses which it also accepts, the claim that the novel assimilates both male conduct books and feminist treatises assumes a poststructuralist perspective, yet Johnson defends the egalitarian feminism of Wollstonecraft and the authorial feminists, not the subjective, difference feminism of Irigaray and the poststructuralists.

Despite this inconsistency, she reveals the novel's forceful social criticism more fully than other feminist critics do. For instance, like Poovey, Auerbach, and others, Johnson admits that, even though Mrs. Bennet and

Lady Catherine forcefully reject male economic privileges, their vulgar notions of money or power condemn strong women, not aristocratic privileges; she argues nonetheless that, far from condemning individual autonomy or humiliating independent characters, this comic novel justifies the characters' individual ideas of happiness and fosters the liberal ideals of John Locke or Samuel Johnson. Elizabeth wittily rebukes Darcy and resolutely opposes Lady Catherine because in Samuel Johnson's liberal manner Elizabeth decides for herself what is wise, good, and even laughable.

Johnson also admits that in *Pride and Prejudice* the ideal society successfully balances social hierarchy and individual energy, or patriarchal tradition and satirical wit, as authorial and historical critics say. She argues, nonetheless, that this social balance implicitly critiques the era's rigid conservative social structures because the balance requires not only the characters' intense arguments but also Darcy's profound reform.[85] That is, when Darcy insults Elizabeth, he does not momentarily forget himself or act out of character; he shows an elitist or aristocratic refusal to consider anything outside of his family pleasing. Similarly, Elizabeth's criticisms of him do not show her blind partiality; they restate the objections which Samuel Johnson and other eighteenth-century social critics raised against such aristocratic indifference to others' feelings. What's more, since Darcy and Elizabeth establish a sensual, erotic relationship, the novel undermines conservative strictures against sexual freedom as well.

In a skeptical poststructuralist fashion, Johnson and Stewart show that, far from asserting universal moral truth, the novel produces valuable feminist insights and undermines conservative views, yet, like Newton and Auerbach, they inconsistently preserve the positive historical truth which justifies Austen's moral authority and resists cultural fragmentation. In general, the poststructuralist authorial, formal, and historical feminists acknowledge the novel's diverse interpretive frameworks and grant the novel the forceful social criticism which, for the most part, traditional critics ignore or deny; still, the poststructuralists limit the import of the novel's criticism and defend a purely feminist literary tradition or conventional eighteenth-century context because they too fear literary and cultural fragmentation.

In the next chapter, which examines the opposition of high and popular culture, I will show that the poststructuralist critique of this opposition shows an equally inconsistent accommodation of literature's traditional authority. To justify the progressive import of the humanities' new cultural program, I indicated in the last chapter that, like Austen's *Pride and Prejudice*, Zora Neale Hurston's *Their Eyes Were Watching God* also critiques romantic illusions and misunderstandings and oppressive marriages, yet, by revealing the debilitating aftermath of plantation slavery, Hurston's novel produces a more profound critique of liberal ideals and middle-class propriety than Austen's does. Thanks to this greater depth, *Their Eyes* vindicates both feminist criticism and a Black aesthetics, both women's studies and African American studies.

In this chapter, I have argued that the poststructuralist feminist critics grant *Pride and Prejudice* more forceful social criticism than its traditional critics do, yet the poststructuralists do not go on to justify the humanities' new programs, as post-Marxist reception study does; rather, they implicitly accept the novel's unifying moral truth because they too fear that modern criticism's numerous schools and approaches fragment the literary enterprise or the feminist movement or fail to resist the literary establishment. I have also argued that, especially in the feminist versions, the many interpretations of this novel have more progressive import than this traditional fear acknowledges. The Victorian liberals and the modern authorial critics, who establish Austen's high canonical status, high moral authority, and good Aunt Jane stereotype, consider the novel a literal chronicle of rural eighteenth-century British life but endow the study of literature with broad political ends: to promote the neoclassical rhetoric, liberal agenda, moral values, or separate spheres of middle-class British society. The authorial feminists, who in a remarkable way break down the Victorian liberals' "separate spheres" and establish and maintain women's studies programs, critique the moral truth of the authorial view but preserve the traditional duality of aesthetic ideals and practical reform. The formal feminists, who also resist the liberals' broad political ends and depict a hostile, angry Austen, foster the autonomy of women's literature courses and women's studies programs. The poststructuralist authorial, formal, and New Historical feminists, who emerge within the established English department and women's studies programs, acknowledge the novel's diverse and incompatible interpretive frameworks and its forceful social criticism, yet these feminists inconsistently accept the Arnoldian cultural ideal whereby the moral authority of literature overcomes linguistic, class, or methodological differences and unifies society. Winning feminist criticism greater academic respectability, these critics preserve the formal autonomy of literary study but do not consistently accommodate the fragmented character of modern culture.[86]

Notes

1. Edward Neill, *The Politics of Jane Austen*, ix.

2. Roger Gard, *Jane Austen's Novels*, 24; similarly, the Marxist James Thompson says that readers who construe Austen's views as progressive or reactionary, feminist or sexist, elitist or democratic ignore the objective eighteenth-century experience of capitalist alienation and anomie. See *Between Self and World*, 18.

3. Elaine Showalter, "Feminism in the Wilderness," 246-47; See also Rosemary Hennessy, *materialist feminism*, 2; Judith Newton and Deborah Rosenfelt, "Toward a materialist-feminist criticism," xxix-xxx; and Mary Poovey, "The Differences of Women's Studies," 135-40.

4. Susan Gubar, "What Ails Feminist Criticism?," 881.

5. Jane Austen, *Pride and Prejudice: An Authoritative Text, Backgrounds and Sources, Criticism* (1993), 46. All further citations are from this edition.

6. Roger Chartier, "Du Livre au lire," 89-101.

7. Scott, cited in B. C. Southam, ed., *Jane Austen: The Critical Heritage I*, 59, 63.

8. Austen, cited in Donald J. Gray, ed., Pride and Prejudice: *An Authoritative Text, Backgrounds and Sources, Criticism* (1993), 255.

9. See Ina Feris, "From trope to code," 20, and Clifford Siskin, "Jane Austen and the Engendering of Disciplinarity," 58-59.

10. See, for example, B. C. Southam, *Critical Heritage* II, 124-26; see also Barbara Hardy, *A Reading of Jane Austen*, 11-12, and Ian Watt, *Jane Austen*, 12. In *Jane Austen: Feminism and Fiction,* Margaret Kirkham, a feminist critic, shows that the biographical notice written by Austen's brother Henry, the biography written by her nephew Austen-Leigh, and the interpretations produced by Scott and other nineteenth-century critics concealed her feelings as an eighteenth-century feminist and a professional writer. See also Judith Newton, *Women, Power, & Subversion*, xix, and Gilbert and Gubar, *The Madwoman in the Attic*, 3-20. For interpretations of the movie adaptations and the English tourism promoted by the Austen industry, see Roger Sales, *Jane Austen and Representations of Regency England*, 10-16.

11. Whately, cited in Gray, ed., *Pride and Prejudice* (1993), 285.

12. Whately, cited in Gray, ed., *Pride and Prejudice* (1993), 285.

13. Lewes, cited in Southam, ed., *Heritage* I, 127.

14. Smith, cited in Southam, ed., *Heritage* I, 190.

15. See Jan Fergus, *Jane Austen: A Literary Life*.

16. Oliphant, cited in Southam, ed., *Heritage* I, 225.

17. Nancy Streuver, "The Conversable World," 79.

18. Tony Crowley, *Standard English*, 132; Thomas Miller, *The Formation of College English*, 3-19.

19. See K. C. Phillips, *Jane Austen's English*, 11-12, and Kenneth Moler, *Pride and Prejudice: A Study in Artistic Economy*, 73-80.

20. Tony Tanner, *Jane Austen*, 38.

21. Twain, cited in Southam, ed., *Heritage* I, 232.

22. See Howard Caygill, *The Art of Judgment*, 100-01; Thomas Miller, *The Formation of College English*, 13-25.

23. Trevor Ross, *The Making of the English Literary Canon*, 225.

24. Harold Orel, *Victorian Literary Critics*, 17-19.

25. See Elizabeth Wallace, *Goldwin Smith, Victorian Liberal*.

26. Thomas Miller, *The Formation of College English*, 262-63.

27. Jonathan Arac, "Peculiarities of (the) English," 195.

28. See Chris Baldick, *The Social Mission of English Criticism*, 71; and *Heritage*, II, 5.

29. Martin Wiener, *English Culture*, 23; Mary Poovey, *Uneven Developments*, 9; see also Claudia Johnson, *Jane Austen*, xvi.

30. See Franklin Court, *Institutionalizing English Literature*, 39-52; Jane Rendall, *Women in an industrializing society*, 3.

31. See Jane Rendall, *Women*, 3, and Doyle, *English and Englishness*, 3.

32. Lord David Cecil, *Poets and Story-Tellers*, 120. Cecil praises her precise depictions of life's surfaces (104), her "power to create living characters" (109), and her "profoundest vision," "unwavering recognition of fact," and "unerring perception of moral quality" (121). Like the liberals, he considers her an impartial author who rightly despises all ideals, sentimentality, and credulousness; however, taste, sense, and virtue, the criteria by which she judges a character, do not simply chronicle eighteenth-century mores.

33. Cecil, *Poets and Story-Tellers*, 122.

34. Mudrick, cited in Gray, ed., *Pride and Prejudice* (1993), 324; Some of these critics maintain that, although Elizabeth prides herself on her quick discernment, her witty rebukes of Darcy and warm partiality for Wickham reveal her emotional, one-sided state of mind. Once she discovers the humiliating truth of Wickham's evils, Darcy's virtues, and, most importantly, her own faults, she learns to appreciate Darcy's rational view of traditional social practices (See Samuel Kliger, "Jane Austen's *Pride and Prejudice*," Stuart Tave, "Affection and the Amiable Man," and Andrew Wright, "Heroines, Heroes, and Villains in *Pride and Prejudice*"). Others say that both Elizabeth and Darcy reveal faults which they learn to overcome. While Elizabeth recognizes the limits of her judgment and comes to value traditional norms, Darcy recognizes the excesses of his pride and learns the virtues of energy and spontaneity (See Howard Babb, "Dialog with Feeling," and Alistair Duckworth, "Jane Austen and the Conflict"). Still others say that Elizabeth, despite her objectivity, falls victim to aristocratic stereotypes encouraged by Wickham and her family. Thanks to Pemberley and Darcy, however, she learns better. Similarly, despite a rational outlook, Darcy accepts middle-class stereotypes promoted by Miss Bingley and Lady Catherine. Because of the Gardiners' polite

manners, he too sees through these stereotypes and acknowledges others' feelings (See David Monaghan, "*Pride and Prejudice*: Structure and Social Vision").

35. Mudrick, cited in Gray, ed. *Pride and Prejudice* (1966), 396.

36. Mudrick, cited in Gray, ed. *Pride and Prejudice* (1966), 408.

37. Mudrick, cited in Gray, ed. *Pride and Prejudice* (1966), 403-5. See also Reuben Brower, "Light and Bright and Sparkling."

38. Mary Poovey, *The Proper Lady*, 194-207.

39. Anne Ruderman, *The Pleasures of Virtue*, 1, 4-14.

40. Martha Satz, "An Epistemological Understanding of *Pride and Prejudice*," 182-83.

41. Morgan, cited in Gray, ed. *Pride and Prejudice* (1993), 360-62.

42. See, for example, Alistair Duckworth, "Jane Austen and the Conflict," 40, and Ralph Rader, "Literary Permanence and Critical Change,"11. See also Mary Poovey, who complains that postmodern criticism fragments the feminist movement ("The Differences of Women's Studies," 135-40).

43. See Morgan, cited in Gray, ed. *Pride and Prejudice* (1993), 352. See also Luce Irigaray, *The Speculum of the Other Woman*, 133-46.

44. Claudia Johnson, "The Divine Miss Jane," 150-51.

45. See Brian Doyle, *English and Englishness*, 102-10.

46. See also Lionel Trilling's "*Emma* and the Legend of Jane Austen," which says that Austen believed that, to escape France's revolutionary violence, a democratic England would resist the reactionary snobbery of the wealthy and the nobility and ensure the social mobility of able, intelligent individuals (37).

47. See Florence Howe, *Myths of coeducation*. See also Ellen Carol DuBois and others, *Feminist Scholarship,* which describes the "dual nature" of women's studies in a similar way: "[W]hile women's studies has often seen itself in opposition to the academic establishment and to the organization of knowledge by discipline, it also builds upon those disciplines, being as much shaped by them as by the transdisciplinary political interests of feminism" (5).

48. Fredric Jameson, *Fables of Aggression*, 14.

49. Q. D. Leavis, "A Critical Theory," 19.

50. Harding, cited in Southam, ed., *Heritage* II, 173

51. Harding, cited in Southam, ed., *Heritage* II, 170.

52. Harding, cited in Southam, ed., *Heritage* II, 170-71.

53. Q. D. Leavis, "A Critical Theory," 4.

54. Q. D. Leavis, "A Critical Theory," 7.

55. Sandra Gilbert and Susan Gubar, *The Madwoman in the Attic*, 161.

56. Gilbert and Gubar, *The Madwoman*, 85.

57. Fraiman, cited in Gray, ed. *Pride and Prejudice* (1993), 372.

58. Fraiman, cited in Gray, ed. *Pride and Prejudice* (1993), 379.

59. Southam, *Heritage* II, 124-26.

60. Mary Lascelles, *Jane Austen and Her Art*, 90.

61. Lascelles, *Jane Austen and Her Art*, 42.

62. Lascelles, *Jane Austen and Her Art,* 172 and 101.
63. Lascelles, *Jane Austen and Her Art,* 203.
64. Lascelles, cited in Gray, ed., *Pride and Prejudice* (1966), 347.
65. Jan Fergus, "The Comedy of Manners," 107.
66. Fergus, "The Comedy of Manners," 108-9.
67. Fergus, "The Comedy of Manners," 118; see also D. W. Harding, in Gray, ed., *Pride and Prejudice* (1993), and Brower, "Light and Bright and Sparkling."
68. Karen Newman, "Can this Marriage be Saved?" 195.
69. Fergus "The Comedy of Manners" 125-26; In *Jane Austen: A Literary Life* (1991), Fergus goes on to grant that Elizabeth consistently defends her independence and, as a result, acts "impertinent" not only to Lady Catherine but to Darcy as well. She also praises the "public sexuality" not only of the reckless Lydia but of the persistent Darcy and the flirtatious Elizabeth. Indeed, Fergus maintains that the novel's "great triumphs" are its structural ironies, sexual antagonism, and emotional incongruities, which resist both its ironic moral truth and its Cinderella fantasies (82-84). Fergus still claims, however, that feminist critics troubled by the novel's happy ending forget that comedies "demand marriage" (87).
70. Francis Mulhern, *The Moment of* 'Scrutiny,' 115-20.
71. Mulhern, *The Moment of* 'Scrutiny,' 199.
72. For instance, in *A Reading of Jane Austen,* Barbara Hardy says that critics were slow to recognize Austen's "formal achievements" because "[t]he criticism of fiction scarcely concerned itself with form before Henry James started to mature its infantilities" (11-12). Similarly, B. C. Southam, who edited the Critical Heritage volumes on Jane Austen, says that the "rigorous, critical analysis" favored by modern scholarship gradually overcomes the "dogmatic pronouncements" and the "silly" and "sentimental" myths promoted by the "old style men-of-letters" (*Heritage* II, 124-26). The more political Ian Watt admits that after World War II a conservative "respect for the traditional" revived Austen studies, but he still considers the 1950s the first decade "in which the main literary problems raised by the novels" were "systematically investigated" (See *Jane Austen,* 12).
73. See, for example, Gerald Graff, *Professing Literature,* 14-15, 204-8.
74. Brown, cited in Gray, ed. *Pride and Prejudice* (1993), 350-51; see also James Thompson, *Between Self and World,* which suggests that readers who construe Austen's views as progressive or reactionary, feminist or sexist, elitist or democratic, fail to see that the novel depicts Austen's experience objectively (6). Rising above partisan feminist or liberal politics, the novel shows that in the eighteenth century the individual experienced a new alienation from social life, what modern social theorists consider the anomic effects of the emerging capitalist economy (18). Similarly, in Pride and Prejudice: *A Study in Artistic Economy* (1989), Kenneth Moler says that we "ought to approach Austen's novel thinking not of nineteenth- and twentieth-century models, but of the cultural traditions of the eighteenth century" (19; see also Kliger, "Jane Austen's *Pride and Prejudice* in the Eighteenth-Century Mode," 58). He presents, just the same, a sociohistorical

version of the liberal Victorian and modern authorial account. In the liberal manner, he appreciates the standard English whose stylistic norms establish a character's status or virtue (73-80). Like Lewes, Simpson, and others, he grants that the novel lacks deep philosophical insight or emotional profundity, but he construes this lack as a philosophical virtue; as he says, the eighteenth century believed that "it is not man's business to speculate about metaphysical questions, nor within his capacity to do so profitably" (18-21). Like Cecil, he esteems Austen's high moral authority and limited perspective because he too believes that the true depth of an artist comes "far more from his handling of his subject matter than from the subject matter itself" (20).

75. Moler, Pride and Prejudice: *A Study in Artistic Economy*, 49.

76. Auerbach, cited in Gray, ed. *Pride and Prejudice* (1993), 336-40; see also Marilyn Butler, who says that Elizabeth's spontaneity "rebukes the contemporary doctrine of faith in the individual" (cited in Gray, ed. *Pride and Prejudice* [1993], 332-33, 335).

77. Judith Newton, *Women, Power, & Subversion*, 16-19, and 57-58.

78. Auerbach, cited in Gray, ed. *Pride and Prejudice* (1993), 345-46.

79. See also Julia Prewitt Brown, who, in keeping with Poovey's egalitarian feminism, complains that feminists fail to grasp Austen's complex moral truth because they hold "a present-day conception of social organization." In Austen's era, women believed that marriage was a "practical and moral enterprise" enabling them to resist sexual passion and to "know themselves and control their lives" (cited in Gray, ed. *Pride and Prejudice* (1993), 349).

80. Newton, *Women, Power, & Subversion*, xvi; see also Judith Newton and and Deborah Rosenfel, "Toward a materialist-feminist criticism," xxii.

81. For example, the Marxist James Thompson maintains that, by depicting the antagonistic relationship of the eighteenth century's feminine domestic sphere and male capitalist economy, Austen's fiction overcomes the traditional divisions of Marxists and feminists as well as fragmentary formal, authorial, historical, and poststructuralist approaches (See *Models of Value*, 185-98). Similarly, Judith Newton says that, "[r]ather than elucidating a complex web of relations—social, economic, linguistic—of which literature is a part," poststructuralist theories "dissociate ideas from material realities" (See "Toward a materialist-feminist criticism," xvi).

82. Maaja Stewart, *Domestic Realities and Imperial Fictions*, 42.

83. Stewart, *Domestic Realities and Imperial Fictions*, 64; see Paul De Man, "The Epistemology of Metaphor," 15.

84. See also Margaret Kirkham, *Jane Austen: Feminism and Fiction*; Mary Poovey, *The Proper Lady and the Woman Writer*; and Alison Sulloway, *Jane Austen and the Province of Womanhood*.

85. Claudia Johnson, *Jane Austen: Women, Politics, and the Novel*, 369-70.

86. Jane Gallop, *Around 1981*, 6.

Chapter Four
Conformity and Resistance in High Art:
From Thomas Hardy to Toni Morrison

Formal critics of high art dismiss, while generic critics of popular culture esteem, the thematic truth and formulaic types of popular fiction.[1] Formal critics maintain that, while high art subverts the humanist ideals of *Hamlet* or the liberal values of Jane Austen, popular culture imposes a mindless acceptance of conventional doctrines and generic types. The Frankfurt School of Social Theory also claims that, while high art resists these doctrines and types, popular culture accepts them, but the Frankfurt School argues that the instrumental reason of the Enlightenment era imposes this mindless conformity; as Theodor Adorno and Max Horkheimer say, the Enlightenment, not just communism or fascism, is "totalitarian."[2] Generic critics maintain, by contrast, that, unlike "elitist" high art, popular culture esteems everyday life; as Ray Browne says, "Popular culture democratizes society and makes democracy truly democratic."[3] Browne, who founded the Popular Culture Association in 1968, adds that, "[a]lthough the tug-of-war might seem a tempest in a teapot . . . actually it was and it remains to a certain extent a radical revolution in the making."[4] Both formal and generic critics agree, however, that the irreducible literary devices or profound insights of high art undermine established humanist values and/or liberal beliefs and preserve the imagination's autonomy, whereas popular fiction dismisses the evanescent ambiguity of purely literary forms and intransigently affirms its thematic truth and formulaic types.

I do not mean to deny that the readers of popular culture esteem its thematic truth and formulaic types, while readers of high art esteem its subversive practices; nonetheless, as John Frow says, to insist that all criticism employ a "single scale" or a "uniform criterion" of aesthetic evaluation is to repress "the differences and specificity" of cultural practices.[5] I will argue that to acknowledge the "differences and specificity" of "subversive" high art and "conformist" popular fiction is to recognize that neither one is inherently more subversive than the other. The opposition between "subversive" high art and "conformist" popular fiction breaks down because both kinds of art affirm and undermine conventional doctrines and stereotypes and because the vast expansion of higher education gives professional literary study a new influence on popular taste.

In the next chapter, I will maintain that traditional critics of high art and popular culture preserve the opposition between "subversive" high art and "conformist" popular fiction because, like the defenders of *Hamlet*'s humanism and Austen's cultural authority, they oppose the specialized disciplines of the modern university and the fragmentation and decline of modern cultural life. Drawing on a few representative texts and their receptions, rather than a single text and its extensive reception, I will also argue that, like high art, popular spy and detective fiction undermines itself, resisting its generic forms and chauvinist and anti-communist stereotypes. In this chapter, which also discusses a few texts and their receptions, I acknowledge that the high modernist and postmodernist fiction of Thomas Hardy, Vladimir Nabokov, Milan Kundera, Philip Roth, and Toni Morrison opposes the optimistic liberalism and humanist ideals of the Enlightenment era, as the traditional critics suggest; this fiction does not consistently exclude the conventions and discourses of popular culture. Hardy adopts an irrationalist pessimism, Nabokov, Kundera, and Roth parody Enlightenment ideals of utopian communism; and Morrison critiques liberal, middle-class notions of beauty and propriety; however, the fiction of these writers still accommodates liberal doctrines and popular stereotypes.

Pessimism in Thomas Hardy's *Tess of the D'Urbervilles*

Tess of the D'Urbervilles preserves the omniscient narration and communal values of George Eliot and nineteenth-century realist fiction but expresses a modernist pessimism which derives from popular detective fiction and subverts the liberal, Enlightenment faith in progress and justice. While the narrator of *Tess* adopts a neutral omniscience, the novel depicts human action as impulsive, blind, and unprincipled, not purposive nor rational. To use Hardy's terms, chance, "hap," the "immanent will," accident, and injustice articulate the "ache of modernism," a pointless, impulsive restlessness undermining the Enlightenment's liberal and/or religious norms and conventions. As Raymond Williams suggests, Hardy turns pessimistic because modern social life destroys traditional social ties and undermines our Enlightenment ideals.[6]

Some scholars assume, by contrast, that the philosophy of Arthur Schopenhauer explain his pessimism;[7] actually, in a letter to Helen Garwood, whose doctoral dissertation examined Schopenhauer's influence on him, Hardy insisted that he developed a pessimistic view of life himself.[8] Moreover, the influence of Victorian social science and detective fiction account for his pessimism more fully than Schopenhauer's notion of a blind will governing the universe. While David Hume and the eighteenth-century empiricists analyzed the "simple" empirical grounds of complex terms or dismissed them as metaphysical rubbish, John Stuart Mill, Herbert Spencer, and August Comte, who were esteemed by Hardy, produced a positive science of social life. Popular murder mysteries, which become a distinct genre in the 1860s and 1870s, reflect this shift from analysis to positive fact. In rejecting *The Poor Man and the Lady,* Hardy's first novel, George Meredith and other editors advised him to imitate the murder mysteries of the successful Wilkie Collins. In later fiction, Hardy explores the breakdown of the rural community but adopts the neutral omniscience which characterizes detective fiction and disrupts the humanist values and liberal ideals of the Enlightenment.

For example, the narration of *Tess* explains why she murders her lover Alec and why the state hangs her but does not evaluate these brutal actions. The neutral tone of the narrator provides an impersonal account of Tess's life, rather than a liberal defense of her virtues or of social justice. While Hamlet manages finally to kill the king and to provide for the succession and Mr. Darcy saves the Bennet family from disgrace, the omniscient narrator regrets that no one comes in time to stop Alec from raping Tess or to secure her family's home after her father dies. It is true, however, that, like William Faulkner's depiction of the antisocial Joe Christmas, whose life and outlook "explain" why he decapitates Anne Burden, or Toni Morrison's depiction of Cholly Breedlove, whose "free" existence tells us why he rapes his daughter Pecola, Hardy's explanations of why Alec rapes Tess, she hangs, and the community breaks down depict what Hardy calls "impressions," not scientific causes nor rational motivations.

The narrator also critiques the social conventions esteemed by Enlightenment liberals and humanists. He insists, for instance, that, sexual desire is a positive force representing ancient, pagan traditions opposed to the "unnatural" social convention. Hardy's account of Tess's rape presents Tess as a reluctant victim and Alec as a melodramatic villain with a black mustache, a big cigar, and a fast buggy. Editors reluctant to publish such sensational events imposed this melodramatic depiction on Hardy, who in an original draft showed Tess and Alec engaged in the open relationship that Sue and Jude eventually establish in *Jude the Obscure*. When Tess gets pregnant and feels guilty, the narrator says, "She had been made to break an accepted social law, but no law known to the environment in which she fancied herself such an anomaly."[9] Here in a traditional omniscient manner the narrator explains Tess's misunderstanding of her environment; however, instead of exposing private interests or defending the community's liberal values, the narrator blames her unhappiness on "accepted social law."

Similarly, as Tess and her brother Abraham drive the wagon carrying the family's beehives to the train station, the narrator says that Abraham reveals middle-class desires—a rich Tess and a large "spy-glass." These desires echo those of his parents, who hope that Tess can wed her wealthy cousin, and those of Enlightenment liberals, who thought that a woman's marrying above her class, as Elizabeth does in *Pride and Prejudice*, represents social improvement. Implying that such views are vain, if not absurd, the neutral narrator juxtaposes this liberal faith with the "cold pulses" and "serene dissociation" of the stars. Abraham hopes that his spyglass will let him draw the stars near, but drawing near that which feels "serene dissociation" and shows "cold pulses" is an existential impossibility undermining both the traditional faith in divine providence and the liberal hope of social improvement.

In a similar manner the narrative juxtaposes the sensational death of the family's horse and Abraham's "prattle" about stars, creation, and marriage. The narrator emphasizes the gruesomeness of the event: the blood spouts and hisses and splashes Tess, and the horse collapses abruptly. The violence of the mail cart's pointed shaft is gratuitous and malevolent, yet the shaft acts "like a sword," which suggests intelligent guidance, not accident or chance. Similarly, Tess tries to stop the horse's bleeding, but that futile act colors her life with a comparable futility: just as she cannot stop the hole or the blood, so too she cannot overcome sex or death. As a consequence, the "shaft" which enters the horse and the blood which stains Tess anticipate Alec's seduction of Tess and Tess's murder of Alec. In these events also, accident seems malevolent: it represents blind but implacable forces disturbing the reader's liberal optimism.

The collapse of Angel and Tess's marriage also undermines liberal ideals. For example, in a nightmarish scene, the sleepwalking Angel carries Tess across a raging river and deposits her in an ancient tomb. As the narrator says, Angel dreamed that Tess was dead and carried her to "the empty stone coffin of an abbot. . . . In this Clare carefully laid Tess" (221). The "empty stone coffin of an abbot" effectively emphasizes Angel's hypocrisy: Angel rejects the D'Urbervilles' aristocratic lineage, the established church, and his father's religion, yet he still takes a woman's loss of innocence to destroy her. His sleepwalking suggests that Angel has repressed or "unconscious" feelings of desire but cannot acknowledge them, at least not until after he leaves Tess and travels to Argentina, where a dying friend urges him to. The sleepwalking shows the reader what the hypocritical Angel does not see—that conventional religious and liberal discourses ironically repress his feelings of desire.

Angel and Tess's flight after Alec's murder also undermines Enlightenment ideals. The flight ends at the ancient Stonehenge, which stands for ritual sacrifice, not social justice. Like the pheasants wounded by careless hunters and the field mice trapped by threshing machines, Tess is a victim, not a criminal: the forces of justice reveal the destructiveness of social law, not the legitimate judgment of a rational will or a progressive community. Camus's Meursault and Faulkner's Joe Christmas die once they have learned to love, and as a result they triumph over their executioners; similarly, Tess hangs once she regains her lover Angel, and her death too indicts her destroyers. Legal justice conceals existential injustice: "'Justice was done, and the President of the Immortals . . . had ended his sport with Tess" (489).

In *Hardy in History* Peter Widdowson complains that traditional critics made Hardy into a Shakespearean realist who, despite his atheistic pessimism and his faulty plots, depicts living characters and preserves the lost rural community. It is true that many traditional critics consider the novel high realist art and ignore the influence of popular detective stories, but many of these critics appreciate its modernist pessimism. In addition, formal, reader-oriented, and Derridean critics reject its metaphysical realism, yet they do not consistently acknowledge the subversive pessimism or its popular influences.

In a fashion which I call realist because it takes art to assert conceptual truth, Irving Howe claims, for example, that *Tess* depicts a living woman whose loyalty, truth, and warmth enable her to exist beyond the novel's pages. Howe still says, however, that *Tess* reveals the anomie and alienation characteristic of modern life. In other words, Howe does not neglect the novel's subversion of humanist values and Enlightenment ideals; rather, he construes it as metaphysical realism excluding Victorian popular culture. Hence, he complains, as many critics do, that the plot has too much improbable metaphysical weight because too many bad things happen in too short a time.[10] He adds that Joyce's *Ulysses* and Woolf's *Mrs. Dalloway's Party* also depict the anomie and alienation of modern social life, but they emphasize a character's inner psychological tensions and denigrate the external dramatic development of the typical Victorian plot.[11] In other words, Howe praises the novel's depiction of the "living" Tess and the modern anomie and censures the "improbable" plot because he constructs the text as an exemplar of Joyce's or Woolf's high modernist art and therefore divorced from popular culture. Although the novel preserves the scientific neutrality of the Victorian detective story and critiques the humanist values and liberal ideals of the Enlightenment, Howe emphasizes the novel's autonomy but ignores its Victorian cultural context.

Formal textual critics, who take a text's figural devices to unify it, also construe the novel as high modernist art excluding popular culture, but, inverting Howe's realism, these critics appreciate Hardy's artistic devices and reject his "didactic" pessimism. Early formal critics like Barbara Hardy and Albert Guerard consider Hardy a weak novelist whose didactic pessimism ruins what his artistic imagination enables him to achieve; as Guerard says, "We must also recognize that his rich and human imagination accompanied a plodding and at times even commonplace intellect."[12] Later formal critics like Tony Tanner and Peter Brooks, who trace the "creative energy" praised by Guerard to the imagery and symbols unifying the fiction, assume that the language of the fiction itself excludes Hardy's didactic intellect and its "extrinsic" sources;[13] however, even though these critics go on to construe these images as unconscious mythopoetic or artistic symbols, rather than philosophical statements or didactic assertions, this construction, like Guerard's "creative energy," dismisses the didactic narration of Hardy's fiction and consequently ignores its subversive treatment of popular culture or Enlightenment values.

In *The Forms of Tragedy*, the reader-oriented critic Dale Kramer also faults the didactic narration, but he grants that Hardy's pessimism subverts Enlightenment values. He argues, however, that the pessimism expresses the subjectivity of the narrator, the characters, and the readers, not the critical insights of the author. When the narrator complains about the indifference of the universe, the quagmires of sexuality, and the degradations of married life, the realist Howe says that the narrator insightfully depicts modern alienation and anomie; formal critics find the narrator intrusive and unacceptably didactic; whereas Kramer takes the narrator and the characters to express different points of view. Moreover, the resulting discrepancies between the narrator's and the characters' perspectives and values free readers to judge the narrator and the characters for themselves. Kramer objects, just the same, that the characters lack drive, energy, or initiative. For example, he claims that, because of Tess's mystical oneness with nature, she brings her tragedy on herself. Like the other critics, the reader-oriented Kramer also construes the novel as high art divorced from popular detective stories or Victorian science; however, instead of resenting the intrusive character of the didactic author or deploring the anomic state of modern life, he regrets the characters' unenterprising lives.[14]

Deconstructive critics also claim that the novel allows many divergent views of Tess's life and that the pessimism undermines Enlightenment ideals; the Derrideans argue, however, that the text's figural language subverts these views and preserves the autonomy of the text, not the judgment of the reader. For example, in *Fiction and Repetition*, Miller says that the tragic suffering of Tess makes the reader want to know why she suffers, but the figural language of the text keeps the reader from figuring out the reasons. In the formal manner, Miller takes red things, the sun, copulation, writing, and other chains of imagery and patterns of repetition to express Hardy's pessimistic faith in the immanent will, but he argues that these chains repeat with a difference, undermining the explanatory power of established interpretations. The pessimistic motif of life's immanent will does not fully explain Tess's suffering because the images repeat themselves but "with a difference." In addition to the immanent will, critics have found a number of motifs explaining Tess's suffering; however, because repetition transforms images, these motifs too are, Miller says, "cancelled almost as soon as they are put forward."[15] In the reader-oriented manner, Miller expects the reader to interpret the chains of imagery and patterns of repetition but claims that the resulting interpretation can never reach "a sovereign principle of explanation" because the novel justifies what he considers "multiple incompatible explanations of what happens to Tess. They cannot all be true, and yet they are all there in the words of the novel."[16] As this claim implies, the Derrideans emphasize the troubling import of Tess's suffering and the subversive effects of Hardy's pessimism but, construing the text as autonomous high art, maintain that the novel itself refutes its own explanations.

In *Thomas Hardy and Women*, Penny Boumelha repudiates the skeptical nihilism of Miller and the formal Derrideans; however, she too says that the many gaps, incoherent revisions, and inconsistent philosophical speculations of the text subverts its ideologies, not the reader's interpretations. Boumelha claims, for example, that through genre and point of view, the narrative places Tess, but this placing also subverts the narrator's hierarchic view of gender and his scientific depiction of Tess's consciousness.[17] The narrator means to describe intellect and culture as male and sex and nature as female, but the narrative makes feminine sexuality more important than male intellect.[18] While the narrator depicts Tess as a transparent consciousness, Tess's sexuality resists the narrator's drive to "penetrate" and to "possess" her.

Widdowson claims that such poststructuralist feminism ruptures neatly with traditional realism and "humanist essentialism."[19] It is true that, more radically than the realist, formal, reader-oriented, and Derridean accounts, Boumelha's feminist account shows that the novel's modernist pessimism undermines the liberal ideals and humanist values of the Enlightenment; still, while the novel adopts the detached neutrality and the "sensationalist" accidents of popular mysteries, she assumes, as the other critics do, that the novel resists the conventions of popular culture. She effectively explains the positive feminist insights of the novel, yet her Derridean belief that the novel undermines its own ideologies preserves the traditional opposition of high and popular art.

Communist Stereotypes in Vladimir Nabokov's *Invitation to a Beheading*, Milan Kundera's *The Unbearable Lightness of Being*, and Philip Roth's *The Prague Orgy*

Nabokov's *Invitation to a Beheading* (1959), Kundera's *The Unbearable Lightness of Being* (1984), and Roth's *The Prague Orgy* (1985) also undermine liberal Enlightenment ideals, but these novels repudiate the scientific neutrality of Hardy's *Tess*. In the modernist *Invitation*, the autonomy of the artistic imagination subverts Enlightenment ideals, whereas in the postmodernist *Unbearable* and *Prague Orgy* a comic sexuality turns subversive. Moreover, like Cold War spy fiction, these novels debunk the utopian ideals which the Enlightenment bequeathed to totalitarian communism.[20] These novels accept, just the same, the chauvinist and communist stereotypes of Cold War spy fiction.

To parody the Enlightenment's utopian communist ideals, *Invitation* shows that Cincinnatus, who possesses an intense inner life but cannot communicate feelings or formulate writing projects, pointedly lacks the chauvinist virtues of a James Bond. When a totalitarian regime finds him guilty of an opaque nonconformity and sentences him to death, he does not battle his opponents and their supporters; he fearfully awaits execution in a prison cell where the guards spy on him and the warden and his family berate and betray him. He does not seduce or manipulate weak, gullible women; he timidly resents the promiscuity of his wife Marthe, whose last minute sexual favors he peevishly refuses. When his long-lost mother returns only to complain about his messy prison cell and his unmade bed, he patiently tolerates her criticisms and hygienic advice. Although he faces death on the guillotine, his wife and his father-in-law urge him to remember their difficulties and to confess his faults; his lawyer, jailer, and prison director require him to appreciate all that they do for him; and Monsieur Pierre, who turns out to be his executioner, offers him his friendship and expects him to esteem the offer. These Kafkaesque demands that the victim assist his or her destroyers forcefully parody utopian Enlightenment ideals of public truth and social responsibility.

Invitation excludes the idealized chauvinist virtues of a Bond but still favors the irreverent skepticism and the pleasurable gaze of a chauvinist voyeur.[21] For example, Cincinnatus enjoys watching the sinewy limbs and "silky blonde hair" of Emmie, a thirteen-year-old girl who dances in and out of his cell, lies on top of him, and proposes marriage to him. He likes seeing the river, fountains, pond, and trees of the beautiful Tamara Gardens and remembering the round face of the youthful Marthe or the early morning activities of the town. *Invitation* also preserves the mystery novel's irreverent skepticism. For instance, even though Cincinnatus does nothing to save himself, he expects Emmie to save him. To his delight, she finally leads him out of the prison, but she brings him to the prison director's apartment, not to freedom. Similarly, at night, when Cincinnatus hears a tapping sound behind his prison wall, he anticipates a rescue with delight and relief. The laughter of Rodrig and Monsieur Pierre, who faked the rescue, mocks his ungrounded faith in human salvation.

In addition to the voyeurism and skepticism of the Bond thrillers, *Invitation* preserves their heroism. Cincinnatus does not battle or kill the communists, as Bond does; rather, he discovers that, since the oppressive totalitarian regime does not allow him to express his inner life, he cannot destroy it until he learns to treat his enemies as absurd figments of his imagination. At the end, when the executioner's ax falls upon his head, a skeptical Cincinnatus finally recognizes that the interested discourses of this bizarre world lack meaning. Just as Alice escapes Wonderland because she defies the queen, so Cincinnatus the artist/hero trusts his imagination and like Bond destroys his totalitarian oppressors: "Cincinnatus slowly descended from the platform and walked off through the shifting debris. . . . Little was left of the square. The platform had long since collapsed. . . . Everything was coming apart. Everything was falling."[22]

Defenders of this novel maintain that its self-conscious modernist conventions resist not only the Enlightenment's utopian communist ideals but all ideological conformity. Robert Alter says, for example, that the novel's ostentatious artifice implicitly recognizes that life's complex, wondrous, and myriad forms invariably escape conventional art.[23] Richard Rorty also argues that critics cannot fault Nabokov's "eccentrically large capacity" for aesthetic "bliss" because art has no ethical or metaphysical foundations.[24] At the same time, Rorty too assumes that, since Nabokov depicts a nightmarish totalitarian society, his "ungrounded" pursuit of aesthetic bliss has justifiable ethical and political grounds: both Orwell and Nabokov rightly "warn the liberal ironist intellectual against temptations to be cruel."[25] It is true that the narrators of detective and spy fiction dissipate illusion and uncover objective facts, whereas, reminding us that *Invitation* is fictive, its narrator describes numerous violations of everyday reality and the world's many aesthetic features—light, color, gardens, paintings. Despite this aesthetic self-consciousness, *Invitation* shares spy fiction's skeptical view of social life, voyeuristic delight in looking, and stereotypical views of totalitarian communism.

The reflexive narration of Milan Kundera's *The Unbearable Lightness of Being* (1984) also subverts Enlightenment ideals but does not escape popular Cold War stereotypes; however, instead of defending the reflexive self-consciousness of high art, this novel shows that life's "unbearable lightness" undermines both conventional moral and religious truths and totalitarian communism. Life's unbearable lightness contravenes the moral heaviness of traditional humanist virtues and the utopian ideals of an insurgent communism but still accepts popular stereotypes of women and communism.

The reflexive narrator says that his characters "were born of a stimulating phrase or two or a basic situation."[26] He calls them his "own unrealized possibilities" (221), wishes that the perfect symmetry and the mysterious coincidences of novels could beautify their lives, (51-52), and explains the diverse meanings which the characters attribute to various terms, a bowler hat, an old church, New York City, and love. More importantly, citing Nietzsche's doctrine of eternal return, the narrator argues that, since events happen only once, everything is permitted, and the world shows a "profound moral perversity" (4).

To illustrate this "perversity," he shows that, out of "co-feeling," Tomas marries Tereza but continues his sexual affairs with Sabina and others. Although he believes that love and sexuality occupy different zones of mental life, he brags that he has made love to over two hundred women (198). The apologetic narrator denies that like the chauvinist James Bond Tomas reduces women to impersonal objects of conquest; rather, the narrator claims that, using a scalpel to carve up the world, Tomas seeks the women's individual styles of sexual intercourse. By contrast, the narrator of the later *Immortality* (1990) readily grants that, unlike Goethe, who has also had many affairs but who, to protect his reputation, resists his desire for Bettina, his would-be biographer,

Rubens is a conventional womanizer. Indeed, he engages in so many sexual affairs that he eventually loses his lust for sex. The difference is that *Immortality*, which considers the media of the Western world to be as oppressive as the former communist countries were, values the image or reputation of the characters more highly than their sexual freedom, whereas the earlier *Unbearable* assumes that Cold War oppression gives the sexuality of the characters a radical import undermining Enlightenment ideals and values.

Unbearable's strong and weak females also resist but do not escape popular stereotypes. Sabina the émigré artist shows a strong will, sexual independence, and practical interests, yet she betrays her father, her lover Franz, her native country, her fellow émigrés, and even her American sympathizers. In the end, wandering through the United States, the lonely Sabina confirms the popular stereotype of the calculating, uncommitted female professional. By contrast, Tereza confirms the stereotype of the weak traditional woman. For instance, Tomas's "erotic friendships" give Tereza fearful nightmares. In one repeated nightmare Tomas shoots naked women walking around a pool if they fail to obey his commands. In another, Tereza is dead and buried, yet Tomas's affairs make her so anxious that she cannot sleep and feels constantly exhausted. In a third, Tomas sends Tereza to a hill where sharpshooters offer to execute her. She declines their offer at the last minute but fears that Tomas will be disappointed.

Asserting herself, she leaves Tomas in Geneva and returns to Prague, but, when Tomas comes after her, she accepts him and fatalistically identifies with Dubcek's and Czechoslovakia's weak state—oppressive forces make both her and Czechoslovakia suffer. To divide her body from her dominating soul, as Tomas does, and thereby to overcomes her weakness, she has exciting sexual relations with an unfamiliar engineer; however, when, when the engineer never returns, she fears that the communists plotted her affair and will expose her infidelity and destroy her marriage. Under communism Tomas finds an unrestrained sexuality liberating, whereas Tereza's fears of a communist conspiracy show her stereotypical female weakness. Lastly, when Tomas and Tereza die in a truck crash, the countryside has contented them. The philosophical narrator ridicules biblical accounts of Eden and the fall, theological views of paradise, and the Cartesian ideal of scientific rationality, yet in the countryside Tomas and Tereza find an Edenic happiness. As the only Czechoslovakian region beyond sexual temptation and communist control, the countryside represents a lost Eden, and Tereza, who blames Tomas's lost stature on her weakness, represents a guilty but contented Eve.

The novel also stereotypes the communists, who, except for Dubcek, are deceptive, degrading, torturous, and oppressive. All they do is intimidate rebels, terrorize citizens, degrade social life, invade other countries, and brutally murder various populations. It is true that in an unconventional fashion Tomas describes Tereza and the communists as wandering orphans. That is, like the infant Moses floating in the Nile, Tereza arrives at Tomas's door and demands his compassion. Similarly, like the ill-fated Oedipus, the Dubcek the liberal communist committed evil but acknowledged his guilt and punished himself. It is the case, however, that, morally obtuse, the other communists self-righteously proclaim their innocence and cruelly persecute Tomas. (In the movie, Dubcek's supporters naively brag that the Soviets would never destroy their "communism with a human face"). To explain this evil, the narrator says that communist enthusiasts, not criminals, bring about the atrocities (176). This claim restates the pessimistic theme of George Orwell's *Animal Farm.*

Unbearable preserves the evil communist other of Cold War spy fiction but does not accept their blind anticommunism. For instance, the communists force Tomas to quit his position at the hospital and eventually to give up medicine altogether, yet he will not sign his neglected son's petition denouncing the communist treatment of Czechoslovakia's intellectual rebels. The painful loss of his career does not reduce him to his son's fanatic anticommunism. Similarly, Franz interprets the struggle against communism as part of the liberal "grand march," but, when he travels to Cambodia to march in protest of communist oppression, muggers beat him to death and his estranged wife reclaims him. Sabina finds the realist kitsch of socialist art disgusting, but she considers the sentimental kitsch of American life equally disgusting. As she says, "[B]ehind Communism, Fascism, behind all occupations and invasions lurks a more basic, pervasive evil" (100).

Unbearable preserves the evil communist and chauvinist male and female stereotypes of spy fiction but opposes both communism and anticommunism.[27] Most critics argue, just the same, that the self-conscious art of Kundera undermines conventional doctrines and popular stereotypes. Some of those who praise Kundera's self-conscious art complain that his aesthetic opposition to modern life's vulgarity denies that the evil of totalitarian society overrides other social evils.[28] This complaint mistakenly assumes that art which accepts the familiar stereotype of the evil communist does not preclude aesthetic independence and artistic nonconformity. Other critics esteem Kundera's self-conscious depiction of modern "concentration camp" life but simply ignore or deny the chauvinist and anticommunist prejudices and stereotypes accepted by the novel.[29] For example, Terry Eagleton says that the fiction's corrosive self-consciousness or "undecidability" effectively frees us from pro- or anticommunism, religious virtue, romantic devotion, or some other intolerant goodness; at the same time, Eagleton, who, in the conservative fashion which I explain in chapter 6, blames the horrors of Soviet communism on Marx's Enlightenment optimism, rather than the Russian tradition of oppressive states,[30] maintains that this comic self-consciousness resists ideological notions of class, race, gender, and nation.[31]

In *The Prague Orgy*, Philip Roth, who published Kundera's *The Farewell Party* in the series titled Writers from the Other Europe, also portrays a comic sexuality which undermines Enlightenment ideals but does not escape popular stereotypes or ideologies. For example, Zdenec Sisovsky, a Czech novelist in exile, convinces Zuckerman to save his father's unpublished Yiddish manuscripts from the Czechoslovakian communists. Similarly, Lieutenant Colonel Trautman persuades Rambo to join an espionage mission in which he saves forgotten American prisoners of war trapped in a Vietnamese labor camp. Of course, Rambo defeats the whole communist army as well as his disloyal American leaders; by contrast, when the Czech communists seize the unpublished manuscripts and label Zuckerman a Zionist agent, Zuckerman, who feels as timid and helpless as Cincinnatus feels, fearfully imagines himself forced to spend the rest of his life sweeping streets.

The concealed truth about the enslaved veterans, the insidious evasions of Murdock the liberal bureaucrat, and the overwhelming evil of the communists justify Rambo's spectacular displays of chauvinist violence. Zuckerman faces a sexually licentious world, not a chaotic Vietnamese jungle, but his mission acquires a comparable moral justification. For instance, he calls himself "an American gentleman abroad, with the bracing if old-fashioned illusion that he is playing a worthwhile, dignified, and honorable role," and he likens his artistic quest to that of a hero who "searches for a kind of holiness, or holy object, or transcendence."[32] In *The Anatomy Lesson*, the third volume of the Zuckerman trilogy, aggressive admirers make Zuckerman worry about his image or reputation as a writer, just as in Kundera's *Immortality* the aggressive Bettina made Goethe restrain his desire and protect his reputation; still, to overcome the writer's block which Zuckerman attributes to his bad back, he engages in sexual intercourse with four different women and even poses as a frank and unusually graphic pornographer. In *The Prague Orgy*, the epilogue of the trilogy, he righteously resists the city's seductive appeals even though he believes that in a communist regime anarchic sexual freedom undermines totalitarian oppression. On this "holy" basis, he resists the beautiful Olga, who caresses his penis, reveals her legs, breasts, and vagina, and repeatedly demands intercourse. She complains that "[a]ll the great international figures come to Prague to see our oppression, but none of them will ever fuck me," but her frank sexual demands, the highly praised orgies at Krenek's palazzo, or the artist Bolotka's sixteen young girlfriends do not tempt or seduce him.[33] Like Rambo, he remains true to his mission.

In Roth's earlier *The Professor of Desire* (1977), which also suggests that sexual freedom undermines communist oppression, David Kepesh resists communist seduction in an equally self-righteous way. In the United States he tries but fails to seduce his college girlfriends, who want to talk, not to make love; as he sadly notes, in his college years he achieved "full penetration" only twice.[34] In Sweden, he establishes an orgiastic relationship with Elizabeth and Birgitta, who accept a ménage à trois which stimulates and gratifies him. Only when he travels to communist Prague does he resist his sexual desire and, like Zuckerman, turn morally superior. For instance, he dreams that the old whore of Kafka offers him a chance to touch her genitals and thereby to destroy the communist state. He refuses the whore's offer even though his guide ominously warns him that his refusal could mean "nothing less than the final victory of the Bolsheviks over free men."[35] In addition, he and a dissident Czechoslovakian intellectual dispute the import of Franz Kafka's fiction. The sad dissident says that Kafka depicts the irrational truths of communist life, while the proper David, who equates the sexual demands of the body and the totalitarian powers of the government, says that Kafka shows the comic nature of sexual impotence.[36]

Like Kepesh, Zuckerman preserves his sexual propriety in the face of communist oppression; however, Zuckerman imagines that writers, artists, and philosophers living under the communist regime tell the same sort of sexually licentious comic stories as Old World Jews resisting their anti-Semitic oppressors. More importantly, Zuckerman accepts Sisovsky's complaint that the communist vice minister of culture called his mistress Eva Kalinova a Jew and a Jew's whore because she played Anne Frank in a Prague theater, divorced an artist with high official status, and married a Jewish artist considered a Zionist agent. Because of this complaint, Zuckerman decides to save Sisovsky's father's unpublished Yiddish manuscripts from the Czechoslovakian communists. Roth shares Kundera's existential belief that a comic sexuality undermines intolerant Enlightenment notions of goodness or badness; Kundera goes on, however, to oppose the vulgarities of all kitsch, communist and capitalist, whereas Roth critiques communist anti-Semitism and preserves Zuckerman's moral virtue.

Some critics claim that this identification of oppressed Jewish people and Czechoslovakian dissidents vindicates Roth's art, whose notorious difficulties with Jewish readers form the subtext of the *Zuckerman Bound* trilogy. These critics suggest that, once Zuckerman discovers the limits of the modernist's severe, aloof style and withdrawn, lonely existence, he goes on to reaffirm his religious identity and communal obligations in the larger sociohistorical world.[37] This realist account clarifies the narrative structure of the trilogy but treats the chauvinist and communist stereotypes as positive sociohistorical truth.

Other accounts suggest, by contrast, that in New York, when a mysterious but unremitting back pain disables Zuckerman, he sadly recognizes that the Jewish community no longer suffers the oppression which motivated his earlier writing. In communist Prague, the minister of culture faults decadent artists in the same terms in which his father and his brother condemned his irreverent stories. As a result, Zuckerman does not overcome his artistic isolation and affirm his Jewish identity; he confronts another version of himself. In other words, Zuckerman's nihilistic imagination enables him to adopt many identities but not to escape himself or accept his communal obligations; as Jonathan Brent says, there is "Zuckerman the Zionist agent, the anti-Semitic Jew, the treacherous brother, the ungrateful son, the monkish artist, the celebrity star, the would-be doctor, the maniacal pornographer king," but no true Zuckerman.[38]

More importantly, Brent admits that Roth betrays chauvinist views of art and women, mingles the devices of high art and mass culture, and, because of the artist's celebrity status, allows readers' responses to influence the artist's work.[39] Similarly, my account says that, like *Invitation* and *Unbearable*, *The Prague Orgy* accepts such influences and stereotypes. Brent and others claim, however, that these stereotypes show the failures of the artistic imagination, which may end up as what Brent terms a "tool of advertising" or "self-help programs" or a "badge" of middle-class virtue, or which allows intolerant readers to impose their misconceptions on an author unable to resist or deny them.[40] Such defenses of the autonomous artistic imagination reinstate the opposition of high art and popular culture or accept its traditional justifications, which, as I indicate in the next chapter, include the fears of the culture industry, totalitarian oppression, middle-class decline, academic specialization, and "political correctness."

Middle-Class Conformity in Toni Morrison's *The Bluest Eye* and *Sula*

In *The Bluest Eye* and *Sula*, Morrison also critiques liberal Enlightenment ideals, but she debunks its norms of beauty and propriety, not its utopian ideal of communist life. Like Hardy, Morrison laments the breakdown of the rural community and debunks liberal ideals of progress and justice. Since these novels grant their African American characters their own narrative voices in a modernist fashion, these novels also undermine the standard English promoted by Austen's liberal Victorian defenders. Morrison still accepts conventional doctrines and popular stereotypes, but, instead of spy fiction's communist and chauvinist others, her novels accommodate degraded middle-class stereotypes of the Black community, what Linda Ditmar calls the social pathology of Morrison's White readership.[41]

Consider, for example, *The Bluest Eye*'s Mrs. Breedlove. In a stereotypical fashion, she finds fulfillment as a White family's maid, not as a mother or a wife. When Pecola brings her the laundry to fold and inadvertently spills the hot berry cobbler, Mrs. Breedlove condemns and strikes her but comforts the White family's blonde daughter, who is the only one free to call Mrs. Breedlove Polly. In addition, to stop Cholly's drinking and his other vices, Mrs. Breedlove fights with him. The fighting gratifies her feelings of righteousness but makes Sammy want to run away and Pecola, to disappear bit by bit. The narrator complains that Mrs. Breedlove treats her family so badly because she accepts the middle-class standards rendering her ugly, yet the novel grants her a moving narrative in which she explains that, when she ran her parents' house, she acquired a love of order which her job as a maid fulfilled. She also explains that, when she made love with Cholly, she experienced a special rainbow and a personal value and beauty: "I feel a power. I be strong, I be pretty, I be young."[42] Undermining liberal norms, these explanations turn Black English into poetry.

Pecola also rebels against but ultimately accepts middle-class White values, yet she is their most terrible victim. On the one hand, she gets sexual climaxes from eating Mary Janes and interesting stories from visiting the whores, who befriend her but never explain what love is. The boys insult her because they think she saw her father naked—another middle-class taboo. When Junior invites her into his house and hurls the cat at her, his mother Geraldine, a middle-class "nest builder" who has always hated "niggers," blames Pecola. She wanders off, her dress and stockings torn. Like Mrs. Breedlove, she considers herself ugly, but she believes that the blue eyes which Soaphead Church gave her overcome her ugliness. After Cholly rapes Pecola and she gets pregnant, Mrs. Breedlove blames her. After the second rape, she feared that she enjoyed it. She assumes that the community envies her new blue eyes, and, becoming schizophrenic, she talks only to an invisible friend; actually, cold and indifferent, the community disdains her and her family. In middle-class fashion, the community purifies itself by purging her.

Unlike Pecola and the Breedloves, Claudia MacTeer, who destroys her Shirley Temple doll and calls the popular, light-skinned Maureen Peel "six-finger-dog-tooth-meringue-pie" (61), rebels against White middle-class norms. When the Breedloves are driven out of doors, Claudia and Frieda befriend Pecola, explaining menstruation to her and stopping the vicious ridicule of the playground boys and of Maureen Peel. Despite this rebellion, Claudia does not entirely escape middle-class norms. After Mr. Henry fondles her sister Frieda, Frieda fears that she is ruined, and, to cure this middle-class vice, she and Claudia run off to find some alcohol. Ironically, they find Miss Marie, a whore, and, by refusing to associate with her, reassert their middle-class integrity. When Pecola's baby dies, they blame the bad soil, which did not grow their seeds, but they no longer communicate with Pecola. Like the indifferent community, they cleanse themselves by purging her.

Soaphead Church, an isolated misanthrope turned fortune teller, finds sexual activity so disgusting that his wife Velma leaves him.

Violating middle-class norms, he fondles young girls' breasts despite his aversion to sex. Morrison still gives him a virtue—compassion. He convinces Pecola that, if she feeds the dog the poisoned food, she will have the blue eyes she desires. In addition, he writes God a letter protesting that the world which He created allows such mistaken faith in middle-class standards.

Cholly rapes his daughter Pecola twice, yet the narrative also app reciates his virtue—he lives free of middle-class values. His many degradations explain this freedom. For instance, two White hunters discover Cholly making love for the first time and force him to continue his lovemaking while they watch. His Aunt Jimmy raised him after his mother abandoned him, and, when his father rejects him, he soils his pants and misses his dead Aunt Jimmy terribly. "With a longing that almost split him, he thought of her handing him a bit of smoked hock out of her dish" (125). Because of these and other degradations, Cholly lives so free of middle-class ethical and social conventions that only a jazz musician, the narrator tells us, could put his life together. When Pecola's gestures with her foot remind him of his wife's youthful lameness, he rapes her "tenderly." As a transgression, the rape excites him; at the same time, because he feels burnt out, with nothing to pass on to her, the rape gives her all the love that he can give her. As Terry Otten says, Morrison's novels turn "incestuous rape, infanticide, and murder" into "acts 'signifyin(g)' a profound if often convoluted love."[43]

Sula also shows that the Black community accommodates middle-class norms, but this novel emphasizes the virtues enabling the community to subvert those norms. Because a White farmer played a joke on his freed slave, the Bottom, located up in the barren hills, has the region's worst soil and the Black community the worst jobs. Such an unjust turn of events invokes liberal ideals; at the same time, when, because of racial integration, the Blacks get better jobs and homes in town, the narrator regrets that the Blacks have lost the valuable sense of place or neighborhood provided by the Bottom. As in Hardy's *Tess,* such regrets undermine Enlightenment ideals of progress. Similarly, after the army hospital releases Shadrack because it needs the space, not because he has recovered his sanity, he returns to Medallion, where he promptly institutes a National Suicide Day march. The community does not treat his illness or lock him up; it just fits his march into its regular affairs. Adopting a mythical, rather than an enlightened, middle-class viewpoint, the community comes to consider Shadrack's insanity normal.

Unlike Shadrack and the community, Eva Peace preserves middle-class norms. She faults the newlywed who cooks her husband the same dinner day after day. Eva complains that Sula fails to make babies and burns up her son Plum because, instead of accepting his male responsibilities, he stays home and smokes dope. In her terms, he tried to crawl back into her "womb." She enjoys hating BoyBoy, who left her and her children to starve, and plays checkers with men who admire her one good leg. By contrast, her daughter Hannah, a widow, likes some touching every day, but, to make love, she takes a man to the cellar, not the bedroom, because the bedroom means middle-class commitment and responsibility. In keeping with its mythical perspective, the community identifies Hannah's burning with Eva's dream, the dry wind, and Sula's sexuality or "nature" and Sula's return with the plague of robins.

Like Cholly, Sula is free of middle-class norms. As a child, she likes the calm peacefulness of Nel's middle-class home, but, after Hannah says that Hannah loves but does not like her, she grows increasingly wild and irreverent. Thus, to intimidate the Italian boys, who bully her and Nel, she cuts her fingertip off. She throws Chicken Little in the river and watches him drown, and enjoys the twitches and the bizarre dancing of the burnt-up Hannah. When Sula returns from college and various big cities and puts Eva in a retirement home, Nel objects, but Sula insists that, if she does not make babies, Eva may burn her up too.

In other words, she is as free of middle-class norms as Cholly is, but her freedom improves the community, which, in response to her rebellion, treats its children and its husbands much better. Her relationship with Nel collapses because, to her surprise, Nel accepts the middle-class possessiveness so foreign to the Peace household. As she is dying, she defends the autonomy which Nel considers impossible for women: "Girl, I got my mind";[44] still, when Ajax takes up with her, she turns middle class. After Ajax spots her nest building and abandons her, she dies because, acting in Nel's middle-class fashion, she compromised her autonomy.

Initially, Nel too rebels against middle-class norms. Her mother, Helene, forces her to pinch her nose and straighten her hair so she can look more middle class, but, once the train ride to New Orleans reveals the weak custard inside Helene, Nel finds relief in Sula. Her chaotic home and wild bravado free Nel to be herself, yet, because Helene rubbed out her imagination, she grows more and more middle class. In marrying Jude, Nel effaces herself and bolsters his wounded ego, but, after Jude sleeps with Sula and leaves Nel, Nel, in great misery, blames Sula for her loss because she accepts a middle-class possessiveness. At the end, when the community is breaking up, Eva reminds Nel that Nel watched Chicken Little drown. She recognizes then that she has been missing Sula, not Jude: "girl, girl, girlgirlgirl" (174). Nel defends middle-class norms, but, like the disintegrating Bottom, her defense of them breaks down.

Some critics claim that *The Bluest Eye* and *Sula* reveal the debilitating impact of conventional, middle-class virtues, but, to preserve the autonomy of high art, these critics do not admit that these novels also accommodate those values. For instance, Herbert Rice says that in *The Bluest Eye* "Black experience was shown to be unintelligible in the context of White reality," whereas in *Sula* "the reverse is true. Black experience becomes the focus, and White misunderstanding the point."[45] Since Black experience and White reality oppose each other, Black experience does not accommodate White reality or middle-class norms. More negative, Barbara Christian, who assumes that the novels' symbols and the community's mythology give a public or objective meaning to the characters' "private" lives, draws a pessimistic moral: "Nature will always inflict disasters on them, . . . the evil of racism will result in jobless men and women, and . . . death will always be with them."[46] This pessimistic notion that evil is inevitable emphasizes the subversive import of high art. That is, this notion implies that, far from accommodating liberal ideals, the novels undermine them as harshly as *Tess, Invitation,* and *Unbearable* do.

Other critics grant that the novel accommodates the middle-class values which it also opposes but, to preserve the autonomy of high art, treats accommodation as critique. Susan Willis maintains, for example, that in the South, the Black community of Cholly and Mrs. Breedlove preserved its integrity, but in the North, where middle-class virtues dominate, Cholly and Mrs. Breedlove are isolated and defeated. In Willis's terms, "Morrison develops the social and psychological aspects that characterize the lived experience of historical transition. For the black emigrant to the North, the first of these is alienation."[47] This claim indicates the breakdown of community and the terrible alienation and repression imposed by the North's reified middle-class culture, but, instead of acknowledging that the novel also accepts this reified culture, Willis argues that the novel's "eruptions of funk" resist it. In both *The Bluest Eye* and *Sula,* alienation or "otherness" becomes a virtue, changing at times into "an explosive image of a utopian mode" or "alternative social world."[48]

Michael Awkward also argues that the novels reveal the alienating effects of middle-class norms, but he maintains that these effects reveal Morrison's Black feminism.[49] For instance, he grants that in *Bluest* the community tacitly accepts middle-class standards but argues that, because Morrison depicts its double or divided consciousness, it actually repudiates them. He also claims that it scapegoats Pecola not because in a conservative fashion it assumes that Pecola must have deserved or enjoyed her rape but because it recognizes that she accepts middle-class standards and rejects her Blackness.[50] He also suggests that scapegoating Pecola has positive benefits: it lets Claudia and the omniscient narrator form a united voice and the community reestablish its wholeness. This argument forcefully depicts Morrison's Black feminist critique of middle-class life but, preserving the conventional opposition of high and popular art, denies that *Sula* and *Bluest* also accommodate the bitter middle-class virtues.

Other critics grant that the novels reveal the debilitating effects of middle-class ideals but still claim that the novels undermine them.[51] These critics admit that *Bluest*, for example, reveals a cycle of defeat and despair but maintain that the redemption inherent in the narrator's eloquence and the novel's many voices opposes this acceptance of middle-class life; as Elliott Butler-Evans says, "Through complex strategies of representation, shifts in perspective, and fragmented stories of feminine or feminist desire, the Morrison narrative, in spite of its apparent single voice, is marked by ideological rupture and dissonance."[52] Such "rupture and dissonance" leave the novels ambiguous, neither supporting nor undermining White middle-class norms. These critics acknowledge that the nursery rhyme at *Bluest*'s beginning evokes the middle-class values which destroy the Breedloves, but they maintain that, open or dialogical, the novel remains ambiguous because it allows gaps, employs a rich, redemptive narrative style, and evokes many different African American voices, including Mrs. McTeer, Mrs. Breedlove, Aunt Jimmy, and Soaphead Church. In Page's terms, the novel "embraces the postmodern acceptance of an always already disunified condition."[53]

Christian complains that, co-opted by the racist literary establishment, such Black poststructuralist criticism engages in esoteric formal analyses and ignores or dismisses the pessimistic truths of African American life.[54] It is true that the poststructuralist accounts emphasize the subversive rhetoric and minimize the stereotypical middle-class others of *Bluest*'s Black community. Neither these accounts nor the traditional realist or historical accounts explain, moreover, how Morrison's fiction could resist middle-class stereotypes and still acquire high status or establish a Black feminist tradition. Denise Heinze claims, for example, that, because of Morrison's ambiguous "double consciousness" her novels subverted middle-class values and still impressed the literary establishment even though its values and codes "perpetuate the system."[55] Such claims reduce the establishment to foolish conservatives and ignore the political conflicts and institutional divisions making Morrison's success possible. As I indicate in chapter 7, it is the growth of Black and women's studies, the emergence of a Black aesthetic, the revival of Zora Neale Hurston, and the success of other Black feminist writers which, as Houston Baker says, "made it possible for literary-critical and literary-theoretical investigators to . . . include previously 'unfamiliar' objects in an expanded (and sharply modified) American artworld."[56]

Although the traditional and the poststructuralist accounts ignore these institutional changes, the poststructuralist accounts still suggest that in *Sula* the rich lyric tone, multiple voices, and many gaps open positive interpretive possibilities involving the reader and contravening the pessimistic middle-class views. More fully than the other accounts, which emphasize the conformity with Nature or the resistance of middle-class norms, the poststructuralist accounts demonstrate that the multiple voices and fragmented narrative of these novels both accept and subvert conventional middle-class values.

High/Popular Art

Initiating a Black feminist tradition, *The Bluest Eye* and *Sula* critique the liberal ideals of beauty and propriety, not the Enlightenment's utopian communism, yet *Tess, Invitation, Unbearable,* or *The Prague Orgy* all undermine the humanist values and liberal ideals which traditional critics of *Hamlet* and *Pride and Prejudice* defend. Indeed, these novels all critique liberal ideals and conventional ideologies and stereotypes, as traditional and postmodern critics claim, but the opposition of high art and popular culture still breaks down because the critique does not preclude conformity with conventional ideologies and stereotypes. In the

136   Chapter Four

next chapter, I also show that the opposition breaks down, but I argue the contrary view: popular culture does not simply accept its generic conventions and ideological commitments; rather, like high art, it also undermines them. In addition, I discuss more fully the theoretical issues raised by the breakdown of the opposition.

Notes

1. In *The Modern Psychological Novel*, Leon Edel says that modernist art describes the subconscious actions of the mind, rather than the empirical features of external realities. Brought on by World War I, modernist art repudiates liberal ideals of progress and morality as well as the clichéd language and public conventions of popular culture. Similarly, in *The Act of Reading*, Wolfgang Iser praises the harsh negativity of the high modern novel. The popular "commercial" novel describes an external, predetermined system; tells the reader what to think; spells out the meaning of the plot, the characters, the narrator, or the symbols; and confirms the reader's interpretative schema and ideological commitments. By contrast, the modern novel negates these features of commercial fiction and frees the reader to produce her own interpretations and to improve her life. The absences, gaps, and blanks of the modern novel imply an alienated world which goads the reader into producing a redemptive meaning (229). For a repudiation of this negativity and and defense of popular formulas, see John Cawelti, *Adventure, Mystery, and Romance*, 5-20.

2. *Dialectic*, 6. This view is especially characteristic of the Frankfurt School's first generation. In *The Dialectic of Enlightenment*, for instance, Adorno and Horkheimer claim that the empirical science of the Enlightenment era sought to dismiss primitive mythology and superstition and to control nature but produced instead its own scientific mythology, which denigrated nature; reified logic, aesthetics, information, and the status quo; and thereby ensured the conformity and the repression of the masses. Unlike popular culture, which accepts this ideological conformity and capitalist domination, high art resists them and preserves a utopian vision. Similarly, in *One-Dimensional Man*, Herbert Marcuse says that popular culture produces that immediate gratification which defuses resistance and desublimates desire. Moreover, just as Martin Heidegger maintained that being explodes the scientific technology grounding modern illusions of happiness and mastery, so does Marcuse, his student, claim that high culture resists the technological reason on the basis of which popular culture deflates rebellion and induces an illusory happiness and short-lived gratification.

3. Browne, cited in Gary Hoppenstand, "Ray and Pat Browne," 61.

4. Ray Browne, *Against Academia*, 2.
5. John Frow, *Cultural Studies*, 132.
6. Raymond Williams, "Love and Work," 470-71.
7. See, for example, J. Hillis Miller, *Thomas Hardy*, 16-17.
8. F. B. Pinion, *A Hardy Companion*, 106.
9. Thomas Hardy, *Tess of the D'Urbervilles*, 75. All further citations are from this edition.
10. Irving Howe, *Thomas Hardy*, 114.
11. Howe, *Thomas Hardy*, 144-45.
12. Albert Guerard, *Thomas Hardy*, 1-2, 60; Barbara Hardy, *The Appropriate Form*, 41; Arthur Mizener, "Jude the Obscure," 193; E. M. Forster, *Aspects of the Novel*, 94.
13. Tony Tanner, "Colour and Movement," 407-31; Peter Brooks, *Thomas Hardy*, 233-53.
14. Dale Kramer, *Thomas Hardy*, 138-43.
15. J. Hillis Miller, *Fiction and Repetition*, 128.
16. Miller, *Fiction and Repetition*, 126-27.
17. Penny Boumelha, "*Tess of the D'Urbervilles*," 128.
18. Boumelha, "*Tess of the D'Urbervilles*," 123.
19. Peter Widdowson, *Tess of the D'Urbervilles*, 5.
20. See Zbigniew Brzezinski and Carl J. Friedrich, *Totalitarian Dictatorship and Autocracy*. As I explain in chapter 6, it shows that the rational ideals which Marx acquired from the French Enlightenment account for the characteristics of the communist state—a dogmatic ideology sanctioned by the state, a monolithic party ruled by a dictator, a terrorist system of police control, and a monopoly of communications, arms and weapons, and economic production (56). See also Herbert Marcuse, *One-Dimensional Man*, which says that Soviet Marxism perpetuates what he calls "technical progress as the instrument of domination"; similarly, Brzezinski and Friedrich claim that, as the product of Enlightenment science, Western technology explains totalitarian practices.
21. See Teresa De Lauretis, *Technologies of Gender*, 25-26.
22. Vladimir Nabokov, *Invitation to a Beheading*, 222-23.
23. Robert Alter, "*Invitation to a Beheading*," 42, 57-58. Alter grants that the novel depicts a stereotypical totalitarian state in which its conformist citizens make themselves "transparent," but, (mis)taking the stereotype for historical realism, Alter says that, far from permitting aesthetic self-indulgence, the novel shows how valuable these reflexive practices are (44, 59).
24. Richard Rorty, *Contingency, Irony, Solidarity*, 155.
25. Rorty, *Contingency, Irony, Solidarity*, 144.
26. Milan Kundera, *The Unbearable Lightness of Being*, 39. All further citations arel be from this edition.
27. *The Book of Laughter and Forgetting* also depicts communists in an unqualified or stereotypical manner, but, instead of resisting the conventional

anticommunism, this novel moves beyond Cold War politics. In *Unbearable*'s absurdist style, this novel juxtaposes comic devils, who deny life any meaning, and pompous angels, who occupy all "the general staffs" and include "the left and the right, Arab and Jew, Russian general and Russian dissident" (70-72); however, the novel construes the conflicts of these devils and angels as an allegory explaining the characters' experiences.

28. For example, Roger Kimball complains that Kundera mistakenly equates the spiritual evil of totalitarian society with the cultural failings of the West (see "The ambiguities of Milan Kundera," 12). Similarly, Robert Boyers, who addresses Kundera directly, says, "You know that conditions in the West are much closer to what you want, yet you insist that they are awful and that to accept them is to make a shabby compromise" (see *Atrocity and Amnesia*, 229).

29. Similarly, Richard Rorty maintains that Kundera accepts the optimistic liberal faith that "everybody can do what they want if they don't hurt anybody else while doing it" (See *Essays on Heidegger and Others*, 75). At the same time, Rorty argues that in Kundera's fiction "[n]obody stands for Truth, or for Being, or for Thinking. Nobody stands for anything Other or Higher." In *Milan Kundera & Feminism* John O'Brien grants that Kundera's novels depict gender stereotypes but still argues that Kundera deconstructs such "either/or thinking" (69). See also John Sisk, "Art, Kitsch, & Politics," and John Bayley, "Fictive Lightness, Fictive Weight," 90-1.

30. Terry Eagleton, *The Ideology of the Aesthetic*, 219-25.

31. Terry Eagleton, "Bakhtin, Schopenhauer, Kundera," 187-88.

32. Philip Roth, *Zuckerman Bound*, 462.

33. Roth, *Zuckerman Bound*, 443.

34. Philip Roth, *The Professor of Desire*, 20.

35. Roth, *The Professor of Desire*, 182-83.

36. Roth, *The Professor of Desire*, 162-63.

37. In *Understanding Philip Roth* Murray Baumgarten and Barbara Gottfield claim that, as Zuckerman "searches for his identity as an artist, he discovers the meanings of familial and communal obligations" (155). Similarly, Eugene Goodheart says that Zuckerman envies the East European artists, who live "in a larger political and historical world in which the writer cannot simply indulge his narcissism" or permit so much "self-indulgence" (see "Writing and the Unmaking of the Self,*"* 446). Goodheart also suggests that, while Kundera and Roth share the postmodernist belief that anarchic fantasy and erotic desire free the self from conventional outlooks, morals, and truths, including totalitarian domination, Kundera and Roth also oppose an "imaginative licentiousness and extremism which threaten reality" (453). See also Martin Tucker, who says that in *Zuckerman Bound* "words bring us back to the family of man we are inevitably cast out of" (see "The Shape of Exile in Philip Roth," 48).

38. Jonathan Brent, "The Unspeakable Self," 181; Brent denies that sexual license or imaginative liberty provides genuine freedom; rather, just as an unre-

strained sexuality can readily turn oppressive, so too the imagination may end up a "tool of advertising" or "self-help programs" or a "badge" of middle-class virtue. In *Comic sense* Thomas Pughe also argues that Zuckerman embodies many distinct selves who never achieve authenticity. Pughe also suggests that the "counterlife" of the imagination or sexual life does not preserve individual autonomy or artistic independence; on the contrary, just as Zuckerman suffers from his public's and even his family's misreadings of his work, so too Roth's questioning of artistic conventions opens his fiction to misreadings which he cannot dismiss.

39. See Jonathan Brent, "The Unspeakable Self," 108-9, 99-100.

40. See, for instance, Thomas Pughe, *Comic sense*, 19-20.

41. Linda Ditmar, "Will the Circle Be Unbroken?," 139-41; see also Deborah McDowell, "The Self and the Other," 78, and Philip Weinstein, "David and Solomon," 53.

42. Toni Morrison, *The Bluest Eye*, 121. All further citations are from this edition.

43. Terry Otten, "Horrific Love," 652; see also Denise Heinz, *The Dilemma of "Double-Consciousness,"* 29.

44. Toni Morrison, *Sula*, 143. All further citations are from this edition.

45. Herbert Rice, *Toni Morrison and the American Tradition*, 52.

46. Barbara Christian, *Black Women Novelists*, 173; see also Carolyn Denard, "The Convergence of Feminism and Ethnicity."

47. Susan Willis, "Eruptions of Funk," 310.

48. Willis, "Eruptions," 323.

49. Houston Baker argues that in *Sula* Morrison creates a sense of community or place which expresses Black domesticity and which, reworking Toomer's or Hurston's fiction, establishes a Black feminist tradition. See "When Lindbergh Sleeps with Bessie Smith," 236-45.

50. Michael Awkward, "The Evil of Fulfillment," 188-89.

51. See Linda Ditmar, "Will the Circle Be Unbroken?"; Deborah McDowell, "The Self and the Other"; Terry Otten, "Horrific Love"; and Philip Page, *Dangerous Freedom*.

52. Elliot Butler-Evans, *Race, Gender, and Desire*, 63.

53. Philip Page, *Dangerous Freedom*, 56; see also Linda Ditmar, "Will the Circle Be Unbroken?,"140-46.

54. See Barbara Christian, "The Race for Theory."

55. Denise Heinz, *The Dilemma of "Double-Consciousness,"*4-5.

56. Houston Baker, *Blues, Ideology, and Afro-American Literature*, 76-77; see also Henry Louis Gates, Jr., "Afterword," 190; In *The Crime of Innocence* Terry Otten also claims that *Sula* requires a "double reading" which situates it in the American (post)modernist and African American traditions, but he still derives the notion of the fall and the divided self of *Sula* from the British Romantic tradition, which esteems the good import of the evil other.

Chapter Five
Gender, Spies, and Art: Ian Fleming, John Le Carré, Mickey Spillane, and Sara Paretsky

The traditional opposition of high and popular art breaks down because neither kind of art undermines liberal ideals, generic conventions, popular stereotypes, and ideological doctrines more forcefully than the other. Moreover, different reading formations explain why readers of high and popular art explain and evaluate this fiction in such different terms. The previous chapter indicated that the fiction of Hardy, Nabokov, Kundera, Roth, and Morrison critiques the liberal ideals and humanist values of the Enlightenment but still accepts generic conventions and popular ideologies and stereotypes. This chapter argues that detective and spy fiction does not simply conform to its generic conventions and ideological commitments, as the generic critics say; this fiction also challenges them.

For example, in A. C. Doyle's *The Sign of Four*, Sherlock Holmes complains that Dr. Watson's accounts of his adventures describe much more than his solution of the crime. This complaint repudiates the novel's literary conventions, which include the traditional romance's resourceful hero, evil genius, riverboat chase, and worldwide adventures. Miss Morstan, by contrast, praises Watson's account, which she considers an epic romance in which Holmes and Watson are valiant knights rescuing damsels in distress.[1] By the end, Holmes's view has triumphed, but the story does not reconcile this opposition between the scientific truth and the mystical romance. Even though Watson ultimately accepts Holmes's reasoning, Watson criticizes his intellectual arrogance, physical self-indulgence, cold calculations, and overconfidence. These criticisms preserve the romance's opposition to narrow scientific expertise and relentless logic.

Popular culture's traditional generic critics, who claim that particular detective and spy novels imitate the established conventions of their type, ignore or deny such tensions, incoherence, or ideological critique and emphasize the conventions' objective truth.[2] The generic critics get the conventions right. That is, the hardboiled detective and spy fiction of Ian Fleming, John Le Carré, Mickey Spillane, and Sara Paretsky show that, as the generic critics say, in the modern world, where cunning, terror, and violence, not Enlightenment ideals, prevail, the grand and brutal violence of the villain justifies the equally grand and brutal violence of the hero. I will argue, however, that, while the feminist novels of Sara Paretsky subvert the ideological oppositions and mechanical certainty of such generic conventions more radically than the novels of Fleming, Le Carré, and Spillane do, these novels all accept and undermine these conventions and their Enlightenment ideals.

Ian Fleming

Ian Fleming's *Live and Let Die* and *From Russia with Love* both value the Enlightenment ideals of the West over the totalitarian communism of the East but go on to subvert these ideological differences in the name of a brutal and cunning chauvinism. In Hemingway's detailed fashion, *Live and Let Die* (1954) names American brands of cars or cigarettes, describes the distinctive mannerisms and the "uneducated" dialectic of the "Negroes," and satirizes greedy, crass American businesses, yet, far from Hemingway's famous understatement, the narrative loads the evil Mr. Big with negative features. As Tony Bennett points out, Fleming's novels usually include an extremely evil character, who compels innocent workers or natives to serve his self-aggrandizing ends, spies for communist countries, acts as a Third World terrorist exploiting East/West conflicts, and subjugates and even destroys female spies or adventurers.[3] In this case, Mr. Big, a "Negro genius" whose disproportionately large head, not racial prejudice, made him a rebel, eloquently explains his artistic genius as well as "Negro" emancipation, smuggles gold coins into the United States, passes secret government information to SMERSH (the Soviet terrorist agency), makes the lady Solitaire read the future from her playing cards, and with voodoo and terror turns Black workers into his "eyes."

The narrative also loads Bond with contrasting positive features, including confidence, taste, strength, encyclopedic wisdom, extraordinary resourcefulness, and enlightened Anglo-American ideals. He too acts as a secret agent and employs terrorist tactics, but he remains loyal and factual, not eloquent nor superstitious. For example, sharks mutilated the American Felix Leiter before he could discover that Mr. Big hides ancient coins in his fish tank's false bottom in order to smuggle them into the United States. The tight-lipped Bond discovers the hiding place easily enough but does not tell anyone. As this silence implies, the text values factual detail over broad generalities, restrained speech over formal rhetoric, and enlightened Anglo-American ideals over terrifying superstition and dominating organizational structures.

Generic critics maintain that Ian Fleming's Bond novels have established the paradigm of the spy romance whose grand, even mythic evil justifies the hero's epic resourcefulness, intellectual genius, or equally grand and brutal violence.[4] Umberto Eco explains the novels in terms of structural and ideological oppositions and literary devices, but his widely praised account also claims that the novels mechanically repeat their structural oppositions and sequences of actions and, as a result, deny the ordinary reader much sophistication.[5] What's more, his account reduces the novels to myths or fairy tales lacking any critical force: Fleming's "is the static, inherent, dogmatic conservatism of fairy tales and myths, which transmit an elementary wisdom, constructed and communicated by a simple play of light and shade, by indisputable archetypes which do not permit critical distinction."[6] The narrative of *Live and Let Die* does reduce the cultural differences of the East and the West to "a simple play of light and shade," but the narrative still undermines these differences.

In a pessimistic fashion, the repeated images of zombies, sharks, barracudas, snakes, wolves, and voodoo dancers, together with the sarcastic descriptions of commercial American culture, imply, for instance, that in this world the dominant virtues are not those of factual truth or enlightened Anglo-American life but those of the brutal and cunning underworld. Since these images characterize both Bond and Mr. Big, they share the chauvinist virtues demanded by this treacherous underworld. While generic critics take the novel to affirm the East and the West's cultural differences, the ocean's violent imagery implies that these cultural ideals lack substance and weight. Their brutal, chauvinist masculinity reduces their ideological differences to a thin veneer of polite, civilized life. At the end, a convenient rock enables Bond to wreck the luxurious yacht of Mr. Big, who tied him and Solitaire up and towed them through a sea filled with hungry sharks. As the sharp coral cuts the bare feet of the tied-up Bond and the sharks bite off and swallow huge chunks of the drowning Mr. Big, he and Bond still manage to stare resolutely into each other's eyes. Omitted in the movie version, which preserves Bond's mythic superiority, this steady look underlines the chauvinism which they share and which effaces the cultural differences which the novel initially emphasized.

Opening with a seventy-one-page description of a violent communist assassin, an autocratic communist government, and its sadistic military and political officials, *From Russia with Love* also emphasizes the differences between totalitarian Communism and Western free enterprise only to undermine them; however, *From Russia* turns espionage into a game played by both the communist and the Western agents. Kronstein, the Soviet chess champion, interprets the Soviet plan to kill Bond as a match with elaborate, well-prepared moves. Grant, the Soviet assassin, mechanically carries out the moves planned by Kronstein. The lovely Tatiana and the spektor decoding machine represent a gambit which Bond takes readily enough. Unlike Darko Kerim, the Turkish agent whose fear of the game foreshadows his death, Bond insists on playing the game to the end. Of course, Bond defeats Grant because the asexual, uncouth Grant plays in a mechanical way, while the flamboyant Bond plays in the individualist's spontaneous, unplanned manner; nonetheless, when Bond and Grant first meet, they, like Bond and Mr. Big, exchange significant glances. Bond mistakes Grant for a British agent sent by the concerned M, but that mistake underlines the recognition and unity which such glances produce.[7] A moment of mutual recognition, their glances emphasize what they share—a brutal, domineering masculinity confident in its prowess and its virility. Generic critics take this brutal masculinity to show that the hero must cultivate great independence, strength, and cunning if he is to defeat an even more anarchic, brutal, and cunning enemy;[8] however, in this novel and in *Live and Let Die*, this chauvinist strength and brutality also undermine the novel's ideological assumption that a liberal Western democracy is superior to Soviet totalitarianism. If, like Bond and Mr. Big, Bond and Grant are in the end only two tough guys fighting each other, their heavily emphasized ideological differences do not matter so much after all.

John Le Carré

The fiction of John Le Carré also assumes that in the modern world cunning, terror, and brutality, not ethical norms nor ideological ideals, prevail. Jerry Palmer argues that Le Carré's brutal competitors and villainous conspirators create a paranoid world which, instead of engaging in ideological critique, simply fails to annul all threat of conflict;[9] however, more like modernist high art than Fleming's novels are, this fiction also critiques the spy novel's ideological faith in liberal Western ideals and tough, violent men.

For example, in *The Spy Who Came in from the Cold* (1963) the loyal Alex Leamus accepts the role of a disaffected British spy only to turn genuinely disaffected with liberal British ideals. After Hans-Dieter Mundt, the head of the East German agency, brutally murders Alex's agents, the cynical Leamus colludes with Control, who runs the British intelligence agency, the Circus, to destroy Mundt. Leamus adopts the deceptive role of a drunken, disaffected spy unjustly dismissed from the Circus. Employed at a library, he meets Liz Gold, a "good" communist who tenderly and persistently mothers him when he gets deathly ill. Although he plans to marry her once he defeats Mundt and retires from the Circus, he remains aloof and contemptuous and sticks to his deceptive role. When Mundt's agents enable him to go to East Germany to sell British intelligence, he meets Karl Fiedler, a "good" communist who brings charges against the neofascist Mundt and inadvertently exposes the Circus's plan. At the ensuing East German tribunal, Alex praises the integrity of Fiedler, but Liz, invited to East Germany to learn about its communist party, reluctantly testifies that Smiley, a British agent, visited her and aided Alex, paying off, for instance, the lease on Alex's apartment. Since Alex concludes that the Circus bungled the plan, he tries to save the principled Fiedler and eliminate the detestable Mundt by admitting that he faked his disaffection. The tribunal condemns him, Liz, and Fiedler to death, but Alex does not realize how drastically he mistook the Circus's plan until in a dramatic midnight appearance Mundt, a double agent, helps Alex and Liz flee East Germany. "And suddenly, with the terrible clarity of a man too long deceived, Leamus understood the whole ghastly trick."[10] He realizes that, to protect the double agent Mundt, a detestable neofascist, Control, Smiley, and the British Circus conspired to sacrifice their own agents, him, Liz, and Fiedler. When East German border guards shoot Liz as she climbs over the Berlin Wall, Alex, turning suicidal, lets them shoot him too.

John G. Cawelti and Bruce A. Rosenberg say that *The Spy* establishes a familiar romantic opposition between innocence and experience. Since Leamus recognizes the devastating brutality of both sides, his cynical view represents experience or truth; by contrast, even though Liz has had a good deal of experience, she remains innocent. Liz does preserve her innocence but not because her dogmatic communist ideology does not permit her to think, as Cawelti and Rosenberg claim;[11] rather, *The Spy* draws an unconventional contrast of good and bad communists. Like Ernest Hemingway's

For Whom the Bell Tolls, in which the Soviet journalist Karkov bravely opposes the paranoid communist functionary Marty, *The Spy* positively depicts Liz, who condemns British immorality, and Fiedler, whose interrogation of Alex poses serious theoretical issues and whose charges against Mundt could reform the East German government. Leamus shows, moreover, the reluctant sexuality, uncertain loyalties, and suicidal impulses of Hemingway's Robert Jordan, and the communists, the ambiguous virtues of Hemingway's Spanish loyalists. More sharply than the Bond novels, which preserve the evil communist stereotypes, *The Spy* breaks down its traditional faith in liberal ideals and chauvinist virtues; however, it also undermines Alex's and the reader's belief that the good British state may use any means necessary to defeat evil East German communism. Control's devious plan to save Mundt is tragic not only because it costs Liz and Leamus their lives but also because it destroys Fiedler's chance to reform the Abteilung and East Germany.[12]

In *Fiction, Crime, and Empire*, Jon Thompson concedes that in *The Spy* "the West is no different from the East. Each political system is regulated and overseen by massive intelligence conglomerates."[13] Thompson claims, however, that Leamus's "heroic" suicide at the Berlin Wall overcomes the novel's "postmodern" uncertainty and reaffirms the traditional ideals of the spy romance.[14] Thompson is right to suggest that, in Bond's fashion, Leamus battles tough guys, resists the triumph of a Mundt, and accepts the harsh politics of the West, but Alex commits suicide once he discovers that the Circus had colluded to destroy him, his agents, Liz, Fiedler, and others. Far from restoring Alex's faith in traditional ideals, the suicide emphasizes the breakdown of the East and the West's ideological differences as well as James Bond's heroic agency. Like *For Whom the Bell Tolls*, which shows the sadistic brutality of both the German fascists and the Spanish guerrillas, *The Spy* suggests that the traditional virtues of heroism, faithfulness, and love can also lead to destruction and suicide.

Le Carré's *Tinker, Tailor, Soldier, Spy* (1974), which grants George Smiley, its protagonist, the individual autonomy and reflective mentality which Leamus lacks, also undermines the West's liberal ideals and heroic figures, but this novel approximates the optimistic realism of a Dickens, rather than the pessimistic modernism of a Hemingway. The story depicts the reluctant struggle of the defeated Smiley to expose his leaders' betrayal of England, to return to the Cambridge Circus, and even to win back his estranged wife, Ann. At the end, in a heroic fashion, he saves the Cambridge Circus from communist infiltrators, but he thoughtfully emphasizes the complex human situation whereby we cannot justify our cruelty to each other.

That is, more like Cincinnatus than James Bond, Smiley, the narrative's central consciousness, does not confront the evildoers or take direct action; he questions and analyzes the story's other narrators, who relate their adventures inside and outside the Cambridge Circus. Ricki Tarr, Jim Prideaux, Bill Haydon, Sam Collins, and other agents tell stories, while Smiley asks difficult, penetrating questions. For example, to convince the captured Soviet agent Karla (alias Gerstmann) to defect, Smiley urges him to think of himself and his wife, not the communist cause. Smiley tells him that communist and capitalist societies are too limited and too faulty to warrant the self-sacrifice which Karla's impending return to the USSR would certainly entail. When Karla fails to respond, Smiley condemns Karla's narrow ideological fanaticism but admits later on that his arguments betrayed his own devotion to his wife. Similarly, when Bill Haydon says that he became a Soviet mole because he did not consider the United States much better than the USSR, Smiley does not comment, but toward the end he confesses that, even though he knew all along that Haydon was the mole, he did nothing because he considered Haydon "one of us."[15] Unable to convert the stubborn Karla or to confront his cynical colleague Haydon, an uncertain Smiley repeatedly shows an insightful grasp of life's complexities.

Tony Barley grants that Smiley's interrogation of himself and of the novel's many narrators emphasizes the complexities of life but in the generic fashion denies that they subvert the many ideologies of the diverse characters;[16] however, while Smiley grasps these complexities, other characters, whom the novel depicts as immature or childish, accept the gross simplifications which characterize ideological doctrine. The novel's many unsettling metaphors of childhood, boyhood, girlhood, youthfulness, and true or false adulthood emphasize this dismissal of complexity. For example, to depict Smiley's opponents in the British Circus, the novel presents and refutes a structural metaphor which construes the house of Lacon, a government official, as a "Berkshire Camelot" (32), the spies of the Cambridge Circus as the knights of the Round Table, the Russian counterspy as Merlin, and Bill Haydon, who wins over Guinevere (Smiley's wife, Ann) as Lancelot. The metaphor implies that, because these characters have not grown up, they accept such romantic fantasies and ignore life's complexity.

In addition, a dogmatic nationalist, the former agent Jim Prideaux insists that, unlike Smiley, he is not a complicated "juju man"; however, to describe him, the novel takes the point of view of Bill Roach, a friendless, uncertain, and timid schoolboy. After the angry and vengeful Prideaux kills the mole Bill Haydon, who betrayed and even crippled him, the story leaves Prideaux with Bill Roach and the schoolboys. When Smiley talks to Ricky Tarr, Oliver Lacon, Roy Bland, and the emigré Max, children play in the background. This juxtaposition suggests that, just as George's former colleague Connie is a "girl/woman," so these male agents or officials are boy/men. Ironically, when Percy the corrupt director insists that his supporters are the "grown ups" (185), we feel that they are still children. By contrast, at the end, when Peter Guilliam no longer feels angry at the mole Bill Haydon, the novel rightly suggests that Peter has grown up and can return to the Circus.

Many critics claim that, while the complex heroes of Le Carré's fiction recognize the brutality and ruthlessness of the West and the East, the fiction still affirms the West's tolerant liberalism.[17] It is true that, more than *The Spy*, *Tinker* preserves the liberal belief that mature characters like Smiley grasp the complexities of life, yet this belief does not preclude the ideological critique whereby the "immature" characters accept crude or dogmatic simplifications of life's complexities. In other words, even though the Dickensian *Tinker* does not share the pessimistic uncertainty of *The Spy* and Hemingway's *For Whom*, both *Tinker* and *The Spy* undermine spy fiction's liberal ideals and chauvinist heroism.

Mickey Spillane

In Ian Fleming's fashion, Mickey Spillane's *One Lonely Night* (1951) and *The Girl Hunters* (1962) show that the chauvinist sexuality, sadistic violence, and totalitarian communism of the modern world justify the liberal ideals and chauvinist violence of the hero;[18] at the same time, more like *The Spy* than *Tinker*, the intense paranoia of the protagonist Mike Hammer, not his thoughtful grasp of life's complexities, indicate that a radical uncertainty undermines these ideals. Generic critics maintain that the "political rave and rant" merely increase our conviction that "Hammer's world . . . is a world of valid paranoia with everything and everyone suspect except Velda and Pat";[19] however, unlike the certainty and confidence of Bond, whom Eco calls a perfect machine because he always remains in control of himself, the emotional rants of the uncertain Hammer reveal a hysteria undermining such chauvinist self-control.[20]

For example, in *Lonely*, a judge who condemns Mike's relentless killing haunts him throughout the novel, disturbing his faith in bone-crushing violence. In despair he wanders across the Brooklyn Bridge only to see a fearful, fleeing woman thrown off of it. Curious about her murder, he impersonates a Communist Party official from Philadelphia and infiltrates the New York Communist Party, where he uncovers a brutal communist clique which, led by Soviet general Osilov and two MVD (Soviet) spies, exploits democratic American freedoms for undemocratic ends—a typical Cold War fear. Similarly, in Raymond Chandler's *Farewell, My Lovely*, Philip Marlowe, curious about why a big, loudly dressed White man would fight his way into a "shine joint," involves himself in Moose Malloy's search for his missing girlfriend, Velma. Marlowe, who always demands payment for his services, remains cynical throughout the search; by contrast, Mike's discovery of the Soviet clique reinvigorates Mike, who acquires the ideological potency of the spy romance's hero.

For instance, in several extended rants, he justifies himself to the absent judge:

> *The hell of it is, Judge . . . Your rain of purity has come, and out there in it is the grim specter who is determined that this time he will not miss. He'll raise his vicious scythe and swing at me with all the fury of his madness and I'll go down, but that one wild swing will take along a lot of others before it cuts me in half.*[21]

On the one hand, he assures the judge that, since the "grim specter" in the "rain of purity" threatens him and many others, he is right to fight back. On the other, he warns that the "grim specter" "will take along a lot of others before it cuts" him "in half." Because the rant piles up italicized sentences in an intense Faulknerian manner, the warning betrays a repressed hysteria, not rational self-control.

Similarly, after the communists discover that the disguised Velda, Mike's secretary, has been spying on them, they strip her, tie her up, and beat her. Sadistic voyeurs, they "slobber and drool" with lust and pleasure, yet they do not weaken Velda, who remains silent. Without much difficulty, the reinvigorated Mike frees her and shoots and dismembers them because their communist "slobber and drool" lacks the ideological potency of his Cold War chauvinism. As he watches them, he again rants hysterically: *"[T]he guy in the pork-pie hat grimaced with hate and raised the rope to smash it down, while the rest slobbered with the lust and pleasure of this example of what was yet to come"* (163).

Their sadism and voyeurism reinvigorates Mike, whose renewed violence thereby acquires an ideological justification overlooked by the liberal judge; however, to keep the wealthy and sexy Ethel Bright from aiding the communists or betraying him, he too poses as a sadistic voyeur: as he says, "Maybe I'll see you stripped again. Soon. When I do, I'm going to take my belt off and lash your butt like it should have been lashed when you first broke into this game" (84). A punishing father and an aggressive lover, Mike shares the voyeur's desire to see the lovely Ethel naked and the sadist's desire to hurt her, yet more ideologically potent than the communists, Mike miraculously converts the naive Ethel, who, unlike the strong Velda, admits her errors and abandons communism. As she confesses, lying naked and wounded, "After . . . I met you I saw . . . the truth, Mike. I knew . . . I had been a fool" (130).

Leslie Fiedler suggests that to Spillane's "lower-middlebrow" readers the "sadist fantasies in which they find masturbatory pleasure are revelations of social disorder, first steps toward making a better world."[22] Ethel's conversion and the communists' destruction do affirm the ideological potency of Mike's chauvinist anticommunism—in Fiedler's optimistic terms, they take "first steps toward making a better world"; however, Mike's strangling Oscar Deamer, an escaped lunatic and an intimidating communist functionary, undermines his conservative outlook. The detective Pat, the newspaper reporters, and even the whole American public believe that only Lee Deamer, the last, honest conservative, can end the moral corruption and communist infiltration of the government. At the end, Mike, who outwits them, discovers that the insane communist Oscar has killed and impersonated Lee, his sane, conservative twin brother. Generic critics assume that the spy romance typically conceals the villain's true self until the end, when such a climactic discovery reveals it; however, the discovery breaks down the novel's emphatic opposition between upright, conservative friends and threatening communist enemies.

What's more, like the "rain of purity," the discovery generates a hysteria incompatible with Hammer's masculine self-control. For instance, when Mike says that Lee killed the good communist Paula Riis because she had been his nurse at the mental hospital, he lapses into another rant:

> Then it happened. Somehow she saw the records or was introduced to the big boy in this country. She knew it was you. What happened? Did she approach you thinking you were Oscar's brother? *Whatever happened she recognized you as Oscar and all her illusions were shattered* (171).

This jumbled Faulknerian rant suggests not only that "her illusions were shattered" but also that Mike loses the rational self-control enabling him to impose his ideological authority. This hysteria resists that secure and confident Cold War chauvinism justifying Mike's knightly quest to save the missing Velda and to destroy the communist enemies.

In the more cynical *The Girl Hunters* (1962), such ideological uncertainty also generates disillusion and hysteria, but the Cold War chauvinism has lost its potency. In *Lonely* a clique of manipulative communist soldiers and tough guys reinvigorates Mike, whose renewed violence thereby acquires the ideological justification denied by the judge. In *Hunters* the loss of the loyal Velda turns Mike into a dissipated alcoholic too bleary to care about brutal thugs or communist gangsters. Although he remembers the scene in *Lonely* where the naked and tied-up Velda remained loyal while the sadistic communist voyeurs whipped her, he fears that Velda abandoned him. He goes on to defeat the notorious Dragon, a team of communist assassins, and to save Velda, who awaits his rescue, but he does not regain his lost ideological potency. Written after a ten-year hiatus in which, to answer his critics, Spillane cultivated a more literary style, this novel is more cynical and self-conscious.[23]

For example, the novel plays on the term "nail." One of the communist assassins is called "Nail." Both Richard Coles, the murdered American agent, and Laura Knapp, the disguised communist assassin, manicure their nails very carefully. After Mike knocks out Tooth, the male communist assassin, he nails Tooth's hands to the wood floor and brags that he "nailed" Tooth.[24] Similarly, Mike's traditional ally Pat, who blames him for Velda's ostensible death, and his communist enemies, who want him to reveal Velda's hiding place, threaten to jail, arrest, beat, torture, kill, or otherwise "nail" him. Generic critics take such puns to assert the Hobbesian belief that in a brutal, dog-eat-dog world only the strong survive; still, the puns on "nail" subvert the differences of evil communists and good-guy policemen because the figurative nailing describes communists and Westerners, allies and enemies alike.

The duplicity of the communist assassin Laura, who poses as a respectable Washington hostess and a conservative senator's grieving widow, also undermines this opposition. Still a chauvinist voyeur, he ogles the fetishized body of the usually naked Laura Knapp, who becomes his seductive and persistent lover. Mike discovers, however, that the duplicitous Laura, who, otherwise known as Tooth, belongs to the communist team the Dragon, murdered her husband. Like the discovery that the insane communist Oscar murdered and impersonated the conservative Lee, this discovery breaks down the novel's emphatic opposition between respectable conservative friends and threatening communist enemies. In the generic fashion, Jerry Palmer grants that in such novels the "paradoxical combination of apparently unequivocal self-certainty and constantly being on the look-out for conspiracies" produces a disconcerting paranoia, but he maintains that, far from undermining generic conventions, such thrillers depict a brutal, treacherous jungle in which a competitive hero like Mike must struggle to prove that "he is better than his opponents" and "his collaborators."[25] The world of the thriller is certainly such a jungle, but the fluctuating, uncertain ideological differences described by both *Lonely* and *Girl Hunters* do not indicate that Mike's paranoia simply enables him to survive in this jungle; rather, generating hysteria, the uncertainty resists that secure, confident chauvinist identity represented by Mike's knightly quest for the missing Velda and destruction of the communist villains.

Sara Paretsky

In *Deadlock* (1984) and *Burn Marks* (1990), Sara Paretsky also depicts the world as a brutal jungle in which the heroine must prove her superiority to her opponents and her collaborators; however, these novels challenge the liberal ideals and chauvinist heroism of the conventional spy romance more sharply than Fleming's, Le Carré's, or Spillane's novels do.

In *Deadlock*, for example, unlike Bond, who remains supremely confident, and Hammer, who lapses into hysteria, Paretsky's heroine V. I. doubts herself in a radical fashion. When she investigates the death of her cousin Boom Boom, a retired hockey star who allegedly fell into a lake and was killed by a nearby barge's churning propeller, no one, except for Lotty, her friend and doctor, encourages her. Bobby Mallory, the police captain and her dead father's old friend, considers Boom Boom's death accidental. When she tells Mallory that Boom Boom was murdered, he tells her to find a husband and take a long vacation. Her family, which always resented Boom Boom's playing hockey, suspects that, after his bad knees forced him to give up hockey, he suffered from depression and committed suicide. Clayton Phillips, vice president of the Eudora Grain Company, obstructs her investigation of the company and Boom Boom's work there, and she gets the one secretary who aids her investigation fired. When she questions Paige Carrington, Boom Boom's lovely girlfriend, V. I. regrets that, allied against a conservative family, she and Boom Boom were friends but not lovers, and she fears that a traditional female envy may motivate her, as Paige claims. Encouraged by Lotty, V. I. goes ahead, but she worries that her investigation may show little more than her sadness and anger at her cousin's untimely death or her jealousy of his lover.

Although the death of a friend or an innocent person also motivates the investigations of Hammer, he never doubts that the death was a brutal murder or that the criminals will suffer a just punishment, not even when his friend Pat the police detective warns him about his investigation's dangers. By contrast, the doubts of V. I. approximate the radical uncertainty of Pynchon's *The Crying of Lot 49*. In it, Oedipa the detective/heroine discovers the conspiratorial activity and the pervasive symbols and icons of the mysterious Trystero, which may have fostered the French Revolution and established a private, underground postal service. She admits, however, that the Trystero may also be a delusion which Inverarity and his associates produced and which reveals only her paranoia.

The Crying never resolves this uncertainty, whereas *Deadlock* depicts an apparently unrelated series of serious accidents which, preserving the generic form, gradually convince V. I. that Boom Boom was definitely murdered. When her cousin's apartment is robbed, a Black security guard is killed; after her brakes fail, her car crashes, sending her to the hospital; and, when she sneaks aboard the Lucella, Bledsoe's grain-hauling barge, it blows up spectacularly, blocking the Great Lakes shipping trade for weeks. Merging two lines of investigation—Boom Boom's death and the barge's destruction—these unrelated accidents overcome V. I.'s uncertainty and reveal the deep, subtle crime required by a thriller.

Generic critics complain that, even though V. I. is a feminist, her investigations of crime and criminals ultimately reestablish the patriarchal order.[26] It is true that, while Mike Hammer rants about communist subversion or Mafia hit men and Philip Marlowe advocates a moral crusade against corruption, she adopts the professional manner of a Sherlock Holmes. Despite Mallory's chauvinist hostility or Bledsoe's sexual advances, she preserves a formal indifference. Still, in a feminist fashion, she resents her family's opposition to her profession, aids abused or oppressed women, and rarely cleans her apartment, puts on makeup, or wears fancy clothes. Unlike the anomic Hammer or Bond, she cultivates a supporting circle of friends, who include the doctor Lotty Herschel and the reporter Murray Ryerson. Moreover, she has sex with Ryerson and Bledsoe the shipping director, but, instead of dramatizing the seductive appeal of her lovers' tantalizing bodies, as the Bond and Spillane novels do, she considers sex a calisthenic activity; as she says after she sleeps with Ryerson, "I found out how much exercise my dislocated shoulder was up to."[27] At the end the violent Mike Hammer usually acts as both judge and executioner, whereas, floating in the ocean, an exhausted and helpless V. I. can only watch as the trapped Greyfaulk aims his rifle at her and then kills himself.

What's more, the investigation of the deep crime opens various lines of ideological critique. For instance, when V. I. links the death of the Black security guard, Boom Boom's death and her traffic accident, Mallory dismisses her claims in a chauvinist manner. On the one hand, like Pat, Mike Hammer's friend, he protects her after he finds her fingerprints in Clayton Phillips's burglarized office. On the other, he regrets that V.I's father never beat her properly and that she took up detective work, instead of devoting herself to the kitchen and a family. When V. I. attends the funeral of the murdered guard, his angry family complains, moreover, that the racist police do not investigate his death because they do not take the murder of a Black person very seriously.

Lastly, V. I. exposes the financial machinations whereby the rich and powerful Neils Greyfaulk manipulated the shipping industry to his advantage. Unable to modernize Greyfaulk Lines, Greyfaulk colluded with Phillips to destroy Bledsoe's shipping company instead. Moreover, he murdered Phillips and Boom Boom, who discovered the plan, and tried to eliminate V. I., who also uncovered his machinations. While the success of the poor but enterprising Martin Bledsoe, whose abilities enabled him to rise in the industry even though in his youth he went to jail for embezzling company funds, vindicates the American business world, the schemes of Greyfaulk the family heir condemn it.

In *Deadlock* V. I.'s self-doubt, unfeminine lifestyle, and persistent investigation subvert spy fiction's conventional liberal ideals and chauvinist values, yet her professional manner preserves her neutral or "patriarchal" objectivity. In the later *Burn Marks* (1990), which also undermines the ideological commitments of the conventional thriller, V. I. has less of Sherlock Holmes's professional indifference and more of Hammer's angry ranting and Kundera's and Roth's reflexivity.

In this novel, V. I. aids her meandering aunt Elana even though her family has long resented Elana's alcoholism. After Elana's hotel burns down, V. I. finds her another apartment, but, when Elana disappears, V. I. gets involved in an insurance fraud investigation which eventually uncovers a ruthless clique of policemen, businessmen, and politicians. Once again, V. I. doubts her investigation until converging family and business events imply a deep and subtle crime; this time, however, she criticizes the men's sexism. As she tells Michael Furey, her would-be lover, "[Y]ou belong to a crowd where the girls sit on blankets waiting for the boys to finish talking business and bring them drinks. . . . I think that style—the segregated way you and Ron and Ernie work—its too much part of you. I don't see how you and I can ever move along together."[28] V. I. also engages in polemical conversations and reflections about the "good" housewife, abused women, possessive or domineering men, and belittled policewomen. These reflections are more sophisticated and more feminist than Hammer's diatribes but just as outraged.

Her many opponents, enemies, and hostile acquaintances also give the novel an angry, ranting tone as well as an aesthetic reflexivity. For instance, in this novel too Mallory berates her for neglecting her proper station in life and getting police work all mixed up. In addition, in a long harangue, the irate detective Roland Montgomery charges that she investigates the arson because she committed it, not because she means to aid the insurance company. When V. I. attends Roz's fund-raising party and contributes $250 to her campaign, Roz and her friend Ralph MacDonald do not thank her; they irately demand that she stay out of Roz's and Boots's business. To an extent, such angry attacks on her motives work as a rhetorical device making the reader imagine that something is terribly amiss. To a greater extent, these attacks emphasize her reputation as an outsider who forcefully challenges the establishment. Unlike Roth's Zuckerman or Kundera's Goethe, V. I. does not try to protect her image, but she too recognizes that she encounters hostile characters who feel vulnerable and act angry because they know her intimidating reputation or her exploits in previous novels.

A supporting circle, which in this novel includes the doctor Lotty Herschel and the reporter Murray Ryerson as well as the neighbor Mr. Contreras, his golden retriever Peppy, and Rick, the gay boyfriend of V. I.'s angry neighbor, still distinguish the social or feminine V. I. from the anomic Hammer or Bond; this time, however, not only does the novel have a ranting, angry tone and a reflexive self-consciousness, the crime also has broad political dimensions. The clique, which destroys the hotel and nearly kills V. I. and Aunt Elena, includes Ralph MacDonald, a billionaire businessman who plans to bid for a new stadium, Roz, a Hispanic woman campaigning for high political office, and Boots, a shady Democratic Party leader who, to stop a progressive alliance of Blacks and Hispanics, supports Roz. Eileen, Mallory's wife, considers the policeman Michael Furey, a protégé of Mallory, to be the perfect husband for V. I., but he is an important part of the clique. At the end, as she drives through the neighborhood in which she, Elena, Michael, Bobby, Roz, Boots, and her parents grew up, she thinks, "Where they all grew up together and helped each other out because the one thing you must never forget in Chicago is to look out for your own" (336). Even though they never forgot "to look out for 'their' own," Michael and others have gone to jail for arson and murder, Bobby has apologized for underestimating V. I.'s integrity, and Boots and Roz have been forced to deny involvement in the clique's schemes. Free indirect discourse, her reflection forcefully critiques the community ideology justifying the deep crime of the political clique. As a result, more sharply than *Deadlock*'s radical uncertainty and ideological critique, the political commentary and feminist polemics of this novel undermine the generic conventions and chauvinist ideals of hardboiled mystery and spy fiction.

Theoretical Defenses of High Art

Paretsky's *Deadlock* and *Burn Marks* critique the ideological oppositions and generic conventions of detective and spy fiction more forcefully than the novels of Fleming, Le Carré, or Spillane do, but, read figuratively, all of their work challenges the fiction's generic ideals and ideological commitments. Indeed, the radical uncertainty of their work undermines the opposition of high art and popular culture. In the previous chapter, I argued that the high modernist and postmodernist art of Vladimir Nabokov, Milan Kundera, Philip Roth, or Toni Morrison undermines the Enlightenment ideals of liberal and humanist criticism but does not consistently resist the nightmarish communists, chauvinist heroes, or racist stereotypes of popular fiction. A skeptic may object, however, that this approach, which claims that popular fiction and high art both affirm and undermine their liberal ideals, generic forms, popular stereotypes, or ideological oppositions, mixes up the fiction's audiences: the sophisticated readers of high art appreciate its subtle figures or profound ironies, not its obvious stereotypes, while ordinary readers of detective and spy fiction enjoy its broad themes, not its subversive metaphors, looks, parody, or hysteria.

For instance, Dana Polan grants that the traditional opposition of high and popular art breaks down but complains that the critique of this opposition denigrates ordinary readers, denying them much sophistication. In her terms, the critique "reserves a privilege for the critic as someone who has the superiority over mass taste by being able to cognize and render explicit what that taste can only miss or, at most, uncritically intuit."[29] As I indicate in the next chapter, the New York intellectuals also fault academic elitism and defend high art, but, more negative than Polan, they go on to oppose "dictatorial" intellectuals, "vacuous" academic formalism, "mindless" popular culture, "politically correct" feminists, Blacks, or radicals, and "nihilistic" postmodern anti-aesthetics. Neither the receptions of *Tess, Invitation, Unbearable, The Prague Orgy, The Bluest Eye* and *Sula* nor those of *From Russia, The Spy Who Came in from the Cold, One Lonely Night,* and *Deadlock* show, however, that literary institutions defend elitist privileges or impose a tyrannical political correctness; rather, as I indicated in the introduction, these institutions have grown in number and in importance and as a result have acquired greater influence upon and responsibility for popular culture as well as women's and African American literature.

As Bennett points out, literature is a historical construct whose opposition to nonliterary discourses has changed markedly, especially in the twentieth century, when the media have been so influential;[30] however, these defenses of high art ignore those changes. Moreover, the opposition of high art and popular culture developed in very different conditions. The opposition first emerged in the Romantic era, when, as I noted in chapter 2, to accommodate the newly established public sphere of the British middle classes, Samuel T. Coleridge and William Wordsworth forcefully defended the autonomy of Shakespeare's imagination and rejected the "mechanical" genres of the neoclassical critics and the sensationalist dramas of the urban theater. In the same era, the traditional man of letters defended the liberal public sphere established by neoclassical humanism, but in the late nineteenth and early twentieth centuries the corporate expansion of the popular media, together with the emergence of elite modernist and postmodernist art, degraded this fragile public sphere and greatly exacerbated the conflict of high art and popular culture. To oppose this fragmentation and decline, traditional critics, who founded the modern English department, defended the unifying cultural authority of Austen and other canonical writers; nonetheless, by the 1940s and 1950s, expanding Anglo-American universities absorbed avant-garde artists and liberal intellectuals, making their work more influential but further exacerbating the conflict of high and popular art. As I noted in previous chapters, at this time traditional critics of *Hamlet* and *Pride and Prejudice* accommodated the historical and formal methods which in earlier eras had so sharply opposed each other. Turning eclectic, these critics not only assimilated contrary methods, they defended the autonomy of high art because they feared that the liberal public was fragmented and degraded by what Irving Howe called "[t]he spreading blight of television, the slippage of the magazines, the disasters of our school system, the native tradition of anti-intellectualism, the cultivation of ignorance by portions of the counterculture, the breakdown of coherent political and cultural publics, [and] the loss of firm convictions within the educated classes."[31]

Scholars point out that a broad range of critics, including the New Critics, the New York intellectuals, and the Frankfurt School of Social Theory, justified the subversive force of modern high art because they feared totalitarian communism, liberal fellow travelers, industrial or capitalist production, and the fragmentation and decline of the public sphere.[32] For example, after World War II the New Critics, who dominated major American universities at that time, promoted the modernist avant-garde and dismissed popular culture. Originally supporters of the Southern Agrarian movement, they defended the organic community and patriarchal traditions of the Old South and condemned the "progress," industry, liberalism, science, wealth, bureaucracy, and democratic equality of the Yankee North. When the Cold War began, they grew more liberal but still considered communism and popular culture totalitarian threats to individual artistic freedom.[33] The New York intellectuals, whose most important members included Richard Chase, Irving Howe, Alfred Kazin, Philip Rahv, and Lionel Trilling, feared that the economic security, ideological conformity, and alienating professional jargon of the burgeoning modern university would isolate them from the fragile space of the public sphere;[34] nonetheless, to secure their position in the university, these intellectuals allied themselves with the dominant formal critics, turning high modern art into what Lionel Trilling called "a polemical concept" and condemning the ideological conformity and cultural decline imposed by Stalinist intellectuals and popular culture.[35]

The New Critics and the New York intellectuals defend high art because of the Cold War, intellectual isolation, the degraded public sphere, and other post-World War II conditions which no longer obtain—communism has ended, the university has expanded, and, far from dominating their consumers, the popular media compete for influence and support. Formulated in the World War II era as well, the Frankfurt School's influential sociohistorical defense of high art also takes for granted these outdated conditions.

In *The Dialectic of Enlightenment* (1944), Adorno and Horkheimer claim, for example, that, while high art resists its degraded character as a commodity, popular culture, so blatantly governed by capitalist enterprises, always accepts its "commodified" nature.[36] Moreover, to explain why high art alone resists the commodified character of capitalist production, Adorno and Horkheimer maintain not only that under monopoly capitalism specialized universities divorce the intellectual from the public sphere but also that Enlightenment science dominates and dehumanizes the modern era; however, as I noted in the introduction, the vast expansion of the modern university has positive import: it greatly increases the accessibility and influence of literary studies and, as a result, counters the dehumanizing import of Enlightenment science. As Habermas says, the Enlightenment tradition overcomes the disciplines' reified character by making expert knowledge accessible to the public sphere, not by speculatively reconstructing the social totality.[37] The opposition of high art and popular culture breaks down because this expansion, accessibility, and new influence enable literary studies to distinguish the diverse interpretive communities of high art and popular culture and to influence public taste and popular culture.

In these new conditions, the specialized literary study of modern educational institutions fosters enlightenment and democracy and does not simply obscure the underlying totality or impose ruling-class domination. Fredric Jameson acknowledges the new conditions, yet he defends Adorno and Horkheimer's belief that, while high art resists capitalist commodity production, popular culture supports it.[38] Assimilating postmodern theory and art to a traditional historical period, he argues that the postmodern era effaces the "older (essentially high modernist) frontier between high culture and so-called mass or commercial culture," integrating them both into "commodity production generally." This argument acknowledges that the historical conditions justifying the Frankfurt School's defense of high art have changed but nostalgically laments high art's lost ability to resist "commodity production." Indeed, Jameson warns us that, by destroying this resistance, the postmodern era fosters "a whole new wave of American military and economic domination throughout the world";[39] still, if the expansion of the modern university enables literary criticism to exercise positive social influence, as post-Marxist reception theory claims, then the high art and popular culture of the postmodern era promotes democratic reforms, not "American military and economic domination."

Cultural studies and poststructuralist theorists who grant that, like popular culture, high modern art has been integrated into commodity production as Jameson and the Frankfurt School say, also acknowledge that the historical conditions justifying the Frankfurt School's defense of high art have changed, but these theorists claim that, even though high art now accommodates commodity production, high art still resists its commodified character and subverts established ideologies and stereotypes.[40] Like the poststructuralist critics of *Hamlet* and *Pride and Prejudice*, many of these theorists are, nonetheless, inconsistent: they repudiate the traditional opposition of high and popular art but still defend the subversive force of high modern and postmodern art. For example, Patricia Waugh maintains that postmodern culture subverts the traditional aesthetic foundations of high art and in a democratic way accommodates the practices of popular culture and modern social life; at the same time, she defends the oppositional force of postmodernism: "Instead of defending Postmodernism as an authentic response to the exhaustion of other modes of art or knowledge or attacking it as an inauthentic capitulation to commercial culture, why not see it as an attempt to modify the past . . . in the light of a present in which recognition of the pervasiveness of consumer culture is not, necessarily, total capitulation to it."[41] Along with the New Critics, the New York intellectuals, Jameson, and the Frankfurt School, poststructuralist critics like Waugh accept conservative fears of cultural decline, totalitarian conformity and oppression, and academia's disciplinary divisions and "political correctness" and, to overcome them, justify theoretical critique and/or the public sphere.

The changes of the late twentieth century, however, have made academic literary studies a potential arbiter of public taste, not a reified or elitist discourse divorced from public life and blind to the underlying socio-economic system. To critique the opposition of high art and popular culture is not to impose political values or intellectual dictates but to acknowledge criticism's new responsibility for and influence upon public taste. The high art of Nabokov, Kundera, Roth, and Morrison and the detective and spy fiction of Fleming, Le Carré, and Paretsky both affirm and undermine their generic conventions and ideological commitments not because academia seeks a dangerous self-aggrandizement or shows an elitist arrogance but because literature courses in schools, colleges, and universities can teach students to judge popular and high art in a more enlightened way. John Frow rightly says that "the 'question of value' is always involved in social struggle and continues to pose urgent political questions."[42]

Notes

1. Arthur Conan Doyle, *The Sign of Four*, 204.
2. For example, in *Adventure, Mystery, and Romance* (1976), John Cawelti explains the generic formula of the classical detective story but, instead of analyzing its incoherence, regrets its conservative import. He says that, originated by Edgar Allan Poe, the detective story has many features, including an unsolved crime which the story investigates, a narrator who like Watson effectively manipulates the reader, and a detective whose status as a gentlemanly amateur justifies his detachment, brilliance, eccentricity, insight, analytic power, and so on. Cawelti adds that his solution of the crime provides "the single right perspective and ordering of events" (89) but allows the middle-class reader to preserve his or her serenity and ignore social injustice (95-98). John Docker, who emphasizes the rich variety and continuing vitality of both detective and spy fiction, defines it more broadly: its generic conventions include not only the gentlemanly amateurs of Poe's fiction but the resourceful heroes and chivalrous knights of classical narratives and medieval romances. He grants that these conventions do not form a coherent whole or reflect middle-class norms, but, like Cawelti, he denies that detective fiction undermines its

conventions or engages in ideological critique. As he says, "[F]orm cannot be identified with ideology, cultural conventions are not the same as discourse" (*Postmodernism and Popular Culture*, 221). For a contrary view, see Tony Bennett, who says that, popular culture reveal richness of meaning and complexity of form, yet formal critics attribute a nonreferential, complex, ambiguous essence to high art but reduce popular culture to a mechanically reproduced object or "message" ("Marxism and Popular Fiction," 142).

3. Tony Bennett and Janet Woollacott, *Bond and Beyond*, 33-42.

4. For example, in *The Spy Story* John Cawelti and Bruce Rosenberg say, "No other writer so simply and forcefully expresses the basic formulaic structure of the heroic spy romance" (154). Similarly John Atkins says that "it would be pointless to enumerate all the occasions on which Bond has been held up as a standard" (*The British Spy Novel*, 90; See also Michael Woolf, "Ian Fleming's Enigmas and Variations," 96). By contrast, Tony Bennett and Janet Woollacott argue that in the 1960s and 1970s, when the Bond novels and films became popular, they effectively subverted the older spy fiction in which a prudish but gentlemanly British agent wards off threats to Britain's national integrity (*Bond and Beyond*, 83).

5. Umberto Eco, *The Role of the Reader*, 161. For Tony Bennett's critique, see *Bond and Beyond*, 76-77.

6. Eco, *The Role of the Reader*, 162.

7. See Tony Davies, "The divided gaze."

8. Bruce Merry, *The Anatomy of the Spy Thriller*, 219.

9. Jerry Palmer, *Thrillers*, 66, 86-88.

10. John Le Carré, *The Spy Who Came in from the Cold*, 202.

11. John G. Cawelti and Bruce A. Rosenberg, *The Spy Story*, 166.

12. The post-Cold War *Our Game* (1995) also shows a (post)modernist uncertainty undermining liberal Western ideals, but, more alienated than Leamus, Tim Cranmer, the first-person narrator, is disaffected with the West's liberal politics. The West supports Boris Yeltsin's postcommunist regime even though it represses the Ingush, a rebellious Russian nationality, as harshly as the czars and the former USSR did. Initially, he believes that, out of jealousy, he killed his former colleague Larry Pettifer, a university professor and a double agent, whose lectures and activism on behalf of the Ingush seduce Emma, Cranmer's mistress. Subsequently, he learns that Larry and various Russians schemed to steal millions of Russian rubles in order to arm the insurgent Ingush. Prosecuted for aiding Larry, not killing him, he travels to the East to find Larry and, if possible, to win Emma back, but he discovers that Larry may be dead and Emma in permanent seclusion. Like Leamus, who commits suicide after he recognizes that the East and the West colluded to maintain the brutal Mundt, Cranmer joins a suicidal Ingush attack on the Russian army.

13. Jon Thompson, *Fiction, Crime, and Empire*, 158; see also LynnDianne Beene, *John le Carré*, 48-49.

14. Jon Thompson, *Fiction, Crime, and Empire*, 159-62; see also LynnDianne Beene, *John le Carré*, 51, 59.

15. John Le Carré, *Tinker, Tailor, Soldier, Spy*, 346. All further citations are from this edition.

16. Tony Barley, *Taking Sides*, 10-11.

17. For example, in *The British Spy Novel* John Atkins says that, to make sense of this "muddled situation," Le Carré distinguishes "ideology and philosophy." "Ideology is largely a matter of unquestioned and unchanging ends, and it is governed by strict authority; philosophy means looking straight at life and deciding, an individual and with only individual sanction, what steps to take" (179). Tony Barley also says that in Le Carré's fiction, oppressive, irrational, eastern communism represents an "unnatural" "foreign" ideology "superimposed by idealists, intellectuals and/or power seekers," while Anglo-American liberal beliefs remain "national, democratic, humanist, individualist, natural" (*Taking Sides*, 15).

18. See John Cawelti, *Adventure, Mystery, and Romance*, 186-89.

19. Max Collins and James Traylor, *One Lonely Knight*, 19.

20. Umberto Eco, *The Role of the Reader*, 144-46.

21. Mickey Spillane, *One Lonely Night*, 154. All further citations are from this edition.

22. Leslie Fiedler, *Love and Death in the American Novel*, 499-500.

23. Max Collins and James Traylor, *One Lonely Knight*, 24-27.

24. Mickey Spillane, *The Girl Hunters*, 186. All further citations are from this edition.

25. Jerry Palmer, *Thrillers*, 86-88.

26. For example, in "Detecting the Phallus," Teresa Ebert says, "This is especially the case in regard to mainstream women detectives, even feminist ones such as Paretsky's V. I. Warshawski . . . the woman detective functions as an agent of patriarchy, and if she is a feminist she often does so in spite of herself and her politics" (14). See also Glenwood Irons, "New Women Detectives," 138; and Kathleen Klein, *The Woman Detective*, 201.

27. Sara Paretsky, *Deadlock*, 176.

28. Sara Paretsky, *Burn Marks*, 48. All further citations are from this edition.

29. Dana Polan, "Postmodernism and Cultural Analysis Today," 50.

30. Tony Bennett, *Formalism and Marxism*, 15.

31. Irving Howe, *A Critic's Notebook*, 128.

32. See Thomas Schaub, who suggests that after World War I liberal thought needed to "preserve high culture from the degradations of mass culture . . . [which] was associated with totalitarian control" (*American Fiction in the Cold War*, 17). Similarly, Alan Sinfield suggests that the "myths of free literary endeavour and the Free World help to generate each other" (*Faultlines*, 102). In "Mapping the Postmodern," Andreas Huyssen also claims that "the age of Hitler, Stalin, and the Cold War produced specific accounts of modernism . . . whose aesthetic categories cannot be totally divorced from the pressures of that era" ("Mass Culture as Woman," 26). William Pietz points out that in the post-World War II era Cold War ideologues insisted that the genuine intellectual resists the party's "total control" and defends

rational ideals ("The 'Post-Colonialism' of Cold War Discourse," 65). Christopher Norris insightfully suggests that, thanks to *1984*, these views "ended up as second nature, not only for Orwell but for a whole generation of collusive Cold-War ideologues" ("Language, Truth and Ideology," 242). See also Andrew Ross, *No Respect*, 42-64.

33. See Mark Jancovich, *The Cultural Politics of the New Criticism*, 71-101.

34. For a full account of the New York intellectuals, see Vincent Leitch, *American Literary Criticism*, 81.

35. Lionel Trilling, *Sincerity and Authenticity*, 94; see also Leitch, *American Literary Criticism*, 109-14, and Shumway, *Creating American Civilization*, 279-87.

36. Theodor Adorno and Max Horkheimer, *Dialectic of Enlightenment*, 352-53.

37. Jürgen Habermas, "Modernity—An Incomplete Project," 9.

38. Fredric Jameson, *Late Marxism*, 229-31.

39. Fredric Jameson, "Postmodernism, or The Cultural Logic of Late Capitalism," 54-57.

40. Some of these theorists say that "postmodern" fiction fails to produce a rational or coherent answer and, as a result, undermines the generic conventions of popular culture. For example, William Spanos, who considers the "anti-detective" story the "paradigmatic literary archetype" of the postmodern imagination, suggests that such stories violently frustrate the "programmed expectations" of the detective drama series, including those expectations which find their "fulfillment in the imposed and habituating certainties of the well-made world of the corporate and totalitarian states" (See *Repetitions*, 24-25; see also Stefano Tani, *The Doomed Detective*, 46). Other theorists grant that popular culture subverts its generic conventions and ideological commitments or that high art assimilates the practices of popular culture. For example, Jim Collins dismisses the traditional belief in high art; as he says, to suggest that "[a]vant-garde textuality is the only course of resistance (and therefore the only 'authentic' art) reveals a profoundly disturbing elitism"(*Uncommon Cultures*, 14; see also John Docker, *Postmodernism and Popular Culture*). Collins argues that popular detective fiction critiques its own ideological distinctions and establishes its own discursive realm with its own sense of justice. He goes on to claim, however, that popular detective fiction does not resist the sociohistorical realm of established beliefs or institutional practices. As a consequence, he preserves the traditional autonomy of figural forms.

41. Patricia Waugh, *Practicing Postmodernism*, 61. Similarly, in *Literary into Cultural Studies* Anthony Easthope complains that in the Frankfurt School's account popular culture dupes ordinary readers into enjoying it (79), but he still shows that the modernist text *Heart of Darkness* is ironic, "always meaning more than it says" (91), while the popular *Tarzan*, for example, is "unironic, literal, closed, delivering a single meaning with the signifier of a single lexemic item . . . an effect reinforced by what has often been noted in popular culture, the formulaic and re-

petitive nature of the material" (91). Easthope denies that this literal, unironic meaning makes the popular text inferior to the high modernist text; however, he concludes that the Frankfurt School rightly construes popular cultural discourse as a matter of "consumption, not production, entertainment, not work," because he favors its theoretical critique of popular fantasy and wish-fulfillment (100). In *Crusoe's Footprints*, Patrick Brantlinger also admits that Adorno and Horkheimer's critique of Enlightenment science is too negative and despairing (185). Like Easthope, he claims that "art or high culture is no more radical or liberating in and of itself than is commodified mass culture" (196); however, he still defends the mimetic realism and the utopian potential with which humanist Marxism and the Frankfurt School endow art. He argues that these traditional approaches more effectively affirm "the promise of a future authentic social rationality" than the postmodern critique of objectivity and representation does (185). See also Richard Johnson, who argues in "What is cultural studies anyway?" that cultural studies can retain its subversive force if it resists assimilation by established departments.

42. John Frow, *Cultural Studies and Cultural Value*, 4.

Chapter 6
Orwell as a Neoconservative: The Reception of *1984*

> Our whole project of "human liberation" has rested on a series of gigantic illusions. The catastrophic consequences of our failures during this century . . . cannot be dismissed as aberrations. . . . The allegedly high ideals we placed at the center of our ideology and politics are precisely what need to be reexamined, but they can no longer even be made a subject for discussion in the mass media and our universities, to say nothing of the left itself.[1]
> —Eugene Genovese, Marxist historian

The emergence of poststructuralist theory, women's studies, and African American and other new programs has exposed the humanities to the neoconservative polemics represented by Eugene Genovese's condemnation of Marxism, the universities, and the left. Reception theory repudiates such polemics, examines the humanities' diverse interpretive communities and their changing sociohistorical contexts, and fosters a progressive coalition of "new social movements" because in the 1990s academic literary study grew so diverse and influential. On that basis, the last chapter suggested that the traditional opposition of high art and popular culture breaks down because both high art and popular culture accept and undermine their liberal ideals, generic conventions, and ideological commitments. The reception of *1984* suggests, by contrast, that, while the liberal realism of the New York intellectuals and others justifies the novel's historical truth, this liberal criticism, like Genovese's Marxism, supports the neoconservative politics whose triumphs in the 1990s have undermined the humanities, minorities, women, homosexuals, the working classes, and higher education. As I noted in chapter 3, the Victorian liberals who established Austen's high canonical status and the modern authorial critics who justified her high moral authority reject the neoclassical ideals of Shakespeare's humanist defenders and advocate the plain language of the "common man." So do the New York intellectuals and other liberal realists, but, instead of repudiating the opposition of popular culture and high modernist art, they go on to assimilate modernism to this public sphere. Indeed, Lionel Trilling termed the authenticity of high modernist art "a polemical concept" resisting the ideological conformity and cultural decline imposed by Stalinist Marxism, liberal fellow travelers, and popular culture.[2] As a result, just as traditional Marxists defend humanist ideals of *Hamlet* and ignore the progressive import of poststructuralist accounts, traditional critics of *Pride and Prejudice* emphasize the moral truth of the novel and deny the progressive import of its diverse readings, generic critics of Cold War detective and spy fiction describe the sociohistorical truths of its conventions and overlook its critique of its ideologies, so liberal realists like the New York intellectuals and others esteem *1984*'s historical truth and support neoconservative politics.

Of course, critics of all types—radical and conservative, formal and historical, traditional and poststructuralist—praise *1984* not only because it critiques the Enlightenment ideals of totalitarian regimes but also because it forcefully defends the public sphere, which, as I noted in previous chapters, the neoclassical humanists established in the eighteenth century and which the twentieth-century expansion of the culture industry and of the university fragments and degrades. It is true that Orwell condemned imperialist oppression in Burma, the suffering of impoverished city dwellers, the exploitation of British coal miners, the fascist victory in Spain, and the Stalinist influence on the left, yet, far more influential than other accounts, the liberal realist account of *1984* maintains that, as a defense of the common man or the liberal "public sphere," *1984* condemns "dictatorial" intellectuals, "vacuous" academic formalism, "mindless" popular culture, "politically correct" feminists, Blacks, or radicals, and "nihilistic" postmodern anti-aesthetics—the familiar targets of neoconservative polemics. Formal, feminist, Frankfurt School, and postmodern critics oppose this neoconservative account of the novel, but, since they too defend the common man or the liberal public sphere, they do not escape key neoconservative doctrines, including the nightmare of totalitarian communism, ideological conformity, and cultural decline.

Dystopian Pessimism in *1984*

1984 is a dystopian satire, as most critics say, but it does not defend the common man or the public sphere; rather, *1984* allows only a metaphysical opposition to totalitarian communism. *1984* depicts a future totalitarian society which accepts the Enlightenment belief that science and technology produce a better society but actually blends twentieth-century fascism and communism.[3] The high modernist and postmodernist fiction of Nabokov, Kundera, and Roth also satirizes the utopian ideals of Enlightenment science, but, as I noted in the last chapter, the reflexive self-conscious art of this fiction undermines the traditional public realism of a Dickens or a Fielding. In Charles Dickens's liberal fashion, *1984* promotes, by contrast, the realist faith that facts, ideas, information, and personal values provide a meaningful opposition to a mad totalitarian world; however, that liberal faith reduces the novel's opposition to a metaphysical quest for truth and endows the totalitarian government with omnipotent, godlike powers which render the novel, in Williams's terms, "profoundly damaging" to "socialism and a centralized economy."[4]

For example, Goldstein's book indicates that Oceania blends and exceeds twentieth-century fascism and communism. Written by O'Brien, this book restates the Enlightenment belief that modern science produces freedom and equality, but, to preserve the social hierarchy, the ruling elites institute war, limit education, and destroy technology. Oceania, Eastasia, and Eurasia, the three totalitarian states which divide the world of *1984*, constantly fight for dominance because, intolerant and oppressive, the ruling party fosters hatred, warfare, sexual repression, and ideological conformity.

In addition, the intense sexual love and painful physical torture depicted in *1984* parody the utopian belief that the rational society of the future eliminates volcanic human emotions.[5] O'Brien's tortures of Winston and Julia adapt them to Oceania but leave them passionless and miserable. Similarly, when O'Brien says that two and two can equal five, or when Oceania's ruling party announces great improvements in chocolate production, the Party, like Swift's Houyhnhnms, shows a horrifying desire for power and domination, not a commitment to a rational society.

This satire forcefully undermines the Enlightenment's utopian faith in science and progress; however, influenced by James Burnham, Orwell accepted the totalitarian view of communism. Gary Dorrien points out that, even though Orwell faulted James Burnham's power worship, "Orwell's intellectual debt to Burnham was . . . considerable."[6] Initially a radical Marxist but eventually honored by President Reagan, Burnham, along with Sidney Hook, Lionel Trilling, Norman Podhoretz, Hilton Kramer, Irving Kristol, and others, led "the neoconservatives' ideological war against communism."[7] As Dorrien says:

> [T]he key conceptual categories of neoconservativism were formulated by Burnham. It was Burnham who theoretically generalized the symmetry between Nazi and communist forms of totalitarianism. . . . And when the war turned out rather differently than he expected, it was Burnham who provided the ideological apparatus for fighting what he called the Third World War.[8]

This "ideological apparatus" included Burnham's *The Managerial Revolution*, which provided Orwell his description of the world's divisions as well as Goldstein's account of "Oligarchical Collectivism" and established the familiar belief that totalitarian communism originates in the liberal Enlightenment but allows no differences of opinion and no resistance or opposition.

As I noted in the introduction, like the post-Marxists Laclau and Mouffe, liberal Russian historians claim that the "uneven development" of feudal Russian institutions explains this oppression more than the Enlightenment's ideals of objectivity, science, and historical truth.[9] Moreover, the historians grant that the Stalinists did some good: they changed the backward, agricultural USSR to a progressive, urban society, with many large cities, an educated population, and a public culture;[10] similarly, Laclau and Mouffe say that the working class, which built factories and schools, educated the population, and developed the cities, accomplished the positive modernizing tasks of the Russian bourgeoisie. By contrast, demonizing communism, totalitarian theorists emphasize the Enlightenment origins and evil consequences of the Stalinist regime but ignore its feudal roots and positive achievements.[11] Both Mikhail Gorbachev and Boris Yeltsin came out of the Soviet Communist Party, whose internal reforms destroyed it and the former USSR, yet totalitarian theorists consider any positive reform of it an impossibility.[12]

As a consequence, *1984* allows only vacuous, empiricist grounds of resistance. In Oceania's history, Winston's memory, an old photo, a forgotten jingle, a converted church building, a dreamy paperweight, Goldstein's subversive book, and the vacuous prols, Winston repeatedly seeks but fails to find undeniable empirical grounds on which to resist Big Brother and the Party. As Anthony Easthope says, Winston mixes up the undemocratic manipulation of documents, records, and the media with the metaphysical pursuit of an absolute ground or "immobility."[13]

For example, Winston considers the cult of Big Brother appropriate for kids and immature adults but still imagines that in a dream O'Brien told Winston to expect to meet him where there is no darkness. Since during a two-minute hate O'Brien briefly glances at him, Winston also imagines that O'Brien supports Goldstein and the Brotherhood even though O'Brien belongs to the Inner Party. By contrast, when Julia first glances at him, he wants to cut her throat because, as Jenny Taylor says, she amounts to a "fetishized" projection of "male sexual obsessions and fears."[14] Although Winston derisively terms her "a rebel from the waist down,"[15] she resists his desire to tell O'Brien about their rebellion, whereas he imagines that whether O'Brien is a friend or a foe will make no difference. Indeed, just as in his dreams he survives while his mother and younger sister drown, so in room 101 he sacrifices Julia to escape the rats ready to eat his face: "Do it to Julia!"(236). O'Brien's torture and omniscience—he read Winston's diary and taped his conversations—expose the vacuity of Winston's metaphysical opposition. Two plus two can be five if the Party wishes it.

Doublethink prevails since the novel allows no grounds for resistance besides Winston's metaphysical quest. Unlike other dystopias, this novel reduces the Brotherhood to just another fantasy concocted and perpetuated by the Party. Winston says, "If there is hope, it lies in the prols" (60), yet he dismisses the old prol, who remembers that he nearly beat up one of the rich capitalists and once wore a top hat like theirs. These memories are too rambling and unsystematic. Winston and Julia pursue "a hopeless fancy," yet he also dismisses the washerwoman's song about a hopeless fancy because he considers the song and the woman mindless. The Party does not regulate the prols or their popular culture because it amounts to a mindless diversion. Julia, who works in the Pornosec division but has no literary sensibility, just operates a writing machine. Winston eventually accepts Newspeak, repudiates sexual, gendered love, and worships Big Brother and the Party not only because a virtually omnipotent O'Brien intimidates and tortures Winston but also because in the paperweight, the photo, Goldstein's book, the prols, popular culture, and even Julia Winston can find no opposition better than the metaphysical. Williams, who calls Orwell "brave, generous, frank, and good,"[16] rightly says that, because of his paradoxical isolation, the novel exaggerates the coercive powers of Big Brother and the Party, which could not stamp out all resistance or render itself impregnable and unchanging and the prols vacuous and passive.[17]

Realist Accounts of *1984*

Those critics whom I call realist expect good art to conceal its figural devices and to depict deep conceptual truth or, as Lionel Trilling says, "great ideas." These critics rightly interpret the novel as a dystopian satire undermining Enlightenment ideals but, unlike Williams, go on to claim that the novel depicts the objective truth of totalitarian society; as Irving Howe says, "[W]e have come close enough during the last half-century to a society like Oceania for the prospect of its realization to be within reach of the imagination."[18] I also call the realists liberals because the realists, who have made *1984* a virtual primer on communist work, sex, speech, family, art, government, warfare, language, intellectuals, or scholarship and "Doublethink," "Newspeak," and "Big Brother" household words, claim that the novel satirizes the ideals of the Enlightenment and vindicates the public values of the common man.[19] Certainly Trilling, who considered Orwell a great writer because he set the "plain truth" above "fashion" and "abstraction," maintains that Orwell reestablishes "the democracy of the mind," restoring "the society of thinking men."[20]

The liberal realist considers the novel's dystopian satire of the Party's irresistible powers truthful because, unlike Williams, the realist accepts the neoconservative belief that totalitarian communism permits no disagreement or opposition. O'Brien's triumph does not show the limits of Winston's metaphysical opposition; the triumph reveals, instead, what William Steinhoff terms "the logical consequences of the totalitarian ideas which had taken root in the minds of intellectuals."[21] I have argued, however, that *1984*'s dystopian parody does not justify the common man or public values, as the realists claim; the parody exposes Winston's metaphysical pretensions. The parody does not indicate Orwell's profound grasp of totalitarian communism; rather, the changes of the USSR refute the totalitarian theory which he acquired from Burnham.

Why then does the liberal realist praise so highly the novel's defense of public values and insightful depiction of totalitarian communism? The reason may be that, in addition to communist oppression, the realist fears the decline of the public sphere. As I noted in chapter 4, in the early twentieth century, the great corporate expansion of the media and the modern university, together with the emergence of elite modernist and postmodernist art, destroyed the fragile public space of the traditional realist and man of letters. To secure positions in the university, the New York intellectuals, the central group of *1984*'s liberal realists, allied themselves with the dominant formal critics but feared just the same that the economic security, ideological conformity, and alienating professional jargon of the burgeoning modern university would isolate them from this fragile public sphere. To defend it, they esteemed Orwell's commitment to plain speech and the common man. As Rodden says, they considered him their hero and, with their high praise of *Animal Farm* and *1984*, helped to make him a major writer.[22]

In the 1960s and 1970s, the New York intellectuals went on to condemn the newly established women's, Marxist, and African American studies and postmodern theorists.[23] These neoconservative jeremiads continued into the 1990s, when communism had disintegrated. As Dorrien points out, Midge Decter insisted even then that "American freedom would not be secure . . . as long as the media demoralized Americans . . . and America's schools inculcated racism through affirmative action and multiculturalism, and universities packaged anti-intellectual sophistries as learning."[24] Neil Jumonville rightly suggests, however, that the neoconservatism of the New York intellectuals and other liberal public critics did not begin in the 1970s and 1980s, when these polemics took place; it began in the 1940s, when Howe, Trilling, and others abandoned the radical Marxist politics of their youth and advocated a liberal realism defending Orwell and the vanishing public sphere.[25]

Dissenting Views

Of course, Howe never abandoned his commitment to democratic socialism. He praised the realism of *1984*, condemned the merely literary or linguistic interests of formal or postmodern critics, and founded *Dissent* in order to oppose the neoconservatives. Alan Wald points out, however, that "[n]eoconservatives Nathan Glazer and Hilton Kramer" considered "Howe's differences with them . . . more rhetorical than real . . . Howe has been partly captured by the very forces he himself set out to influence."[26] Feminist and formal critics and critical and postmodern theorists also oppose the realist orthodoxy, but their opposition too may be "more rhetorical than real." That is, the differences of the neoconservatives and their formal, historical, and postmodern opponents readily break down because even the radical proponents of the Frankfurt School or of postmodern theory do not consistently reject key neoconservative views, including the demonic communist other of totalitarian theory, the nightmarish decline of modern culture, or the political correctness of the humanities.

For example, Daphne Patai, a feminist critic, argues that O'Brien's triumph shows the patriarchal order bonding Winston to O'Brien and Big

Brother, not the inescapable domination of the totalitarian party. Patai reminds us that, during the two-minute hate which begins the novel, Winston is attracted to O'Brien, whom he considers trustworthy, and hostile to Julia, whose throat he would like to cut. At the end, when he faces electric and rat torture, he abjures Julia and loves O'Brien and Big Brother, but this painful result simply extends the male bonding indicated by the opening scenes. Patai, whose *Professing Feminism* faults the intolerance and ideological conformity of women's studies, goes on to accept, just the same, the realist belief that the novel reveals the bureaucratic intellectual's true motive—power for power's sake. In her terms, the Party cultivates and destroys worthy opponents like Winston because the Party treats the struggle for power as a competitive game played for its own sake.[27]

By contrast, Bernard Bergonzi considers the artistic traditions of *1984* literary, not dystopian or political. He points out that the London of *1984* draws upon the Victorian slums depicted by George Gissing's *The Nether World* and that the "golden country" of Winston's dreams echoes the classical tradition of a golden age. Like a Proustian artist/hero, Winston preserves his memories of his family, the "golden country," and London, makes sense of an old prol's memories, and recreates a traditional romantic relationship and even an old-fashioned domestic retreat. Bergonzi claims that this pursuit of the past, "a major theme of the literature of the past two hundred years," gives the novel a purely literary import, yet he still assumes that the novel depicts totalitarian communism objectively.[28] In addition, since the Party cannot finish translating Shakespeare, Milton, and others into Ingsoc before the twenty-first century, Bergonzi suggests that in literature, not in political engagement, Orwell found communism's most effective opponent.[29]

Patrick Reilly also esteems the novel's literary import, but he argues that in general Orwell's pessimism restates the philosophical despair of Eliot and other modernist writers, who doubted the Enlightenment belief that science and technology produce social progress and human betterment. Reilly claims that, like Jonathan Swift, whom Orwell greatly admired, Orwell satirizes modern humanity, which confuses genuine salvation with the lies and distortions of Big Brother. Reilly says that, in particular, *1984* retells the story of Milton's *Paradise Lost*. In Orwell's version, Julia and Winston come to occupy an Edenic world which permits love, privacy, and femininity, but, tempted by Julia, Winston bites the apple of knowledge and destroys their Eden.[30] The resistance of Winston, whom Reilly considers a "holy fool," amounts to a self-defeating pride enabling O'Brien to destroy him and Julia easily. Reilly believes, just the same, that the novel's historical objectivity makes Orwell a great writer: "He is the prime example in our time of the writer as hero . . . insisting on the unwelcome, unfashionable truth . . . that the *apparatchik* is ready to suppress."[31]

1984 and the Frankfurt School

The social theorists of the Frankfurt School reject the liberal realist orthodoxy more radically than these feminist and formal critics do but still do not escape the realist's neoconservative views. For example, Eric Fromm claims that O'Brien's victory does not show how oppressive life in the totalitarian future will be; O'Brien's victory indicates that modern life in both the communist and the Western "free" world also tends toward an oppressive totalitarian condition. Doublethink and Newspeak do not apply to a communist society alone; they apply to the Western world too. The leaders of totalitarian parties seek the power to create reality and truth, but so do the heads of the West's giant corporations. As Fromm says, *1984* reveals a new "managerial industrialism, in which man builds machines which act like men and develops men who act like machines."[32] This new industrialism characterizes the whole modern era, not just totalitarian communism, yet, like communism, this new era is "conducive to . . . dehumanization and complete alienation" (267). What's more, Fromm maintains, this era produces a cultural decline in which "men are transformed into things and become appendices to the process of production and consumption."[33]

Mark Crispin Miller, another proponent of the Frankfurt School, also dismisses the realist orthodoxy and its totalitarian theory and applies *1984* to modern Western life as a whole, not to communist societies alone. Miller argues, however, that *1984* depicts a "radically uncertain" dream world in which Oceania, "like some monstrous psyche," "ingests and transforms everything and everyone into its own dark element."[34] Winston unsuccessfully opposes this monstrous dream world not because the novel allows no opposition besides the metaphysical but because his internal and external worlds are equally uncertain and insubstantial.[35]

Miller grants that Winston expects pictures, memories, or facts to enable him to prove that the Party has fabricated history, but Miller argues that the differences between Winston and O'Brien break down because O'Brien, who quotes Winston's diary or records and plays back his words to him, adopts the same strategy.[36] Miller complains that the realists, who construe *1984* as an "anti-Stalinist allegory," fail to understand that the Party assimilates all oppositions: city and country, body and soul, thought and nature, and free, democratic world and Soviet dictatorship,[37] but Miller still considers the novel truthful, not fantastic. As he says, "This, then, is the real horror at the heart of *1984*—not that the Party is too devious . . . but that it sees through everything itself, so that any effort to subvert it can do nothing but resemble it."[38] Like Fromm, Miller claims that this relentless subversion also characterizes the Western corporate world. Its advertising destroys all resistance, producing an individual who "yearns and buys and yearns as if responding only to his heart's desires."[39] Like Fromm too, Miller suggests that the Party's evils stem from the Enlightenment, whose subversive practices have become what he terms an "oppressive orthodoxy." He too takes the relationship of Winston and O'Brien to indict intellectuals; as he says, "Orwell perceived a totalitarian tendency in all of modern intellectual culture."[40] Lastly, he too construes popular culture as a nightmarish decline whose restless commodification of art has not only deadened us to *1984*'s true horror but has made the consumer's life an equally horrifying obsession.[41] In the neoconservative manner, he adds that, since modernist and postmodernist theories construe all oppositions as linguistic and not historical, these theories reaffirm the Enlightenment's practices and thereby ensure the triumph of Big Brother and the Party.[42]

Postmodern Readings

Miller and Fromm critique the realist orthodoxy and repudiate totalitarian theory but still affirm the realist's nightmare vision of Enlightenment (ir)rationality and cultural decline. Poststructuralist critics also do not escape the realist's neoconservative views, but poststructuralist critics challenge not only the realist orthodoxy and its totalitarian theory but the nightmare vision of Enlightenment reason and cultural decline as well.

For example, Anthony Easthope grants that *1984* insightfully embodied the general ideas of totalitarian theory, as the realists claim, but considers this theory ideological, not objective, because, like the post-Marxists and the liberal Russian historians, he claims that the theory cannot explain the "development of Stalinist Russia out of Czarist absolutism."[43] More importantly, he argues that, constructing a liberal ideology or "subject position," *1984* grants Winston self-consciousness and individual autonomy and the state unconscious orthodoxy but cannot successfully distinguish fact and fantasy even though the novel denies its status as writing and emphasizes the empirical immediacy of "facts" and the transcendental status of the knower. Far from affirming individuality, love, and other public values, Winston and

Julia's resistance reveals the impossibility of such empiricist grounds of truth. O'Brien's triumph does not show the dangers posed by totalitarian intellectuals;[44] instead it expresses a sexual fantasy in which Winston, who frequently shows misogynistic feelings, disavows Julia and heterosexual desire, accepts his unconscious homosexuality, and loves O'Brien and Big Brother.

More forcefully than the formal, feminist, or Frankfurt School critics, Easthope demonstrates that the novel's rhetorical practices undermine its realist or empiricist ideology, but he goes on to suggest that the novel's dystopian fantasy reveals the paranoia produced by Winston's repressed homosexuality and, more generally, the "anonymous social repression" characteristic of twentieth-century monopoly capitalism.[45] As I noted in chapter 4, this theoretical critique of repression restates the fears of cultural decline shared by Howe and the neoconservative realists and Fromm, Miller, and the Frankfurt School, who also maintain that the fantasies revealed by great art resist the repression and decline imposed by capitalist rationality.

The liberal neopragmatist Richard Rorty also rejects the novel's pretension to historical objectivity and subversive satire, but, unlike Easthope, whose theoretical critique of capitalist repression defends the capacity of great art to undermine capitalist rationality, he argues that the traditional categories of high art and popular realism draw an empty, metaphysical distinction between moral seriousness and aesthetic value. As I indicated in the last chapter, reception theory describes both high and popular art as conformist and subversive; similarly, he considers the high art of, say, Nabokov different from, not better or worse than, the popular fiction of Orwell.[46]

This critique of traditional aesthetic categories forcefully debunks the "foundational" realist belief in art's neutral truths or independent realities but, unlike Easthope, preserves many of the liberal realist's neoconservative views. For example, while Easthope treats totalitarian theory as ideological, Rorty says that O'Brien's triumph condemns intellectuals who, because of the Enlightenment's failed ideals, "allied themselves" with a "spectacularly successful criminal gang."[47] Rorty grants, in other words, that *1984* rightly describes the former USSR, but he claims that *1984* indicates a contingent historical possibility, rather than the objective truths of totalitarian communism or modern social life. He also grants that, by "redescribing the Soviet Union," *1984* redescribes "the postWWII political situation,"[48] but he takes this redescription to show us "what vocabulary to stop using," not the era's underlying historical or political framework.[49] Rorty admits as well that the novel describes bureaucratic intellectuals like O'Brien truthfully but takes the novel to show that, when an O'Brien tears down the beliefs and the language of intellectuals, they suffer a "special pain": they lose the capacity to restore their coherence and selfhood.

Rorty also preserves the liberal ideal of public values. For instance, Easthope says that the text undermines its ideological project, revealing a modernist paranoia or an impossible quest for metaphysical truth, but Rorty insists that such ideological critique mixes up the public space of literal statement and the private space of figural ("ironic") theory. Thus, while Nabokov and Orwell both preserve liberal values, Nabokov's aesthetic concern with individual betterment is private, whereas Orwell's emphasis on social welfare is public.[50] More forcefully than formal, feminist, and Frankfurt School critics, Rorty and Easthope oppose the realist belief that *1984* depicts the historical truths of communist or modern life and vindicates the public values of the common man; nonetheless, because they wish to preserve the liberal values of the public sphere or the oppositional force of theoretical critique, they do not escape key neoconservative doctrines, including the nightmare of totalitarian communism, public values, or cultural decline.

Conclusion

The liberal realist view of the New York intellectuals and others rightly esteems the novel's dystopian satire but claims that *1984* embodies the historical truth of totalitarian societies and justifies the common man's opposition to an oppressive establishment. Scholars say that this liberal, public criticism can answer the neoconservatives and revive the Anglo-American cultural left;[51] however, even though Orwell's experience with Burmese natives, British coal miners, the Spanish Civil War, German fascists, and Soviet communists made him a forceful defender of democratic ideals, the liberal realist view has fostered the neoconservative belief that a nightmarish totalitarian communism justifies a tenacious opposition not only to communist parties but also to popular culture, liberal intellectuals, and feminist, multicultural, and postmodern critics. Formal, feminist, Frankfurt School, and poststructuralist critics reject the realist view, but their defense of the text's or of theory's subversive force implicitly accommodates this neoconservative opposition to totalitarian communism, theoretical language or "jargon," specialized discourses, and the humanities' new cultural and multicultural programs. Similarly, many critics defend the autonomy of high art because, as I noted in chapter 4, they fear that the great corporate expansion of the media and of the modern university, together with the emergence of elite modernist and postmodernist art, has imposed ideological conformity and degraded the public sphere. It is true, however, that, as I argued in previous chapters, the growth of higher education has positive import: it incorporates previously excluded populations of students, and it has made academic literary studies a potential arbiter of public taste. The previous two chapters suggested that, as a consequence, popular spy and detective fiction and high modernist and postmodernist art both affirm and undermine their generic forms, popular stereotypes, or ideological motifs. Because of this expansion and new influence, the next chapter suggests that the feminist and African American revaluation of Zora Neale Hurston's *Their Eyes Were Watching God* vindicates the humanities' new women's and African American studies.

Notes

1. Eugene Genovese, "Eugene Genovese asks the North American left, 'What did you know, and when did you know it?," 375.

2. See Vincent Leitch, *American Literary Criticism*, 109-14; David Shumway, *Creating American Civilization*, 279-87; and Lionel Trilling, *Sincerity and Authenticity*, 94.

3. See *Problems of Materialism and Culture*, in which Raymond Williams says that dystopias like *1984* emerge from the failed rationality which utopian societies would impose on our future social life (196-212). See also William Steinhoff, who says that in this novel the optimistic utopian equation between science and progress conceals a deep ignorance of blind human irrationality and fanatic dogmatism (*George Orwell*, 8).

4. Raymond Williams, *George Orwell*, 77.

5. Vita Fortunati, "It Makes No Difference," 119.

6. Gary Dorrien, *The Neoconservative Mind*, 42.

7. Dorrien, *The Neoconservative Mind*, 40.

8. Dorrien, *The Neoconservative Mind*, 40.

9. For example, in *Russia Under the Old Regime* Richard Pipes shows that communism elaborates the social and political traditions of Imperial Russia. He says that under the czars Imperial Russia never developed familiar Western distinctions between state and society, private property and public wealth, individual rights and executive power, or regional independence and central authority. Rather, in keeping with what Pipes terms an ancient "patrimonial mentality," the czars treated the Russian people and Russian wealth as their private goods, part of their royal family (54). Pipes admits that in the eighteenth and nineteenth centuries the czars initiated reforms which granted independence to middle-class entrepreneurs, university

scholars, and others, but Pipes argues that basically the patrimonial czars owned or controlled all land, industry, and commerce (194). Moreover, from the fifteenth to the nineteenth century, the czars set up a centralizing bureaucracy, including a pervasive and autonomous secret police. The communists resisted the bureaucracy and the police, but, when the communists came to power, they vastly expanded the czar's bureaucratic apparatus, including the police. Other Russian historians also argue that Stalin's tyrannical regime came to approximate the equally tyrannical regimes of the eighteenth- and nineteenth-century czars, who also built huge projects, forced the peasants into slave labor camps, censored the work of artists and intellectuals, established a strong, modernizing central government, and organized an extensive secret police and a highly ritualized bureaucracy. However, unlike Pipes or Brzezinski, these historians sharply distinguish Stalinism from communism. They argue that the Stalinist variety emerged because World War I, the revolution, the civil war, and the foreign invasion devastated Soviet industry and business. By the mid 1920s the country reverted to a primitive kind of agriculture, the triumphant alliance of peasants and workers broke down, and the Communist Party grew isolated and alienated. This internal isolation, growing Russian nationalism, and unceasing Western hostility led the Stalinists to adopt Imperial Russia's medieval practices, including the czar's belief in "revolution from above." Not only did the Stalinists impose collective farming, liquidate the kulaks (rich peasants), and purge agricultural and industrial specialists, they built up the secret police and eliminated their communist opposition. See Stephen Cohen, *Rethinking the Soviet Experience*, 38-70; Moishe Lewin, *The Making of the Soviet System*, 13-82; and Robert Tucker, "Stalinism," 94-104.

10. See Moishe Lewin, *The Gorbachev Phenomenon*, 30-82, and Robert Daniels, *The End of the Communist Revolution*, 67-69.

11. Many political scientists accept this view of the Soviet state. For example, in *Totalitarian Dictatorship and Autocracy* (1956), Zbigniew Brzezinski and Carl J. Friedrich, distinguished proponents of this view, say that, with a dogmatic ideology sanctioned by the state, a monolithic party ruled by a dictator, a terroristic system of police control, and a monopoly of communications, arms and weapons, and economic production, Soviet communism relentlessly imposed violent, totalitarian rule. Moreover, Brzezinski and Friedrich claim that "totalitarian ideology is rooted in the totality of Western ideas" (87). Brzezinski and Friedrich admit that the Soviet constitution accorded its people many democratic rights, but Brzezinski and Friedrich argue that actually the party, its administrators, its secret police, its armed forces, and its media simply implement the will of the dictator, who seeks a mystical unity of self and people (27-30). Although naive liberals may imagine that communists can and do reform the party and the society, the party allows no differences of opinion and no resistance or opposition (56). In *The Grand Failure* (1989), Brzezinski even insists that communist doctrine, especially the refusal to accept a multiparty system, is too rigid and too deeply entrenched to permit the reforms sought by Gorbachev (102). Sigmund Krancberg also says that "the now-

defunct Soviet Union retained totalitarian techniques uniquely adapted to its power in the modern world" (*A Soviet Postmortem*, 24). In *Today's Isms: Communism, Fascism, Capitalism, Socialism*, which reached its ninth edition in 1985, William Ebenstein and Edwin Fogelman admit that Marx had humanist leanings and that Lenin developed a Russian viewpoint, but they still explain Soviet communism as the systematic application of Marx's "principles." See also James R. Ozinga's *Communism: The Story of the Idea and Its Implementation*, 72-94. More liberal totalitarian theorists claim that after Joseph Stalin's era the USSR evolved beyond this model of communism. They grant that the Soviet Union outlined and applied Marx's scientific account of history's "laws" and socialism's "inevitability" but still maintain that Soviet communism violates Marx's humanist ideals. See A. G. Meyer, *Communism*, 121.

12. See Robert Daniels, *The End of the Communist Revolution*, 8, and Gary Dorrien, *The Neoconservative Mind*, 381.

13. Anthony Easthope, "Fact and Fantasy in '*Nineteen Eighty-Four*,'" 273.

14. Jenny Taylor, "Desire is Thoughtcrime," 29-30.

15. George Orwell, *1984*, 129. All further citations are from this edition.

16. Raymond Williams, *Culture and Society*, 294.

17. Raymond Williams, *george orwell*, 80-81; See also Alexander Dallin, "Big Brother Is Watching You," and Isaac Deutscher, "*1984*—The Mysticism of Cruelty."

18. Irving Howe, "*1984*: Enigmas of Power," 6; see also "*1984*: History as Nightmare," 53.

19. In *The Politics of Literary History* John Rodden points out that, while most critics, unlike Trilling, ranked the historical objectivity of *1984* below the formal self-consciousness of Joyce's *Ulysses* or Faulkner's *The Sound and the Fury*, they too valued Orwell's appeal to our common humanity (75-83). Similarly, Bernard Crick, who believes that Orwell "had the literary genius to go right to the heart" of totalitarianism's dilemmas ("*Nineteen Eighty-Four*: Satire or Prophecy?," 19), claims that the novel bitterly satirizes "power hungry" intellectuals and affirms democratic equality, personal trust, private memory, and plain language. See also Alex Zwerdling, who says that, since Orwell expected ordinary people, not powerful intellectuals, to resist the onslaught of a totalitarian society, he wrote a book "that would bridge the gap between popular and elitist culture"("Rethinking the Modernist Legacy in *Nineteen Eighty-Four*," 19); Carl Freedman, "Antinomies of *Nineteen Eighty-Four*"; Stephen J. Greenblatt, "Orwell as Satirist," 103-18; and Steven Spender, "Introduction to *1984*."

20. Lionel Trilling, *Sincerity and Authenticity*, 137-39.

21. William Steinhoff, *George Orwell*, 57-62, 221; see also Irving Howe, "*1984*: Enigmas of Power," 13; Robert Nisbet, "*1984* and the Conservative Imagination," 180; Lionel Trilling, "Orwell on the Future," 27-28; and Michael Zuckert, "Orwell's Hopes, Orwell's Fears," 41-52.

22. John Rodden, *The Politics of Literary History*, 10, 43-46.

23. See Harvey Teres, *Renewing the Left*, 242-43.
24. Gary Dorrien, *The Neoconservative Mind*, 350.
25. Neil Jumonville, *Critical Crossings*, 185.
26. Alan Wald, *The New York Intellectuals*, 332. Wald adds that most of those "integrated into the *Dissent* circle" moved "almost invariably and steadily to the right" (332).
27. Daphne Patai, *The Orwell Mystique*, 222.
28. Bernard Bergonzi, "*Nineteen Eighty-Four* and the Literary Imagination," 228.
29. Bergonzi, "*Nineteen Eighty-Four* and the Literary Imagination," 227.
30. Patrick Reilly, Nineteen Eighty-Four: *Past, Present, and Future*, 62-67.
31. Reilly, Nineteen Eighty-Four: *Past, Present, and Future*, 6.
32. Eric Fromm, Afterword, 267.
33. Fromm, Afterword, 267.
34. Mark Crispin Miller, "The Fate of *1984*," 25.
35. Miller, "The Fate of *1984*," 25.
36. Miller, "The Fate of *1984*," 33-44.
37. Miller, "The Fate of *1984*," 27.
38. Miller, "The Fate of *1984*," 41.
39. Miller, "The Fate of *1984*," 45.
40. Miller, "The Fate of *1984*," 36.
41. Miller, "The Fate of *1984*," 43-46.
42. Miller, "The Fate of *1984*," 39.
43. Anthony Easthope, "Fact and Fantasy in '*Nineteen Eighty-Four*,'" 267.
44. Easthope, "Fact and Fantasy," 280-83.
45. Easthope, "Fact and Fantasy," 280; see also Anthony Easthope, *Literary into Cultural Studies*, 100.
46. Richard Rorty, *Contingency, Irony, Solidarity*, 146, 170.
47. Rorty, *Contingency, Irony, Solidarity*, 171.
48. Rorty, *Contingency, Irony, Solidarity*, 171.
49. Rorty, *Contingency, Irony, Solidarity*, 175.
50. Rorty, *Contingency, Irony, Solidarity*, 146, 170.
51. See, for example, Harvey Teres, *Renewing the Left*, 12-13, 242-43.

Chapter Seven
Critical Realism or Black Modernism? The Reception of *Their Eyes Were Watching God*

In 1973 Alice Walker flew to Eatonville, Florida, to plant a tombstone on Zora Neale Hurston's unmarked grave. She posed as Hurston's niece so as to interview Hurston's physician, undertaker, and neighbors, wandered through the cemetery's waist-high grass in search of the forgotten grave, and commissioned a tombstone whose inscription declared Zora Neale Hurston "a genius of the South novelist folklorist anthropologist 1901 1960."[1] Walker says, "A people do not throw their geniuses away,"[2] yet, even though her historic trip to Eatonville initiated the recovery of Hurston's forgotten work, she does not explain why her people threw away Hurston's genius in the first place. More suspicious of such recovered work, Harold Bloom fears that "contemporary work by women and by minority writers becomes esteemed on grounds other than aesthetic," but he assures us that "[r]eading *Their Eyes Were Watching God* dispels all skepticism."[3] This assurance is welcome, yet, like Walker's visit, it does not explain why the novel was forgotten. If just reading the novel dispels "all skepticism," why was it neglected until the 1970s, when feminist and African American writers and scholars recognized its aesthetic value?[4] Did Richard Wright and its other detractors never get around to reading it?

Like Walker's tombstone and Bloom's reading, many accounts of Hurston's work seek to rehabilitate it, but, in explaining why the novel was forgotten, these accounts single out its Marxist detractors, who adopted the objective sociohistorical view of the realist approach, rather than the textual, figural, or rhetorical view of the formal or poststructuralist approach. Like the Marxist and authorial humanist views of *Hamlet*, the modern authorial and feminist views of *Pride and Prejudice*, the generic critic's defense of popular detective and spy fiction, and the liberal realist accounts of *1984*, the main accounts of why *Their Eyes* was forgotten, as well as what the novel is about, establish a debilitating opposition between the novel's realist detractors and its formal and poststructuralist defenders; however, while the previous accounts defend the common values and plain speech of the public sphere and in the case of *1984* go on to condemn "vacuous" academic formalism, "mindless" popular culture, "politically correct" feminists, Blacks, or radicals, and "nihilistic" postmodern anti-aesthetics, the main accounts of *Their Eyes* condemn the realists and, to justify the humanities' new programs and theories, defend formal textual and poststructuralist approaches.

To overcome this opposition, reception theory, which repudiates foundational aesthetic norms and examines the literary studies' reading formations and their sociohistorical contexts, construes realism as a changing institutional "apparatus" governing the reader's activity, not a fixed objective content excluding formal interpretations. As my accounts of the Victorian liberals establishing Austen's reputation, the generic critics defending the historical truth of detective and spy fiction's generic conventions, and the liberal realists justifying *1984*'s historical truth suggest, realism, part of what Bennet calls the "literary-pedagogical apparatus," evolves and changes with literary studies' changing practices. As a result, it is not the failures of the Marxist realists but the profundity of feminist and African American criticism that overcomes the debilitating opposition of realist and formal and poststructuralist views and that justifies the revaluation of *Their Eyes*. Scholars complain that, essentially "ideological," the feminist, African American, or postcolonial critique of the canon implies that, as Wendell Harris says, "no text is to be preferred for its presumed truth-value."[5] Reception theory does not accept the neutral objectivity of such pure "truth-value," what Hans-Georg Gadamer terms the Enlightenment prejudice against prejudice.[6] I will maintain as a result that, as both a realist critique of slavery and its aftermath and a modernist evocation of Black dialect and myth, the forgotten *Their Eyes* achieves greater depth than Jane Austen's realist *Pride and Prejudice* and William Faulkner's modernist *As I Lay Dying*. First, however, I will explain how the standard accounts of the novel's neglect and the novel's meaning preserve the realist/formalist opposition which reception study overcomes.

Explanations of the Novel's Neglect

To explain the novel's neglect, many critics fault the social or Marxist realists who, like Richard Wright and Ralph Ellison, considered the novel indifferent to social injustice and class conflict. As Mary Helen Washington says, "By the end of the forties, a decade dominated by Wright and the stormy fiction of social realism, the quieter voice of a woman searching for self-realization could not, or would not, be heard."[7] I grant that realists like Wright dismissed the novel because they believed that, as Georg Lukács said in *realism in our time*, great literature reveals the causal nexus of social forces bringing about progressive social change. While in exile in Paris, Richard Wright no longer shared Lukács's faith in communism, yet in "The Literature of the Negro in the United States," he declared that the "voice of the American Negro is rapidly becoming the most representative voice of America and of oppressed people anywhere in the world today."[8] More importantly, Lukács feared that modernist fiction disintegrates the subject, encouraging its solipsistic withdrawal from social life and from historical reality; in a harsher way, Wright simply complained that *Their Eyes* "carries no theme, no message, no thought." After Hurston graduated from Barnard, she acquired the reputation of a perfect "darkie," simple, childlike, and primitive, because she successfully entertained and flattered the very controlling philanthropist Mrs. Osgood-Mason, who financed her research and writing.[9] Alluding to this demeaning reputation, Wright adds that *Their Eyes* entertains White readers "in minstrel fashion."[10]

Scholars claim that, because of this harsh criticism, Hurston's work was forgotten by the 1960s, yet in the 1930s William Faulkner's work faced similar criticisms. That is, in the 1930s his work, like Hurston's, was attacked on the grounds that it indulged sensationalist interests, neglected social justice, and fostered modernist nihilism and absurdity. In the early 1940s, his major fiction was out of print, and, like Hurston, he was desperate for cash, which he earned by churning out short stories and Hollywood film scripts. After World War II, Hurston's work was neglected, and she was forced to accept employment as a maid and welfare support from the state; by contrast, Faulkner's work acquired a new importance.

For instance, in an influential essay, the New Critic John Crowe Ransom labeled Faulkner the preeminent postwar American moralist. As Lawrence Schwartz says, Ransom considered him "imbued with tradition, yet with an avant garde, modernist core."[11] To justify American postwar dominance, the New York intellectuals also praised the work of Faulkner, not of Hurston, but they construed him as an American modernist asserting the universal values of tradition, endurance, and individual will. Schwartz says that "the sharpest definition of Faulkner's role in the 'vital center' of politics and culture came . . . from Irving Howe, in whose reading Faulkner turned 'the southern myth' into a universal vision of the human condition."[12] Moreover, in the 1960s, when student rebellions initiated campus programs in African American literature and culture, these critics repudiated the "nationalist" African American critics reviving the work of Hurston.[13] Robert Penn Warren maintained that, if Western culture acknowledged its denial of African American humanity, Western culture would redeem itself.[14] Similarly, Howe claimed that Wright's protest fiction does not reduce Black life to traumatic violence, as Baldwin and Hurston said. Such fiction transforms American culture, forcing the White man "to recognize himself as an oppressor,"[15] rather than the integrity of African American culture.

While Faulkner's reputation rose, Hurston's reputation declined sharply not only because Marxists realists failed to appreciate Hurston's feminist or artistic concerns but also because the leading scholars and critics who defended the modernism of Faulkner and others adopted these conservative views; James Baldwin rightly complained that it was "literary politicians" who changed Faulkner "from struggling individual to cultural symbol . . . rendering Afro American writers invisible."[16]

It was not until the 1960s and 1970s that African American literary study, established in major Anglo-American universities, went on to revalue Hurston's *Their Eyes*. At that time, it underwent what Houston Baker, echoing Thomas Kuhns, terms a "paradigm shift": the Black Power movement gave rise to a new Black aesthetics, which dismissed the realist belief that African American literature adhered to common American ideals and which identified African American literature with peculiarly African American experience, culture, language, and history.

Baker says:

> Prior to the mid-1960s, scholars were led by an integrationism that permitted them to apprehend as "literature" or "art" only those Afro-American expressive works that approached or conformed to a "single standard of criticism." . . . The integrationists assumed as a first principle that art was an American area of achievement in which race and class were not significant variables. To discover or assert that the "Negro-ness" or "Blackness" of an expressive work was a fundamental condition of its "artistic-ness" was for a new generation to "flip over" the entire integrationist field of vision. Such a reversed, or inverted, perceptual reorientation is precisely what Henderson and his Black Aesthetic contemporaries achieved. Their efforts made it possible for literary-critical and literary-theoretical investigators to . . . include previously "unfamiliar" objects in an expanded (and sharply modified) American art world.[17]

Hurston's work was initially reclaimed by Alice Walker, not by these Black aestheticists; nonetheless, since this paradigm shift "made it possible for literary-critical and literary-theoretical investigators to . . . include previously 'unfamiliar' objects in an expanded (and sharply modified) American art world," the shift to a Black aesthetics explains what made the rediscovery of *Their Eyes* possible.[18]

Baker claims, however, that, once the Black power movement faded, the Black aesthetic movement revealed theoretical limitations overcome by the next generation: new formal or figural Black critics, whom he calls "reconstructionists" because they "reconstruct" pedagogy or criticism as a matter of close textual analysis. This claim implies that the African American realists, who demanded a single, universal standard of aesthetic value, rather than a Black or a formal standard, caused the novel's neglect; however, as the case of Faulkner shows, after World War II literary historians, the New Critics, the New York intellectuals, and other critics and scholars absorbed by expanding American universities adopted conservative assumptions and neglected *Their Eyes*. David Shumway points out, for example, that in the early twentieth century literary historians assumed that American literature shared the White, male, aristocratic, Anglo-Saxon roots of English literature.[19] In the 1920s and 1930s, when the study of American literature acquired professional status, historians adopted what Shumway calls the positivist microanalysis of a text's sources or influence or a writer's biography, era, or culture but preserved the traditional canon and its conservative assumptions.[20] Unlike the historians, the New Critics, who supported the southern agrarian movement, promoted the modernist avant-garde. As I noted in chapter 4, when the Cold War began, they grew more liberal, but they never gave up their faith in the Old South's organic community and patriarchal traditions or appreciated Hurston's work.[21]

Allied with the New Critics, the New York intellectuals also defended the modernist avant-garde, but they treated conservative modern writers as an oppositional force undermining the indiscriminate liberal faith in human equality and social progress. In the 1930s and 1940s, liberals and communists struggled for racial equality and social progress—American communists defended Stalin's regime but effectively promoted African American culture, albeit a masculine sort.[22] Despite this promotion, the New York intellectuals reduced communist practices to a totalitarian nightmare and liberal writers and critics to fellow travelers whose tolerance of communism showed their blindness to impending evil. Lionel Trilling maintained, for example, that the aristocratic ideals and religious piety of great modern art produced works of much greater value than those of liberal American intellectuals and democratic writers who, because of what he termed their "Stalinist proclivities," accepted simplistic abstractions and stylistic ineptitude.[23]

More fully than the conventional accounts, Baker's history of African American criticism explains why the novel was neglected until African American criticism was established in major universities; still, Baker's history too faults the realists even though conservative literary historians, New Critics, and New York intellectuals also neglected *Their Eyes*. What's more, far from vanquished, contemporary African American realists still condemn the withdrawn or apolitical character of formal criticism and defend the critic's obligation to his or her community. For instance, Barbara Christian says that "some of our most daring and potentially radical critics (and by our I mean black, women, third world) have been influenced, even co-opted, into speaking a language and defining their discussion in terms alien to and opposed to our needs and orientation."[24] Christian opposes modern Black criticism and defends critical realism on the grounds that it remains responsive to the community, not the literary establishment; Baker grants, by contrast, that the formal "reconstructionists" accommodate the "literary professional-managerial classes" but still insists that their work establishes a "paradigm shift" positively reconfiguring critical practice.

As these differences of Christian and Baker imply, the realists have not been vanquished. Indeed, their accounts of *Their Eyes* have evolved from Wright's negative traditionalism to more positive feminist and New Historicist varieties. For example, in the 1940s and 1950s, traditional realists, who, like Wright, found little social protest in the novel, claimed that it told an exciting and romantic story of Janie's adventures or asserted universal truth. In *Negro Voices in American Fiction* (1948), Hugh Gloster admits that Hurston is "more interested in folklore and dialect than in social criticism," as Wright says, but still praises the novel's "vivid pictures of social life in Eatonville, gambling dives in Jacksonville, and bean-picking communities in the Everglades" and "the social tension of the Southern scene."[25] Richard Bone, who considers the novel "Miss Hurston's best novel, and possibly the best novel of the period, excepting *Native Son*,"[26] also appreciates the story's action, but he interprets the novel in historical and universal, not feminist or African American terms. On the one hand, the novel's "dramatic structure" shows "the familiar cultural dualism of the Negro Renaissance";[27] on the other, the novel reveals the universal truths of the human condition: "Yet if mankind's highest dreams are ultimately unattainable, it is still better to live on the far horizon than to grub around on shore."[28]

In the 1970s and 1980s, when major American universities began to recruit Black scholars and to establish programs in African American and women's studies, the realists acknowledged the novel's feminist and African American sentiments but produced both harsh negative and positive laudatory readings. For example, in Wright's harsh manner, Darwin Turner treats the novel as a bad tragedy showing "Miss Hurston's continued emphasis upon intraracial and intrafamilial hatred."[29] More positive, Roger Rosenblatt claims that Janie's progress in the novel is "toward personal freedom."[30] In *Black Fiction* (1974), he terms the love and marriage of Tea Cake and Janie a rare achievement because the characters in Black romances usually seek both love from each other and success in the White world; nonetheless, in Wright's harsh manner, he calls their avoidance of the White world "a fantasy of independence." Rejecting any notion of Black autonomy or aesthetics, he claims that, like Romeo and Juliet, they recognize their tragic inability to escape the outside world waiting to destroy them.[31] In *The Way of the New World* (1975) Addison Gayle also grants that Janie's rebellion against racial and sexual tradition does not lead her to oppose "restrictive patterns" based on class, as Wright says, but, unlike Rosenblatt, he appreciates Janie's rebellions against traditional women's roles as well as middle-class, White culture. In *Their Eyes*, which, he says, "evidences the strength and promise of African American culture," Janie, an "outsider," emerges as a "modern Black woman" who is "strange and alien to American thought."[32]

Realist Black feminists also say that Janie develops a Black female self which no longer needs to identify with a man's life or aims or with White, middle-class culture; the Black feminists argue, however, that, far from recounting Janie's romantic adventures, the novel shows Janie's growth of a feminist as well as a communal identity. Nellie McKay claims, for instance, that, melding the narrator's standard English and the community's folk dialect, Janie's "[v]oice constitutes a force for liberation within the community of women."[33] Hazel Carby too claims that Janie develops a Black feminist self and that Pheoby's mediation may well liberate the community; nonetheless, more skeptical than McKay, Carby considers the liberation difficult and complicated because Hurston's "subject position" as a woman, a writer, an intellectual or anthropologist, and a Black aestheticist alienated her from Black folk culture. In Wright's negative manner, Carby complains, moreover, that, instead of warning us about the Black community's suffering and misery, the novel encourages us to believe that the community is happy and healthy.[34]

While the realists of the 1940s and 1950s find in the novel an exciting account of Janie's romantic adventures or an assertion of universal truth, the realists of the 1980s and 1990s consider the novel a forceful defense of Black women's independence and the Black community's integrity. In this way, the realist approach has evolved from Wright's harsh negativism to positive feminist and African American accounts, yet many of the critics who blame Wright for the novel's neglect claim that the novel develops the rhetorical devices of modernist fiction, not the independent self and community of the realist view. For example, both Henry Louis Gates Jr. and Barbara Johnson appreciate the metonymic projection and metaphoric assertion with which the novel expresses Janie's self-division. Johnson takes these figural devices to justify the novel's literary value. She says, for instance, that, after Joe slaps Janie for preparing a bad dinner, she imagines that her image of him fell off her mental shelf. Johnson considers this fallen image of him both a metaphoric description of his lost status and a metonymic introjection of her oppressive domestic life.[35] Citing Johnson, Gates also says that the novel employs these rhetorical devices, but he takes them to show African American concerns about which voice best represents Black life. Moreover, far from faulting Janie's lack of voice, he considers that the novel's use of free indirect discourse—the narrator, who speaks in the third person, reports Janie's or Joe's thoughts, rather than her own—initiates the multi-voiced narration of Black modernist art.

Michael Awkward complains that this formal reading divorces voice from action or social context. Janie develops a divided self, as the formal critics say, but, a version of what W. E. B. Du Bois called double consciousness, that self-division indicates the dilemmas of everyday Black life, not a purely rhetorical practice. Awkward grants that the novel's involved narration describes this complex consciousness but maintains that Janie achieves a "unified sensibility" reflecting the African American "precultural" unity of voice and action.[36] By contrast, considering Janie's deadly insult of Joe characteristic of African American "Signifyin(g)," Gates says that Janie's voice "is an outcome of her consciousness of division," not "a sign of a newly found unified identity."[37] Similarly, Johnson says that Janie's figural forms resist the unified, universal self to which realists like Eric Auerbach reduce modernist fiction. More generally, Johnson considers the realists' pursuit of a unified, universal human or Black female self a fantasy of male domination resisted by Hurston's figural art. In Johnson's feminist terms, "A woman's work is never done."[38]

The realists esteem the novel's sociohistorical insight and deny its formal autonomy; the formal critics dismiss its historical insight and unity and appreciate its autonomous rhetorical devices—as Robert Stepto says, the novel "forwards the historical consciousness of the tradition's narrative forms."[39] In Wright's manner, the realists still complain that, ignoring the disabling effects of racial discrimination, modernist or formal accounts of the novel divorce voice and action, subject and object, self and community, while the poststructuralists argue that the novel's figural forms, folk dialect, and free indirect discourse undermine realism's totalizing unities and preserve an autonomous Black literary tradition.

Reception theory claims that, by repudiating the foundational aesthetic norms of the realist and the figural approaches and acknowledging their changing contexts, criticism can escape the opposition of realists and poststructuralists.[40] To clarify this claim, I return to the text, which I situate between Jane Austen's *Pride and Prejudice* and William Faulkner's *As I Lay Dying*. On the one hand, the forgotten *Their Eyes* and the classic *Pride and Prejudice* both expose romantic illusions and misunderstandings and oppressive marriages in a realist fashion, but, instead of preserving Enlightenment optimism and middle-class propriety, *Their Eyes* reveals the debilitating effects of plantation slavery. On the other, in a modernist fashion *Their Eyes* and *As I Lay Dying* both repudiate middle-class propriety, elevate dialect to lyrical or mythical levels, and expose the metaphysical absurdity of life, yet *Their Eyes* achieves greater profundity.

Pride and Prejudice and *Their Eyes* examine the female characters' romantic and marital difficulties, including their gradual division into a public and a private self. In *Pride*, Mrs. Bennet insists that Elizabeth marry Mr. Collins, who will inherit the estate when Mr. Bennet dies. Nanny also tells Janie to marry Logan Killicks in order to gain economic security; however, more serious and practical than Mrs. Bennet, Nanny claims that Logan's farm will save Janie from the pain, torment, and abandonment which Nanny suffered during and after slavery. Elizabeth considers her mother's insistence ridiculous and with her father's help rejects Mr. Collins's hand, whereas Janie cooperates after Nanny slaps her and pleads with her: "Put me down easy, Janie. Ah'm a cracked plate."[41] Accepting Nanny's fear that romantic love will reduce her to little more than a man's "spit cup," she marries Logan only to discover a limit to or absurdity in Nanny's realism—his toenails are too dirty and his neck too fat for her to love him: "Some folks never was meant to be loved and he's one of them" (22). Nanny defends her realism: "Heah you got uh prop tuh lean on all yo' bawn days, and big protection, and everybody got tuh tip dey hat tuh you and call you Mis' Killicks, and you come worryin' me about love" (22). Janie's complaints kill her ("she dwindled all the rest of the day"[23]) because Nanny's realism cannot exclude Janie's "absurd" belief in love; however, Janie matures: "Janie's first dream was dead, so she became a woman" (24).

Elizabeth's friend Charlotte Lucas faces spinsterhood and economic dependence, rather than a dominating grandmother, but like Janie she marries to gain economic security. To Elizabeth's amazement, the unromantic Charlotte accepts Mr. Collins's offer but, unlike Janie, adroitly adjusts to Collins's absurdities and even to Lady Catherine's officious attentions. Even though Charlotte does not rebel against them, Elizabeth still finds in Charlotte's domestic arrangements and her tactful silences her unstated resistance to them. More importantly, while Elizabeth ridicules and rejects the pompous Mr. Collins and the wealthy Darcy, she, like Charlotte, divides into a public and a private self. For example, Darcy's letter refuting her criticisms of him depresses Elizabeth terribly because she had not expected that his treatment of Wickham or his sister "was capable of a turn which made him entirely blameless throughout the whole."[42] Retiring to her chamber to read the letter or to consult her thoughts, she conceals her private feelings more and more, even from her dear sister Jane. After she decides that he is just the right man for her, she does not admit it publicly, not even when her father ridicules Mr. Collins's warning against her marriage to Darcy. At the end, the novel celebrates their marriage, which unifies their public and private selves; still, as Darcy's influence steadily grows on her, she loses her inclination to laugh at him, and, like Charlotte, develops a meaningful private and an empty public self.

Jody Starks saves Janie from Logan but imposes on Janie a similar but much harsher self-division, as the formal critics say. For instance, he talks with the "big picture" talkers sitting on the porch, but he will not allow her to talk with them. He attends the mule's funeral, delivers an oration, but keeps her at home because he cannot believe that a lady should associate with "such commonness." Most importantly, when she spoils his dinner, he beats her, and, like the town, which keeps its resentment of Jody to itself, she divides into a silent but meaningful private self and a conventional but insignificant public self: "She had an inside and an outside now and suddenly she knew how not to mix them" (68).

Both Hurston and Austen assume that public speech overcomes the division between the characters' public and private selves. For example, Elizabeth often engages in witty public discourse. Unlike Jody Starks, Mr. Bennet grants Elizabeth this (male) privilege, but it embarrasses her mother, who orders her not to "run on in the wild manner that you are suffered to do at home" (29). Elizabeth freely disputes the opinions of one and all, just the same, and thereby wins the ardent admiration of Darcy. After she marries him, she teaches his sister to laugh at him too; still, once she can no longer hate Darcy, she loses her enthusiasm for witty disputation ("It is such a spur to one's genius, such an opening for wit to have a dislike of that kind" [145]).

Austen, who shares the Enlightenment belief that women and men have the same rational faculties, esteems public disputation; by contrast, as Cynthia Bond shows, Hurston considers the porch's "big picture" talk both impotent speech and male domination.[43] At the end Janie has discovered the "impotence" of the public speech, which at the beginning the narrator terms the "mass cruelty" of "the skins" (2); still, to overcome the self-division imposed by Jody, she struggles to engage in public talking. This struggle culminates when, after Joe calls her an old woman, she ridicules his sexual potency: "When you pull down yo' britches, you look lak de change uh life" (75). Jody retreats to his deathbed, sick from a bad liver and a wounded ego. When she tells him that he has never known her true self, he promptly dies—realism precipitates absurdity once again. More importantly, after Jody's death, Janie realizes that she had accepted her grandmother's blind faith in the slave owners' ideals—that owning things counts more than exploring the horizon. Like Sethe, who, as Toni Morrison indicates in *Beloved*, would rather kill her baby than allow Schoolteacher to return it to slavery, she angrily condemns those ideals and, by implication, middle-class realism as well.

Although *Pride* and *Their Eyes* both show that the romantic and marital difficulties faced by the female characters impose on them a self-division alleviated by public speech, *Pride* does not produce such a profound critique of middle-class marriage. Moreover, gradually restricted to Elizabeth's point of view, Austen's third-person narrator demonstrates a limited omniscience which, as I indicated in chapter 3, preserves a sharp distinction between standard English and the "vulgar" regional dialects. By contrast, *Their Eyes*, which destroys the opposition of dialect and standard speech, effectively depicts the folk mind of ordinary Blacks, not just the middle classes. In keeping with the Harlem Renaissance, which sought to demonstrate that Black folk culture was not simply the subject of comic minstrelsy but worthy of serious artistic depiction, Hurston, an accomplished anthropologist, cultivated an exceptionally insightful grasp of African American folk culture.

Janie's involved narration and Black dialect and folk culture bring *Their Eyes* closer to Faulkner's *As I Lay Dying*. Since these novels construe folk dialect and culture as an aesthetic object and reduce the narrator to a viewpoint different from, not superior to, that of the characters, these novels undermine the conventional opposition of Southern folk culture and the national middle-class culture. *Their Eyes* achieves greater depth, but with their multivoiced narratives these novels both depict absurdities subverting traditional realism's privileged omniscience and middle-class propriety.

On the one hand, while the Bundrens struggle to preserve their dignity, their trip to Jefferson to bury Addie reduces her death and their grief to absurdity. Cash's building the coffin of Addie, his mother, makes a terrible noise, yet he will not stop even when the dying Addie calls to him. Despite the cost, the pain, and the worsening smell, Anse won't begrudge the dead Addie the trip he promised her and won't impose on the neighbors on whom he does impose, while, having helped Anse so much already, the neighbors can no longer stop. Darl's practical decision to burn down the barn storing the coffin and the wagon for the night could have ended the painful trip to Jefferson, yet, betrayed by Dewey Dell, the sensitive Darl is sent to an insane asylum to save the Bundrens the expense of a new barn. Burying Addie in Jefferson costs Darl his sanity, Cash a leg, Dewey Dell her abortion, and Jewel his horse but brings Anse new teeth and a new Mrs. Bundren.

These absurdities of the Bundrens' trip undermine the middle-class propriety of Austen and other traditional realists. So do the highly distinct rhetorics of the young Vardaman, the sensual Dewey Dell, the omniscient Darl, the angry Jewel, the sententious Anse, and the other narrators, whose mutual incoherence puts the historical truth of the novel in question. While Peabody the physician says, for example, that Addie has been dead for ten days, Cash says that, while he was building her coffin, the dying Addie sat up in bed and yelled, "You, Cash." The religious neighbor Cora, who considers Addie's death a blessing because she is free of Anse, regrets that in a vain way Addie set her son Jewel above God, whereas, oppressed by her husband Anse and her self-righteous neighbor Cora, Addie resists this rhetoric of family and religion and defends silence and withdrawal. In a belated narration, the dead Addie complains that, far from signifying what they should, words enable people to avoid experience and to seek an empty salvation. Moreover, with a Joycean indifference, Faulkner describes not only the narrators' incoherence but also their moments of formal absurdity or stasis. For example, while Anse watches Cash build Addie's coffin, the narrator says that Anse, "from behind his slack-faced astonishment . . . muses as though from beyond time, upon the ultimate outrage."[44] To emphasize Anse's astonishment as this "ultimate outrage," the narrative places Anse's musing "beyond time."

In an equally modernist fashion, *Their Eyes* repudiates realism's omniscience and reveals middle-class absurdity, but, instead of such formal stasis and incoherence, *Their Eyes* achieves substantial insight. Janie's intense, romantic relationship with Tea Cake develops this profound insight. His playful, imaginative courtship shocks the town, which sees in it only mercenary motives, but pleases Janie, who rejects the town's (and realism's) middle-class assumption that without a wealthy husband she will not survive. Although Tea Cake eventually supports her financially, like Jody he initially treats her as a private possession. After he excludes her from his all-night party, she protests angrily, and he proceeds to teach her the rich games, work, talk, music, and food of Black folk culture. They move to the Florida muck, where she learns to shoot a gun, pick beans, talk porch talk, and to enjoy life in general. Interested in Tea Cake, Nunky makes her angry and jealous. Mrs. Turner's racial hypocrisy and unmarried brother anger Tea Cake, who turns jealous and violent, beating Janie and destroying Mrs. Turner's restaurant. Despite this brutality, the intense playing, fighting, working, socializing, and lovemaking fulfill her, yet metaphysical absurdity still informs this naturalist paradise. When a hurricane threatens the Florida swamp, an overconfident Tea Cake ignores the fleeing animals and Indians only to get caught in the hurricane's high winds and floodwaters. Tea Cake and Janie escape them but not the jaws of a mad dog, whose rabies drive Tea Cake mad as well. Overcome with jealousy and thirst, he reverts to a domineering chauvinist manner and tries to shoot her. She shoots him first—an absurdity of tragic proportions: "It was the meanest moment of eternity" (175).

After the trial and the funeral gain Janie the absolution of the curious White women and Tea Cake's angry Black friends, she retreats to her Eatonville home, where she tells Pheoby the lessons of her story—"tuh go to God" and "tuh find out about livin' fuh theyselves" (183). Pheoby, who feels as though Janie's story has made her a bigger person, promises to mediate Janie's differences with the contemptuous community; as Janie says, "My tongue is in mah friend's mouf" (6). In general, the involved narration of both *Their Eyes* and *Dying* undermines the privileged omniscience of traditional fiction and reveals the absurdity of established social practices; however, while the studied indifference of Faulkner's narration emphasizes the incompatibility of the narratives or the characters' formal absurdity or stasis, Hurston's involved narrator teaches the reader substantial truths—"tuh go to God" and "tuh find out about livin' fuh theyselves."

Although this account of the novel divorces it from its African

American context, the account emphasizes the profundity of the novel and thereby justifies the African American revaluation of it and, more generally, the critique of the Anglo-American canon. That is, Hurston's *Their Eyes* exposes its culture's absurdity in a substantial fashion, whereas *Dying* reveals only its formal absurdity; still, unlike *Their Eyes*, Faulkner's work acquired high canonical status. Hurston's *Their Eyes* also criticizes romance and marriage more profoundly than Austen's *Pride*, but *Their Eyes* was neglected, while *Pride* retained its canonical status. The main accounts of why the novel was forgotten and what it is about also esteem its critiques of romance, marriage, and middle-class conventions and justify its revaluation; however, my study of the novel's reception maintains that it is not so much the limited vision of Marxist realists as the conservative ideals and Cold War preoccupations of modern literary study that explain the novel's neglect. In other words, *Their Eyes*'s main accounts, which blame the Marxist realists for the novel's neglect, perpetuate the debilitating "culture wars" dividing traditional and Marxist realists from formal and poststructuralist critics, yet the formal analyses of the poststructuralists do not preclude a profound realist critique of social life because realism itself is a changing critical practice, not a fixed sociohistorical content excluding figural analyses. The Marxist and authorial humanist account of *Hamlet*, the modern authorial and feminist accounts of *Pride and Prejudice*, the generic accounts of detective and spy fiction, and the liberal realist account of *1984* also establish a debilitating opposition between traditional and poststructuralist critics, but these accounts dismiss the poststructuralist concern with race, gender, class, ethnicity, and other multicultural values in the name of humanist, ethical, formal, historical, or neoconservative ideals; by contrast, the profundity of *Their Eyes* indicates that realism does not escape or resist literary study's diverse reading formations or their institutional "apparatus" and that, as a consequence, its feminist and African American accounts have progressive import. The revaluation of *Their Eyes* and, more generally, the critique of the Anglo-American canon does not indicate that feminist and African American scholars dismiss literature's truth value or adopt politically correct ideals and values but that realism evolves in keeping with criticism's interpretive communities and their institutional "apparatus."

Notes

1. Alice Walker, "Looking for Zora," 307.
2. Alice Walker, "A Cautionary Tale and a Partisan View," 69.
3. Harold Bloom, *Zora Neale Hurston*, 1.
4. See Mary Helen Washington, "Foreword," x; Michael Awkward, *New Essays on* Their Eyes Were Watching God, 7.
5. Wendell Harris, "Canonicity," 118; see also Charles Altieri, *Canons and Consequences,* and, for a more radical view, Paul Lauter, "History and the Canon."
6. See Hans Robert Jauss, *Toward an Aesthetic of Reception*, 16-22, and Steven Mailloux, *Rhetorical Power*, 140-45.
7. Mary Helen Washington, "Foreword," viii; In a similar vein, Michael Awkward says, "Wright's view of literature [e.g., as a "blunt weapon"], along with his apparent lack of interest in the significance of female oppression, rendered him unable to appreciate Hurston's subtle critiques of . . . American society" (*New Essays on* Their Eyes Were Watching God, 12). Similarly, Henry Louis Gates Jr. says that "What we might think of as Hurston's mythic realism, lush and dense within a lyrical black idiom, seemed politically retrograde to the proponents of a social or critical realism" ("Afterword," 190). Echoing Bloom, Gates adds that Hurston's "complexity . . . refuses to lend itself to the glib categories of 'radical' or 'conservative,' 'black' or 'Negro,' 'revolutionary' or 'Uncle Tom'—categories of little use in literary criticism" ("Afterword," 186).
8. Richard Wright, "The Literature of the Negro in the United States," 145.
9. Mary Helen Washington, "Foreword," 9-11.
10. See K. A. Appiah and Henry Louis Gates Jr., *Zora Neale Hurston*, 17.
11. Lawrence Schwartz, *Creating Faulkner's Reputation*, 28.
12. Schwartz, *Creating Faulkner's Reputation*, 208.
13. Schwartz, *Creating Faulkner's Reputation*, 136-39.
14. See Mark Jancovich, *The Cultural Politics of the New Criticism*, 132.
15. Lawrence Schwartz, *Creating Faulkner's Reputation*, 121.
16. See Craig Werner, *Playing the Changes*, 28.
17. Houston Baker Jr., *Blues, Ideology, and Afro-American Literature*, 76-77.
18. Similarly, Barbara Herrnstein Smith says that a text may be rediscovered as an "unjustly neglected masterpiece" when "different of its properties and possible functions become foregrounded by a new set of subjects with emergent interests and purposes" (*Contingencies of Value*, 49).
19. David Shumway, *Creating American Civilization*, 123-28.
20. Shumway, *Creating American Civilization*, 189-90.
21. See Mark Jancovich, *The Cultural Politics of the New Criticism*, 71-101.
22. See Robin Kelley, *Race Rebels*, 120-21.

23. Lionel Trilling, *The Liberal Imagination*, 277-87; see also Daniel O'Hara, who points out that Trilling accepted Henry James's belief that "to question the last principle of coherence, the masculine character, is to undermine society completely, as the women take over the culture and the men 'lite out for the territories,' to their mutual destruction" (*Radical Parody*, 168).

24. "Race," 52; see also Cornel West, who argues that the "glacier shift from an African American literature of racial confrontation during the four decades of the forties through the seventies to one of cultural introspection in our time is linked in some complex and mediated way to the existential needs and accommodating values of the black and white literary professional-managerial classes who assess and promote most of this literature" (*Keeping Faith*, 39).

25. Hugh Gloster, *Negro Voices in American Fiction*, 237.

26. Richard Bone, *The Negro Novel in America*, 128.

27. Bone, *The Negro Novel*, 129.

28. Bone, *The Negro Novel*, 131-32.

29. Darwin Turner, *In a Minor Chord*, 108. He also finds some social protest in the novel: "Through Nanny, Miss Hurston denounced slavery and the wives of slave owners; through Teacake she ridiculed the southerners' habit of selecting certain blacks as their pets while abusing the others; and through Mrs. Turner she ridiculed Negroes who hate their race" (108; see also Ann Rayson). In addition, Turner finds some improvement—less caricature, more feeling—but many aesthetic flaws. For example, like French critics who considered Shakespeare's tragedies flawed, he complains that, despite the tragic conclusion, a "lighter mood develops . . . from her frequent admixtures of comedy and her tendency to report dramatic incidents rather than to involve the reader with the emotions of the characters" (106). He appreciates the serious tone of the first four chapters but finds the "impudent jovial chatter of the Eatonville folk" included in chapter 6 "[d]igressive and unnecessary" (107). More importantly, he considers Janie a perceptive delineation of "a woman whose simple desires mystify the men in her life" (108), but he labels her stinging insult of the dying Jody Starks "aesthetic inappropriateness": "Never was his conduct so cruel as to deserve the vindictive attack which Janie unleashes" (108).

30. Roger Rosenblatt, *Black Fiction*, 29; see also *Black Writers of the Thirties* (1973), in which James Young maintains that in *Their Eyes* Hurston wove the novel's "romantic elements into a pattern of protest; not race or class protest, but feminine and individual protest" (220).

31. Roger Rosenblatt, *Black Fiction*, 33.

32. Addison Gayle Jr., *The Way of the New World*, 147.

33. Nellie McKay, "Crayon Enlargements of Life," 68.

34. Hazel Carby, "The Politics of Fiction," 89-90.

35. Barbara Johnson, *The Critical Difference*, 163.

36. Michael Awkward, *Inspiriting Influences*, 55-56.

37. Henry Louis Gates Jr., "*Their Eyes Were Watching God*: Hurston and

the Speakerly Text," 187.

38. Barbara Johnson, *The Critical Difference*, 171.

39. Robert Stepto, *From Behind the Veil*, 166.

40. Similarly, in *Fables of Aggression* Fredric Jameson suggests that modernist fiction like *Their Eyes* possesses the resources to overcome its opposition with traditional realism. Even though modernist art derives from modern capitalism's reified social and artistic life, this art still resists reification and produces critical insight (14).

41. Zora Neale Hurston, *Their Eyes Were Watching God*, 19. All further citations are from this text.

42. Jane Austen, *Pride and Prejudice*, 133. All further citations are from this text.

43. See Appiah and Gates, *Zora Neale Hurston*, 24-26.

44. William Faulkner, *As I Lay Dying*, 72.

Conclusion: The Limits of Reception Study

My argument has been that post-Marxist reception study, which denies that literary theory can improve readers, resolve interpretive disputes, or transform institutional practices, explains the changing sociohistorical contexts of literary study's divided schools and movements and clarifies the progressive import of the humanities' new theories and programs. In Jauss's modern fashion, post-Marxist reception study maintains that the study of the reader's interpretive practices, rather than the author's intention or the text's figural devices, explains the history of a text. In Fish's or Mailloux's poststructuralist fashion, post-Marxist reception study repudiates the transformative force of canonical literature and traditional theory and explains the divisions and conflicts of modern interpretive communities. In keeping with Foucault's notion of knowledge as power and Laclau and Mouffe's concept of radical democracy, the post-Marxist reception study describes the sociohistorical contexts of literary study's established communities and clarifies the conservative and progressive aspects of literary study and the modern university. The objections raised to reception study of all types include the following: (1) instead of promoting a consensus or preserving the aesthetic norms, reception study accepts a relativist notion of literary division and fragmentation; (2) far from acknowledging the subversive rhetoric undermining the interpretive practices of the reader or the bureaucratic layers of academic institutions, reception theory accepts dead conventions and ossified institutions; and (3), rather than foster the revolutionary transformation of social life or ensure the agency and political will of the feminist, African American, and other new movements, post-Marxist (reception) theory accepts the status quo, with its class divisions, racial biases, and alienating commodity production. Reception study has value, especially since the conservative and radical polemics of the 1990s have so sharply divided and discredited the literary profession; however, there is much truth to these objections, which I will now discuss in more detail.

The first objection, that reception study lapses into relativism, means that, producing incommensurable results, reception study cannot establish a consensus or promote rational communication.[1] Reed Way Dasenbrock complains, for example, that, if our interpretations embody our beliefs or those of our communities, as Fish says, then criticism turns self-identical or solipsistic and fails to learn from experience or to recognize alterity or difference. Moreover, since the public accepts traditional notions of truth and objectivity, literary critics who accept such relativism cause the humanities' divisions and conflicts. As he says, "We've Done It to Ourselves." Such objections blame the messenger for the message. Unlike Protagorus, whose belief that the context of a statement always establishes its truth is self-refuting, reception study maintains that it is not the divisions and conflicts of all times but the divided conditions established in the 1990s and still influential which justify its critiques of theoretical norms and textual or figural practices and its defense of the humanities' new programs.

It is also true that, with concentrations, majors, and programs in women's, African American, gay, cultural, and multicultural or postcolonial studies, many departments and colleges have accommodated the new programs and theories and preserved consensus and rational communication. Reception study does not suffer from a vitiating relativism if it acknowledges the influence of the divisions and conflicts, yet the critique of reception study's relativism rightly emphasizes the times of unity and compatibility, when departments can assimilate new programs and approaches because critics may work in different areas but employ compatible methods and assumptions. As my studies of *Hamlet* and other texts noted, literary history shows many such moments, including the period from the 1950s to the 1970s, when expanding Anglo-American universities encouraged the mutual accommodation of the formal, textual and the historical, authorial methods, but, as my account of the 1990s and its influence indicated, there are also times when the profession is divided because scholars adopt incompatible methods and contrary beliefs. These moments of division do not take precedence over the moments of coherence, nor does what Foucault terms a ruptured, discontinuous history displace a continuous one. While the critique of relativism privileges unity over disunity, coherence over division, continuity over discontinuity, literary history includes both moments.

Indeed, as my book indicated, the receptions of *Hamlet, Pride and Prejudice, 1984, Their Eyes Were Watching God*, detective and spy fiction, and modernist and postmodernist art reveal moments of unity and affiliation as well as moments of division and conflict. For example, chapter 2 shows that the Marxist account of *Hamlet* sharply opposes the traditional and the poststructuralist or New Historicist accounts; however, although the traditional authorial, formal, and historical accounts oppose the Marxist accounts, the traditional and the Marxist accounts justify the ideals of modern humanism. Moreover, these accounts oppose the "antihumanist" poststructuralist accounts even though they promote contemporary interests in race, class, and gender. In chapter 3, Austen's traditional critics oppose feminist as well as poststructuralist approaches, but the traditional and the feminist critics both consider the sheer diversity of contemporary interpretations an embarrassment even though the many approaches to this novel have progressive feminist import. For instance, the Victorian liberals considered Austen's novels a humble chronicle of her era's customs but established the high canonical status and moral authority of Austen as well as the academic study of her fiction and other modern literature. The authorial, formal, and historical approaches, which evolved out of the liberal Victorian view, acquired progressive feminist import once female students and faculty broke down the liberals' "separate spheres" and gained equal status and independent women's studies and departmental programs. The poststructuralist feminists oppose established English department and women's studies programs, yet these feminists preserve the formal autonomy of literary study and accommodate the fragmented character of modern criticism.

Chapters 4 and 5, which examine the opposition of high and popular art, rather than poststructuralism and Marxism or feminism, show that the high modernist and postmodernist fiction of Thomas Hardy, Vladimir Nabokov, Milan Kundera, Philip Roth, and Toni Morrison opposes the optimistic liberalism and humanist ideals of the Enlightenment era, as traditional critics say; however, this fiction does not exclude popular stereotypes and established doctrines and conventions. Similarly, far from precluding subversive aesthetic practices, popular spy and detective fiction also undermines itself, resisting its generic forms and chauvinist and anticommunist stereotypes. Cultural studies and poststructuralist theorists acknowledge that the opposition of high and popular art breaks down in this way but still defend the subversive force of high modern and postmodern art.

In chapter 6, the public cultural criticism dominating the reception of *1984* highly esteems the novel's sociohistorical critique of totalitarian communism and of Western culture's decline and fragmentation and, like the traditional critics of *Hamlet*, *Pride and Prejudice*, and high modern art, bitterly opposes the subjective, "irrational" views of postmodern theory as well as "naive" liberals, "power hungry" intellectuals, "misguided" feminists, and the "complicit" media. Formal, feminist, Frankfurt School, and postmodern accounts of the novel resist this neoconservative approach but do not consistently overcome it. Lastly, the main accounts of Hurston's *Their Eyes Were Watching God* esteem its critiques of romance, marriage, and middle-class conventions and justify its revaluation; however, these accounts blame the Marxist realists for the novel's neglect and thereby perpetuate the debilitating culture wars dividing traditional and Marxist realists from formal and poststructuralist critics. My study of the novel's reception suggests, however, that the formal analyses of the poststructuralists do not preclude a profound realist critique of social life because it is not so much the limited vision of Marxist realists as the conservative ideals and Cold War preoccupations of modern literary study that explain the novel's neglect.

Theorists may argue that criticism ought to transcend its divisions and establish consensus and unity; these practical reception studies show, however, that, along with the unified or coherent moments, modern literary study also shows moments of division and conflict. John Guillory acknowledges this disunity, but, as I noted in the introduction, he still dismisses "relativist" reception study and defends theoretical critique.[2] He argues in addition that, since post-Marxist reception study fails to engage in "historical self-reflection," it cannot adequately explain how the changing institutional contexts of criticism influence it.[3]

My post-Marxist reception studies have nonetheless sought to explain these changing institutional contexts. For example, the reception of *Hamlet* showed that the humanist ideals defended by Marxist and non-Marxist views evolved in the nineteenth century, not the sixteenth. Moreover, while poststructuralist readings foster the multicultural practices of the modern university and state, the authorial, formal, and historical readings from which the poststructuralist readings evolve fostered the professional unity of the modern English department and of independent English associations and the national unity of Britain and the United States. These eclectic readings themselves evolved from the neoclassical humanism and romantic formalism by virtue of which Coleridge, Hazlitt, Johnson, and other early modern critics resisted the aristocratic classical ideals of the Renaissance humanists and the Tudor court and promoted the language and the literature of the British middle classes. Moreover, chapters 3, 4, and 5 show that in the late nineteenth and early twentieth centuries the corporate expansion of the popular media, together with the emergence of elite modernist and postmodernist art, degraded the middle-class public sphere established by the neoclassical humanists and romantic formalists and greatly exacerbated the conflict of high art and popular culture. To oppose this fragmentation and decline, traditional critics, who founded the modern English department, defended the unifying cultural authority of Austen and other canonical writers; nonetheless, by the 1940s and 1950s, expanding Anglo-American universities absorbed avant-garde artists and liberal intellectuals, making their work more influential but further exacerbating the conflict of high and popular art. At this time traditional critics of *Hamlet* and *Pride and Prejudice* not only assimilated contrary methods, they also defended the autonomy of high art because they feared that the liberal public was fragmented and degraded. Reception study argues, by contrast, that the vast expansion of the modern university greatly increases the accessibility and influence of literary studies. Because of this expansion and new influence, literary studies can influence public taste and popular culture. In chapter 6, the realist accounts of *1984* claim that it embodies the historical truth of totalitarian theory and justifies the common man's opposition to the oppressive establishment because they too fear that the great corporate expansion of the media and of the modern university, together with the emergence of elite modernist and postmodernist art, has imposed ideological conformity and degraded the public sphere. Formal, feminist, Frankfurt School, and poststructuralist critics reject the realist view, but their defense of the text's or of theory's subversive force implicitly accommodates this neoconservative opposition to the technical language or "jargon," specialized discourses, and new cultural and multicultural programs of the modern humanities. By contrast, the last chapter suggests that, because of the literary studies' expansion and new influence, the African American revaluation of Zora Neale Hurston's *Their Eyes Were Watching God* vindicates the humanities' African American programs.

As these studies indicate, reception study explains the moments of unity and disunity of modern literary schools and movements as well as their changing sociohistorical contexts and conservative and progressive aspects; however, scholars like Dasenbrock and Guillory find reception study too radical and ahistorical. By contrast, Derrideans consider it insufficiently radical. Derrideans say that, irreducible and hence subversive, the figural language or rhetorical forms of a text sustain many different interpretations and, as a result, undermine the ideologies of a text or a reader. The Derrideans argue, moreover, that to grant the reader control of the text is to accept established interpretive practices and their ideological justification.[4] For instance, Paul De Man claims that, since Jauss treats interpretation as the individual concretization of a "polysemic" textual structure which remains inexhaustible, his reader's "horizon of expectation" successfully articulates the relationship of poetics and hermeneutics, textual structure and interpretive activity, and semiotics and literary history. De Man still argues, however, that the irreducible "play" of the signifier undermines this relationship of textual structure and reader's interpretation. Jauss does not rigorously pursue the logic of the signifier; rather, he quickly reaestheticizes the signifier's effects so that nothing "unpleasant can occur."[5]

It is true that not only Jauss but all reception theory takes the conventions of interpretive practice to limit the play of the signifier and, instead of revealing and critiquing the choices and decisions animating dead conventions and established institutions, accepts them. What justifies reception study is in part the pedagogical practices whereby readers learn to read. As Jonathan Culler points out, someone has to teach readers that the aporias, gaps, and figural play subverting interpretive norms or aesthetic ideals require what De Man terms rigorous reading.[6] The Derridean objection ignores this institutional influence on interpretive practices, which the text's polysemic figural language may resist but from which it cannot altogether escape. To acknowledge the influence of these academic contexts is not, moreover, to adopt a conservative politics or to choose "the professional game"; indeed, there is no way to escape the game. As Fish says, the opposition to criticism's professional contexts is itself a professional gambit.[7]

Political objections to post-Marxist reception theory also range from the insufficiently to the excessively radical. On the one hand, John Ellis says that "race-gender-class critics" critique the establishment in Rousseau's radical fashion but ignore the critique's historical consequences: totalitarian communism;[8] on the other, Fredric Jameson equates post-Marxist theory with Edward Bernstein's late nineteenth-century revisionist socialism, not revolutionary Marxist theory.[9] Similarly, Michèle Barrett fears that the poststructuralist critique of foundational theory denies the human agency and the political will of the feminist or African American liberation movements.[10]

As I noted in the introduction, post-Marxist theory maintains that literary institutions produce their own social relations and do not simply reflect predetermined contexts and structures and fixed historical stages of traditional Hegelian Marxism. The post-Marxists claim, moreover, that the tragedies of the Soviet experience justify their critiques of traditional Hegelian Marxism and their radical extension of the Enlightenment tradition. Laclau and Mouffe grant the totalitarian theorist's belief that the Leninist account of the vanguard party explains the Stalinist features of Soviet communism. Laclau and Mouffe accept, at the same time, the liberal historians' belief that, more than Marxist theory, the authoritarian character and the socioeconomic difficulties of late nineteenth-century Russia explain the growth of the Stalinist system (see chapter 6).

In other words, post-Marxists critique the establishment in Rousseau's fashion and still acknowledge the critique's historical consequences. By contrast, traditional Marxists grant that the Stalinist regime acquired a dogmatic, oppressive character but, unlike the post-Marxists, deny that their broad dialectical view of history has anything to do with one-sided Stalinist dogma. Certainly Lukács, who supported the Stalinist regime and still praised Solzhenitsyn's dissident fiction, believed that the Soviet government would evolve, not collapse. Frankfurt School theorists also admit that Stalinist communism was dogmatic and oppressive, but they claim that the whole modern world is equally oppressive because they consider Enlightenment reason totalitarian, not a justification of a radical democracy. Scientific Althusserians also recognize the oppressive, dogmatic character of Stalinist communism but simply dismiss totalitarian theory—Robert Resch calls it an "oxymoronic anti-Marxist myth" catering to middle-class fears.[11]

Jameson also dismisses totalitarian theory, but he argues that Stalinism was a positive modernizing force whose enviable successes gave it worldwide influence. Moreover, although his innovative assimilation of structuralist and poststructuralist views has distinguished his work, he defends Marxism's traditional Hegelian doctrines, which include a "complex" distinction of base/superstructure, objective accounts of class contexts, systematic practices of revolutionary change, and the critique of the global economy and of commodity fetishism. No doubt such totalizing theory forcefully illuminates the social relations concealed by specialized, disciplinary discourses and, as a consequence, exposes the ideological illusions generated by these capitalist divisions and ultimately by commodity production. Still, the extravagant theoretical autonomy sought by the Hegelians so disgusted Marx that in *The German Ideology* he ridiculed their pretensions: such theorists foolishly imagine, he says, that men drown because they cannot get the idea of gravity out of their heads.[12] Marx would rather report the death of philosophy than acknowledge theory's ability to change material conditions. Even though Hegelian theorists are among the most critical in the Western tradition, I think Marx was right: the force of speculative thought is too limited. Defending Marxism's Hegelian doctrines may show that artists, rebels, and other marginal groups create alternative worlds and utopian visions which undermine the rigid structures and loosen the restricted possibilities of our "fetishized" society; however, such totalizing theory construes institutional practices as repressive and "one dimensional" and neglects their internal divisions or progressive and conservative import. Indeed, Jameson derides the revisionist post-Marxism of Bennett but praises Derrida's "radical politicization" of Marxist theory even though what Derrida terms the "affirmative messianic and emancipatory promise" of Marxism dismisses not only all versions of scientific Marxism but academic policies and institutional practices and programs as well.[13]

In general, it is true that post-Marxism, which promotes a democratic coalition of the humanities' new programs and, more generally, the "new social movements," defends the status quo; still, while the status quo has conservative aspects, it also has progressive aspects, which include broadly inclusive admissions policies and widely influential literary and cultural programs. Scholars assume that a properly ethical, aesthetic, or objective scholarship asserts universal norms of rationality, purely formal versions of rhetoric, or traditional notions of historical development and political agency; however, such proper scholarship ignores the policies of literary study's institutional context or implicitly accepts outmoded conservative fears, which, as I have noted, include the communist nightmare, cultural fragmentation and decline, the "obfuscating jargon," "self-defeating relativism," poststructuralist "complicity," and the "political correctness" of feminist, African American, gay, cultural, and multicultural studies. It is true, however, that, to the extent that the literary profession remains divided and conflicted, aesthetic standards and philosophical methods do not consistently transcend these divisions. In other words, reception study critiques the foundational norms of aesthetic theory and examines the interpretive communities and institutional contexts of literary study because in the postcommunist era the vast expansion and increased accessibility of higher education have given literary studies new influence and importance. Indeed, the coalitions fostered by reception study support the threatened working-class, African American, postcolonial, female, or gay constituencies, both inside and outside the university. As Michael Bérubé says, if left-wing cultural theory wins the support of the liberals, intellectuals, progressive trade unionists, feminists, African Americanists, and other oppositional groups and social movements loosely associated with the Democratic Party, this theory can more effectively defend higher education against its right-wing detractors.[14]

Notes

1. See Paul Bové, *In the Wake*, 5; Reed Way Dasenbrock, "Truth," 552; John Guillory, 272-77; and Michael Sprinker "The War," 155. Étienne Balibar and other Marxists address Althusserian theory, not reception study, but they too maintain that "genuine" Marxist theory "takes its distance from any form of 'constructivism' or relativism, even in the sophisticated form given it by Foucault" (Balibar, "Object," 163; see also Kai Nelson, 166-67; Resch, 166; Smith, 81-82, 215; Sprinker, "Current Conjuncture," 829-31). See also John Ellis, who also faults the relativism of radical postmodern theory, but he says that a "logically inadequate notion of what a definition is" explains why "race-gender-class" critics oppose traditional views of literature (45).

2. John Guillory, *Cultural Capital*, 272-77.

3. Guillory, *Cultural Capital*, 324. Similarly, in *In the Wake of THEORY* Paul Bové rejects reception study not only because it accepts the conservative scholars' hostility to "oppositional" theory and multicultural studies (5) but also because it lacks what he terms "[c]ritical intelligence" which "involves a demystification of intellectuals' sense of their independence, a constant genealogical self-criticism, and research into specific discourses and institutions as part of the struggle against oppressive power" (47); see also Reed Way Dasenbrock, "We've Done It," 182; Michael Sprinker, "The War," 155; and Brook Thomas, who says that reception study's critique of theory discredits the "very possibility of a new historicism" (*The New Historicism*, 79).

4. For example, in *What's Wrong with Postmodernism* Norris argues that Fish accepts conventional practices because Fish denies the subversive import of figural language (109; see also Daniel O'Hara, *Radical Parody*, 133-43).

5. Paul De Man, "Introduction," 10-25.

6. Jonathan Culler, *Structuralist Poetics*, 114.

7. Stanley Fish, "Anti-Professionalism."

8. John Ellis, *Literature Lost*, 12-32.

9. Fredric Jameson, "Actually Existing Marxism," 21.

10. Michèle Barrett, *The Politics of Truth*, 90-96.

11. Robert Paul Resch, *Althusser*, 17.

12. See Karl Marx and Friedrich Engels, *The German Ideology*, 1-2.

13. Fredric Jameson, "Marx's Purloined Letter," 104; Jacques Derrida, *Specters of Marx*, 75. For another positive appraisal of Derrida's Marxism, see Ernesto Laclau, "'The time is out of joint,'" 91. For a fuller discussion of Derrida's Marxism, see my essay "Communism and Postmodern Theory." For an extensive

account of Jameson and the Frankfurt School, see my book *The Politics of Literary Criticism*.

14. Michael Bérubé, *Public Access*, 34.

Bibliography

Adelman, Janet. *Suffocating Mothers: Fantasies of Maternal Origin in Shakespeare's Plays,* Hamlet *to* The Tempest. New York: Routledge, 1992.

Adorno, Theodor, and Max Horkheimer. *Dialectic of Enlightenment.* Trans. by John Cumming. New York: Continuum, 1972.

Akenson, Donald H. *A Protestant in Purgatory; Richard Whately, Archbishop of Dublin.* Hamden, Conn.: Archon, 1981.

Alexander, Nigel. *Poison, Play and Duel: A Study of* "Hamlet." Lincoln: University of Nebraska, 1971.

Alter, Robert. "*Invitation to a Beheading*: Nabakov and the Art of Politics," *Triquarterly,* 17 (Winter 1970), 41-59.

Althusser, Louis. *Essays in Self-Criticism.* London: New Left Books, 1976.

———. *Lenin and Philosophy.* Trans. by Ben Brewster. London: Monthly Review Press, 1971.

———. *For Marx.* Trans. by Ben Brewster. New York: Random House, 1969.

Altick, Richard D. *The English Common Reader: A Social History of the Mass Reading Public, 1800-1900.* Chicago: University of Chicago Press, 1957.

Altieri, Charles. *Canons and Consequences: Reflections on the Ethical Force of Imaginative Ideals.* Evanston, Ill.: Northwestern University Press, 1990.

Appiah, K. A., and Henry Louis Gates Jr., eds. *Zora Neale Hurston: Critical Perspectives Past and Present.* New York: Amistad, 1993.

Apple, Michael. *Official Knowledge: Democratic Education in a Conservative Age.* New York: Routledge, 1993.

Arac, Jonathan. "Peculiarities of (the) English in the Metanarrative(s) of Knowledge and Power." In *Intellectuals: Aesthetics, Politics, Academics.* Ed by Bruce Robbins. Minneapolis: University of Minnesota Press, 1990: 189-99.

———. Huckleberry Finn *as Idol and Target: The Functions of Criticism in Our Time.* Madison: University of Wisconsin Press, 1997.

Aronowitz, Stanley. *Science as Power: Discourse and Ideology in Modern Society.* Minneapolis: University of Minnesota Press, 1988.
Atkins, John. *The British Spy Novel: Styles in Treachery.* New York: Riverrun Press, 1984.
Auerbach, Erich. *Literary Language and Its Public in Late Latin Antiquity and in the Middle Ages.* Trans. by Ralph Manheim. Princeton, N.J.: Princeton University Press, 1993.
Austen, Jane. *Pride and Prejudice: An Authoritative Text, Backgrounds and Sources, Criticism.* 2nd edition. Ed. by Donald J. Gray. New York: Norton, 1993.
Austin, John. *How to Do Things with Words.* 2nd Edition. Ed. by J. O. Urmson and Marina Sbisà. Cambridge, Mass.: Harvard University Press, 1975.
Awkward, Michael. "'The Evil of Fulfillment': Scapegoating and Narration in *The Bluest Eye.*" In *Toni Morrison: Critical Perspectives Past and Present.* Ed. by K. A. Appiah and Henry Jouis Gates Jr. New York: Amistad, 1993: 175-209.
———. *Inspiriting Influences: Tradition, Revision, and Afro-American Women's Novels.* New York: Columbia University Press, 1989.
Awkward, Michael, ed. *New Essays on* Their Eyes Were Watching God. Cambridge: Cambridge University Press, 1990.
Babb, Howard S. "Dialog with Feeling: A Note on *Pride and Prejudice.*" In Pride and Prejudice: *An Authoritative Text, Backgrounds and Sources, Criticism.* 1st edition. Ed. by Donald J. Gray. New York: Norton, 1966: 421-31.
Baker, Houston A. Jr. *Blues, Ideology, and Afro-American Literature: A Vernacular Theory.* Chicago: University of Chicago Press, 1984.
———. "When Lindbergh Sleeps with Bessie Smith: The Writing of Place in *Sula.*" In *Toni Morrison: Critical Perspectives Past and Present.* Ed. by K. A. Appiah and Henry Jouis Gates Jr. New York: Amistad, 1993: 236-60.
Baldick, Chris. *The Social Mission of English Criticism, 1848–1932.* Oxford: Oxford University Press, 1983.
Barker, Francis. *The culture of violence: tragedy and history.* Chicago: University of Chicago Press, 1993.
Barley, Tony. *Taking sides: the fiction of John le Carré.* Philadelphia: Open University Press, 1986.
Barrett, Michèle. *The Politics of Truth: From Marx to Foucault.* Stanford, Calif.: Stanford University Press, 1991.
Barthes, Roland. *Mythologies.* Trans. by Annette Lavers. New York: Hill and Wang, 1972.
Baumgarten, Murray, and Barbara Gottfried. *Understanding Philip Roth.* Columbia: University of South Carolina Press, 1990.
Bayley, John, "Fictive Lightness, Fictive Weight,"*Salmagundi*, 73 (Winter 1987):

84-92.
Beene, Lynn Dianne. *John le Carré*. New York: Twayne, 1992.
Bennett, Tony. *Culture: A Reformer's Science*. St. Leonards, Australia: Allyn & Unwin, 1998.
———. *Formalism and Marxism*. London: Methuen, 1979.
———. "Marxism and Popular Fiction." *Literature & History*, VII (Autumn 1981), 149-64.
———. *Outside Literature*. New York: Routledge, 1990.
———. "Texts in History: The Determinations of Readings and Their Texts." *The Journal of the MMLA*, 18 .2 (1985), 1-16; rpt. In *Post-structuralism and the question of history*. Ed. by Derek Attridge, Geoff Bennington, and Robert Young. Cambridge: Cambridge University Press, 1987: 63-81.
———. "Texts, Readers, Reading Formations." *The Bulletin of the Midwest Modern Language Association*, XVI, 1 (1983), 3-17.
Bennett, Tony, and Janet Woollacott. *Bond and Beyond: The Political Career of a Popular Hero*. New York: Methuen, 1987.
Bergonzi, Bernard. *Exploding English: Criticism, Theory, Culture*. Oxford: Clarendon Press, 1990.
———. "*Nineteen Eighty-Four* and the Literary Imagination." In *Between Dream and Nature: Essays on Utopia and Dystopia*. Ed. by Dominic Baker-Smith and C. C. Barfoot. Amsterdam: Rodopi Publishers, 1987: 211-28.
Bernal, Martin. *Black Athena: The Afroasiatic Roots of Classical Civilization*. New Brunswick, N.J.: Rutgers University Press, 1987. Vol 1.
Bérubé, Michael. *Public Access: Literary Theory and American Cultural Politics*. London: Verso, 1994.
———. *The Employment of English: Theory, Jobs, and the Future of Literary Studies*. New York: New York University Press, 1998.
Bloom, Allan. *The Closing of the American Mind: How Higher Education Has Failed Democracy and Impoverished the Souls of Today's Students*. New York: Simon & Schuster, 1987.
Bloom, Harold, ed. *Zora Neale Hurston*. New York: Chelsea House, 1986.
Bone, Robert A., *The Negro Novel in America*. New Haven, Conn.: Yale University Press, 1958.
Boumelha, Penny. "*Tess of the D'Urbervilles*: Sexual Ideology and Narrative Form." In *Tess of the D'Urbervilles: Thomas Hardy*. Ed. by Peter Widdowson. New York: St. Martin's, 1993: 44-62.
Bové, Paul. *Intellectuals in Power: A Genealogy of Critical Humanism*. New York: Columbia University Press, l986.
———. *In the Wake of THEORY*. Hanover, N.H.: Wesleyan University Press, 1992.
Boyers, Robert. *Atrocity and Amnesia: The Political Novel Since 1945*. New York: Oxford University Press, 1985.
Bradley, A. C. *Shakespearean Tragedy: Lectures on Hamlet, Othello, King Lear,*

Macbeth. London: Macmillan, 1911.
Bradshaw, Graham. *Misrepresentations: Shakespeare and the Materialists*. Ithaca, N.Y.: Cornell University Press, 1993.
Brantlinger, Patrick. *Crusoe's Footprints: Cultural Studies in Britain and America*. New York: Routledge, 1990.
Brent, Jonathan. "The Unspeakable Self: Philip Roth and the Imagination." In *Reading Philip Roth*. Ed. by Asher Z. Milbauer and Donald G. Watson. New York: St. Martin's, 1988: 180-200.
Bristol, Michael D. *Big-time Shakespeare*. New York: Routledge, 1996.
Brooks, Peter. *Thomas Hardy: The Poetic Structure*. Ithaca, N.Y.: Cornell University Press, 1971.
Brower, Reuben A. "Light and Bright and Sparkling: Irony and Fiction in *Pride and Prejudice*." In *Jane Austen: A Collection of Critical Essays*. Ed. by Ian Watt. Englewood Cliffs, N.J.: Prentice-Hall, 1963.
Brown, Julia Prewitt. "The Feminist Depreciation of Austen: A Polemical Reading," *The Novel*, 23 (1990): 303-13.
Browne, Ray B. *Against Academia: The History of the Popular Culture Association/American Culture Association and the Popular Culture Movement 1967-1988*. Bowling Green, Ohio: Bowling Green State University Popular Press, 1989.
Brzezinski, Zbigniew. *The Grand Failure: The Birth and Death of Communism in the Twentieth Century*. New York: Scribner, 1989.
Brzezinski, Zbigniew, and, Carl J. Friedrich. *Totalitarian Dictatorship and Autocracy*. Cambridge, Mass.: Harvard University Press, 1956.
Butler, Marilyn. *Jane Austen and the War of Ideas*. Oxford: Oxford University Press, 1975.
Butler-Evans, Elliot. *Race, Gender, and Desire: Narrative Strategies in the Fiction of Toni Cade Bambara, Toni Morrison, and Alice Walker*. Philadelphia: Temple University Press, 1989.
Calderwood, James L. *To Be and Not to Be: Negation and Metadrama in* Hamlet. New York: Columbia University Press, 1983.
Carby, Hazel. "The Politics of Fiction, Anthropology, and the Folk: Zora Neale Hurston." In *New Essays on* Their Eyes Were Watching God. Ed. by Michael Awkward. Cambridge: Cambridge University Press, 1990: 71-93.
Carr, Jean Ferguson. "The Polemics of Incomprehension: Mother and Daughter in *Pride and Prejudice*." In *Tradition and the Talents of Women*. Ed. by Florence Howe. Urbana: University of Illinois Press, 1991.
Caute, David. *The Illusion: An Essay on Politics, Theatre and the Novel*. London: Andre Deutsch, 1971.
Cawelti, John C. *Adventure, Mystery, and Romance: Formula Stories as Art and Popular Culture*. Chicago: University of Chicago Press, 1976.
Cawelti, John G., and Bruce A. Rosenberg. *The Spy Story*. Chicago: University of Chicago Press, 1987.

Caygill, Howard. *The Art of Judgment*. London: Basil Blackwell, 1989.
Cecil, Lord David. *Poets and Story-Tellers*. New York: Macmillan, 1949.
Chartier, Roger. "Du Livre au lire," *Pratiques de la lecture*. Ed. by Roger Chartier. Paris: Éditions Payot & Rivages, 1993: 79-114.
———. *On the Edge of the Cliff: History, Language, Practices*. Baltimore, Md.: Johns Hopkins University Press, 1997.
———. *The Cultural Uses of Print in Early Modern France*. Trans. by Lydia G. Cochrane. Princeton, N.J.: Princeton University Press, 1987.
———. *The Order of Books: Readers, Authors, and Libraries in Europe between the Fourteenth and Eighteenth Centuries*. Trans. by Lydia G. Cochrane. Cambridge: Polity Press, 1992.
Christian, Barbara. *Black Women Novelists: The Development of a Tradition, 1892-1976*. Westport, Conn.: Greenwood, 1980.
———. "The Race for Theory," *Cultural Critique*, 6 (Spring 1987), 51-64.
Cohen, Stephen F. *Rethinking the Soviet Experience: Politics and History since 1917*. New York: Oxford University Press, 1985.
Colebrook, Claire. *New Literary Histories: New Historicism and Contemporary Criticism*. Manchester: Manchester University Press, 1997.
Coleridge, Samuel Taylor. "Notes on the Tragedies: Hamlet." In *Hamlet*. 2nd edition. Ed. by Cyrus Hoy. New York: Norton, 1992: 157-64.
Collins, Jim. *Uncommon Cultures: Popular Culture and Post-modernism*. New York: Routledge, 1989.
Collins, Max Allan, and James L. Traylor. *One Lonely Knight: Mickey Spillane's Mike Hammer*. Bowling Green, Ohio: Bowling Green University Popular Press, 1984.
Conklin, Paul S. *A History of Hamlet Criticism: 1601-1821*. New York: Columbia University Press, 1947.
Conley, Thomas M. *Rhetoric in the European Tradition*. Urbana-Champaign: University of Illinois Press, 1990.
Conquest, Robert. "Totaliterror." In *On* Nineteen Eighty-Four. Ed. by Peter Stansky. New York: W. H. Freeman, 1983: 177-87.
Cooke, Katharine. *A.C. Bradley and his influence in Twentieth-Century Shakespeare Criticism*. Oxford: Clarendon Press, 1972.
Court, Franklin E. *Institutionalizing English Literature: The Culture and Politics of Literary Study, 1750-1900*. Stanford, Calif.: Stanford University Press, 1992.
Crick, Bernard. "*Nineteen Eighty-Four*: Satire or Prophecy?" In *The Future of 1984*. Ed. and intro. by Ejner J. Jensen. Ann Arbor: University of Michigan Press, 1984.
Crowley, Tony. *Standard English and the Politics of Language*. Urbana: University of Illinois Press, 1989.
Culler, Jonathan. *Structuralist Poetics: Structuralism, Linguistics and the Study of Literature*. Ithaca, N.Y.: Cornell University Press, 1975.

Dallin, Alexander. "Big Brother Is Watching You." In *On Nineteen Eighty-Four*. Ed. by Peter Stansky. New York: W. H. Freeman, 1983: 188-96.

Daniels, Robert V. *The End of the Communist Revolution*. London: Routledge, 1993.

Dasenbrock, Reed Way. "Do We Write the Text We Read?" In *Literary Theory After Davidson*. Ed. by Reed Way Dasenbrock. University Park: Pennsylvania State University Press, 1993: 18-36.

———. "Truth and Methods." *College English*, 57 (1995): 546-61.

———. "We've Done It to Ourselves: The Critique of Truth and the Attack on Theory." In *PC Wars: Politics and Theory in the Academy*. Ed. by Jeffrey Williams. London: Routledge, 1995: 172-83.

Davies, Tony. "The divided gaze: Reflections on the political thriller." In *Gender, Genre and Narrative Pleasure*. Ed. by Derek Longhurst. London: Unwin Hyman, 1989: 118-35.

———. *Humanism*. London: Routledge, 1997.

De Lauretis, Teresa. *Technologies of Gender: Essays on Theory, Film, and Fiction*. Bloomington: Indiana University Press, 1987.

De Man, Paul. "The Epistemology of Metaphor," *Critical Inquiry* (Autumn 1978): 13-30.

———. "Introduction." In *Toward an Aesthetic of Reception* by Hans Robert Jauss. Trans. by Timothy Bahti. Minneapolis: University of Minnesota Press, 1982.

———. *The Resistance to Theory*. Minneapolis: University of Minnesota Press, 1986.

Denard, Carolyn. "The Convergence of Feminism and Ethnicity in the Fiction of Toni Morrison." In *Critical Essays on Toni Morrison*. Ed. by Nellie Y. McKay. Boston: G. K. Hall, 1988: 171-78.

Derrida, Jacques. "The Principle of Reason: The University in the Eyes of Its Pupils." *Diacritics*, III.3 (1983): 3-20.

———. "Signature, Event, Context." *Glyph*, 1 (1977), 172-97.

———. *Specters of Marx: The State of the Debt, the Work of Mourning, and the New International*. Trans. by Peggy Kamuf. New York: Routledge, 1994.

Deutscher, Isaac. "*1984*—The Mysticism of Cruelty." In *George Orwell: A Collection of Critical Essays*. Ed. by Raymond Williams. Englewood Cliffs, N.J.: Prentice-Hall, 1974: 119-32.

Ditmar, Linda. "'Will the Circle Be Unbroken?' The Politics of Form in *The Bluest Eye*." *The Novel*, 23 (1990): 137-55.

Docker, John. *Postmodernism and Popular Culture: A Cultural History*. Cambridge: Cambridge University Press, 1994.

Dollimore, Jonathan. "Introduction." In *Political Shakespeare: Essays in Cultural Materialism*. 2nd edition. Ed. by Jonathan Dollimore and Alan Sinfield. Ithaca, N.Y.: Cornell University Press, 1994.

Dorrien, Gary. *The Neoconservative Mind: Politics, Culture, and the War of Ideol-*

ogy. Philadelphia: Temple University Press, 1993.
Dowden, Edward. *Shakespeare: A Critical Study of his Mind and Art*. In *A New Varorium Edition of Shakespeare*. 5th edition. Ed. by Horace Howard Furness. Philadelphia: Lippincott, 1877.
Doyle, Arthur Conan. *The Sign of Four*. New York: Berkeley Medallion, 1975.
Doyle, Brian. "The Invention of English." In *Englishness: Politics and Culture, 1880-1920*. London: Croom Helm, 1986.
———. *English and Englishness*. London: Routledge, 1989.
DuBois, Ellen Carol et al. *Feminist Scholarship: Kindling in the Groves of Academe*. Urbana: University of Illinois Press, 1985.
DuCille, Ann. *The Coupling Convention: Sex, Text, and Tradition in Black Women's Fiction*. Oxford: Oxford University Press, 1993.
Duckworth, Alistair M. "Jane Austen and the Conflict of Interpretations." In *Jane Austen: New Perspectives*. Ed. by Janet Todd. New York: Holmes & Meier, 1983.
Dworkin, Dennis. *Cultural Marxism in Potwar Britain: History, the New Left, and the Origins of Cultural Studies*. Durham: Duke University Press, 1997.
Eagleton, Terry. "Bakhtin, Schopenhauer, Kundera." In *Bakhtin and Cultural Theory*. Ed. by Ken Hirschkop and David Shepherd. New York: Manchester University Press, 1989: 178-88.
———. *Criticism and Ideology*. London: Verso, 1978.
———. *The Function of Criticism: From The Spectator to Post-Structuralism*. London: Verso, 1984.
———. *The Ideology of the Aesthetic*. Cambridge: Basil Blackwell, 1990.
———. *Literary Theory: An Introduction*. Minneapolis: University of Minnesota Press, 1983.
———. *Marxism and Literary Criticism*. Berkeley: University of California Press, 1976.
———. *Walter Benjamin, Or Towards a Revolutionary Criticism*. London: Verso Editions, 1981.
———. *William Shakespeare*. London: Basil Blackwell, 1986.
Easthope, Anthony. *British Post-structuralism since 1968*. London: Routledge: 1988.
———. "Fact and Fantasy in '*Nineteen Eighty-Four*.'" In *Inside the Myth: Orwell: Views From the Left*. Ed. by Christopher Norris. London: Lawrence and Wishart, 1984: 263-85.
———. *Literary into Cultural Studies*. London: Routledge, 1991.
Ebenstein, William, and Edwin Fogelman. *Today's Isms: Communism, Fascism, Capitalism, Socialism*. 9th edition. Englewood Cliffs, N.J.: Prentice-Hall, 1985.
Ebert, Teresa. "Detecting the Phallus: Authority, Ideology, and the Production of Patriarchal Agents in Detective Fiction." In *Rethinking Marxism*, 5, 3 (Fall 1992): 6-28.

Eco, Umberto. *The Role of the Reader: Explorations in the Semiotics of Texts*. Bloomington: Indiana University Press, 1984.

Edel, Leon. *The Modern Psychological Novel*. Gloucester, Mass.: Peter Smith, 1972.

Ellis, John. *Literature Lost: Social Agendas and the Corruption of the Humanities*. New Haven, Conn.: Yale University Press, 1997.

Fairlamb, Horace L. *Critical Conditions: Postmodernity and the question of foundations*. Cambridge: Cambridge University Press, 1994.

Farley-Hills, David. *Critical Responses to Hamlet, 1790-1830*, vol. 2. New York: AMS, 1996.

Faulkner, William. *As I Lay Dying*. New York: Vintage, 1957.

Felperin, Howard. *The Uses of the Canon: Elizabethan Literature and Contemporary Theory*. Oxford: Clarendon Press, 1990.

Fergus, Jan. "The Comedy of Manners." In *Jane Austen's* Pride and Prejudice. Ed. and intro. by Harold Bloom. New York: Chelsea House Publishers, 1987: 107-26.

———. *Jane Austen: A Literary Life*. New York: St. Martin's, 1991.

Ferguson, Margaret. W. "Hamlet: letters and spirits." In *Hamlet*. 2nd edition. Ed. by Cyrus Hoy. New York: Norton, 1992.

Feris, Ina. "From trope to code: the novel and the rhetoric of gender in nineteenth-century critical discourse." In *Rewriting the Victorians: Theory, history, and the politics of gender*. Ed. by Linda M. Shires. New York: Routledge, 1992: 18-30.

Fiedler, Leslie. *Love and Death in the American Novel*. Revised edition. New York: Stein and Day, 1966.

Finkelstein, Sidney. *Who Needs Shakespeare?* New York: International Publishers, 1973.

Fish, Stanley. "Anti-Professionalism." *New Literary History*, XVII (1985): 89-108.

———. "Being Interdisciplinary Is So Very Hard To Do." *Profession* 89: 15-22.

———. "Boutique Multiculturalism, or, Why Liberals Are Incapable of Thinking of Hate Speech." *Critical Inquiry*, 23 (1997): 378-95.

———. "Consequences." *Critical Inquiry*, XI (1985): 433-58.

———. *Is There a Text in This Class? The Authority of Interpretive Communities*. Cambridge, Mass.: Harvard University Press, 1980.

———. *professional correctness: literary studies and political change*. Oxford: Clarendon Press, 1995.

Fleishman, Avrom. *The Condition of English*. Westport, Conn.: Greenwood Press, 1998.

Fleming, Ian. *From Russia With Love*. New York: New American Library, 1957.

Folsom, Marcia McClintock, ed. *Approaches to Teaching Austen's* Pride and Prejudice. New York: Modern Language Association of America, 1993.

Forster, E. M. *Aspects of the Novel*. New York: Harcourt, Brace & World, 1927.

Fortunati, Vita. "'It Makes No Difference': A Utopia of Simulation and Transparency." In *George Orwell's 1984*. Ed. by Harold Bloom. New Haven, Conn.: Chelsea House Publishers, 1987: 109-20.

Foucault, Michel. *The Archaeology of Knowledge*. Trans. by A. M. Sheridan Smith. New York: Harper & Row, 1976.

———. *Discipline and Punish: The Birth of the Prison*. Trans. by Alan Sheridan. New York: Random House, 1979.

———. *Madness and Civilization: A History of Insanity in the Age of Reason*. Trans. by R. Howard. New York: Random House, 1973.

———. *The Order of Things: An Archaeology of the Human Sciences*. Trans. by Alan Sheridan. New York: Pantheon, 1970.

———. *Power/Knowledge: Selected Interviews and Other Writings 1972-1977*. Ed. by Colin Gordon. Trans. by Colin Gordon and others. New York: Pantheon, 1980.

Freedman, Carl. "Antinomies of *Nineteen Eighty-Four*." In *Critical Essays on George Orwell*. Ed. by Bernard Oldsey and Joseph Brown. Boston: G. K. Hall, 1986: 90-110.

———. "Rhetorical Hermeneutics, Huckleberry Finn, and Some Problems with Pragmatism." In *Reconceptualizing American Literary/Cultural Studies: Rhetoric, History, and Politics in the Humanities*. Ed. by William E. Cain. New York: Garland, 1996: 117-28.

French, A. L. *Shakespeare and the critics*. London: Cambridge University Press, 1972.

French, Marilyn. *Shakespeare's Division of Experience*. New York: Summit, 1981.

Fromm, Eric. "Afterword." *1984*. New York: New American Library, 1981: 257-67.

Fromm, Harold. *Academic Capitalism and Literary Value*. Athens: University of Georgia Press, 1991.

Frow, John. *Cultural Studies and Cultural Value*. Oxford: Clarendon Press, 1995.

———. *Marxism and Literary History*. Cambridge, Mass.: Harvard University Press. 1986.

Frye, Northrop. *Northrop Frye on Shakespeare*. Ed. by Robert Sandler. New Haven, Conn.: Yale University Press, 1986.

Gallop, Jane. *Around 1981: Academic Feminist Literary Theory*. New York: Routledge, 1992.

Garber, Marjorie. *Shakespeare's Ghost Writers: Literature as uncanny causality*. New York: Methuen, 1987.

Gard, Roger. *Jane Austen's Novels: The Art of Clarity*. New Haven, Conn.: Yale University Press, 1992.

Gardner, Helen. *The Business of Criticism*. Oxford: Clarendon Press, 1959.

Gates, Henry Louis Jr. "Afterword." *Their Eyes Were Watching God*. New York: Harper & Row, 1990.

———. "*Their Eyes Were Watching God*: Hurston and the Speakerly Text." In *Zora Neale Hurston: Critical Perspectives Past and Present*. Ed. by K. A.

Appiah and Henry Louis Gates Jr. New York: Amistad, 1993: 154-203.
Gayle, Addison Jr. *The Way of the New World: The Black Novel in America*. Garden City, N.Y.: Anchor, 1975.
Gendron, Bernard. "Theodor Adorno Meets the Cadillacs." In *Studies in Entertainment: Critical Approaches to Mass Culture*. Ed. by Tania Modleski. Bloomington: Indiana University Press, 1986: 18-38.
Genovese, Eugene D. "Eugene Genovese asks the North American left, 'What did you know, and when did you know it?' about the crimes of communism." *Dissent* (Summer 1994): 371-76.
Gilbert, Sandra M., and Susan Gubar. *The Madwoman in the Attic: The Woman Writer and the Nineteenth-Century Literary Imagination*. New Haven, Conn.: Yale University Press, 1979.
Gloster, Hugh M. *Negro Voices in American Fiction*. Chapel Hill: University of North Carolina Press, 1948.
Glucksmann, André. *The Master Thinkers*. Trans. by Brian Pearce. New York: Harper & Row, 1980.
Goldstein, Philip. "Communism and Postmodern Theory: A Revaluation of Althusser's Marxism." *Rethinking Marxism*, 10, 3 (1997): 79-98.
―――. *The Politics of Literary Criticism: An Introduction to Marxist Cultural Theory*. Tallahassee: University of Florida Press, 1990.
Goodheart, Eugene. "Writing and the Unmaking of the Self." *Contemporary Literature*, 29, 3 (1988): 438-53.
Gottschalk, Paul. *The Meanings of Hamlet: Modes of Literary Interpretation Since Bradley*. Albuquerque: University of New Mexico Press, 1972.
Grady, Hugh. *The Modernist Shakespeare*. Oxford: Clarendon Press, 1991.
Graff, Gerald. *Professing Literature: An Institutional History*. Chicago: University of Chicago Press, 1987.
Grafton, Anthony, and Lisa Jardine. *From Humanism to the Humanities: Education and the Liberal Arts in Fifteenth and Sixteenth-Century Europe*. Cambridge, Mass.: Harvard University Press, 1986.
Gray, Donald J., ed. Pride and Prejudice: *An Authoritative Text, Backgrounds and Sources, Criticism*. New York: Norton, 1966, 1993.
Greenblatt, Stephen J. "Orwell as Satirist." In *George Orwell: A Collection of Critical Essays*. Ed. by Raymond Williams. Englewood Cliffs, N.J.: Prentice-Hall, 1974: 103-18.
―――. *Shakespearean Negotiations: The Circulation of Social Energy in Renaissance England*. Berkeley: University of California Press, 1988.
―――. "Towards a Poetics of Culture." In *The New Historicism*, Ed. by H. Aram Veeser. New York: Routledge, 1989: 1-14.
―――. "What Is the History of Literature?" *Critical Inquiry*, 23 (1997): 460-81.
Gubar, Susan. "What Ails Feminist Criticism?" *Critical Inquiry* 24 (1998): 878-902
Guerard, Albert. *Thomas Hardy: The Novels and the Stories*. Cambridge, Mass.: Harvard University Press, 1949.

Guillory, John. *Cultural Capital: The Problem of Literary Canon Formation*. Chicago: University of Chicago Press, 1993.
Gunn, Giles. "Approaching the Historical." In *Reconceptualizing American Literary/Cultural Studies: Rhetoric, History, and Politics in the Humanities*. Ed. by William E. Cain. New York: Garland, 1996: 59-72.
Guy, Josephine M., and Ian Small. *Politics and Value in English Studies: A discipline in crisis?* Cambridge: Cambridge University Press, 1993.
Habermas, Jürgen. *The Philosophical Discourse of Modernity*. Trans. by Frederick Lawrence. Cambridge, Mass.: MIT Press, 1987.
———. "Modernity—An Incomplete Project." In *The Anti-Aesthetic: Essays on Postmodern Culture*. Ed. by Hal Foster. Port Townsend, Wash.: Bay, 1983: 3-15.
Halpern, Richard. *Shakespeare among the Moderns*. Ithaca, N.Y.: Cornell University Press, 1997.
Hanmer, Sir Thomas. "Some Remarks on the *Tragedy of Hamlet*." In *Shakespeare: The Critical Heritage*. Ed. by Brian Vickers. London: Routledge & Kegan Paul, 1975: III, 40-69.
Hardy, Barbara. *The Appropriate Form: An Essay on the Novel*. London: University of London Press, 1964.
———. *A Reading of Jane Austen*. New York: New York University Press, 1979.
Hardy, Thomas. *Tess of the D'Urbervilles*. Ed. by William E. Buckler. 1891; Boston: Houghton Mifflin, 1960.
Harris, Wendell. "Canonicity." *PMLA* 106 (1991): 10-21.
Hawkes, Terence. *Meaning by Shakespeare*. New York: Routledge, 1992.
———. "Telmah." *Shakespeare and the Question of Theory*. Ed. by Patricia Parker and Geoffrey Hartmann. New York: Methuen, 1985: 310-32.
Heilbrun, Carolyn. "The Character of Hamlet's Mother." In *The Tragedy of Hamlet Prince of Denmark*. 2nd edition. Ed. by Edward Hubler. New York: New American Library, 1987.
Heinz, Denise. *The Dilemma of "Double-Consciousness": Toni Morrison's Novels*. Athens: University of Georgia Press, 1993.
Hennessy, Rosemary. m*aterialist feminism and the politics of discourse*. New York: Routledge, 1993.
Herron, Jerry. *Universities and the Myth of Cultural Decline*. Detroit: Wayne State University Press, 1988.
Hinnant, Charles. H. "*Steel for the Mind*": *Samuel Johnson and Critical Discourse*. Newark: University of Delaware Press, 1994.
Hirsch, E. D. Jr. *Cultural Literacy: What Every American Needs to Know*. New York: Vintage, 1988.
———. *Validity in Interpretation*. New Haven, Conn.: Yale University Press, 1967.
Holub, Robert C. *Crossing Borders: Reception Theory, Poststructuralism, Deconstruction*. Madison: University of Wisconsin Press, 1992.

———. *Reception Theory: A Critical Introduction*. London: Methuen, 1985.
Hoppenstand, Gary. "Ray and Pat Browne: Scholars of Everyday Culture." In *Pioneers in Popular Culture Studies*. Ed. by Ray Browne and Michael T. Marsden. Bowling Green, Ohio: Bowling Green State University Popular Press, 1999: 33-66.
Horwitz, Howard. "'I Can't Remember': Skepticism, Synthetic Histories, Critical Action." *SAQ*, 87 (88): 787-820.
Howe, Florence. *Myths of coeducation: selected essays, 1964-1983*. Bloomington: Indiana University Press, 1984.
Howe, Irving. *A Critic's Notebook*. Ed. and intro. by Nicholas Howe. New York: Harcourt Brace, 1994.
———. "*1984*: Enigmas of Power." In *1984 Revisited: Totalitarianism in Our Century*. Ed. by Irving Howe. New York: Harper & Row, 1983.
———. "*1984*: History as Nightmare." In *Twentieth Century Interpretations of 1984: A Collection of Critical Essays*. Ed. by Samuel Hynes. Englewood Cliffs, N.J.: Prentice-Hall, 1971: 41-53.
———. *Thomas Hardy*. New York: Macmillan, 1967.
Hoy, Cyrus, ed. *Hamlet*. 2nd edition. New York: Norton, 1992.
Hubler, Edward, ed. *The Tragedy of Hamlet Prince of Denmark*. 2nd edition. New York: New American Library, 1987.
Hunter, Ian. *Culture and Government: The Emergence of Literary Education*. London: Macmillan, 1988.
Hurston, Zora Neale. *Their Eyes Were Watching God*. New York: Harper & Row, 1990.
Huyssen, Andreas. "Mass Culture as Woman: Modernism's Other." In *Studies in Entertainment: Critical Approaches to Mass Culture*. Ed. by Tania Modleski. Bloomington: Indiana University Press, 1986.
Irigaray, Luce. *The Speculum of the Other Woman*. Trans. by Gillian C. Gill. Ithaca, N.Y.: Cornell University Press, 1985.
Irons, Glenwood. "New Women Detectives: G is for Gender-Bending." In *Gender, Language, and Myth: Essays on Popular Narrative*. Toronto: University of Toronto Press, 1992: 127-41.
Iser, Wolfgang. *The Act of Reading*. Baltimore, Md.: Johns Hopkins University Press, 1972.
Jameson, Fredric. "Actually Existing Marxism." In *Marxism Beyond Marxism*. Ed. by Saree Makdisi, Cesare Casarino, and Rebecca Karl. New York: Routledge, 1996: 14-54.
———. *Fables of Aggression: Wyndham Lewis, the Modernist as Fascist*. Los Angeles: University of California Press, 1979.
———. *Late Marxism: Adorno, or The Persistence of the Dialectic*. New York: Verso, 1990.
———. "Marx's Purloined Letter." *New Left Review*, 209 (January/February 1995): 75-108.

———. *Marxism and Form: Twentieth-Century Dialectical Theories of Literature*. Princeton, N.J.: Princeton University Press, 1971.

———. *The Political Unconscious: Narrative as a Socially Symbolic Act*. Ithaca, N.Y.: Cornell University Press, 1981.

———. "Postmodernism, or The Cultural Logic of Late Capitalism." *New Left Review*, 146 (July/ August 1984): 53-92.

———. *The Prison-House of Language*. Princeton, N.J.: Princeton University Press, 1972.

———. "Regarding Postmodernism—A Conversation with Fredric Jameson." *Social Text*, 17 (1987): 29-54.

Jancovich, Mark. *The Cultural Politics of the New Criticism*. Cambridge: Cambridge University Press, 1993.

Jauss, Hans Robert. *Question and Answer: Forms of Dialogic Understanding*. Ed. and trans. by Michael Hays. Minneapolis: University of Minnesota Press, 1989.

———. *Toward an Aesthetic of Reception*. Trans. by Timothy Bahti. Minneapolis: University of Minnesota Press, 1982.

Johnson, Barbara. *The Critical Difference: Essays in the Contemporary Rhetoric of Reading*. Baltimore, Md.: Johns Hopkins University Press, 1980.

———. "Thresholds of Difference: Structures of Address in *Their Eyes Were Watching God*." In *A World of Difference*. Baltimore, Md.: Johns Hopkins University Press, 1987: 172-83.

Johnson, Claudia L. *Jane Austen: Women, Politics, and the Novel*. Chicago: University of Chicago Press, 1988.

———. "The Divine Miss Jane: Jane Austen, Janeites, and the Discipline of Novel Studies." *boundary 2*, 23. 3 (1996): 143-63.

Johnson, Richard. "What is cultural studies anyway?" In *What Is Cultural Studies? A Reader*. Ed. by John Storey. London: Arnold, 1996: 75-114.

Johnson, Samuel. "Preface." *The Plays of William Shakespeare*. Ed. by Donald Greene. New York: Oxford University Press, 1984: 419-56.

Jones, John. *Shakespeare at Work*. Oxford: Clarendon Press, 1995.

Jumonville, Neil. *Critical Crossings: The New York Intellectuals in Postwar America*. Berkeley: University of California Press, 1991.

Kamps, Ivo. "Introduction." In *Materialist Shakespeare: A History*. Ed. by Ivo Kamps. London: Verso, 1995.

Kamuf, Peggy. *The Division of Literature: Or The University in Deconstruction*. Chicago: University of Chicago Press, 1997.

Kelley, Robin D. G., *Race Rebels: Culture, Politics, and the Black Working Class*. New York: Free Press, 1994

Kernan, Alvin. *The Playwright as Magician: Shakespeare's Image of the Poet in the English Public Theater*. New Haven, Conn.: Yale University Press, 1979.

———. *Samuel Johnson and the Impact of Print*. Princeton, N.J.: Princeton University Press, 1989.

———. *The Death of Literature.* New Haven, Conn.: Yale University Press, 1990.

Kerrigan, William. *Hamlet's Perfection.* Baltimore, Md.: Johns Hopkins University Press, 1994.

Kettle, Arnold. "From Hamlet to Lear." In *Shakespeare in a Changing World.* Ed. by Arnold Kettle. New York: International Publishers, 1964: 146-71.

———, ed. *Shakespeare in a Changing World.* New York: International Publishers, 1964.

Kiernan, Victor. *Eight Tragedies of Shakespeare: A Marxist Study.* London: Verso, 1996.

Kimball, Roger. "The ambiguities of Milan Kundera." *The New Criterion* 4 (January 1986): 5-13.

———. *Tenured Radicals: how politics has corrupted higher education.* New York: Harper & Row, 1990.

Kirkham, Margaret. *Jane Austen: Feminism and Fiction.* Totoway, N.J.: Barnes & Noble, 1983.

Kitching, Gavin. *Marxism and Science: Analysis of an Obsession.* University Park: Pennsylvania State University Press, 1994.

Klein, Kathleen Gregory. *The Woman Detective: Gender and Genre.* 2nd Edition. Urbana: University of Illinois Press, 1995.

Kliger, Samuel. "Jane Austen's *Pride and Prejudice* in the Eighteenth-Century Mode." In *Twentieth-Century Interpretations of* Pride and Prejudice. Ed. by E. Rubinstein. Englewood Cliffs, N.J.: Prentice-Hall, 1969: 46-58.

Knapp, Steven, and Walter Benn Michaels. "Against Theory." *Critical Inquiry*, 8 (1982): 723-42.

Knight, G. Wilson. *The Wheel of Fire: Essays in Interpretation of Shakespeare's Somber Tragedies.* London: Oxford University Press, 1930.

Kramer, Dale. *Thomas Hardy: The Forms of Tragedy.* London: Macmillan Press, 1975.

Krancberg, Sigmund. *A Soviet Postmortem: Philosophical Roots of the "Grand Failure."* Lanham, Md.: Rowman & Littlefield, 1994.

Kreiger, Murray. *The Institution of Theory.* Baltimore, Md.: Johns Hopkins University Press, 1994.

Kundera, Milan. *The Book of Laughter and Forgetting.* Trans. by Michael Henry Heim. New York: Penguin, 1980.

———. *Immortality.* Trans. by Peter Kussi. New York: HaperCollins, 1991.

———. *The Joke.* Trans. by Michael Henry Heim. New York: Penguin, 1987.

———. *The Unbearable Lightness of Being.* Trans. by Michael Henry Heim. New York: Harper & Row, 1984.

LaCapra, Dominick. *Soundings in Critical Theory.* Ithaca, N.Y.: Cornell University Press. 1989

Laclau, Ernesto. *New Reflections on the Revolution of Our Time.* London: Verso,

1993.
———. "'The time is out of joint.'" *Diacritics*, 25, 2 (1995): 86-97.
Laclau, Ernesto, and Chantal Mouffe. *Hegemony and Socialist Strategy*. London: Verso, 1985.
Larrain, Jorge. *Ideology and Cultural Identity: Modernity and the Third World Presence*. Cambridge: Polity, 1994.
Lascelles, Mary. *Jane Austen and Her Art*. London: Oxford University Press, 1939.
Lauter, Paul, "History and the Canon." *Social Text*, 12 (Fall, 1985): 94-101.
———. "'Political Correctness' and the Attack on American Colleges." In *Higher Education Under Fire: Politics, Economics, and the Crisis of the Humanities*. Ed. by Michael Bérubé and Cary Nelson. New York: Routledge, 1995: 73-90.
Leavis, Q. D. "A Critical Theory of Jane Austen's Writings." In *A Selection from Scrutiny*. Ed. by F. R. Leavis. Cambridge: Cambridge University Press, 1968, II, 1-80.
Le Carré, John. *Our Game*. New York: Ballantine, 1995.
———. *The Spy Who Came in from the Cold*. New York: Dell, 1963.
———. *Tinker, Tailor, Soldier, Spy*. New York: Bantam, 1975.
Leitch, Vincent B. *American Literary Criticism from the Thirties to the Eighties*. New York: Columbia University Press, 1988.
Lentricchia, Frank. *After the New Criticism*. Chicago: University of Chicago Press, 1980.
Lerner, Lawrence. *Thomas Hardy's* The Mayor of Casterbridge: *Tragedy of Social History*. London: Sussex University Press, 1975.
Levin, Harry. *The Question of Hamlet*. New York: Oxford University Press, 1959.
Levin, Richard. *New Readings vs. Old Plays: Recent Trends in the Reinterpretation of English Renaissance Drama*. Chicago: University of Chicago Press, 1979.
———. "The Poetics and Politics of Bardicide." *PMLA*, 105 (1990):491-504.
Levine, Lawrence W. *The Opening of the American Mind: Canons, Culture, and History*. Boston: Beacon, 1996.
Lewin, Moshe. *The Gorbachev Phenomenon: A Historical Interpretation*. Berkeley: University of California Press, 1988.
———. *The Making of the Soviet System: Essays in the Social History of Interwar Russia*. New York: Pantheon, 1985.
Lewis, C. S. "Hamlet The Prince or the Poem?" In *Hamlet: Enter Critic*. Ed. by Claire Sacks and Edgar Whan. New York: Appleton-Century-Crofts, 1960: 170-87.
Lowe, John. *Jump at the Sun: Zora Neale Hurston's Cosmic Comedy*. Urbana: University of Illinois Press, 1995.
Lucas, Christopher J. *American Higher Education: A History*. New York: St. Martin's, 1994.
Lukács, Georg. *Marxism and Human Liberation*. Ed. by E. San Juan Jr. New York:

Dell, 1973: 61-71.
———. *Realism In Our Time: Literature and the Class Struggle*. New York: Harper & Row, 1971.
Lyotard, Jean-François. *The Postmodern Condition: A Report on Knowledge*. Trans. by Geoff Bennington and Brian Massumi. Minneapolis: University of Minnesota Press, 1984.
Macaulay, Thomas Babington. "The London University." In *Selected Writings*. Ed. by John Clive and Thomas Pinney. Chicago: University of Chicago Press, 1972, 4-33.
Macherey, Pierre. *A Theory of Literary Production*. Trans. by Geoffrey Wall. London: Routledge and Kegan Paul, 1978.
———. *The Object of Literature*. Trans. by David Macey. Cambridge: Cambridge University Press, 1995.
Mailloux, Steven. "Articulation and Understanding: The Pragmatic Intimacy between Rhetoric and Hermeneutics." In *Hermeneutics and Rhetoric in Our Time*. Ed. by Walter Jost and Michael Hyce. New Haven, Conn.: Yale University Press, 1995: 1-33.
———. *Interpretive Conventions: The Reader in the Study of American Fiction*. Ithaca, N.Y.: Cornell University Press, 1982.
———. *Reception Histories: Rhetoric, Pragmatism, and American Cultural Politics*. Ithaca, N.Y.: Cornell University Press, 1998.
———. *Rhetorical Power*. Ithaca, N.Y.: Cornell University Press, 1989.
Marcuse, Herbert. *One-Dimensional Man*. Boston: Beacon, 1964.
Margolies, David. *Monsters of the Deep: Social Dissolution in Shakespeare's Tragedies*. Manchester: Manchester University Press, 1992.
Margolis, Joseph. *Pragmatism Without Foundations: Reconciling Realism and Relativism*. London: Basil Blackwell, 1996.
Marx, Karl and Friedrich Engels. *The German Ideology*. Ed. R. Pascal. New York: International Publishers, 1947.
McCormick, Kathleen. *The culture of reading and the teaching of English*. New York: Manchester University Press, 1994.
McDowell, Deborah E. "'The Self and the Other': Reading Toni Morrison's *Sula* and the Black Female Text." In *Critical Essays on Toni Morrison*. Ed. by Nellie Y. McKay. Boston: G. K. Hall, 1988: 77-89.
McGann, Jerome J. *The Beauty of Inflections: Literary Investigations in Historical Method and Theory*. Oxford: Clarendon Press, 1985.
McGee, Arthur. *The Elizabethan Hamlet*. New Haven, Conn.: Yale University Press, 1987.
McKay, Nellie. "'Crayon Enlargements of Life': Zora Neale Hurston's Their Eyes Were Watching God as Autobiography." In *New Essays on* Their Eyes Were Watching God. Ed. by Michael Awkward. Cambridge: Cambridge University Press, 1990: 51-70.
Merry, Bruce. *The Anatomy of the Spy Thriller*. Montreal: McGill-Queen's Univer-

sity Press, 1977.
Meyer, A. G. *Communism*. 3rd edition. New York: Random House, 1967.
Miller, J. Hillis. *Fiction and Repetition: Seven English Novels*. Oxford: Basil Blackwell, 1982.
———. *Thomas Hardy: Distance and Desire*. Cambridge, Mass.: Harvard University Press, 1970.
Miller, Mark Crispin. "The Fate of *1984*." In *1984 Revisited: Totalitarianism in Our Century*. Ed. by Irving Howe. New York: Harper & Row, 1983: 19-46.
Miller, Thomas P. *The Formation of College English: Rhetoric and Belles Lettres in the British Cultural Provinces*. Pittsburgh: University of Pittsburgh Press, 1997.
Miller, Toby. *The Well-Tempered Self: Citizenship, Culture, and the Postmodern Subject*. Baltimore, Md.: Johns Hopkins University Press, 1993.
———. *Technologies of Truth: Cultural Citizenship and the Popular Media*. Minneapolis: University of Minnesota Press, 1998.
Mizener, Arthur. "*Jude the Obscure* as a Tragedy." *Southern Review*, 6(1940), 193-213.
MLA Committee on Professional Employment, *Final Report* (December 1997)
Moler, Kenneth L. Pride and Prejudice: *A Study in Artistic Economy*. Boston: Twayne Publishers, 1989.
Monaghan, David. "*Pride and Prejudice*: Structure and Social Vision." In *Jane Austen's* Pride and Prejudice. Ed. and intro. by Harold Bloom. New York: Chelsea House Publishers, 1987: 59-83.
Montrose, Louis. "Professing the Renaissance: The Poetics and Politics of Culture." In *The New Historicism*. Ed. by H. Aram Veeser. New York: Routledge, 1989: 15-36.
Morrison, Toni. *The Bluest Eye*. New York: Plume, 1994.
———. *Sula*. New York: Plume, 1973.
Mudrick, Marvin. *Jane Austen: Irony as Defense and Discovery*. Princeton, N.J.: Princeton University Press, 1952.
Mulhern, Francis. *The Moment of* 'Scrutiny.' London: New Left Books, 1979.
Nabokov, Vladimir. *Invitation to a Beheading*. Trans. by Dmitri Nabokov. New York: Putnam, 1959.
Neill, Edward. *The Politics of Jane Austen*. New York: St. Martin's, 1999.
Nelson, Cary. "Always Already Cultural Studies: Two Conferences and a Manifesto." *The Journal of the Midwest Modern Language Association*, 24, 1 (July 1991): 24-38.
———. "Against English: Theory and the Limits of the Discipline." *Profession* 87: 46-52.
Nelson, Kai. "The Concept of Ideology: Some Marxist and Non-Marxist Conceptualizations." *Rethinking Marxism*, 2, 4 (1989): 146-73.
Newman, Gerald. *The Rise of English Nationalism: A Cultural History, 1740-1830*.

New York: St. Martin's, 1987.
Newman, Karen. "Can This Marriage Be Saved? Jane Austen Makes Sense of an Ending." In *New Casebooks*: Sense and Sensibility *and* Pride and Prejudice. Ed. by Robert Clark. New York: St. Martin's, 1994.
Newton, Judith Lowder. *Women, Power, & Subversion: Social Strategies in British Fiction, 1778-1860*. New York: Methuen, 1981.
Newton, Judith Lowder, and Deborah Rosenfelt. "Toward a materialist-feminist criticism." In *Feminist Criticism and Social Change*. Ed. by Judith Lowder Newton and Deborah Rosenfelt. New York: Methuen, 1985, xv-xxxix.
Nigel, Alexander. *Poison, Play and Duel: A Study of Hamlet*. Lincoln: University of Nebraska Press, 1971.
Nisbet, Robert. "*1984* and the Conservative Imagination." In *1984 Revisited: Totalitarianism in Our Century*. Ed. by Irving Howe. New York: Harper and Row, 1983: 180-206.
Norris, Christopher. "Language, Truth and Ideology: Orwell and the Post-War Left." In *Inside the Myth; Orwell: Views From the Left*. Ed. by Christopher Norris. London: Lawrence and Wishart, 1984: 242-62.
———. *What's Wrong with Postmodernism: Critical Theory and the Ends of Philosophy*. Baltimore, Md.: Johns Hopkins University Press, 1990.
O'Brien, John. *Milan Kundera & Feminism: Dangerous Intersections*. New York: St. Martin's Press, 1995.
O'Hara, Daniel. *Radical Parody: American Culture and Critical Agency After Foucault*. New York: Columbia University Press, 1992.
Ong, Walter. J. *Rhetoric, Romance, and Technology: Studies in the Interaction of Expression and Culture*. Ithaca, N.Y.: Cornell University Press, 1971.
Orel, Harold. *Victorian Literary Critics*. London: Macmillan, 1984.
Orwell, George. *1984*. New York: NAL Penguin, 1981.
Otten, Terry. *The Crime of Innocence in the Fiction of Toni Morrison*. Columbia: University of Missouri Press, 1989
———. "Horrific Love in Toni Morrison's Fiction." *Modern Fiction Studies*, 39, 3&4 (Fall/Winter 1993): 651-68.
Ozinga, James R. *Communism: The Story of the Idea and Its Implementation*. 2nd Edition. Englewood Cliffs, N.J.: Prentice-Hall, 1991
Page, Philip. *Dangerous Freedom: Fusion and Fragmentation in Toni Morrison's Novels*. Jackson: University of Mississippi Press, 1995.
Palmer, Jerry. *Thrillers: Genesis and Structure of a Popular Genre*. New York: St. Martin's, 1979.
Paretsky, Sara. *Burn Marks*. New York: Dell, 1990.
———. *Deadlock*. New York: Ballantine Books, 1984.
Parrinder, Patrick. *Authors and Authority: A Study of English Literary Criticism and Its Relation to Culture, 1750-1900*. London: Routledge & Kegan Paul, 1977.

Patai, Daphne. *The Orwell Mystique: A Study in Male Ideology*. Amherst: University of Massachusetts Press, 1984.

Patterson, Annabel. "The Very Age and Body of the Time His Form and Pressure." In *Shakespeare and Deconstruction*. Ed. by G. Douglas Atkins and David M. Bergeron. New York: Peter Lang, 1988: 47-68.

Pechter, Edward. "The New Historicism and Its Discontents: Politicizing Renaissance Drama." *PMLA*, 101 (1987): 292-303.

Perkins, David. *Is Literary History Possible?* Baltimore, Md.: Johns Hopkins University Press, 1992.

Petry, Sandy. *Speech Acts and Literary Theory*. New York: Routledge, 1990.

Phillipps, K. C. *Jane Austen's English*. London: Andre Deutsch, 1970.

Pietz, William. "The 'Post-Colonialism' of Cold War Discourse." *Social Text*, 19/20 (Fall 1988), 56-76.

Pinion, F. B. *A Hardy Companion*. London: St. Martin's, 1968.

Pipes, Richard. *Russia Under the Old Regime*. New York: Scribner, 1974.

Polan, Dana. "Postmodernism and Cultural Analysis Today." In *Postmodernism and Its Discontents*. Ed. by E. Ann Kaplan. London: Verso, 1988: 45-58.

Poovey, Mary. "The Differences of Women's Studies: The Example of Literary Criticism." In *Feminisms in the Academy*. Ed. by Donna C. Stanton and Abigail J. Stewart. Ann Arbor: University of Michigan Press, 1995: 135-56.

———. *The Proper Lady and the Woman Writer: Ideology as Style in the Works of Mary Wollstonecraft, Mary Shelley, and Jane Austen*. Chicago: University of Chicago Press, 1984.

———. *Uneven Developments: The Ideological Work of Gender in Mid-Victorian England*. Chicago: University of Chicago Press, 1988.

Porter, Carolyn, "Are We Being Historical Yet?" *SAQ*, 87 (1988), 743-86.

Poster, Mark. *Foucault, Marxism, & History: Mode of Production versus Mode of Information*. Cambridge: Polity, 1984.

Price, Joseph, ed. Hamlet: *Critical Essays*. New York: Garland, 1986.

Prosser, Eleanor. *Hamlet and Revenge*. Stanford, Calif.: Stanford University Press, 1967.

Pughe, Thomas. *Comic sense: reading Robert Coover, Stanley Elkin, Philip Roth*. Basel, Switzerland: Birkhäuser Verlag, 1994.

Rader, Ralph. "Literary Permanence and Critical Change." *Works and Days 7: Essays in the Socio-Historical Dimensions of Literature and the Arts*, 4, 1 (1986), 9-16.

Raval, Suresh. *Grounds of Literary Criticism*. Urbana: University of Illinois Press, 1998.

Rayson, Ann L. "The Novels of Zora Neale Hurston." *Studies in Black Literature*, 5, 2 (1974): 1-10.

Readings, Bill. "The University Without Culture?" *New Literary History*, 26 (1995): 465-92.

Reilly, Patrick. Nineteen Eighty-Four: *Past, Present, and Future*. Boston: Twayne, 1989.
Rendall, Jane. *Women in an Industrializing Society: England 1750-1880*. Oxford: Blackwell, 1990.
Resch, Robert Paul. *Althusser and the Renewal of Marxist Social Theory*. Berkeley: University of California Press, 1992.
Rice, Herbert William. *Toni Morrison and the American Tradition: A Rhetorical Reading*. New York: Peter Lang, 1996.
Robbins, Bruce. *Secular Vocations: Intellectuals, Professionalism, Culture*. New York: Verso, 1993.
Rodden, John. *The Politics of Literary History: The Making and Claiming of 'St. George' Orwell*. New York: Oxford University Press, 1989.
Rorty, Richard. *Consequences of Pragmatism (Essays: 1972-1980)*. Minneapolis: University of Minnesota Press, 1982.
———. *Contingency, Irony, Solidarity*. Cambridge: Cambridge University Press, 1989.
———. *Essays on Heidegger and Others*. New York: Cambridge, 1991.
———. "Response to Ernesto LaClau." In *deconstruction and pragmatism*. Ed. by Chantal Mouffe. New York: Routledge, 1996: 69-77.
Rose, Jacqueline. "Sexuality in the Reading of Shakespeare: *Hamlet* and *Measure for Measure*." In *Hamlet*. 2nd edition. Ed. by Cyrus Hoy. New York: Norton, 1992: 262-83.
Rosenblatt, Roger. *Black Fiction*. Boston: Harvard University Press, 1974.
Ross, Andrew. *No Respect: Intellectuals & Popular Culture*. New York: Routledge, 1989.
Ross, Trevor. *The Making of the English Literary Canon: From the Middle Ages to the Late Eighteenth Century*. Montreal: McGill-Queen's University Press, 1998.
Roth, Philip. *The Professor of Desire*. New York: Bantam, 1977.
———. *Zuckerman Bound*. New York: Fawcett Crest, 1985.
Rowe, John Carlos, ed. *"Culture" and the Problem of the Disciplines*. New York: Columbia University Press, 1998.
Ruderman, Anne Crippen. *The Pleasures of Virtue: Political Thought in the Novels of Jane Austen*. Lanham, Md.: Rowman & Littlefield, 1995.
Russell, Bertrand. "On the Nature of Acquaintance." In *Logic and Knowledge: Essays 1901-1950*. Ed. by Robert C. Marsh. New York: Macmillan, 1966: 125-74.
Ryan, Michael. *Literary Theory: A Practical Introduction*. Malden, Mass.: Blackwell, 1999.
Ryle, Gilbert. *The Concept of Mind*. Barnes & Noble, 1949.
Said, Edward. *The World, the Text, and the Critic*. Cambridge, Mass.: Harvard University Press, 1983.
Sales, Roger. *Jane Austen and Representations of Regency England*. London:

Routledge, 1994.
Sarchett, Barry W. "Russell Jacoby, Anti-Professionalism, and the Politics of Cultural Nostalgia." *Minnesota Review*, 39 (1992/3): 122-42.
Satz, Martha. "An Epistemological Understanding of *Pride and Prejudice*: Humility and Objectivity." In *Jane Austen: New Perspectives*. Ed. by Janet Todd. New York: Holmes & Meier Publishers, 1983: 171-86.
Schaub, Thomas. *American Fiction in the Cold War*. Madison: University of Wisconsin Press, 1991.
Scholes, Robert. *The Rise and Fall of English: Reconstructing English as a Discipline*. New Haven, Conn.: Yale University Press, 1998.
Schwartz, Lawrence H., *Creating Faulkner's Reputation: The Politics of Modern Literary Criticism*. Knoxville: University of Tennessee, 1988.
Searle, John. "Literary Theory and Its Discontents." *New Literary History*, 25 (1994): 637-68.
———. "Reiterating the Differences: A Reply to Derrida." *Glyph*, 1 (1977): 198-208.
Shakespeare, William. *Hamlet*. Ed. by Cyrus Hoy. 2nd edition. New York: Norton, 1992.
Showalter, Elaine "Feminism in the Wilderness." In *The New Feminist Criticism: Essays on Women, Literature, and Theory*. Ed. by Elaine Showalter. New York: Pantheon Books, 1985.
Shumway, David. *Creating American Civilization: A Genealogy of American Literature as an Academic Discipline*. Minneapolis: University of Minnesota Press, 1994.
Siegel, Paul N. *Shakespeare in His Time and Ours*. Notre Dame, Ind.: University of Notre Dame Press, 1968.
Simpson, David. *Romanticism, Nationalism, and the Revolt Against Theory*. Chicago: University of Chicago Press, 1993.
Sinfield, Alan. *Faultlines: Cultural Materialism and the Politics of Dissident Reading*. Berkeley: University of California Press, 1992.
Sisk, John P. "Art, Kitsch, & Politics." *Commentary*, 85, 5 (1988): 50-53.
Siskin, Clifford. "Jane Austen and the Engendering of Disciplinarity." In *Jane Austen and Discourses of Feminism*. Ed. by Devoney Looser. New York: St. Martin's, 1995: 51-67.
Smith, Anthony, and Frank Webster, eds. *The Postmodern University? Contested Visions of Higher Education in Society*. London: Open University Press, 1997.
Smith, Barbara Herrnstein. *Contingencies of Value: Alternative Perspectives for Critical Theory*. Cambridge, Mass.: Harvard University Press, 1988.
Smith, Goldwin. *The Life of Jane Austen*. London: Walter Scott, 1890.
Smith, Rebecca. "A Heart Cleft in Twain: The Dilemma of Shakespeare's Gertrude." In *The Woman's Part: Feminist Criticism of Shakespeare*. Ed. by Carolyn Ruth Swift Lenz, Gayle Greene, and Carol Thomas Neely. Ur-

bana: University of Illinois Press, 1980.

Southham, B. C., ed. *Jane Austen: The Critical Heritage*. 2 vols. New York: Routledge & Kegan Paul, 1987.

Spanos, William V. *Repetitions: The Postmodern Occasion in Literature and Culture*. Baton Rouge: Louisiana State University Press, 1987.

Spender, Stephen. "Introduction to *1984*." In *Twentieth Century Interpretations of 1984: A Collection of Critical Essays*. Ed. by Samuel Hynes. Englewood Cliffs, N.J.: Prentice-Hall, 1971: 62-72.

Spillane, Mickey. *The Girl Hunters*. New York: New American Library, 1962.

———. *One Lonely Night*. New York: New American Library, 1951.

Spivak, Gayatri Chakravorty. "Revolutions That As Yet Have No Model: Derrida's Limited Inc." *Diacritics*, 10, 4 (1980): 29-49.

Sprinker, Michael. "The Current Conjuncture in Theory." *College English*, 51 (1989): 825-34.

———. *Imaginary Relations: Aesthetics and Ideology in the Theory of Historical Materialism*. New York: Verso, 1987.

———. "The War Against Theory." In *PC Wars: Politics and Theory in the Academy*. Ed. by Jeffrey Williams. London: Routledge, 1995: 149-71.

Stanton, Domna C., and Abigail J. Stewart, eds. *Feminisms in the Academy*. Ann Arbor: University of Michigan Press, 1995.

Steinhoff, William. *George Orwell and the Origins of 1984*. Ann Arbor: University of Michigan Press, 1975.

Stepto, Robert B. *From Behind the Veil: A Study of Afro-American Narrative*. Urbana: University of Illinois Press, 1979.

Stewart, Maaja A. *Domestic Realities and Imperial Fictions: Jane Austen's Novels in Eighteenth-Century Contexts*. Athens: University of Georgia Press, 1993.

Struever, Nancy S. "The Conversable World: Eighteenth-Century Transformations of the Relation of Rhetoric and Truth." In *Rhetoric and the Pursuit of Truth: Language Change in the Seventeenth and Eighteenth Centuries*. Los Angeles: William Andrews Clark Memorial Library, 1985.

Sulloway, Alison G. *Jane Austen and the Province of Womanhood*. Philadelphia: University of Pennsylvania Press, 1989.

Swingewood, Alan. *The Novel and Revolution*. London: Macmillan. 1976.

Tani, Stefano. *The Doomed Detective: The Contribution of the Detective Novel to Postmodern American and Italian Fiction*. Carbondale: Southern Illinois University Press, 1984.

Tanner, Tony. "Colour and Movement in Hardy's *Tess of the d'Urbervilles*." In *The Victorian Novel: Modern Essays in Criticism*. Ed. by Ian Watt. London: Oxford University Press, 1971: 407-31.

———. *Jane Austen*. Cambridge, Mass.: Harvard University Press, 1986.

Tave, Stuart M. "Affection and the Amiable Man." In *Jane Austen's* Pride and Prejudice. Ed and intro. by Harold Bloom. New York: Chelsea House,

1987: 21-38.
Taylor, Gary. *Reinventing Shakespeare: A Cultural History from the Restoration to the Present.* New York: Oxford University Press, 1989.
Taylor, Jenny. "Desire Is Thoughtcrime." In Nineteen Eighty-Four *in 1984: Autonomy, Control, and Communication.* London: Comedia Publishing Group, 1983.
Tennenhouse, Leonard. *Power on Display: The politics of Shakespeare's genres.* London: Methuen: 1986.
Teres, Harvey M. *Renewing the Left.* New York: Oxford University Press, 1996.
Thomas, Brook. *The New Historicism and Other Old-Fashioned Topics.* Princeton, N.J.: Princeton University Press, 1991
Thompson, James. *Between Self and World: The Novels of Jane Austen.* University Park: Pennsylvania State University Press, 1988.
———. *Models of value: eighteenth-century political economy and the novel.* Durham, N.C.: Duke University Press, 1996.
Thompson, Jon. *Fiction, Crime, and Empire: Clues to Modernity and Postmodernity.* Urbana: University of Illinois Press, 1993.
Tillyard, E. M. W. *Shakespeare's Problem Plays.* Toronto: University of Toronto Press, 1949.
Tomarken, Edward. *Samuel Johnson on Shakespeare: The Discipline of Criticism.* Athens: University of Georgia Press, 1991.
Tompkins, Jane P. *Sensational Designs: The Cultural Work of American Fiction 1790-1860.* New York: Oxford University Press, 1985.
Trilling, Lionel. "*Emma* and the Legend of Jane Austen." In *Beyond Culture: Essays on Literature and Learning.* New York: Harcourt, Brace, Jovanovich, 1965.
———. *The Liberal Imagination: Essays on Literature and Society.* Garden City, N.Y.: Doubleday, 1953.
———. "Orwell on the Future." In *Twentieth Century Interpretations of 1984: A Collection of Critical Essays.* Ed. by Samuel Hynes. Englewood Cliffs, N.J.: Prentice-Hall, 1971: 24-28.
———. *Sincerity and Authenticity.* Cambridge, Mass.: Harvard University Press, 1972.
Tucker, Martin. "The Shape of Exile in Philip Roth, or the Part Is Always Apart." In *Reading Philip Roth.* Ed. by Asher Z. Milbauer and Donald G. Watson. New York: St. Martin's, 1988: 33-49.
Tucker, Robert C. "Stalinism as Revolution from Above." In *Stalinism: Essays in Historical Interpretation.* Ed. by Robert C. Tucker. New York: Norton, 1977: 77-108.
———. "Does Big Brother Exist?" In 1984 *Revisited: Totalitarianism in Our Century.* Ed. by Irving Howe. New York: Harper and Row, 1983: 89-102.
Turner, Darwin T. *In a Minor Chord: Three Afro-American Writers and Their Search for Identity.* Carbondale: Southern Illinois University, 1971.

Urkowitz, Steven. "'Well-savd olde Mole": Burying Three Hamlets in Modern Editions." In *Shakespeare Study Today: The Horace Howard Furness Memorial Lectures*. Ed. by Georgianna Ziegler. New York: AMS Press, 1986: 36-70.
Vickers, Brian, ed. *Shakespeare: The Critical Heritage*. London: Routledge and Kegan Paul, 1979. 5 vols.
———. *Appropriating Shakespeare: Contemporary Critical Quarrels*. New Haven, Conn.: Yale University Press, 1993.
Wald, Alan. *The New York Intellectuals: The Rise and Decline of the Anti-Stalinist Left from the 1930s to the 1980s*. Chapel Hill: University of North Carolina Press, 1987.
Walker, Alice. "A Cautionary Tale and a Partisan View." In *Zora Neale Hurston*. Ed. and intro. by Harold Bloom. New York: Chelsea House, 1986: 63-69.
———. "Looking for Zora." In *I Love Myself When I am Laughing ... And Then Again When I am Looking Mean and Impressive: A Zora Neale Hurston Reader*. Ed. by Alice Walker. Intro. by Mary Helen Washington. New York: Feminist Press, 1979: 297-313.
Wallace, Elisabeth. *Goldwin Smith, Victorian Liberal*. Toronto: University of Toronto Press, 1957.
Warner, William Beatty. *Chance and the Text of Experience: Freud, Nietzsche, and Shakespeare's* Hamlet. Ithaca, N.Y.: Cornell University Press, 1986.
Warren, Charles. *T.S. Eliot on Shakespeare*. Ann Arbor: University of Michigan Research Press, 1987.
Washington, Mary Helen. "Foreword." In *Their Eyes Were Watching God*. New York: Harper and Row, 1990.
Waswo, Richard. *Language and Meaning in the Renaissance*. Princeton, N.J.: Princeton University Press, 1987.
Watkins, Evan. *Work Time: English Departments and the Circulation of Cultural Value*. Stanford, Calif.: Stanford University Press, 1989.
Watt, Ian, ed. *Jane Austen: A Collection of Critical Essays*. Englewood Cliffs, N.J.: Prentice-Hall, 1963.
Watts, Cedric. *Hamlet*. London: Harvester-Wheatsheaf, 1988.
Waugh, Patricia. *Practicing Postmodernism Reading Modernism*. London: Edward Arnold, 1992.
Weimann, Robert. "Mimesis in Hamlet." In *Shakespeare and the Question of Theory*. Ed. by Patricia Parker and Geoffrey Hartmann. New York: Methuen, 1985: 275-91.
Weinstein, Philip. "David and Solomon: Fathering in Faulkner and Morrison." In *Unflinching Gaze: Morrison and Faulkner Re-Envisioned*. Ed. by Carol A. Kolmerten and others. Jackson: University Press of Mississippi, 1997: 48-76.
Weitz, Morris. Hamlet *and the Philosophy of Criticism*. Chicago: University of Chicago Press, 1964.

Wellek, René. *A History of Modern Criticism: 1750-1950*. New Haven, Conn.: Yale University Press, 1965. 5 vols.
———. *Concepts of Criticism*. Ed. by Stephen G. Nichols Jr. New Haven, Conn.: Yale University Press, 1963.
Wellek, René and Austin Warren. *Theory of Literature*. New York: Harcourt Brace, 1956.
Werner, Craig. *Playing the Changes: From Afro-Modernism to the Jazz Impulse*. Chicago: University of Illinois Press, 1994.
Werstine, Paul. "Narratives About Shakespearean Texts: 'Foul Papers' and 'Bad' Quartos." *Shakespeare Quarterly*, 41 (Spring 1990): 65-86.
West, Cornel. *Keeping Faith: Philosophy and Race in America*. New York: Routledge, 1993.
Whately, Richard. *Elements of Rhetoric Compromising an Analysis of the Laws of Moral Evidence and of Persuasion, with Rules for Argumentative Composition and Elocution*. Carbondale: Southern Illinois University Press, 1963.
Whigham, Frank. *Ambition and Privilege: The Social Tropes of Elizabethan Courtesy Theory*. Berkeley: University of California Press, 1984.
White, Hayden. *Tropics of Discourse: Essays in Cultural Criticism*. Baltimore, Md.: Johns Hopkins University Press, 1978.
Widdowson, Peter. *Hardy in History: A Study in Literary Sociology*. London: Routledge, 1989.
———, ed. *Tess of the D'Urbervilles: Thomas Hardy*. New York: St. Martin's, 1993.
Widgery, David. "Reclaiming Orwell." In *Nineteen Eighty-Four in 1984*. London: Comedia Publishing Group, 1983: 15-23.
Wiener, Martin J. *English Culture and the Decline of the Industrial Spirit, 1850-1908*. Cambridge: Cambridge University Press, 1981.
Williams, Raymond. *Culture and Society*. New York: Columbia University Press, 1983.
———. *The Long Revolution*. New York: Columbia University Press, 1961.
———. "Love and Work." In *Tess of the D'Urbervilles*. 3rd edition. Ed. by Scott Elledge. New York: Norton, 1991: 460-71.
———. *Marxism and Literature*. New York: Oxford University Press, 1976.
———. *george orwell*. New York: Columbia University Press, 1971.
———. *Problems in Materialism and Culture: Selected Essays.*. London: Verso, 1980.
———. *Writing in Society*. London: Verso, 1985.
Willis, Susan. "Eruptions of Funk: Historicizing Toni Morrison." In *Toni Morrison: Critical Perspectives Past and Present*. Ed. by K. A. Appiah and Henry Jouis Gates Jr. New York: Amistad, 1993: 308-29.
Wilson, J. Dover. *What Happens in Hamlet*. London: Cambridge University Press, 1967.

Wilson, John. *The myth of political correctness: the conservative attack on higher education.* Durham, N.C.: Duke University Press, 1995.
Wirth-Nesher, Hana. "From Newark to Prague: Roth's Place in the American-Jewish Literary Tradition." In *Reading Philip Roth.* Ed. by Asher Z. Milbauer, and Donald G. Watson. New York: St. Martin's, 1988: 17-32.
Woodman, Thomas. *A Preface to Samuel Johnson.* London: Longman, 1993.
Woolf, Michael. "Ian Fleming's Enigmas and Variations." In *Spy Thrillers: From Buchan to Le Carré.* Ed. by Clive Bloom. New York: St. Martin's, 1990.
Wright, Andrew H. "Heroines, Heroes, and Villains in *Pride and Prejudice.*" In *Twentieth-Century Interpretations of* Pride and Prejudice. Ed. by E. Rubinstein. Englewood Cliffs, N.J.: Prentice-Hall, 1969: 97-110.
Wright, Richard. "The Literature of the Negro in the United States." In *White Man, Listen!* Garden City, N.Y.: Doubleday, 1957: 105-50.
Young, James. *Black Writers of the Thirties.* Baton Rouge: Louisiana State University Press, 1973.
Young, Robert. "The Idea of a Chrestomathic University." *Logomachia: The Confict of the Faculties.* Ed. by Richard Rand. Lincoln: University of Nebraska Press, 1992: 99-126.
Zuckert, Michael. "Orwell's Hopes, Orwell's Fears." In *The Orwellian Moment: Hindsight and Foresight in the Post-1984 World.* Ed. by Robert L. Savage, James Coombs, and Dan Nimmo. Fayetteville: University of Arkansas Press, 1989: 45-67.
Zwerdling, Alex. "Rethinking the Modernist Legacy in *Nineteen Eighty-Four.*" In *The Revised Orwell.* Ed. by Jonathan Rose. East Lansing: Michigan State University Press, 1992.

Index

Addison, Gayle, 187-88
Adelman, Janet, 61
Adorno, Theodor, realism of, 43, 135-36
aesthetics, Black, 184-85
Alter, Robert, 122, 137
Althusser, Louis, 11
The Anatomy Lesson, 126
Arac, Jonathan, 49
Archaeology of Knowledge, 13
Aronowitz, Stanley, 18-19
As I Lay Dying, absurdity in, 192-93; and *Their Eyes Were Watching God*, 192-94
Atkins, John, 161, 161-62
Auerbach, Nina, 102-3
Austen, Henry, 88
Austen, Jane, as a classical writer, 89; aunt Jane stereotype of, 88; financial success of, 89; and literary study, 90-91; and the new rhetoricians, 89-90; standard English of, 89-90
Austin, John, 33-34
Awkward, Michael, 134, 189, 195-96

Baker, Houston, 138-39, 184-85, 186
Baldwin, James, 184
Balibar, Étienne, 207
Barker, Francis, 73
Barley, Tony, 147, 162
Barrett, Michèle, 204
Barthes, Roland, 40
Baumgarten, Murray, 138
Bennett, Tony, 6, 9, 10, 14-15, 24, 40-47, 49, 160-61; and Althusserian theory, 40-41; the critique of theory of, 45-46, 50-51; and cultural studies, 45-46; institutional technology of, 42-3, 45-6; the reading formations of, 42; and Russian formalism, 41-42
Bergonzi, Bernard, 172
Bérubé, Michael, 2, 23
Bloom, Allan, 28
Bloom, Harold, 181
The Bluest Eye, as high art, 132-33; middle-class norms in, 129-31; poststructuralist accounts of 133-34

Bone, Richard, 187
The Book of Laughter and Forgetting, 137
Boumelha, Penny, 120
Bové, Paul, 207
Boyers, Robert, 137
Bradley, A. C., 59-60, 63
Brantlinger, Patrick, 163-64
Brent, Jonathan, 138
Brooks, Thomas, 26, 207
Brown, Julia Prewitt, 101, 111
Browne, Ray, 113
Brzezinski, Zbigniew, and Carl J. Friedrich, 136-37, 178
Butler, Marilyn, 111
Butler-Evans, Elliot, 134
Burn Marks, aesthetic reflexivity in, 155; ranting in, 154-56
Burnham, James, 168

Calderwood, James, 66
Carby, Hazel, 188
Cawelti, John G., 145, 160, 161
Cecil, Lord David, 92, 108
Chartier, Robert, 17, 85
Christian, Barbara, 132, 134, 186
Colebrook, Clare, 16-17, 80
Coleridge, Samuel T., 59, 60
Collins, Jim, 163
Communism, Soviet, 168; 177-78; liberal historical accounts of, 178; Marxist views of, 205; totalitarian theories of, 168, 178-79
conservatives and radicals, coalition of, 2-3, 18, 20
Crick, Bernard, 179
The Crying of Lot 49, 153
culture wars, 1-3

Dasenbrock, Reed Way, 200
Davies, Tony, 76
De Man, Paul, 9, 26, 34-35, 204
Deadlock, 152-54; feminism in, 153; ideological critique in, 154; uncertainty in, 152-53
Decter, Midge, 171
Derrida, Jacques, 20, 30; and speech-act theory, 34
Descartes, René, 32
Detective and spy fiction, 141-42
The Dialectic of Enlightenment, 135-36, 158
Discipline and Punish, 14
Docker, John, 160
Dorrien, Gary, 167-68, 171
Duckworth, Alistair, 92

Eagleton, Terry, 26, 28-29, 50, 125; and Althusserian theory, 40-41, 43; and poststructuralism, 43; on *Hamlet*, 55
Easthope, Anthony, 163, 168-69, 174-75
Ebenstein, William, and Edwin Fogelman, 179
Ebert, Teresa, 162
Eco, Umberto, 143, 148
Edel, Leon, 135
Eliot, T. S., 64
Ellis, John, 204, 207
Empson, William, 64-65

Farewell, My Lovely, 149
Fergus, Ian, 99-100, 110
Ferguson, Margaret, 65-66
Fish, Stanley, 9, 14, 24, 31, 32-36, 47; anti-theory argument of, 35; interpretive community of, 32-33; and multiculturalism, 35; positivism in, 36; professionalism in, 204; reader response criticism of, 32; and speech-act theory, 34
For Whom the Bell Tolls, 145-46
Foucault, Michel, 12-14, 76; on humanism, 76-77
Fraiman, Susan, 98-99

Index

Addison, Gayle, 187-88
Adelman, Janet, 61
Adorno, Theodor, realism of, 43, 135-36
aesthetics, Black, 184-85
Alter, Robert, 122, 137
Althusser, Louis, 11
The Anatomy Lesson, 126
Arac, Jonathan, 49
Archaeology of Knowledge, 13
Aronowitz, Stanley, 18-19
As I Lay Dying, absurdity in, 192-93; and *Their Eyes Were Watching God*, 192-94
Atkins, John, 161, 161-62
Auerbach, Nina, 102-3
Austen, Henry, 88
Austen, Jane, as a classical writer, 89; aunt Jane stereotype of, 88; financial success of, 89; and literary study, 90-91; and the new rhetoricians, 89-90; standard English of, 89-90
Austin, John, 33-34
Awkward, Michael, 134, 189, 195-96

Baker, Houston, 138-39, 184-85, 186
Baldwin, James, 184
Balibar, Étienne, 207
Barker, Francis, 73
Barley, Tony, 147, 162
Barrett, Michèle, 204
Barthes, Roland, 40
Baumgarten, Murray, 138
Bennett, Tony, 6, 9, 10, 14-15, 24, 40-47, 49, 160-61; and Althusserian theory, 40-41; the critique of theory of, 45-46, 50-51; and cultural studies, 45-46; institutional technology of, 42-3, 45-6; the reading formations of, 42; and Russian formalism, 41-42
Bergonzi, Bernard, 172
Bérubé, Michael, 2, 23
Bloom, Allan, 28
Bloom, Harold, 181
The Bluest Eye, as high art, 132-33; middle-class norms in, 129-31; poststructuralist accounts of 133-34

235

Bone, Richard, 187
The Book of Laughter and Forgetting, 137
Boumelha, Penny, 120
Bové, Paul, 207
Boyers, Robert, 137
Bradley, A. C., 59-60, 63
Brantlinger, Patrick, 163-64
Brent, Jonathan, 138
Brooks, Thomas, 26, 207
Brown, Julia Prewitt, 101, 111
Browne, Ray, 113
Brzezinski, Zbigniew, and Carl J. Friedrich, 136-37, 178
Butler, Marilyn, 111
Butler-Evans, Elliot, 134
Burn Marks, aesthetic reflexivity in, 155; ranting in, 154-56
Burnham, James, 168

Calderwood, James, 66
Carby, Hazel, 188
Cawelti, John G., 145, 160, 161
Cecil, Lord David, 92, 108
Chartier, Robert, 17, 85
Christian, Barbara, 132, 134, 186
Colebrook, Clare, 16-17, 80
Coleridge, Samuel T., 59, 60
Collins, Jim, 163
Communism, Soviet, 168; 177-78; liberal historical accounts of, 178; Marxist views of, 205; totalitarian theories of, 168, 178-79
conservatives and radicals, coalition of, 2-3, 18, 20
Crick, Bernard, 179
The Crying of Lot 49, 153
culture wars, 1-3

Dasenbrock, Reed Way, 200
Davies, Tony, 76
De Man, Paul, 9, 26, 34-35, 204
Deadlock, 152-54; feminism in, 153; ideological critique in, 154; uncertainty in, 152-53
Decter, Midge, 171
Derrida, Jacques, 20, 30; and speech-act theory, 34
Descartes, René, 32
Detective and spy fiction, 141-42
The Dialectic of Enlightenment, 135-36, 158
Discipline and Punish, 14
Docker, John, 160
Dorrien, Gary, 167-68, 171
Duckworth, Alistair, 92

Eagleton, Terry, 26, 28-29, 50, 125; and Althusserian theory, 40-41, 43; and poststructuralism, 43; on *Hamlet*, 55
Easthope, Anthony, 163, 168-69, 174-75
Ebenstein, William, and Edwin Fogelman, 179
Ebert, Teresa, 162
Eco, Umberto, 143, 148
Edel, Leon, 135
Eliot, T. S., 64
Ellis, John, 204, 207
Empson, William, 64-65

Farewell, My Lovely, 149
Fergus, Ian, 99-100, 110
Ferguson, Margaret, 65-66
Fish, Stanley, 9, 14, 24, 31, 32-36, 47; anti-theory argument of, 35; interpretive community of, 32-33; and multiculturalism, 35; positivism in, 36; professionalism in, 204; reader response criticism of, 32; and speech-act theory, 34
For Whom the Bell Tolls, 145-46
Foucault, Michel, 12-14, 76; on humanism, 76-77
Fraiman, Susan, 98-99

French, A. L., 75
From Russia with Love, 142-44
Fromm, Eric, 173
Frow, John, 6, 9, 24, 31, 40-45, 47, 114; the Althusserian theory of, 40-41; and relativism, 44; and Russian formalism, 41
Frye, Northrop, 70

Garber, Marjorie, 61, 78
Gard, Roger, 84
Gardner, Helen, 79
Gates, Henry Louis Jr., 188-89; 195-96
Genovese, Eugene, 165
Gilbert, Sandra, and Susan Gubar, 29, 97-98
The Girl Hunters, 151-52; puns in, 151; paranoia in, 151-52
Gloster, Hugh, 187
Goodheart, Eugene, 138
Gottfield, Barbara, 138
Gottshalk, Paul, 60, 75
Grady, Hugh, 69, 79
Graff, Gerald, 29, 67
Greenblatt, Stephen, 15-17
Guber, Susan, 84
Guerard, Albert, 118
Guillory, John, 23, 202
Guy, Josephine and Ian Small, 3

Habermas, Jürgen, 12
Hall, Stuart, 45
Halpern, Richard, 65, 74
Hamlet, and anti-humanism, 53-54, 71; and economic determinism, 53, 58; and humanism, 53, 54, 57-58; and Protestant theology, 72; and social mobility, 56; eclectic historical readings of, 69-71; figural, Derridean views of, 63, 65-66; formal, textual views of, 63-65; misogyny in, 55-56; neoclassical account of, 59, 77; New Historical accounts of, 71-73; positivist historical readings of, 67-69; psychoanalytic views of, 61; reforms in, 54-55; romantic views of, 59-61; traditional Marxist view of, 53, 54-58, 74
Harding, D. W., 97
Hardy, Barbara, 110
Hardy, Thomas, pessimism of, 114-15
Harris, Wendell, 182
Hawks, Terence, 66, 75
Hazlitt, William, 59-60, 77
hegemony, 11-12
Heilbrun, Carolyn, 78
Heinze, Denise, 134
high art, 113-14, 156; defenses of, 157-60; history of, 157
higher education, expansion of, 19; literary studies in, 19-20, 90-91
Hirsch, E. D. Jr., 6, 28
historical method, traditional, 6-7, 15; reductivism in, 7; New Historical versions of, 16-17
Holub, Robert, 4, 8, 9
Howe, Irving, 118, 157, 170, 171, 184
humanism, as conservative, 76; origins and features of, 57
humanities, decline of, 19
Hurston, Zora Neale, 183, 192; and Faulkner, 183-84; grave of, 181
Huyssen, Andreas, 162

Immortality, 123, 126
Invitation to a Beheading, 120-22; aesthetic self-consciousness in, 122
Iser, Wolfgang, 135

Jameson, Fredric, 29, 45, 159, 197, 205-6; on Derrida, 206; on post-Marxism, 204
Jauss, Hans Robert, 4-6, 7-9, 26, 31, 41, 204
Johnson, Barbara, 34, 188, 189
Johnson, Claudia, 104-5
Johnson, Samuel, 59, 77

Kamuf, Peggy, 45
Kamps, Ivo, 77
Kernan, Alvin, 57-58, 66
Kerrigan, William, 61-62, 75
Kettle, Arnold, 53, 54, 58, 65
Kimball, Roger, 137
Kirkham, Margaret, 107
Knight, G. Wilson, 64
Kramer, Dale, 119
Krancberg, Sigmund, 178-79
Kreiger, Murray, 3

LaCapra, Dominick, 28
Laclau, Ernesto, and Chantal Mouffe, 11-13; and Soviet communism, 27, 168, 204-5
Lascelles, Mary, 99
Leavis, F. R., 63
Leavis, Q. D., 97
Leitch, Vincent, 30
Levin, Harry, 70
Levin, Richard, 73, 79
Lewes, Henry, 88, 90
Lewis, C. S., 75
literary study, conservatism in, 185-86; divisions of, 1-4, 18-23; 200-2; growth of, 62-3; in higher education, 19-20, 90-91; professionalization of, 67, 74
Live and Let Die, ideological subversion in, 142-44
Lukács, Georg, 6

Macauley, Thomas Babington, 90-91

Macherey, Pierre, 49-50
Madness and Civilization, 13
Mailloux, Steven, 9, 24, 31, 47; and anti-theory arguments, 37, 39; and *Huckleberry Finn*, 37-38; and *Protagorus*, 38; and Rorty's neopragmatism, 38; rhetorical hermeneutics of, 36-40
Marcuse, Herbert, 136
Marx, Karl, 11
Marxism, 11; Derridean version of, 14-15; post-Marxist versions of, 10-14; 35, 204-5; on Soviet communism, 205
McGann, Jerome, 25, 26
McKay, Nellie, 188
Meyer, A. G., 179
Miller, J. Hillis, 119-20
Miller, Mark Crispin, 173-74
Miller, Toby, 42-3, 46
Moler, Kenneth, 101, 110-11
Morgan, Susan, 94
Morrison, Toni, 128-29
Mudrick, Marvin, 92-93

Neill, Edward, 83
New Critics, 157-58, 185-86
New York intellectuals, 30, 158, 170-71, 186
Newton, Judith, 102-3, 111
1984, and the Frankfurt School of Social Theory, 173-74; as dystopian satire, 167-69; feminist views of, 171-72; liberal realist accounts of, 166, 170-71; literary views of, 172-73; metaphysical opposition in, 168-69; poststructuralist accounts of, 174-76
Norris, Christopher, 162, 207
O'Brien, John, 137
O'Hara, Daniel, 36, 196
Ong, Walter, 57

One Lonely Night, communism in, 148-49; paranoia in, 149-50
Order of Things, 13
Orwell, George, 166, 176; and totalitarian communism, 167-68
Otten, Terry, 130-31, 139
Our Game, 161

Patai, Daphne, 171-72
Perkins, David, 5-6
philosophy, analytic, 33
Pietz, William, 162
Pipes, Richard, 177-78
Polan, Dana, 156
Poovey, Mary, 93-94, 109
popular culture, 113-14
Poster, Mark, 27-28
The Prague Orgy, anti-semitism in, 127; artistic autonomy in, 128; comic sexuality in, 125-27; realist views of, 127-28
Pride and Prejudice, and *Their Eyes Were Watching God*, 105-06, 189-92; early authorial accounts of, 91-92; later authorial accounts of, 92, 95, 96, 106, 108; feminist authorial views of, 92, 94, 95, 96; formal, feminist accounts of, 96-97, 100-101, 106; formal, textual accounts of, 96-97, 100; historical feminist accounts of, 101-5, 106; liberal Victorian account of, 87-91; post-structuralist feminist accounts of, 105-6; reading in 84-85; realism in, 88; social criticism in, 83-84, 85-87; traditional historical accounts of, 101-2, 106
The Professor of Desire, 126-27
Pughe, Thomas, 138

Ransom, John Crowe, 184
Reading formations, 14-15
reception theory, and canonical art, 2-4, 182, 195; conservatism of, 204, 206; Derridean criticisms of, 203-4; historical justification of, 4; modern version of, 4-6; objections to, 199-200; post-Marxist version of, 10, 14-17, 31, 33, 204-6; poststructuralist version of, 4, 9-10, 24, 25, 31; relativism in, 23, 32-33, 200-2; and realism, 181, 189, 195; and socio-historical change, 202-3
Reilly, Patrick, 172-73
Rice, Herbert, 132
Robbins, Bruce, 30
Rodden, John, 171, 179
Rorty, Richard, 12, 122, 175-76
Rose, Jacquelyn, 61
Rosenberg, Bruce A., 145, 161
Rosenblatt, Roger, 187
Rowe, John Carlos, 1
Ruderman, Anne, 94
Russell, Bertrand, 33, 47-48
Ryle, Gilbert, 33

Said, Edward, 3, 29
Satz Martha, 93-94
Schaub, Thomas, 162
Scholes, Robert, 18
Schwartz, Lawrence, 184
Scott, Sir Walter, on Austen's realism, 88
Searle, John, 34, 48
Showalter, Elaine, 84
Shumway, David, 185-86
The Sign of Four, 141-42
Sinfield, Alan, 72, 162
Smith, Barbara Herrnstein, 9, 24, 31, 45, 50-51, 196
Smith, Goldwin, 88

Southam, B C, 110
Spanos, William, 163
speech-act theory, 33-34
The Spy Who Came in from the Cold, 145; communism in, 145-46; heroism in, 146
Steinhoff, William, 170, 177
Stepto, Robert, 189
Stewart, Maaja, 103-4
Sula, as high art, 132-33; middle-class norms in, 131-32; poststructuralist accounts of, 133-34

Tani, Stefano, 163
Tanner, Tony, 89-90
Taylor, Gary, 79
Tennenhouse, Leonard, 56-7, 72-3
Tess of the D'Urbervilles. 115-17; deconstructive views of, 119-20; feminist views of, 120; formal, textual views of, 118-19; reader-oriented views of, 119; realist views of, 117-18
Their Eyes Were Watching God, absurdity in, 193-94; and *As I Lay Dying*, 192-94; and *Pride and Prejudice*, 189-92; formal, rhetorical views of, 188-89; Marxist views of, 183, 195-96; public speech in, 191-92; neglect of, 181; realist views of, 187-88, 89; romantic difficulties in, 190-91
Theory, crisis of, 3-4; poststructuralist versions of, 2, 3, 11, 12, 15, 16, 21, 25, 27
Thompson, E. P., 58
Thompson, James, 107, 110, 111
Thompson, Jon, 146
Tillyard, E. M. W., 68-69
Tinker, Tailor, Soldier, Spy, 146-48; complexity as critique in, 147-48

Tomarken, Edward, on Johnson, 77
Tompkins, Jane, 9
Trilling, Lionel, 7, 165, 170, 186
Tucker, Martin, 138
Turner, Darwin, 187
Twain, Mark, 90

The Unbearable Lightness of Being, reflexive narration of, 122-23; as self-conscious art, 125; stereotypes in, 123-25

Vickers, Brian, 79

Wald, Alan, 171, 180
Walker, Alice, 181
Warren, Charles, 79
Warren, Robert Penn, 184
Washington, Mary Helen, 183
Watkins, Evan, 19-20
Watt, Ian, 110
Waugh, Patricia, 159
Weimann, Robert, 66
Weitz, Morris, 75
Wellek, René, and Austin Warren, 6
West, Cornel, 196
Whately, Richard, 88, 89
White, Hayden, 16-17
Widdowson, Peter, 117, 120
Williams, Raymond, 7, 115, 167, 169, 177
Willis, Susan, 134
Wilson, J. Dover, 69-70
women's studies, 96, 101, 106, 109
Wright, Richard, 183

Young, James, 197
Young, Robert, 96

Zwerdling, Alex, 179

About the Author

Philip Goldstein earned a B.A. in English from Columbia University in 1966, an M.A. in Philosophy from Temple University in 1970, and a Ph.D. in English from Temple University in 1984. Since 1977 he has taught English and philosophy in the Parallel Program, the Women's Studies Program, and the English Department of the University of Delaware. He was promoted to Professor in 2001. He has published *The Politics of Literary Criticism: An Introduction to Marxist Cultural Theory* (University of Florida Press, 1990) and edited *Styles of Cultural Activism: From Theory and Pedagogy to Women, Indians, and Communism* (University of Delaware Press, 1993). With James Machor, he also edited *Reception Study: Theory, Practice, History* (Routledge Press, 2000). He is currently working on a study of horror and mystery fiction and the literary canon, especially Faulkner's and Morrison's art.